Critics praise Andrew Taylor's Lydmouth mysteries:

An Air that Kills

'Captures perfectly the drab atmosphere and cloying mor-
ality of the 1950s, when surface respectability masked nasty
social and sexual undercurrents. Taylor is an excellent
writer. He plots with care and intelligence and the solution
to the mystery is satisfyingly chilling'

The Times

'There is no denying Taylor's talent, his almost Victorian
prose exudes a quality uncommon among his contempor-
aries . . . his eye for detail and an enviable ability to dissect
relationships and communal habits make for a pleasurable
read'

Time Out

The Mortal Sickness

'The reader sees inside the pressure-cooker of village life and
how it leads to murder and then, as inexorably, to exposure.
Very enjoyable'

Spectator

'A fine, atmospheric thriller'

Daily Mail

'Taylor's remarkable talent shows in his language and his
skilful plotting . . . Wicked and wonderful'

Yorkshire Post

The Lover of the Grave

'The tensions, both emotional and sexual, that run through this deftly plotted novel stretch the reader's nerves almost to breaking point'

Val McDermid, *Manchester Evening News*

'Andrew Taylor was given the thumbs up long ago for beautifully crafted, well written narratives combining subtlety, depth and that vital "Oh my God what the hell is going to happen next" factor, which is the driving force of the storyteller . . . *The Lover of the Grave* . . . makes you long to read the next tale'

Frances Fyfield, *Express on Sunday*

Also by Andrew Taylor

An Air That Kills
The Mortal Sickness
The Lover of the Grave

About the Author

Andrew Taylor is the author of the award-winning crime series featuring William Dougal. He has also written thrillers for adults and teenagers, and novels of psychological suspense, including the much praised THE BARRED WINDOW. He and his wife live with their children in the Forest of Dean.

The Suffocating Night

Andrew Taylor

NEW ENGLISH LIBRARY
Hodder & Stoughton

For
Shoo and the Founder Members of FAW

Copyright © 1998 Andrew Taylor

The right of Andrew Taylor to be indentified as the Author
of the Work has been asserted by him in accordance with
the Copyright, Designs and Patents Act 1988.

First published in Great Britain in 1998
by Hodder and Stoughton
First published in paperback in 1999
by Hodder and Stoughton
A division of Hodder Headline PLC

A New English Library Paperback

10 9 8 7 6 5 4 3 2 1

All rights reserved. No part of the publication may be
reproduced, stored in a retrieval system, or transmitted,
in any form or by any means without the prior written
permission of the publisher, nor be otherwise circulated in
any form of binding or cover other than that in which it is
published and without a similar condition being imposed
on the subsequent purchaser.

All characters in this publication are fictitious
and any resemblance to real persons, living or
dead, is purely coincidental.

A CIP catalogue record for this title
is available from the British Library.

ISBN 0 340 69598 6

Typeset by Hewer Text Limited, Edinburgh
Printed and bound in Great Britain by
Clays Ltd, St Ives plc

Hodder and Stoughton
A division of Hodder Headline PLC
338 Euston Road
London NW1 3BH

AUTHOR'S NOTE

The title comes from poem xxx in *A Shropshire Lad* by A. E. Housman.

THE PRINCIPAL CHARACTERS

NORAH COALWAY – wife and mother; and SIDNEY,
  her husband
JILL FRANCIS – a journalist on the *Lydmouth Gazette*
RICHARD THORNHILL – Detective Inspector
EDITH THORNHILL – his wife; DAVID and
  ELIZABETH, their children
BRIAN KIRBY – Detective Sergeant
RAYMOND WILLIAMSON – Detective Superintendent
PC PORTER – Lydmouth Division, Uniform Branch
CHARLOTTE WEMYSS-BROWN – owner of the *Gazette*
PHILIP WEMYSS-BROWN – husband of Charlotte;
  editor of the *Gazette*
MR QUALE – factotum at the Bull Hotel
OLIVER YATELEY, MP
CAMERON ROWSE – a journalist from London
HAROLD ALVINGTON – landlord of the Bathurst Arms
GLORIA ALVINGTON – his wife; JANE – his
  daughter
JOE VANCE – proprietor of a Lydmouth garage
BERNARD BROADBENT – a County Councillor; cousin
  of Edith Thornhill
ERIC BLAINES – a civil servant from London
HOWARD SIMCOX – the man with the fish

PHYLLIS RICHARDS – companion to MRS PORT-
    LEIGH, of Edge Hill
MRS VEALE – a widow, of Edge Hill
DR BAYSWATER – a general practitioner and police
    surgeon
IVOR FUGGLE – a journalist on the *Post*

ANNOUNCEMENTS

PARRY, Heather Margaret: — With all our love on the anniversary of the day you went away, Mother, Dad, Keith and Granny.

The *Lydmouth Gazette*, 18 April

Chapter One

Timing is all, Cameron Rowse used to say. Get the timing right, and who needs luck? On his trip to Lydmouth, his timing was apparently perfect. But Rowse was murdered a few hours after he arrived so perhaps luck has its uses after all.

On Tuesday morning, Rowse loaded his luggage into the panniers of the Triumph TRW and rode west out of London, enjoying the anonymity of leathers and goggles. The motorbike was army surplus, like all TRWs, a gutless beast but its engine, a 500 Twin, would probably keep going until the end of time. It was still relatively early. He had lunch at a roadside café west of Oxford. While he ate he read the clipping from the *People* once again.

SQUATTERS INVADE CAMP
ARMY HELPLESS

The story below the headline was straightforward. Farnock Camp was a military base outside Lydmouth. The soldiers had left in 1946 and then for a year or two civilians had been allowed to live there while council housing was being built for them in the town. Since then it had been standing empty. Recently, however, a private housing development in Lydmouth had led to the eviction of several families, who had promptly moved into the camp. The army wanted them out, arguing that their occupation was illegal and in any case the international situation meant that the camp would almost certainly be required for military purposes in the near future. A Labour county councillor said that it was tragic that in this day and age any British citizen should not have a roof over his head. A Conservative county councillor said that the needs of the country must come first.

Through the grime on the café window, Cameron Rowse saw a cloudless April sky. *Lydmouth.* The name stirred eddies in his memory. He had driven through the town with his parents on a camping holiday when he was a kid. He remembered a silver river snaking down a valley, old buildings and green hills that shaded to blue in the distance. For some reason the place glowed in his mind like a lost paradise. This was probably because of the contrast with the present. His bank account was overdrawn and his landlady was clamouring for a fortnight's rent.

Well, he had thought that morning, why not take a chance on it? He needed a break, and a working holiday would be just the ticket. Because of the international situation, the piece in the *People* had been slanted against the squatters, though the writer had made a pretence of being even-handed. Rowse hoped he would be able to place a feature, text and photographs, with the *Picture Post*. There were other possibilities – including the reassuring knowledge that if all else failed, he could find a less lucrative but more certain market in the *Empire Lion*.

After lunch, Rowse pressed on to Gloucester. He rode through the city, followed the road westwards and then turned left. According to the map the shortest way to Lydmouth would take him into a forest. The road snaked through a switchback course over hills and along valleys. The trees, which he had assumed would be picturesque, pressed hard on the road as if they planned to smother it. He passed through several mining villages, their stonework dark with coal dust. Passers-by stared at him, their faces neither hostile nor friendly. The area was overrun with sheep. It's springtime, Rowse thought, observing the lambs gambolling on the verges and at times on the road itself. He rounded a bend, taking it a little too fast.

Bloody hell—

There were two lambs in the middle of the road, staggering drunkenly in the same direction as he was going. From the shelter of the trees, a full-grown sheep – presumably their mother – stood with moving jaws, watching the lambs without much apparent interest.

Rowse braked hard to avoid the nearer lamb, swerved, found the second lamb had turned into his path and swerved again, this time with less control than before. The front wheel of the Triumph hit the verge and then a stone that lay on the grass. The motorbike bucked and sliced sideways in a gradually flattening arc. Rowse flung himself clear, his arms round his head. His body hit the ground with a jolt that drove the breath out of his lungs. For a brief, agonising moment he waited for the bike to crash down on his left leg. To his enormous relief, he discovered he had landed inches clear of it.

He stood up, too shaken even to swear. The Triumph's engine had cut out. He stretched cautiously and tried to assess the damage he had done to himself: a few bruises on his left side, he thought; but nothing worse. But it was obvious that the Triumph had fared less well. He pulled the bike up and examined the damage. As it had fallen, the fork had collided with another rock, half hidden in the grass. The fork was bent, and several spokes on the front wheel were damaged as well. It was a garage job, and an expensive one at that.

Rowse set the bike on its stand and checked the panniers. The buckle had been torn off the nearside pannier, but its contents – mainly clothes – were undamaged. The camera and typewriter had been in the other pannier, which had landed on top of the bike. He lit a cigarette and studied the map. Lydmouth could not be more than ten or twelve miles away.

He heard the throb of an engine coming, as he had done, from the Gloucester direction. A moment later, a saloon car swept round the bend. Rowse stuck out his thumb. The car, a large dark green Humber, surged past him. Rowse glimpsed the silhouette of a man behind the wheel.

Toffee-nosed bastard.

A few yards down the road, the car braked, stopped and reversed back to where Rowse was waiting. He opened the passenger door. A smell of leather and cigar smoke swept out to greet him. The driver was a middle-aged man with heavy features.

'Hello. Need a lift?'

'You can say that again.'

The driver saw the motorbike. 'Spot of trouble?'

Rowse snorted. 'That's what comes of trying to avoid a couple of lambs.'

'I'm going to Lydmouth. I can take you there, if you like. Or I can drop you off at a garage on the way.'

'I'm going to Lydmouth myself.'

'Then why don't you look for a garage there? It's not far – they can send someone out for the bike.'

Rowse nodded. 'Is it OK if I bring my things? There's not much.'

The man got out and opened the boot of the Humber. It contained a couple of good leather suitcases. There was ample room for Rowse's belongings. The man eyed the typewriter and camera. 'Tools of the trade, eh?'

Rowse blinked. 'Well, yes.'

'What do you do?'

'I'm a journalist.'

'Oh yes?'

They got into the car. For a few seconds, Rowse relished the quietness, the comfort and the warmth of the Humber. Simultaneously he puzzled about the man's voice. There was a hint of Yorkshire in it, and for some reason it was faintly familiar, even though the man himself was not.

'Who do you work for?' the man said. 'One of the local rags?'

'No, freelance.'

'I shouldn't have thought there's enough work round here for a freelance.'

'I live in London.' Rowse was more comfortable asking questions than answering them.

'So you're following a story?'

Damn the man. 'Not really. Just down here for a little holiday.' He glanced sideways at the driver. 'Of course you never know – there may be a chance to do some work as well.'

'You never know,' the man agreed.

They drove in silence for the next couple of miles, passing through a straggling village. The road began to descend, sweeping in great loops towards the valley below. The familiarity of the man's voice niggled at Rowse.

'Haven't we met somewhere before?' he said.

The man glanced at him. 'No, I don't think we have.'

There was another silence, longer this time. Rowse wondered what the man did for a living. Nice suit, well-cut hair; the hands on the steering wheel had been manicured; there was a box of Havanas from Harrods on the back seat.

'Do you live in Lydmouth?' Rowse asked.

'No.'

The driver blew his horn at a grubby, unshaven man idling on the road. Ahead of them was the stone bridge over the river Lyd. Just beforehand, on the right, there was a turning. Rowse glimpsed the word Farnock on the signpost as they passed it.

'Holiday, then?' Rowse suggested.

'I think there's a garage just over the bridge,' the driver said. 'Just down that side road beyond the station. Want me to drop you on the corner?'

So the man had been to Lydmouth before. 'Yes, please.'

A moment later Rowse was standing on the forecourt of a small garage with his luggage beside him. There were a couple of petrol pumps at the front, then a ramshackle workshop with a corrugated iron roof, and behind that a large yard crammed with rusting vehicles, most of them ex-army. A man in khaki overalls came out of the workshop, rubbing oily hands on an oilier rag. He had red hair, close-set blue eyes and a small moustache like ginger bristles on a pair of toothbrushes. Rowse explained what had happened to the Triumph. It seemed to take much longer than it would have done if he had been in London. Yokels thought slowly as well as spoke slowly.

'When can you collect it?'

The mechanic stared over Rowse's shoulder. 'In an hour or so. Maybe. Depends when our Jack brings the truck back.'

'I don't want it to get nicked.'

'It'll be all right up there. So you'll be wanting a new fork and a new front wheel?'

'Do you have something in stock?'

The man flicked the rag at the mechanical graveyard behind the workshop. 'We've got just about everything.'

'How long will it take to fix?'

'Can't tell. Not till I've seen it. Can't give you a quote, either.'

Rowse sighed. Whatever the price, it wouldn't be cheap. 'Can you suggest somewhere I could stay for a day or two?'

'You could try the Bathurst at the bottom of Lyd Street.'

'Is it far?'

'Not if you walk back past the station to the river and then cut along the towpath. Otherwise you do three sides of a square. Tell them Joe Vance sent you.'

It didn't take long to find the Bathurst Arms. Harold Alvington was the name over the door, but there was no sign of him. A plain, plump girl showed Rowse the guest bedroom, which was over a garage at right angles to the rest of the pub, reached by a separate staircase that went up from the lobby by the back door to the yard. The room had a view across the river to the wooded hills beyond. He opened the window and leaned out.

'Won't take me a moment to make up the bed,' the girl said. 'Will you be wanting an evening meal?'

'I'm not sure.'

Outside, the sun was still shining, still bringing an illusion of warmth to the day. There were ducks on the river, squabbling over a piece of bread, and daffodils were growing wild on the further bank. Just like a picture postcard: just like the country was supposed to be.

'You know Farnock?'

'Yes, sir.'

'How far is it?'

'The camp?'

He nodded.

'You go over the river and turn left down the lane. It's about half a mile.'

'Do you know anything about these squatters?'

She stared at him. 'No, sir.'

Christ. Her face was as expressionless as a scrubbed potato, and probably about as intelligent. Another bloody peasant, he thought, the result of centuries of inbreeding in the long winter evenings. How on earth did they survive in the modern world?

Chapter Two

When the girl had gone, Rowse put a film in his camera and slipped a notebook in his pocket. The damage to his motorbike made it all the more urgent to earn some money from this trip. He admired himself in the dressing-table mirror; his new tweed jacket had a rather dashing hound's-tooth check and a particularly elegant cut – a touch of metropolitan sophistication to dazzle the locals. He sauntered downstairs and was soon walking back along the towpath, cigarette in hand, cap tilted back on his head, the very picture of a tourist. He noticed a tall plant with small purple flowers, growing wild near a bench, and wondered if he should find out its name. Readers liked a splash of local colour. *By the river, the lesser-spotted ragglewort glowed in the spring sunshine* ...

He bought a local paper, the *Gazette*, at the newsagent's near the station. The Farnock Camp story was front-page news. The piece was better written than the one in the *People* but kinder to the squatters. That surprised him – usually you could count on the editors of local papers to support the authorities in any shape or form. They'd do anything rather than run the risk of damaging their advertising revenue.

He stuffed the paper into the pocket of his jacket, crossed the river and turned left into the lane. There were no pavements here, and the lane grew progressively narrower as it wound inland. The hedgerow on the right-hand side gave way to wire fencing, topped with barbed wire. The camp came into view – rows of Nissen huts like the tumuli of a forgotten tribe. At the main entrance, the gates had been pulled off their hinges. A freshly-painted notice ordered people to keep out. Bracken and saplings were colonising the open spaces. Weeds sprouted through cracks in the concrete. Smoke drifted up from the stove chimneys attached to some of the nearer huts. Rowse turned into the camp and walked towards them. He knocked on the door of the nearest hut. A moment later, the door opened to reveal a young woman with a missing front tooth and two toddlers clinging to her skirt.

'Yes?'

Rowse swept off his hat. 'Good afternoon, madam. My name's Cameron Rowse. I work for the *Picture Post.*' He watched her face, watched confusion giving way to suspicion. 'The features editor wants me to do a piece about the camp.' He waved an arm towards the other huts. 'Looks like quite a little community you've got here.' He noticed that someone had dug a little flower bed at the side of the hut, and primroses and more daffodils were growing there. 'I see you've even got a garden.'

'We try to keep things nice. Not that we should have to be here by rights.'

'I should think not. Just what I was saying to the editor. It's a disgrace.' He adopted the expression of sympathetic outrage which had served him well over the years. 'And I gather the army are trying to get you out. That doesn't seem very fair.'

The woman flushed with anger. 'The army! Don't talk to me about the bloody army. Sid spent four years in the army, and look where it's got him.'

'Surely the council should be helping you?'

'Most of them are as bad as the War Office.'

Rowse could believe it. Quite apart from the legal position, water, sanitation and the disposal of rubbish would be a nightmare.

'Anyway, if you want to see Sid, you'll have to come back later.' She was already beginning to close the door. 'I'm busy.'

'But it's the women's side that I'm interested in,' Rowse said quickly. 'My editor wants the family angle, you see. How do the children cope? How do you manage about your shopping? All the little details of life — that's what will interest our readers. That's what people will sympathise with.'

The children stared up at him with wide, wondering eyes. There were grey, moving flecks in their hair. Crawling with lice — vermin attracted to vermin; that's the way it went. Sometimes Rowse felt his job was like a hunter's: you marked down your prey, you pursued them, and then you tasted the best pleasure of all — when you realised that they could not escape you.

'What I'd like to do,' he went on, 'is just wander round and chat to people. Have a word with the men when they get home. Take a few photographs.'

'There was a bit in the *People* the other day.' The woman was still suspicious. 'Buggers said we were unpatriotic.'

'That's downright stupid. You've all done your bit for the country, I'm sure. And now the country has a duty to house you. Where do they expect you to live, anyway?'

Rowse kept talking, relying not so much on the force of his words as the effect of his sympathy. Gradually the woman warmed and began to respond. Her name was Norah Coalway. She introduced him to her neighbours. He took photographs of them and the children. They showed him the insides of their huts — most of them neatly swept and filled with makeshift furniture. Some of them even had ornaments and photographs on the windowsills. There was something pathetic about it all, he thought, like children playing house. These people weren't much more sophisticated than the cows in the lane and the sheep in the Forest.

The story began to take shape as the material accumulated. Seven of the huts were occupied, all of them by families with young children. Until recently they had lived in the Templefields area of Lydmouth which was being systematically pulled down and redeveloped.

'The sods just want to make a profit, and they don't care how they do it,' said Mrs Coalway. 'You put that in your newspaper, all right? We could die on the pavements for all they care.'

Who were *they*? Rowse wondered. The building developers, the bureaucrats at the Ministry, the councillors on the Planning Committee? The faceless ones who always wielded the power.

One by one, the husbands trickled back from work. One of them was a miner from a pit up in the Forest, but the other four worked in the town. The men were a tiresome chore — they had to be won over, and they were tired, hungry and even more suspicious than the wives had been. By the time he had talked to the fifth man, Rowse had had enough.

'I thought I'd have a stroll round the camp and take a few more photos,' he said. 'I need to do it soon, while the light's OK. Is that all right?'

He had the impression they were glad to let him go. Though they appreciated his offer of support, they barely had the time and energy to talk to him. Rowse spent a happy fifteen minutes on his own. This was a part of the job that he really enjoyed. No people to talk to: just himself and the camera.

By now it was late afternoon and the sun was low in the sky. But the light was excellent for photographs. He took a stark shot of the vandalised gates. Nearby was a pile of logs, neat and cylindrical, their sides covered with flaking paint. Those parasites from the huts had evidently sawn up the flagpole to use on their stoves.

A few minutes later, he found what was evidently the squatters' rubbish tip. By one of those flukes that made his job worthwhile, there was a torn Union Jack in one of the empty huts nearby. He took it out and draped it artistically over some of the rubbish. 'Patriots,' he murmured happily to himself, as his forefinger squeezed the shutter.

By now he had reached the far end of the camp. There was a smaller entrance here, protected by a ruined guardhouse. It gave access to a metalled track running parallel with the lane leading to the main gate. On the other side of the track, a steep field, strewn with rocks, sloped up to the Forest. As Rowse approached the guardhouse, he heard the rustle of water. A trickle of urine oozed through the empty doorway. Then a man in an army greatcoat emerged. He was small, lean-faced and unshaven. Dark hair swept back in a cowlick from a widow's peak. The moment he saw Rowse, his eyes widened and his nostrils flared. He stopped, and the two men stared at each other.

'Sorry if I startled you,' Rowse said easily. 'I've just been talking to your friends.' By now the words rolled so glibly off his tongue he barely had to think of them. 'We're doing a feature on the camp for the *Picture Post*.'

'Oh aye.'

'Have you been here long?'

'Too long.'

'Have a cigarette.'

Rowse held out the packet of Woodbines. The man reached out a grimy hand and took one. Rowse glimpsed a tattoo on his wrist – a blue fish with a gaping mouth and red fins. He struck a match and the stranger came closer for a moment, bringing with him a feral smell. Washing must be a problem, Rowse thought, though probably most of the squatters would just as soon be dirty.

'I hear the army are trying to get you all out. Were you in the services yourself?'

'Yes. I've got to go.'

The squatter sidled into the gap between the fence and

the guardhouse. Rowse felt aggrieved. The man had accepted a cigarette. The least he could do was answer a few questions. Rowse raised the camera.

'Hey, you.'

The fish-man turned, a vapour trail of cigarette smoke oozing from the corner of his mouth. Rowse pressed the shutter.

'I'll send you a copy of the magazine.'

The squatter took a step towards him. 'Now look, mister. Who said you could do that?'

Rowse had a good ear for accents. The fish-man had said so little that it was hard to be sure, but his voice had changed. At first it had sounded local, much the same as those of the other men. But those last few words had a trace of education.

In the distance Rowse heard the sound of an engine near the main gate.

'Mr Rowse!' Norah Coalway had appeared fifty yards away. 'Mr Rowse!'

'Sorry,' Rowse said to the man with the fish tattoo. 'Sounds like I'm wanted.'

He walked away, half expecting to hear running footsteps behind him.

Norah beckoned him impatiently. 'The other journalist's here,' she called as he drew nearer.

'The one from the *People*?'

'That bugger wouldn't bloody dare. We'd crucify him, look. No, this one's the lady from the *Gazette*.'

A moment later he reached the cluster of occupied Nissen huts. A Ford Anglia, its wings streaked with mud, was parked just outside the gate. Most of the squatters, men, women and children, were in a group near the car. They parted as Rowse arrived. The newcomer was quite a looker, in her way. She looked at Rowse and smiled.

'Hello. I gather you're from the *Picture Post*.' She held out a hand. 'My name's Jill Francis. I work for the *Lydmouth Gazette*.'

They shook hands. The woman's friendliness surprised him. Usually these provincial hacks were wary of journalists from London, partly from professional jealousy and partly because the newcomers were only there to poach stories which the locals might otherwise have sold to the nationals themselves. She was wearing gloves so he could not tell whether there was a wedding ring on her left hand.

'I used to know some people at the *Post*,' Jill Francis was saying.

'Oh, I'm freelance.' Rowse tried the effect of a smile, aware that the *Picture Post* might prove awkward territory. 'This is by way of a working holiday, really.'

'You saw the piece in the *People*?'

'Yes.' A lot of these local hacks fed promising stories to the nationals. 'Something that came from you?'

'No.'

He sensed that he was losing ground with her so he decided on a change of tack. 'I thought not. I preferred the one in today's *Gazette*. Was that yours, by any chance?'

'As it happens, yes.'

'Have you ever thought of trying your luck in London?'

'Yes, I have.'

'You should.'

'I dare say. So you've actually been commissioned, have you?'

'All being well. But you can never quite believe it until the cheque's in the bank. You know what editors are like – nothing in writing, just a gentleman's agreement. Trouble is, most of them aren't gentlemen.'

She smiled politely. 'How do you see the story? There are two sides to it, especially now the army say they need the camp back.'

He patted the camera. 'A good picture's worth a thousand words. The army doesn't stand a chance against homeless kiddies in their mothers' arms.'

'Do you think that's true?'

Rowse shrugged and tried another smile. Damn the woman, he thought – it was impossible to tell how serious she was. He felt aggrieved – he was doing his level best to be nice to her and she wasn't responding. But he might need a local contact, so best to keep her sweet.

'I'd better be on my way,' he said, glancing at his watch. 'Nice to meet you, Mrs Francis.'

'It's Miss, actually.'

'Sorry ... Yes, I think I've got more or less all I need here, for the time being. Let's see.' He opened his notebook and flicked through the pages he had used. 'Mrs Coalway? There are twenty-six of you, eh? All told. Seven couples and twelve children?'

'No,' said Norah Coalway. 'Betty's Dave was killed last year. Accident down the pit. Roof caved in.'

'Can you check the names for me? The ones I may quote from.' He held out his notebook to her. 'I wouldn't like to get them wrong.'

'They can't do anything to us if you print our names, can they?'

'Don't worry. They'd have a riot on their hands if they tried.'

'We're not criminals,' Norah went on, clearly disturbed by the possibility that they were. She ran her forefinger under the scribbled words, breathing heavily. 'Yes, that's OK.'

'What about the man I met over by the other gate?' He jabbed a thumb behind him. 'Smallish. Dark hair.'

'Don't know who you mean.'

'Man with the fish—'

'Only man you haven't met is my Sid. But he's got fair hair and I wouldn't call him small, neither.'

'Who actually commissioned you?' Jill Francis interrupted.

'Leonard Franks,' Rowse said easily. Len was certainly a features editor at the *Picture Post*, and Rowse had once been introduced to him. Not that Len had found anything to say to him. 'So long, then.' He raised his hand in farewell, including all the group of squatters. 'You've been very helpful. I may be back tomorrow for a few more questions, but if not, I wish you the best of luck. Maybe my piece will help.'

He walked jauntily away and into the lane. No one said anything. Probably they were all staring after him. Everything had been going so well until that Francis woman came along. She might be suspicious, not that it would matter. Almost certainly, she wasn't so much suspicious as annoyed with him for poaching on her turf.

Nothing she could do about it. It was a free country, thank God, though these days even that seemed to be in doubt.

Chapter Three

The bars at the Bathurst Arms did not open until six o'clock. As a resident, Rowse could have got a drink beforehand but he had never enjoyed drinking alone.

When he returned from Farnock Camp, it was almost a quarter past five. He felt excited, as though riding a winning streak in poker. Timing is everything. One way or another, Farnock Camp was going to be a story: it was money in the bank. The only cloud on the horizon was the bill he would soon have to pay for the repair of the Triumph. He wondered if the garage would take credit. You wouldn't get away with it in London, not with a stranger, but country bumpkins could be astonishingly naïve.

Thinking about his accident had reminded him about the well-heeled Good Samaritan who had given him a lift: the man in the Humber, the man with the oddly familiar voice. Everyone needs a hobby, Rowse thought as he went downstairs with the *Lydmouth Gazette* tucked under his arm. Some men played cards, some played football, some played the field: he merely indulged his curiosity, a hobby which at least had the advantage of helping to earn his living. He reached the hall and peered into the lounge bar.

'Can I help?'

Startled, he spun round. The fat girl had appeared

in the doorway of a room at the other end of the hall.

'What's your name?' he said, more sharply than intended.

'Jane, sir.'

Plain Jane, he thought. 'Tell me, what's the biggest hotel in Lydmouth?'

'The Bull.'

'Is it far?'

She shook her head. 'Up the hill to the High Street, turn left and it's on your right. Ten minutes' walk at most.'

'I might stretch my legs.'

'Will you be wanting an evening meal, sir?'

'No, I don't think so.' He put on his cap and examined himself in the hall mirror. 'I'm not sure when I'll be back.'

'The bar at the Bull opens at five-thirty.'

He glanced at the reflection of the girl's fat round face in the mirror. For a moment he thought she had been mocking him. But her expression was perfectly serious. Probably hadn't many more brain cells than one of those damned sheep.

He said goodbye and sauntered outside. At first, as he walked up Lyd Street, he relished the contrast with the streets of London. Coming to this backwater was like travelling back ten or fifteen years in time. Even the people looked old-fashioned. Most of them, anyway – the Francis woman had been reasonably well turned out. She probably dabbled in journalism for a little pin-money. Ten to one her brother or her father was the editor of the local rag, or even its owner. The thought of such an unfair advantage gave him a sensation like the shadow of impending indigestion in the pit of his stomach. Unconsciously he began to walk faster.

At the top of the hill, Rowse turned left into a broad, long street. He saw the façade of the Bull almost at once on the other side of the road. He hesitated outside a newsagent's by the library. A placard said: GLOSTERS – CASUALTIES. The *Empire Lion* was right. This was already World War III in all but name.

As he waited on the kerb for a bus to go by, he noticed a dirty, fair-haired man in a torn jacket leaning against the wall of the library. Bloody tramp, Rowse thought without particular animosity; why can't he have himself a bath and find himself a job? Then a memory clicked up in his mind like a number in a cash register: it was the man he had seen on the bridge when he arrived at Lydmouth, the man the Humber's driver had hooted at.

Rowse crossed the road. The portico of the Bull Hotel reared above him. The place needed a coat of paint. He hesitated on the pavement for a moment, looking up and down the road. The hotel was on a corner. Instead of going inside, Rowse walked along the pavement and into the side road, Bull Lane. On his right, as he had hoped, was an archway leading to a yard at the back of the hotel. As he looked through the archway into the cobbled yard beyond, a tiny thrill of pleasure touched him, the reward of an intelligent guess that happened to be right. The green Humber was parked under a lean-to shelter on the left.

'Help you, sir?'

Rowse turned his head. An elderly man in a striped waistcoat was standing in the shadow of a fire escape which cut across the rear wall of the hotel.

'I was looking for the bar. Can I get through this way?'

The old man dropped a cigarette end to the ground and flattened it under his heel. 'I'll show you, sir.' He led the way to a door beyond the fire escape, opened it and stood back to allow Rowse to pass through. 'Turn left, and then it's on your left beyond the dining room.' The old man glanced up at the clock that ticked away over the reception counter in a case the colour of milk chocolate. 'They'll just have opened.'

Rowse walked slowly along the corridor. On the right was a large lounge. He looked in — no one there except two elderly ladies stranded in armchairs beside the remains of a substantial tea. He heard footsteps on the stairs and turned, just in time to see the driver of the Humber walk quickly down the stairs and into the part of the hall which was beyond Rowse's range of vision.

'Good evening, sir.'

'Evening, Quale. Can you tell me how to get to Church Street?'

Rowse, out of sight round the corner, leant against the wall and listened.

'Turn right out of here, sir, then just follow the High Street. It's the next on your right after Woolworth's.'

'How far is it?'

'Two or three hundred yards.'

'Thank you.'

The man's footsteps clipped across the hall. The front door, the one to the portico, opened and closed. Rowse let a few seconds slip by. Then he sauntered back to the main hall. Quale was in the little half-glazed office behind the reception counter. He came out when he heard Rowse.

'Everything all right, sir?'

'I forgot my cigarettes. Back in a minute.'

Rowse went outside. The Good Samaritan was already fifty yards ahead, striding down the High Street. Rowse followed, accelerating to lessen the distance between them. They passed Woolworth's and a moment later the man turned right into Church Street. He walked down it, glancing at the houses on either side of the road. At last he seemed to reach his destination: he hesitated for a few seconds outside a cottage on the right, just before the road opened out into an irregular quadrilateral with a church in the middle.

Instead of knocking on the door, however, the man with the familiar voice crossed the road and went into the churchyard. He was walking more slowly now, and when he reached the churchyard he wandered, apparently aimlessly, among the graves. Rowse sat down on a bench facing the church outside a row of almshouses. From this vantage point he could see much of the churchyard and also keep an eye on the house, which he now saw was called Church Cottage. He pulled his cap down over his face and pretended to read the newspaper. It was clear that his quarry couldn't make up his mind about something. That was odd in itself, because everything else Rowse knew about him suggested that he was naturally decisive.

After a couple of minutes, the man left the churchyard, crossed the road and went back to the cottage. This time he knocked on the door.

To Rowse's surprise, the door was opened by Jill Francis, the journalist he had met at Farnock Camp. He hastily raised the newspaper a little higher. He heard the murmur of voices but was too far away to distinguish any words. He risked a glance: the man from the Humber had his arms stretched out; it was as if he were asking the woman something. Jill Francis, on the other hand, had one hand on the door and the other on the jamb, forming a human barrier. But something the man said must have achieved the desired effect: she stood back, the man went into the house, and the door closed.

Rowse considered waiting to see what happened. But time was getting on, and a stranger would stick out in a place like this. In any case, there was nothing to show that following this hunch would lead him anywhere.

Nevertheless, as he walked back to the Bull, the incident lingered in his mind, a minor irritation. No doubt there was a simple explanation why a prosperous stranger should visit a local journalist while he was in Lydmouth. Perhaps the man was a civil servant or a soldier in mufti paying a discreet visit to Lydmouth to assess the state of local opinion about the squatters.

Rowse went into the Bull by the front entrance. There was no one behind the reception counter, and the office was empty too. He glanced up the stairs, and then peered round the corner, down the corridor past the lounge to the bar. For the moment, he was alone. He went back to the counter, pulled the leather-bound hotel register towards him and turned it round. He skimmed through the book to the current page. The most recent entry was scrawled in a flowing handwriting which burst above and below the lines meant to contain it. Why the hell couldn't people write legibly?

London, yes – an address in Dolphin Square: that made sense; the man in the Humber was comfortably off. Alan? Patey? Pately?

No, not Alan: *Oliver*. There were footsteps on the landing; someone was approaching the head of the stairs.

The scrawled surname unfolded itself. *Yateley*. Oliver Yateley, by God. No wonder the voice had sounded familiar. But what on earth was he doing in this part of the world? And why was he visiting a reporter working for some tinpot local paper?

The footsteps were on the stairs now. Rowse shut the register and slid it back to its original position. He walked quickly away from the counter – not towards the bar but back to the front door. He slipped into the High Street. The doors to the library were still open, and people were passing up and down the steps. He crossed the road, went into the reference library and asked for *Who's Who*. Soon after he sat down with the fat red book, he noticed the fair-haired tramp, or whatever he was, coming into the reading room. Rowse forgot the tramp and skipped towards the end of the book.

> YATELEY, John Oliver: Born 1911, son of Frederick John Yateley
> of Leeds, and Mary, née Hutton ...

He worked his way through the entry, making notes. Grammar school, a succession of jobs in local government, articled to a firm of solicitors called Prater and Farlow, a Labour councillor, briefly, before the war intervened. Enlisted 1939; soon commissioned into an infantry regiment; DSO in North Africa; came out of the war with the rank of major. MP for a town near Leeds in 1945. Since then, a steady climb through the ranks of the party.

Yateley had married Virginia Mary Prater, the daughter of a man who was almost certainly the senior partner in the solicitors' practice, in 1937. They had two daughters and one son. There was an address in Yorkshire as well as the one in Dolphin Square. Yateley's main home was probably the one in his constituency, with the London flat as a pied-à-terre for the House of Commons.

Rowse jotted down the addresses and the telephone number – the flat was evidently ex-directory – in his notebook – and pushed the book aside. Yateley wasn't any old backbencher. He was on the new Select Committee for Defence. He had the sort of presence that works well on radio – confidential, quietly authoritative, warm-voiced – and he was quick-witted, too. Rowse had heard him on the Brains Trust, demolishing an opponent's argument with wit and efficiency.

So that made it even more curious. What was a busy politician like Yateley doing over a hundred miles from London and several hundred miles from his constituency? For an instant Rowse considered trying to pump Quale, the old man at the hotel. But that would cost money, he suspected, and he was short enough as it was without laying out more on what would probably prove to be a wild-goose chase.

He closed *Who's Who* with a bang which jolted the tramp momentarily from his doze. Why would a man like Yateley want to visit Jill Francis? Why not telephone or write beforehand? It was clear that she hadn't been expecting him.

Two possibilities: they were having an affair or it was something to do with Farnock Camp. On present showing, nothing else would fit. Suppose it was Farnock Camp. Maybe Yateley was planning to ask a question in the House. Or maybe it was the national security issue which had brought him down here. Either way, there could be a story in it.

Alternatively, suppose it was an affair. Jill Francis was an attractive woman, if you liked them ladylike and no longer as young as they had been. No doubt Yateley's position gave him a certain allure. But if Yateley had a bit of skirt, you'd expect him to keep her in London, convenient for the House of Commons, not on the borders of England and Wales. And he would surely have known where to find her; he would not have had to ask Quale where Church Street was.

It was time for that drink.

Rowse left the library and lit a cigarette on the steps. His instincts told him that there was something unusual here. It wasn't so much that Yateley was in Lydmouth, but that curious conversation that Rowse had seen but not heard on the doorstep of Church Cottage. What if there had been no words? What if he had witnessed a mime? What would their movements have been saying?

Yateley had arrived without warning on Jill Francis's doorstep. He had been asking to be allowed in. She had not wanted to allow him, but in the end had given way. It was all speculation, Rowse knew, but something was happening between them. And whatever it was, it was *urgent*.

As he stood there, smoking, the possibilities danced tantalisingly through his mind. On the whole he would prefer an affair. Stories involving national security, however marginally, were always accompanied by the risk of heavy-handed intervention from the goons of Special Branch. Sex was much safer, and probably more lucrative. Rowse could think of several people who would pay handsomely for cast-iron evidence that Yateley was having an adulterous liaison. Yateley might be willing to pay even more handsomely to suppress the story. The second possibility need not exclude the first; it was all a matter of timing.

Rowse had no sympathy for Yateley. Politicians lived their lives in public, and if they strayed from the path of righteousness and ended up in a bog, then they had only themselves to blame. Rowse particularly disliked Labour politicians because of their holier-than-thou attitudes and because he suspected that most of them were the next best thing to Communists. Looked at from that direction, it was almost one's patriotic duty to sabotage the career of an up-and-coming Labour politician. And if one could earn a little money by doing so, well, why not?

Timing, Rowse thought yet again: get the timing right, and who needs luck?

He stared vacantly across the road at Bull Lane. What he needed now was more information about Yateley and Francis. There were people in London who would be able to tell him about Yateley. The trouble was, they would be curious about his reasons. His eyes focused on Bull Lane: on the opposite corner from the hotel was a telephone box, red as a guardsman's tunic and as solid as the Bank of England. At that moment, an idea slipped into his mind fully formed. What had he got to lose? He investigated his trouser pocket and found a handful of change.

The telephone box smelt of vinegar and old newspapers. He nearly changed his mind as he fed the money into the slot – trunk calls were so damned expensive – but his spirits lifted when he heard the voice reciting the number at the other end: not a child, thank God, and probably not a servant.

'Good evening. May I speak to Mrs Yateley?'

'Speaking.'

'Mrs Virginia Yateley?'

'Yes.' There was more than a hint of impatience in the voice. 'Who is this calling, please?'

Rowse looked across the road at the fascia board above the newsagent's: J. Jones and Son. 'My name's Jones, Mrs Yateley. James Jones. I'm a reporter. I'm trying to get in touch with your husband. I wonder if I might have a word with him.'

'He's not here, I'm afraid. He's in London.'

'No, he's not, Mrs Yateley. He left the flat this morning. He was driving the Humber.'

There was a sharp intake of breath at the other end of the line. 'He's sometimes called away unexpectedly. Party business, you understand. If you'd like to leave a message, Mr Jones –?'

'He's in trouble, isn't he?'

'Don't be ridiculous.' Mrs Yateley's voice had a Home Counties coating but Yorkshire vowels were beginning to poke through. 'Anyway, I thought ...'

'What did you think?' Rowse asked.

There was a silence at the other end of the line. Then Mrs Yateley began to cry.

'Tell me,' Rowse said gently. 'Maybe I can help.'

Chapter Four

After his telephone call, Cameron Rowse decided that work should come before pleasure. He went back to the Bathurst Arms and typed up his notes on the two stories, the squatters at the camp and Oliver Yateley. With luck, the squatters should pay for his trip to Lydmouth and the repair to the motorbike. Oliver Yateley, on the other hand, could make him rich.

His good humour was only slightly dented by the discovery that at present he had rather less money than he had thought. He would be able to pay his bill at the Bathurst Arms, but he doubted if he would have much left over for the motorbike. He strolled back up the hill, relishing the contrast between his leisurely progress and the way the adrenaline was flooding through his body. Timing is everything, and tonight his timing was perfect.

Quale was dozing over the *Gazette* at reception.

'Is Mr Yateley in?'

Quale studied him for a moment and then said, 'I believe he's in the bar, sir.'

'Thanks.'

The Bull Hotel was livelier than it had been, or rather slightly less moribund. Rowse followed the now familiar corridor to the bar. Yateley was by himself at a corner table, with a large whisky in front of him. Rowse pulled out a chair and sat down opposite him.

'What can I do for you now?' Yateley demanded, the brusque tone overriding the politeness of the words.

'My name's Jones,' Cameron Rowse said. 'James Jones.'

'And why are you sitting at my table, James Jones?' Yateley's eyes were bloodshot. 'There are several very nice tables over there with no one sitting at them.'

'Because I thought you might like to buy me a drink.'

'You bloody did, did you? And what gave you that idea?'

Five minutes later, Cameron Rowse was fifteen pounds richer and Yateley had left the bar. If only life were always this simple, Rowse thought, as he sipped a pint of mild and bitter. He was sitting in the chair that Yateley had occupied. Look at it any way you like, he was on to a winner with this one.

He lit a cigarette and opened the *Lydmouth Gazette*. The front-page story concerned a local councillor who was arguing that a gateway, part of Lydmouth's mediaeval defences, should not be restored on the grounds that World War III would soon make the expenditure unnecessary and irrelevant. Rowse applauded such realistic sentiments. He finished his drink and decided that, now he had lined his stomach with beer, he would try a large whisky.

The door opened and a large man lumbered into the room. The barman reached for a pewter tankard, one of a row hanging over the counter.

'Evening, Mr Wemyss-Brown.'

'Evening, George.' For a moment the newcomer watched the barman pouring his pint. Then he said abruptly, 'I was wondering if I might find one of your guests here. Mr Yateley.'

The barman's eyes slid momentarily towards Rowse. 'He was here a few minutes ago, sir. Not in his room?'

Wemyss-Brown shook his head. 'Quale says his key's on the board.'

'Probably gone out to dinner.'

'Oh well — doesn't matter.' Wemyss-Brown took a long swallow of his beer, leaving a moustache of foam on his upper lip. 'Did you hear the news about Farnock Camp?'

The barman shook his head. Rowse stood up and wandered over to the bar with his empty glass.

'There's talk of evicting them before the end of the week,' Wemyss-Brown went on.

George drew the pump handle towards him. 'Really?'

'Bloody inhumane, if you ask me. Don't you agree?'

The barman nodded, as barmen do when customers ask their opinion.

'Can't say I do, actually.' Rowse pushed his glass across the bar counter. 'Same again.'

Wemyss-Brown turned to face him. 'I don't think we've met, have we?'

'I don't think we have.'

There was a pause. Then Wemyss-Brown said, 'You can't just turf them out. There are kiddies there. Where are they going to go?'

'That's their affair.' Rowse paid for his drink. 'The point is, we're going to be at war in six months. Maybe sooner. Any fool can see that. The army are going to need that camp. Otherwise they'll be nothing to stop the Russkies dropping atom bombs on us right, left and centre. Then there'll be millions of people who haven't got homes. And that won't be the worst of their problems, either.'

Wemyss-Brown shook his head. 'There's every chance we can keep this business localised in Korea — as long as there aren't too many people going around rattling sabres.'

'If you ask me,' Rowse said, getting into his stride, 'we should get in first. After all, we've got the A bomb too, and now the Yanks have the H Bomb.'

'We can't go dropping bombs on every Communist in sight.'

'Best thing to do with them, in my opinion. Bang, bang, you're dead.'

'Rubbish.' Wemyss-Brown lit a cigarette with a silver lighter. 'Most Communists are just ordinary, decent people, just like us. The only thing that dropping bombs on them will achieve is make them drop bombs on us. When I was in Spain—'

'Oh,' Rowse interrupted, 'you were in Spain, eh? In the Civil War?'

'As it happens, yes.'

Rowse shrugged. 'No prizes for guessing which side *you* were on.'

'What's that supposed to mean?'

'Whatever you want it to.'

Rowse strolled back to his table in the corner. In terms of his alcoholic intake, he had reached the point where he enjoyed a good argument. Not that these provincials were capable of intellectual discussion, even the ones with hyphenated surnames. Still, it was fun to stir things up, safe in the knowledge that in all probability he would never return to Lydmouth.

He picked up the paper again. As his glow of triumph subsided, it occurred to him that perhaps he should have discovered why Wemyss-Brown had been asking for Yateley, and who Wemyss-Brown was. He knew the man was staring at him. He heard the barman ask a question, something about the *Gazette* – probably an attempt to derail an argument that might lead to a possible quarrel. But Wemyss-Brown's answer was cut short by the opening of the door from the corridor. A plump, middle-aged woman advanced towards the bar.

'Philip! I thought I might find you here,' she said in a carrying voice that suggested that here was not where he was supposed to be.

Wemyss-Brown, whose tankard had just been refilled, said, 'I'll just finish this, dear. Would you like one?'

The woman shook her head. Her eyes swept round the

room. Rowse smiled unpleasantly at her. The barman polished a glass assiduously.

A moment later, Rowse went to the lavatory. As he walked across the yard towards the gents, a primitive and evil-smelling affair at the back of the hotel, he noticed that Yateley's Humber had gone. He had hardly begun to relieve himself when he heard footsteps behind him on the concrete floor. He looked up and saw Wemyss-Brown coming into the urinal. Rowse tensed.

'I don't know who you are,' Wemyss-Brown said, 'but if I were you I'd finish your drink and go.'

'What if I don't want to?' Rowse buttoned up his flies. 'It's a free country. Unlike some I could mention.'

'You're being offensive. I assume you're drunk.'

'Whereas you're as sober as a judge. No doubt that's why the stout party came looking for you. Easy to see who wears the trousers in your household.'

As he was speaking, Rowse slipped past Wemyss-Brown and into the open air. His right hand dug into his trouser pocket, the fingers burrowing into the bunch of keys, turning them into a makeshift knuckle-duster. He felt a hand on his arm and spun round, ready to strike.

'Good evening.'

Suddenly the aggression dissolved. Both men turned towards the newcomer, a slim man who had entered the yard through the archway from Bull Lane.

Wemyss-Brown blinked. 'Evening, Thornhill.' He glanced at his watch and mimed surprise. 'Good God. Is that the time? I must be off – I'll just collect Charlotte.' He nodded at Thornhill, glared at Rowse and went back into the hotel.

Rowse's grip relaxed and the keys fell from his fingers and jingled in his pocket. Thornhill went into the lavatory. Feeling cheated, for he had wound himself up like a watch spring but all to no purpose, Rowse lit another cigarette and walked slowly back to the hotel. As he reached the door, it opened and Mrs Wemyss-Brown emerged, towing her husband by the hand. She ignored Rowse and strode towards a Rover 90 which was parked near the archway.

'Got your marching orders, I see.' Rowse smiled at Wemyss-Brown. 'She's wasted in a piddling little town like this. She should be running the War Office.'

Wemyss-Brown said, 'You've got five seconds to produce a compelling reason why I shouldn't knock you down.'

'Oh, *Philip*,' called his wife. 'For heaven's sake!'

'I'm not standing here and letting this dirty little tyke get away with insulting you.' Wemyss-Brown raised his voice. 'Well?'

For an instant, Rowse felt a thrill of pure pleasure. Now this big booby was in a rage, he was really quite terrifying. But the keys were back in his hand now, entwined among his fingers. If Wemyss-Brown was stupid enough to try throwing a punch, he would get more than he bargained for.

There were footsteps, and Thornhill appeared in the doorway of the lavatory.

'Inspector!' Charlotte Wemyss-Brown skimmed across the yard with surprising speed for a lady with her bulk. 'This man is pestering my husband.'

Inspector? Of all the bloody luck.

'I don't think I know this gentleman,' Thornhill said. 'May I ask who you are?'

'You can ask,' Rowse replied. 'Be my guest.' His excitement had receded, and so had the warmth of the alcohol, leaving a residue of tiredness and truculence behind. 'My name's Rowse.'

'And where do you live, Mr Rowse?'

'London.'

'You're a long way from London tonight.'

'I'm a journalist, though I don't see what concern that is of yours, and I'm down here to work.'

'Where are you staying?'

'The Bathurst Arms. Are you planning to keep me here all night, Inspector?'

'I hope not, Mr Rowse.'

'Well,' said Mrs Wemyss-Brown brightly, 'I suppose we'd better be on our way. I'll drive, shall I, Philip?'

The Wemyss-Browns said goodnight to Thornhill and drove off.

'I notice you don't use your finely-honed interrogation technique on them, Inspector.' Rowse took a step towards the door. 'If there's nothing more you want me for, I'll be on my way.'

'When are you leaving Lydmouth, Mr Rowse?'

'Tomorrow morning, I hope. And as far as I'm concerned, the sooner the better.'

Rowse went into the hotel and slammed the door behind him. He went into the bar to soothe himself with another Scotch. No one was behind the bar. Where the hell was George? For a moment he stood there, tapping a half-crown against the mahogany top of the counter. He noticed a cigarette lighter half concealed by the lip of the tray that held the soda siphon and the water jug. Rowse picked it up – it was the one the fat Commie had used. Silver – a Richelieu, too, one of those French imports. On impulse, he slipped the lighter into his pocket, picked up his *Gazette* and left the room. Communists were always going on about the need to redistribute property.

As he passed the reception desk on the way out, Quale raised his lizard-like head. 'Everything all right.' He left a brief pause, the subtlest of insults. 'Sir?'

'Fine,' Rowse said. 'Absolutely bloody fine.'

Chapter Five

Cameron Rowse's evening continued on its steady course towards oblivion.

He considered trying to find Oliver Yateley, which might be entertaining as well as potentially lucrative. Regretfully, however, he was forced to admit to himself that this might not be a good idea. In this sort of affair, timing was everything. If he put too much pressure on Yateley too soon, he might end up forfeiting far more important long-term advantages. Also, he was hungry.

Feeling oddly dejected, he trailed back to the Bathurst Arms in search of a meal and another drink or two. Here, fortune unexpectedly smiled on him. In the lounge bar of the Bathurst Arms, he was expecting to find Jane – Jane who had shown him his room, plain, plump, youthful Jane whom no man in his right mind would find attractive. Instead he found Mrs Alvington, a strawberry blonde and a real stunner from stem to stern. She made that stuck-up Francis woman look dowdy.

'You can't be Jane's mum. You're too young, Mrs Alvington.'

She fluttered blackened eyelashes at him. 'I'm not her mum, Mr Rowse. She's my stepdaughter. Now – are you sure you wouldn't like something to eat?'

Mrs Alvington's name was Gloria; and Rowse soon realised that he and Gloria were destined to get on like a house on fire. She served him a substantial casserole — obviously part of the family's supper — by the fire in the bar. There were few customers, and she lingered to chat. Afterwards, the other customers trickled away. Rowse went to sit at the bar and asked her if she would care to join him for a drink. She said she wouldn't mind if she did. She had one Bloody Mary, then another, and then a third. He told her some of his jokes, which she found wonderfully funny, always a good sign. When she laughed, her breasts trembled and she smoothed the tight, shiny material of her skirt over her hips. Breathless with lust, he feasted his eyes on her.

Then, to Rowse's irritation, an old man with a grey face and a stained cardigan shuffled through the doorway from the private part of the house. The old fellow had the kiss of death on him. Ignoring Rowse, he asked Gloria where the cocoa was. She shepherded the man away and was gone for at least ten minutes.

'Who was that?' Rowse asked when she returned. 'Your dad?'

She leant across the bar towards him, bringing her bright head close to his. 'That's my hubby. Harold.'

He smelled her perfume. 'Your husband? He's—'

'Yes, he's Jane's dad,' interrupted Gloria, raising her voice.

A moment later, her stepdaughter came through the door from the house. 'Shall I lock up?'

Gloria flashed Jane a smile. 'That's OK, dear, you go up. I'll do it.'

Rowse and Gloria listened to the sound of Jane's feet on the stairs. Then Gloria bolted the door to the street. She emptied the ashtrays into the fire and collected empty glasses.

'Would you like a nightcap, Mr Rowse?'

'Why not? A brandy, maybe. But will you have one with me? I don't like to drink alone.'

'All right.'

She poured the drinks, and they toasted each other.

'You know,' he said, leaning confidentially towards her, 'you really are quite something.'

She smiled lazily at him, narrowing her eyes.

He smiled back. 'Maybe I should pay my bill now? Save time in the morning.'

'Please yourself.' Gloria scribbled a figure on a beermat and slid it across the counter. 'That's breakfast, as well.'

He did not look at the beermat. He laid seven pounds on the counter. 'That should cover any – ' he glanced at her ' – any extras as well. Keep the change.'

'Thank you, Mr Rowse.'

'Call me Cameron,' he murmured.

'What would you like now?' Gloria flicked a strand of hair from her right cheek, making her breasts sway. 'Have it on the house.'

'Oh yes,' said Rowse. 'I'd like that.'

Her eyes met his, and she nodded.

Ten minutes later, Rowse made his way up the stairs to his room over the garage. He felt almost sick with excitement. *Gloria – what a girl, eh?* You could tell she was panting for it. When he reached the landing, he stood swaying for a moment, feeling for his key. The only light filtered up the stairs from the lobby below. He groped towards the door knob, and his hand jarred against the key, which was still in the lock. He must have left it there when he came upstairs briefly after his return from the Bull. He twisted the knob and pushed open the door. The room was in darkness. He brushed down the light switch. Nothing happened.

Damn. There were two switches for the single overhead light, one by the door and one a cord dangling from the ceiling by the bed. If you switched off the light with the cord, you would have to turn it on with the cord before the switch by the door would work. But he could have sworn that he had turned off the light at the door as he left the room. He fumbled in his jacket pocket for matches and found the Richelieu lighter instead. He opened it and, after a rasp of flint on steel, a wavering flame appeared. Holding up the lighter, he advanced slowly into the room.

The first thing Rowse saw was the reflection in the mirror of the person who was about to kill him.

Chapter Six

After another restless night, Detective Inspector Richard Thornhill climbed slowly up the stairs at Police Headquarters. Now, at last, he had come to a decision. Or rather, yesterday evening had forced the decision on him. He should feel glad, he told himself. Anything was better than uncertainty. But at the thought of implementing the decision, he felt an ache — not where his heart was supposed to be, but deep in his stomach.

Tension. That's all it was. Only natural.

He walked along the corridor to the CID office. Brian Kirby swung round as the door opened, revealing that he had recently bought yet another vivid tie. This one was covered with maroon zigzags against a lime-green background.

'Morning, sir,' he said. 'Mr Williamson wanted a word.'

'He's in his office?'

Kirby nodded.

'Anything else I should know?'

'Not that I know of.' Kirby brushed a hair from the sleeve of his jacket. 'It's been a quiet night.'

Thornhill went into his room and shut the door. Williamson could wait. He stared at the telephone at his desk with a mixture of longing and loathing. At last he picked up the handset and dialled the number of the *Gazette*.

'Miss Francis, please.'

'I'm sorry, sir – she isn't in yet. I could take a message, or you could speak to—'

'Thank you, but it doesn't matter.' Thornhill cut the connection. Still holding the handset, he looked out of the window and saw nothing but possibilities he did not want to see. Anything would be better than this uncertainty. He dialled the number of Church Cottage from memory.

The phone rang on and on. *She's not there, she's not there.* He did not know whether to feel relieved or sorry. *She's not there, she's not there.* There was even a bitter triumph in knowing—

'Yes?'

Thornhill opened his mouth, but the words he had rehearsed were no longer appropriate, and he had nothing to put in their place.

'Yes? Who is this?'

'Jill, it's me. Richard.'

This time the silence was on her end of the line. Then: 'I'm sorry to sound so stupid. I was asleep.'

He squeezed the phone until his hand hurt.

'I'm glad you woke me,' she went on. 'I – I must go to work. I'm late.'

'Can we meet? I need to talk to you. If it's convenient, that is.'

Another silence. 'Yes, of course. When?'

'Would some time this evening be all right? About six-thirty.'

'All right.'

They said goodbye. Sweat had left smears on the handset of Thornhill's telephone. He glanced at his watch and hurriedly left the room. The Superintendent's office was on the same floor. When Thornhill tapped on the door, the response was a muffled snarl, an invitation to come in.

Williamson had a large room overlooking the High Street. Once it had been even larger but, like most of the rooms at

Headquarters, it had been partitioned at some point during the previous sixty years. The building served as the headquarters for the county as well as for the division, and space was increasingly at a premium. There was a canteen rumour that Williamson was under pressure to move into a smaller room, so his existing office could be subdivided again. If the rumour were true, Williamson would fight the proposal all the way; he had a keen sense of what was due to a man in his position.

The Superintendent waved a hand, dispelling some of the cloud of pipe smoke that hung about his head. 'Ah, Thornhill. Sit yourself down.'

Thornhill pulled up a chair. Williamson often kept him standing. The Superintendent applied another match to his pipe. He had recently returned from sick leave and it seemed that the experience had changed him in a number of ways. His breathing was louder than it had been, as though he could not find quite enough oxygen in the air he sucked into his lungs. His colour was higher, too. And there were other changes, harder to pin down.

'Beautiful morning, eh?' He tossed the dead match in the general direction of his metal wastepaper basket. It missed. 'Wonderful what a bit of spring sunshine can do. Everything well with you?'

'Yes, thank you, sir.'

'And Mrs Thornhill and the children?'

'Yes, sir.'

'Good, good.'

Thornhill felt a twinge of alarm. 'Sergeant Kirby said you wanted a word.'

'Yes – two things. First there's this business of Farnock Camp. The squatters will have to leave within the next few days. We've been asked to stand by.'

'Where will they go?'

'None of our concern. But I wouldn't lose much sleep over them. That crowd are typical Templefields riffraff. Always bob to the surface.' Williamson sniffed. 'Like scum. Now, it shouldn't affect you directly, of course. With luck, they won't need us at all, and even if they do, it'll be a job for Uniformed. But when we get a list of the squatters' names, Mr Hendry wants us to check them against the files. Just in case.'

'Yes, sir.'

'I blame the *Gazette*, myself,' Williamson went on. 'Wemyss-Brown is usually perfectly sensible, but some of his editorials have been almost *sympathetic* to the squatters. Bloody irresponsible, if you ask me.'

So the Chief Constable had ordered Williamson to find out if they had any dirt on the squatters. Just as a precaution, Thornhill thought: if public opinion showed signs of veering towards the squatters' cause, then Hendry – if all went well – would be able to undermine the squatters' case. No doubt Hendry would be doing someone else a favour. That was the way it worked.

'So when we get the names,' Williamson was saying, 'I want you to get on to it right away. It wouldn't surprise me at all if half of them turn out to be card-carrying Communists with criminal records as long as your arm.'

'Yes, sir.'

Williamson fiddled with his pipe stem. His eyes seemed to glaze over. The old man shouldn't have come back to work yet, Thornhill thought. He wondered whether the Superintendent were past it, had permanently lost his grip. His relative benevolence was curiously unsettling, like a giggle at a funeral.

'You said there were two things you wanted to talk to me about, sir,' Thornhill said.

'Eh? Yes.' Williamson's large blue eyes focused on Thornhill. 'Have a look at this.'

He pushed a copy of the *Lydmouth Gazette* across his desk. It was yesterday's edition, folded open to page three where most of the announcements and advertisements were. An item in the personal column had been ringed in red pencil.

> *PARRY, HEATHER MARGARET: — With all our love on the anniversary of the day you went away, Mother, Dad, Keith and Granny.*

Thornhill looked up. 'Went away? Died?'

'No — went away: just that. She packed her bag and vanished into thin air. Must be three years ago now. Time flies. So you haven't heard of her?'

'Before my time, sir.'

For an instant Williamson's mouth clamped shut, as tight and unyielding as a vice. Then he forced a smile. 'I thought you might have come across it. What with the concert on Friday and the fact that Mr Broadbent's taking an interest.'

Thornhill looked down at the newspaper on his lap, just in case his expression revealed something of his feelings. Bernard Broadbent, he thought — so that was the reason for Williamson's uncharacteristic amiability. Bernard bloody Broadbent. A problem at home, and now, it seemed, a problem at work.

'The Parrys live up Narth Road,' Williamson was saying. 'One of those modern houses beyond Mill Place. You know?'

Thornhill nodded.

'Parry's an engineer. They're comfortably off, I'd say. Just the two kids: there's a boy, who's in the RAF now, and then Heather, the baby of the family. Bright kid. She was in her last year at the High School. Just eighteen.' Williamson paused. His eyes drifted down to the pipe in his hands. 'By all accounts she was a nice child. She was a school prefect — hoping to go to teacher-training college — and very musical, apparently. She was in the choir at St John's, and she used to win singing competitions. Then suddenly, one day in April, she's off.' Williamson pulled a file out of his in-tray and opened it. He glanced at one page, licked a finger and turned to the next sheet of paper. 'Here we are. One small suitcase. According to Mrs Parry, the girl just took a change of clothes. Her best clothes – they'd given her a frock for Christmas, a sort of cocktail dress, she'd taken that. Her ration book was missing. So was her Post Office Savings Book. We checked, of course, but there were no withdrawals after the date of her disappearance. Nearly thirty pounds in the account, and it's still there.' Williamson scratched his left armpit with a childlike lack of self-consciousness. 'So – what do you think of that?'

'Boyfriend?' Thornhill asked.

'None known.'

'Who was asked?'

Williamson scratched the other armpit. 'The parents and the brother.'

'What about friends?'

'The parents asked around. We were notified of the disappearance, of course, and we did what we could, but there was nothing to warrant a major investigation.' Williamson stared at Thornhill, his eyes like pale blue frosted glass. 'That was Ian Raeburn's decision, by the way. I was at a conference at Hendon.'

Inspector Raeburn, now safely retired, had been Thornhill's predecessor as Head of CID for Lydmouth Division. If anyone had made a wrong decision, Thornhill thought, it wouldn't have been Williamson.

'Any evidence of arguments in the home? Any sign of strain?'

Williamson shook his heavy head. 'Not according to Mr and Mrs Parry. For what that's worth.'

'Packing a suitcase suggests she went willingly.'

'And that she had time to plan it.'

'Had she any ambitions?'

'She wanted to be a teacher – a music teacher.' Williamson

licked his finger and turned over another sheet. 'Though the brother said she really wanted to be a singer. You know ...' His fingers played inaudible notes on an invisible keyboard. 'Marlene Dietrich. Edith Piaf. You know the sort of nonsense that girls can get in their heads. But the parents had made her see reason.'

Thornhill said carefully, 'I can understand how distressing this must be for the Parrys, but thousands of young people go off every year. There's no evidence of a crime, apart from the fact that Heather was under age. Surely, the odds are that she went off to London, with or without a boyfriend? Maybe life at home wasn't as pleasant as the Parrys make out.'

'She didn't go by train, or not from Lydmouth, and probably not by bus, either.'

'Perhaps she hitched. Or perhaps there was a boyfriend and he had a car.'

'It's possible,' Williamson conceded. 'Even probable. But the Parrys don't agree.' He paused, and this time the silence dragged on until it became uncomfortable. 'In the first few months after Heather went, the Parrys wrote to everyone they could think of. Their MP. Scotland Yard. The *Gazette*. Their county councillor – at that time it was old Hawley-Minton. He wasn't much use to them, of course – wasn't much use to anyone.'

Once again Williamson paused. At 84, Brigadier Hawley-Minton had been the oldest member of the County Council. For many years he had been a by-word for inactivity, but he still commanded substantial support in his ward. The Brigadier had won a VC during the Boer War and there was a vague, but powerful feeling that voting against him would be both ungrateful and unpatriotic. In January of this year, Hawley-Minton had at last succumbed to his many infirmities and there had been a by-election to fill the vacant seat on the Council. Hawley-Minton was notionally Conservative, though his political philosophy had more to do with the Duke of

Wellington's than Mr Churchill's. After his death, the electors had evidently decided that they wanted a complete change. A large majority had voted for the Labour candidate, Bernard Broadbent, a former coal miner who was now the part-owner of a large engineering works outside Lydmouth.

Bernard Broadbent — Edith Thornhill's cousin Bernard.

'Parry asked Mr Broadbent to look into the matter again.' Williamson tapped a typed letter on his blotter. 'And Councillor Broadbent's been in touch with me. We're keen to do anything we can.' Williamson paused and gave Thornhill another frosted blue glare. 'Naturally.'

Naturally? In Thornhill's opinion, there was nothing natural about it. But the whole affair was beginning to make an unpleasant sense at last. Broadbent was a newly-elected county councillor, keen to sweep vigorously, as new brooms are wont to be. But there was more to it than that: Hawley-Minton's death had removed not only a County Councillor but also a member of the Standing Joint Committee, which oversaw the county's police force. In time — probably sooner rather than later — another councillor would fill the vacancy. A monstrous suspicion blossomed in Thornhill's mind.

'But Heather must be over twenty-one by now,' he pointed out, trying to avert the inevitable. 'And there's no evidence that a crime has been committed.'

'That depends how you interpret the evidence, doesn't it, Thornhill? The point is, she was a minor when she disappeared, and there's nothing to show that she left Lydmouth.' He cleared his throat, producing a sound like a strangled growl. 'In my *humble* judgement.'

'Yes, sir.'

Williamson closed the file and pushed it across the desk. 'Everything's there, including a photograph taken just a few weeks before her disappearance. A birthday snap — she was wearing that frock, in fact. I imagine you'll want to talk to the Yard. It might also be worth circulating the details to

Manchester, Birmingham and Cardiff.' He rapped the pipe sharply against the cut-glass ashtray on his desk. 'Might as well try Bristol, as well, and Newport and Swansea. No point in spoiling the ship for a ha'porth of tar. And then you'll also want to go over the ground locally, I dare say. It'll be a useful exercise, whatever the outcome. Co-operation and team work: that's the way we do things in this force, eh? Only the other day I was saying to Mr Hendry—'

One of the telephones began to ring. Williamson picked up the nearer of the two. Thornhill made as if to leave, but the Superintendent waved to him to stay where he was. The conversation which followed was brief. Then Williamson slammed down the phone with such inaccurate violence that it fell out of its cradle and had to be replaced.

'Damn.' His face looked sharper and harder than it had a moment ago, the eyes colder and bluer. 'That's the last thing we need. They've got a body at the Bathurst Arms.'

Chapter Seven

'Next!' bellowed Dr Bayswater, his voice only slightly muffled by the one-and-a-half-inch thick mahogany door which separated his consulting room from the waiting room.

The receptionist, a sternly handsome lady in late middle age, nodded to Phyllis Richards with the stately condescension of a lord chamberlain controlling access to the presence of a monarch. Phyllis smiled her thanks and thought *You nasty woman.* She stood up, gathered up her handbag and gloves and tapped on the door.

'Come!'

Phyllis went into the consulting room and closed the door behind her. Bayswater was writing but he broke off to wave her to a chair. Both the room and the doctor looked as if they had seen better days. Phyllis's eyes darted to and fro, registering the hole in the carpet by the door, the pile of ashes in the grate, the cobwebs along the cornice, the dull, unpolished wood of the desk, the dark stain on the lapel of Bayswater's tweed jacket, and his unbrushed grey hair. She wished with all her heart that she had not come, that she had surrendered to the urge to slip out of the waiting room while there was still time.

Bayswater capped his fountain pen and looked up. 'Mrs – ah –?' He glanced down at her notes – not that there would be anything there apart from her name, age and address. 'Mrs Richards. What can I do for you?'

He spoke abruptly but in a cultivated voice that was at odds with his down-at-heel appearance. Bayswater had a reputation as a ladies' man, Phyllis had heard, which perhaps had something to do with the fact that he so obviously looked as though he needed mothering.

'Well?' he prompted, glancing at his wristwatch.

'I – I haven't been sleeping well – for some time now ...'

'I see.' He looked at her notes again. 'Why is there nothing here?'

'I've only lived in Lydmouth for two years. And I've never had occasion to ...'

'I can see that. But where were you living before? They haven't sent on your notes.'

'My husband and I were living in Singapore before the war. Then I was evacuated to Australia. My husband – he didn't survive.' Phyllis wondered whether to trot out the familiar story about the Japanese prisoner-of-war camp but decided not to; Bayswater was tapping his fingers against the desk. 'And then I came back home.'

Home – such a useful word, she thought: it changes meaning all the time. Is home a country, a town, a house? She looked down at her clasped hands and felt her eyes fill with tears. Or merely where the heart is?

'So you've not been sleeping well?' Bayswater said, more gently than before. 'How long for?'

Months? Years? She said, 'For the last six weeks it's been worse.'

'Any particular reason?'

'I'm a companion-housekeeper to an old lady and – and recently I've begun to wonder what will happen to me if she dies or has to go into a nursing home.' Phyllis looked up and tried to smile. 'I suppose you could say I don't feel very secure. And lately it's been growing worse and worse. It's got so bad that I keep nodding off during the day, sometimes at the most inappropriate times.'

Her employer, Mrs Portleigh, was religiously inclined and liked to begin and end the day with prayers and a reading from the Bible. She had a voice that whispered like the wind in the chimney, and the effect was so soporific that on three occasions Phyllis had dozed off. 'An insult to God,' Mrs Portleigh had said on the third occasion, 'and an insult to me.'

'And what do you expect me to do for you?' Dr Bayswater asked.

'I wondered if you would prescribe me something to help me sleep. Mrs Portleigh's husband used to have barbiturates and I wondered—'

'Barbiturates? Not ideal. But I'll give you something else to take at bedtime. Something to help you get off to sleep. If things don't improve, come and see me again in a fortnight.'

While he was speaking, he had been writing on his prescription pad. He tore off the top sheet of paper and handed it to her.

'Thank you, Doctor.'

'Good morning.'

Phyllis slipped out of the room and closed the door as gently as she could. The receptionist stared at her but said nothing. It seemed to her that everyone in the waiting room was staring at her. But there was nothing personal in that, Phyllis told herself. If you were sitting in a waiting room with nothing to do, you naturally stared at anyone who was moving, at anyone who was leaving the doctor's room. She shouldn't take it personally. It didn't mean that they knew that every day of her life she was living a lie. She smiled apologetically at the receptionist and sidled towards the door to the street.

'Next!' shouted Dr Bayswater.

Chapter Eight

Thank God for Richard, Jill Francis thought. If he hadn't telephoned she might have slept until lunchtime.

It was after half past nine. The unexpected arrival of Oliver Yateley had been not so much the last straw on the camel's back as the last ton of bricks. Jill had lain awake for most of the night with the problems chasing round her mind – singly, in pairs and in crowds. Alice, her heavily pregnant cat, had added insult to injury by sleeping unfeelingly for most of this time. Jill had heard the church clock striking the quarters and the hours. She heard the milkman delivering the milk. Shortly after this, she fell into an uneasy doze, only to be woken by Alice purring loudly and thrusting her head into Jill's face. She staggered downstairs, fed the cat and let her out. Then she went back to bed and this time she slept so solidly that even the clanging of the alarm did not wake her, slept until Richard Thornhill telephoned.

Fifteen minutes later, she was out of the house – washed, dressed and made up; but also hungry, thirsty, heavy-eyed with tiredness and more worried than she remembered being since that terrible week when she first came to Lydmouth.

It was only a short walk to the *Gazette* office on the corner of the High Street opposite the war memorial. She was so late that she dared not even go into the Gardenia for a cup of coffee. As she approached the office, she heard a sash window sliding up above her head.

'Hi, Jill!' Philip Wemyss-Brown called.

She looked up.

Her editor had his elbows on the sill. He was glowering at her. 'Can you spare a moment? I'd like a word.'

The head withdrew and the sash slammed down. Jill went through the front office, up the stairs and along the landing to Philip's office. Miss Gwyn-Thomas, his secretary, peered down her long, wandering nose at Jill and glanced at the clock before wishing her good morning. Jill tapped on Philip's door and went in.

Scowling, he lumbered towards her. 'You're late.'

'I overslept – sorry.'

'And I bet you've come out without any breakfast.' Philip waved her towards one of the armchairs by the fire and went into the ante-room. 'Miss Gwyn-Thomas, be a darling and make us some coffee, would you? And we'll have a biscuit, too. On second thoughts, you'd better bring the whole tin.' He came back into his room, closing the door behind him. His cheeks looked more pouchy than usual and he had cut himself shaving. 'I was late myself, as a matter of fact. Slept badly.'

He felt in his pockets, produced a packet of cigarettes and offered it to Jill. She shook her head. He patted his pockets.

'Damn – can't find anything this morning. Have you got a match?'

She found a box in her handbag and lobbed it to him. He lit the cigarette, inhaling hungrily, and sat down heavily in the other armchair.

'What happened?' Jill asked. 'You look ghastly. More or less as I feel.'

He smiled at her. 'I had one of those evenings. For a start, I was in the Bull and a nasty little man wanted a quarrel. He tried to pick a fight. He tried so hard I nearly gave him one.'

'But why?'

'How should I know? Fellow was half drunk, and it takes people that way sometimes. I was just having a quiet chat about Farnock Camp with George, and this fellow Rowse butted in with some absurd war-mongering rubbish. And later he made some rather personal remarks about Charlotte. Naturally, I wasn't having that. I—'

'Rowse?' Jill interrupted. 'Are you sure?'

'Luckily both Charlotte and Richard Thornhill turned up just as I was about to knock him down.'

Jill looked down at her lap. Secretly she traced an R with her fingertip on the material of her skirt.

'Otherwise I would probably be up before the magistrates at this very moment,' Philip was saying. He glanced sharply at Jill. 'What did you say about Rowse? Do you know him?'

'I think I might have met him. What was he like?'

'Smallish man, bad teeth. A Londoner, by the sound of him, and he had a bit of a lisp. When I saw him he was wearing a frightful tweed jacket.'

'He was at Farnock Camp yesterday afternoon. He said he was doing a piece on the squatters for the *Picture Post.*'

'A journalist? In that case I pity the squatters.'

'He was taking photographs of all and sundry and asking for their life histories,' Jill said. 'He gave the impression he was entirely on their side.'

'He would, wouldn't he?'

There was a knock on the door and Miss Gwyn-Thomas brought in a tray of coffee. Philip poured Jill a cup and passed her the tin. She wolfed down two biscuits.

With her mouth full of the third, she said, 'What did you actually say to Rowse?'

'This and that.'

'Did he know who you were?'

'*I* didn't tell him.'

'Yes, but someone else might. And I dare say you made your personal sympathies quite clear?'

Philip flushed. 'Not in so many words. But I couldn't let him get away completely with such balderdash. I made one or two points – nothing controversial, mind: the sort of thing that any rational man would find perfectly acceptable.' He glanced at Jill and added hastily, 'Or woman, for that matter. I know George agreed with me.'

'George agrees with everyone, Philip.'

He waved a hand. 'He agrees with some people more wholeheartedly than others. You can always tell. Well, at least I can. Anyway, this chap Rowse was the next best thing to a fascist, so—'

'You didn't mention Spain, did you?'

'As a matter of fact, yes. But only in passing. And why not? It's nothing to be ashamed of.'

Jill held her tongue. Philip was an excellent journalist but he had his blind spots. One of them was his inability to believe that anyone could actually dislike him.

He waved a cigarette at her. 'Look, what are you getting at?'

'I didn't take to Rowse. I'm pretty sure he hasn't got any sympathy with the squatters, either. This business at Farnock Camp has all the makings of a juicy story. And from what you've told me, he's trying hard to make it even juicier.'

'Aren't you being a bit Machiavellian?'

'I can see the sort of line he'll take. While our boys are dying in Korea, some of the very people they are protecting are making the army's job more difficult at home. Even worse, the editor of the local paper supports them. Not that that's altogether strange, Rowse'll point out, because the said editor is a Communist sympathiser.'

'Twaddle. I'll have him for libel.'

'No, you won't. All he'll do is mention that you fought

on the Republican side in the Spanish Civil War. That's all he *needs* to do.'

'He doesn't know I fought—'

'He soon will if he doesn't already.'

'I was only out there for two weeks. Less than that.' Philip glared at Jill, who knew better than to take it personally. 'All right, perhaps I should have been more careful. So what do you propose I do about it?'

'As little as possible. Try and ride it out.' Jill hesitated. 'I know someone in the features department at the *Picture Post*. I could ring him if you like. I've a feeling that Rowse is working on spec.'

Philip shrugged. 'Worth a try, I suppose, though I don't see what good it can do.' He took out another cigarette and patted his pockets again. Muttering an excuse, he opened the door of his room. 'Miss Gwyn-Thomas? Would you phone the Bull for me? I think I may have left my lighter there last night.' He closed the door, sat down and refilled the coffee cups. 'It was one of those evenings. Charlotte wasn't best pleased with me, either – dinner was ruined. And afterwards I had to go out and see Bernard Broadbent, for Spews.'

Spews was the nickname for People In The News, an occasional series of short features about county notables which had been running for nearly six months.

'Broadbent?' Jill said. 'He's a bit of an outside candidate, isn't he?'

'I don't know – he's made a dramatic change from Hawley-Minton, and his majority was really quite impressive. There's a rumour he's going places. They want to fill the vacancy on the Standing Joint Committee with a Labour councillor. And then of course, he's a former miner, as he's always telling one. Local boy made good – that's always a popular theme. He's no fool, either, not when it comes to getting himself noticed. You know he's trying to get the Parry case reopened? That won't do him any harm.'

'You make him sound dreadfully calculating.'

'Perhaps he is,' Philip said. 'Or perhaps he just does it naturally. Some people are like that. He certainly enjoys talking about himself. He kept me there until after midnight.'

'The Parry girl – did you know her?'

'No.' Philip leant forward to stub out his cigarette. 'If you believe the parents, she was as angelic as they come.'

'What does Broadbent think?'

'God knows. But at present it suits him to help the parents. He's supporting the madrigal concert at the High School as well – the one on Friday evening that's raising funds for the Parry Music Room. He knows what he's doing.'

'You're much more cynical than you used to be.'

'It's this job.' Philip ran his fingers through his thinning hair. 'Nothing like a local paper for showing you the worst side of human nature. You know that.'

Jill took another biscuit. 'I do have work to do. I know we're having a lovely cosy chat, but is there something else you'd like to say to me?'

'Oh – ah – yes.' Philip looked anxiously at her. 'If you can spare another moment. The thing is, the reason I went to the Bull last night was because old Quale tipped me the wink. It seems that they've got Oliver Yateley staying there.'

Not Oliver, Jill thought: please God – don't say Philip knows about Oliver.

'Good for a few column inches, I thought. Everyone knows Yateley because of the radio work he does. The trouble was, I just missed him. It turned out he'd gone out to dinner. I mentioned it to Charlotte, though, and she said perhaps I'd better have a word with you before going any further. I'd forgotten you actually knew him. Not Charlotte, though – she's got a memory like an elephant's. Didn't he phone you once, when you were staying with us? She thought he did.'

'Yes,' Jill heard herself saying. 'I believe he did.'

She took a cigarette from her bag. Philip leant forward to light it.

'Anyway, seeing as there's a personal connection, perhaps if we do something about him, you'd be the best one to write it. But perhaps you think it wouldn't be ... well, altogether appropriate?'

Philip's voice tailed away. A heavy lorry rumbled down the High Street, making the sash window rattle in its frame. Jill carefully tapped ash into her saucer. Philip's words said one thing but meant much more. She felt angry, mortified and – strangest of all – ashamed, and all because Oliver Yateley had reappeared in Lydmouth like a troublesome ghost. She didn't know what was worst: Charlotte putting two and two together and making five, which Jill suspected she must have done some time ago; or Charlotte telling Philip all about her conclusions.

'Jill? Are you all right?'

She had hoped that no one else need know. Oliver had at least been discreet – he had told her that he had not mentioned her name at the hotel. She looked at Philip, whose face was slightly flushed.

'Yes, I do know Oliver,' she said coolly. 'In fact, when I was in London I knew him quite well. But I don't think he would welcome publicity while he's in Lydmouth.'

'No,' Philip said, displaying the sort of tact that is harder to deal with than a slap in the face. 'I don't suppose he would. I quite understand.'

Jill stood up and thought: *Oh no, you don't.*

Chapter Nine

———◆———

Howard had hoped to find the house before daybreak, but as usual luck was against him.

Edge Hill was only a couple of miles from the centre of Lydmouth, but in the dark he took a wrong turning and ended up down by the river again. Then he nearly fell foul of a policeman on a bicycle. Later still, he tried to shelter in a barn, only to be scared off by a barking dog. When the sky began to lighten in the east, he found a footpath going in what he hoped was the right direction. Unfortunately it led straight through a large field heavily populated with cows. He was afraid of cows, which was something only his mother, long dead, had known. What if a cow took against you? It could crush the life out of you. What could a whole herd do? And then there was the question of whether they were all cows. Maybe some were bullocks or bulls. No doubt about it, it was wiser to find another way.

Howard stumbled through the muddy fields, squeezing through gaps in prickly hedgerows, muttering a steady flow of soft obscenities. He found another footpath, this one safely enclosed by high hedges and running up from the river. But by the time he reached Edge Hill, the day had well and truly begun. He hid for a while in a building site on the east side of the triangular village green. Luckily no one was working there today. He made himself wait, trying to keep warm, trying to ignore the hunger that dug deeper and deeper into his stomach. That and the lack of sleep were making him feel almost unreal.

Someone strange is in my head. Her? Can't be her, you stupid bastard, she's dead.

He forced himself to concentrate. The trouble was, he didn't know which was the house he wanted. He could have asked someone, of course, but that would have been to court disaster. People would remember him. He had slept rough since leaving London, and he'd been forced to walk for the last fifty miles of the way; hitching had been obviously out of the question. He had a three-day beard, and he suspected that he smelt. Even so, someone might recognise him. That was the ever-present danger, the one thing that must not happen. Because if they did, they might remember—

Someone strange is in my head.

So Howard waited and watched as the sun climbed higher in the sky. He made brief, cautious forays around the building site. Once it had been a garden, he thought, and the remains of a shrubbery made it easier than it might have been to move around without advertising his presence. Between the building site and the three-cornered green was a main road, probably the road north from Lydmouth. At the corner furthest from him was a church; to the left was a row of cottages; and to the right were larger houses set back from the green behind walls and trees, and also a small school. Behind the church was what looked like a small council estate, which was unlikely to be much use to him.

Next, he investigated the main road as best he could without giving himself away. In the Lydmouth direction were neat little semi-detached houses, all of them numbered, though some had names as well; but he did not think it could be one of those. In the other direction, there were only fields — fields and more cows.

All he had was the address: Rochester House, Edge Hill, Lydmouth. It sounded a solid, respectable sort of place. If he had to put money on it, he thought, he would go for one of the more substantial houses on the right of the green. He hoped that Rochester House wasn't tucked away somewhere on the outskirts; in that case it could take him days to find. He worked his way nearer the road and settled in the shelter of a lank laurel, its leaves gritty with dirt thrown up by the traffic.

A bus came trundling down the road from Lydmouth and drew up at the stop on the green, almost opposite his laurel bush. He drew back into its dusty green recesses. Three women got off. Tweed coats, headscarves and shopping baskets; dowdy old crones, not worth a second glance. And then without warning his luck changed.

The bus pulled away, revealing a fourth woman who had got off behind the others. Like them, she wore a coat and headscarf and carried a shopping basket. But she was younger, and she could have been reasonably good looking if only she had taken a bit of trouble with her appearance. Then what he saw collided with a memory, and past and present became one.

Phyllis, by God, it's Phyllis.

In his excitement Howard almost said her name aloud, almost called out to her. An instant later, he realised that that would have been suicide. The three old crones were still within earshot. It would have ruined everything. No, the best thing to do was to stay where he was and watch, and wait.

With his eyes, he tracked Phyllis as she crossed the green. She veered to the right and turned into the driveway of one of the houses near the school. The house was set back further from the green than the others, and stood a little apart from them.

Better and better.

There was also the reassuring knowledge that he had been correct: that, just as his intelligence had forecast, Rochester House was one of those on the right. There was nothing wrong with his brain. He'd run rings around them all before he was finished. Confidence surged through him. It was going to be OK. Now he knew which house to go to, why shouldn't he simply cross the road, walk over the green and go boldly up the drive to the front door? The chances of his being noticed were small; and if he picked a time when no one was around, the chances of his being recognised were so minute they barely existed.

Then caution damped the flare of optimism. Why risk it? This was Lydmouth, not London: any stranger was likely to be noticed, particularly one who looked as disreputable as he did. Besides, there was the situation at the house to consider. No point in blundering in without a proper reconnaissance.

Howard stared over the road at Rochester House, framed in the leaves of his laurel bush. It was hard to get a clear idea of its size and appearance because of the high garden wall and the trees. But the chimneys on the gable nearest to him were distinctive – a bank of four in pale yellow clay: square in cross-section, and gently tapering to a toothed rim at the top. It began to rain, a new discomfort.

He could bear the waiting no longer. Any action was better than none. He picked up his knapsack and slipped away from the laurel bush, whose shelter became almost homely at the moment of leaving it. He worked his way through the debris of the building site to its northern boundary.

Feeling uncomfortably exposed, Howard scrambled over the wall. The first field had been ploughed and sown – something green was growing in neat lines like soldiers on parade. He kept close to the line of the hedgerow, his head ducked so that it would not show above the skyline. The next field was used as pasture – fortunately it was empty of cows and humans. This was a large field, and at the far corner was a five-bar gate which must lead on to the main road. The field beyond, however, was full of cows.

He reckoned that he was now almost half a mile north of Edge Hill. He made himself wait until he could hear no traffic before crossing the road. On the other side was another ploughed field. Soon his boots were heavy with the turned clay. The rain was falling harder. He licked drops of water from his face. Strange to be so wet and cold on the outside and so dry and hot on the inside. As he staggered along the line of the hedgerow, it occurred to him that he had not eaten anything for twenty-four hours; no wonder everything was strange.

On the far side of the field were trees, the fringe of what looked like a substantial spinney. Trees were good: they offered shelter and concealment. The advantages outweighed the drawbacks, such as the risk of gamekeepers.

The spinney was fenced with barbed wire, and he tore his coat and cut his left hand as he struggled through it. He leant against a tree and sucked the cut. Nourishment of a sort? The spinney was a quiet, cool place but some of the colours were unbearably vivid. There were buds like green flames on the tips of the branches and there were drops of bright blood on the skin and on his trousers.

'Red for go,' he muttered aloud, 'green for danger. Oh Christ, I'm seeing things.'

He heaved himself away from the tree and blundered on through the wood. Suddenly it became easy. One foot after another, like an endless file of soldiers. He stumbled into a low, cast-iron fence, the sort a child could have climbed or slipped through. And that was odd because for a moment he thought he heard children singing. He shook his head, trying to shake the singing out of it. Beyond the fence was a shrubbery. Beyond the shrubbery were the roofs and chimneys of a house. Tapering chimneys, square in cross-section. His house.

Wouldn't it be lovely, the stranger in his head was saying, if we had our own little house, just you and me, all on our own?

Careful, Howard told himself, forcing himself to concentrate. He could hardly turn up at the back door, cap in hand. In some ways this was the most dangerous part of the whole operation. For all he knew, the house could be packed with people. He needed to watch and wait before he made a move. He needed to be sure.

Howard slipped through the fence. Instinct drew him towards an extension from the main house whose roofs were lower than the rest. The shrubbery was bounded by a stone wall, on the far side of which was a sort of yard. Close to him was an outbuilding, its door hanging by only one of its hinges. With a whimper of relief, he stumbled towards it.

Inside it was dark, but dry and appreciably warmer than it had been outside in the rain. Howard stood for a moment just inside the doorway, leaning with his back to the wall, his limbs trembling. He dropped the knapsack on the ground. Food and sleep, he told himself, that's what I need: then I'll be as right as rain.

The children were singing again, a sort of chanting sound that went round and round. Was it outside or inside his head? He could even make out the words, or thought he could: 'Mrs Nipper! Mrs Yipper! Mrs Slapper! Mrs Crapper!'

Bloody rubbish. Can't be real. Doesn't matter. Ignore it.

Gradually his eyes adjusted to the gloom. He was in a wood store. A long-handled axe leant against a cradle for sawing wood. There was a small pile of chopped logs near the door. At the back was a larger pile of unchopped wood. The air was scented with pine.

He took a few steps towards the darkest corner of the outbuilding. He stumbled on something soft. His stomach lurched as though a cold hand had pressed it towards his spine.

Slowly he bent down, fingers outstretched.

Just a pile of sacks, dry to the touch. Not a body, heavy and yielding. He shook out the sacks, one by one, draped two of them over his shoulders and sat on the rest, with his back against the wall.

Mustn't go to sleep. Too dangerous.

His teeth were chattering, and he drew the sacks more tightly around him. His head felt light and swaying, as though no longer firmly attached to his body. He knew he must concentrate in order to prevent himself from falling asleep. He wished those bloody kids would stop. On and on they went, a waking dream without end.

Mrs Nipper! Mrs Yipper! Mrs Slapper! Mrs Crapper! Mrs Nipper! Mrs Yipper! Mrs Slapper! Mrs Crapper! Mrs Nipper! Mrs Yipper! Mrs Slapper! Mrs Crapper ...!

Time passed, and the children stopped their wretched singing. Perhaps he slept, perhaps he dreamed. Howard wasn't sure. But it was not meant to be like this. He knew that. It wasn't fair.

Then he opened his eyes to find Phyllis looking down at him as he lay, teeth chattering, under sacks smelling of pines and damp earth. He knew it was Phyllis, even though he could not see her face properly. It was something about the shape of her head, silhouetted against the rectangle of grey light from the doorway. Why was it so dark in here? Why couldn't he see properly?

It must be Phyllis's fault.

'Howard,' she was saying. 'Oh my God, Howard, oh my God.'

He would have liked to leap up, grip her by the shoulders and shake her until her teeth rattled in her skull, just as his were doing. But he was unable to move. It was as though a cold weight pressed down on his limbs. Yet he was very thirsty and someone had lit a fire behind his eyes.

What Howard hated more than all the discomfort was the knowledge that he was no longer in control. This was all wrong. He was always in control. That was what made him different from all the others, from the little people who never got what they wanted because they were too scared to try to get it. Not him, though, not him. He was never scared. His eyelids covered his eyes and he was alone once more in the darkness with the singing children.

Mrs Nipper! Mrs Yipper! Mrs Slapper! Mrs Crapper! Mrs Nipper! Mrs Yipper! Mrs Slapper! Mrs Crapper!

Chapter Ten

There was a uniformed officer outside the Bathurst Arms, and in the window of the saloon bar was a notice written in neat round capitals: CLOSED UNTIL FURTHER NOTICE. Thornhill told his driver to wait and went inside.

Brian Kirby was in the saloon bar with Harold, Jane and a woman whom Thornhill did not at first recognise. For a moment, he thought it must be the charwoman. She wore a faded housecoat with a floral pattern and a turban covering curlers. Her face was pale and stern.

'Good morning, sir,' he said to Harold. 'A sad business.' He nodded to Jane. 'Miss Alvington.' An instant later, he realised he was seeing Gloria as had never seen her before. 'Mrs Alvington.'

Nor had he seen the bar like this, with cloths draped over the hand pumps, the fire laid but unlit and only the family there. The room looked as unnatural as a stage set seen from the wings. Usually he would have called Jane and Gloria by their Christian names, which added to the unreality of the occasion.

When the greetings were over, Thornhill beckoned Kirby outside into the passage.

'So what exactly have we got, Brian?'

'We've certainly got a corpse, sir. The bloke was a guest

here – turned up out of the blue yesterday afternoon. Apparently his motorbike had broken down. The boys got here about ten minutes ago. They're upstairs.'

Thornhill nodded. The Scene of Crime Officers could be safely left to their own devices for a while.

'And Bayswater?'

Kirby grinned. 'Said the living had more need of him than the dead. He's coming after he's done his rounds.'

'What does it look like?'

'Could be a knife wound in the chest,' Kirby said. 'Hard to be sure till we move him. Room's been turned over.'

'Any sign of the weapon?'

Kirby shook his head. Then: 'Jane found him. She took him some tea about nine-thirty – realised he was dead and got on the phone right away.'

'Touch anything?'

'She says not. No fool, that girl.'

'Have you got a name?'

'Cameron Rowse. He's some sort of journalist from the Smoke.'

'I think I met him at the Bull last night.' Thornhill frowned, remembering the scene in the yard at the back of the hotel. 'Any idea when he died?'

Kirby jerked a thumb at the lounge bar. 'He was in there until just after midnight. Him and our Gloria were keeping each other company.' He paused and added demurely, 'At least, that's what Jane told me. I haven't had a chance to confirm it with the horse's mouth.'

Thornhill led the way back into the bar.

'Would you like some coffee, Inspector?' Harold croaked.

Gloria opened her mouth as if about to snap something out, but closed it again.

'Nothing for us, thank you, sir.'

Thornhill sat down at the head of the long table. Harold was at right angles to him on a padded settle that ran along the wall, with Gloria and Jane on either side. Kirby took a chair opposite them and pulled out his notebook. Thornhill glanced at Harold, whom he had not seen for several months. The publican had once been a big man, but he was shrinking inside his skin. His complexion was pale, more grey than white, and the black-and-white stubble on his face made him look unwashed. Liver-spotted fingers plucked at the thick flannel of his trousers. He was wearing slippers, two cardigans, a collarless shirt and a muffler. It was a mild spring morning.

'Harold's not well,' Gloria said suddenly. 'Couldn't he go and lie down, Mr Thornhill? I'm sure me and Jane can answer anything you want to ask.'

'I'm all right,' Harold said. 'Don't fuss.'

Jane sucked in her breath. Everyone said that Harold Alvington had cancer, though he and Gloria stoutly denied it. The trouble was, Thornhill thought, everything depended on Harold. If Harold died, then the only common ground between Gloria and Jane was the fact that they would both have a claim on his estate. There might not be much left to quarrel over, either. Since Harold's illness, the business had declined. And it was Harold's name over the door: the Bathurst Arms was a tied house, and there must be a possibility that both the brewery and the magistrates might feel that Gloria was not a fit person to take over as licensee. And it wouldn't help if Rowse had got himself murdered on the premises, especially after a drinking session with Gloria.

'Just a few questions for now,' Thornhill said. 'We need to establish a framework, you see. When did Mr Rowse arrive?'

Gradually the story emerged. To Gloria's obvious chagrin, Jane did most of the talking — inevitably, because Gloria had not met Cameron Rowse until the evening. He had arrived in the middle of the afternoon, sent to the Bathurst by Joe Vance at Vance's Garage. (At this point Thornhill intercepted a glance between Gloria and Jane.) Jane had shown Rowse up to his room. He had asked directions to Farnock Camp and gone out almost immediately afterwards.

Harold stirred. 'Farnock Camp? Isn't Norah Coalway up there?'

'Who?' Gloria said.

'Yes, she is.' Jane looked at Thornhill as she answered Gloria's question. 'She used to work here when she and Sid were courting.'

He nodded. 'Do you know when Mr Rowse got back from the camp?'

Jane shook her head. The next time she had seen him, he was coming down the staircase from the guest bedroom. It had been a little after five o'clock, she thought. He had asked her which was the biggest hotel in town. Then he had left, presumably going to the Bull.

Gloria took up the story. It had been about eight o'clock when Rowse returned to the Bathurst. She had served him a meal in the bar. Yes, he had seemed in quite a cheerful mood, though she hadn't been observing him closely. Yes, he had had a drink or two after closing time and had insisted on buying her a drink as well while she was tidying up before going to bed. She thought he had gone upstairs at about midnight.

While the two women were speaking, dough-faced Harold sat between them, his red-rimmed eyes fixed on Thornhill. An April shower gusted up the river and threw itself against the window of the Bathurst's saloon bar. Gloria broke off, directing a startled glance towards the sound. Like fingernails tapping on the glass, Thornhill thought, startled by his own flight of fancy; a ghostly lover, perhaps.

Let me in, let me in . . . Jill, oh Lord, what the hell are we going to do?

A second later, he became aware that the lounge bar was silent except for the cries of the seagulls over the river, and that Brian Kirby and the other three were looking in his direction, waiting for him to say something.

'And this morning?' he said sharply to Jane.

'I took him some tea. And there he was.'

'Had he asked to be called?'

'No, sir. But it was after half-past nine so I thought I'd better wake him.' She bit her lip.

'Had he been to bed?'

She shook her head. 'I don't think so. The bed's still made. No creases on the pillow.'

'You've been very helpful.' He pushed back his chair and stood up. 'We'll need to talk to you again, of course. All of you. But I'd like to see the room now.'

Jane said suddenly, 'Did you know you can reach it from the yard as well?'

'The Inspector's got eyes in his head, dear,' Gloria said. 'Same as everyone else.'

Jane glanced at her stepmother. 'It might be important.'

Harold nodded. 'The girl's right. If the door to the yard wasn't locked, anyone could have got in.'

'I locked up myself,' Gloria said.

'But when did you do it, my girl?' Harold glared at his wife and, for an instant, the ghost of his old authority clung to him. 'Can't you see? That's the point.'

Chapter Eleven

For several years, Philip had cultivated a useful source at Police Headquarters, a sergeant named Fowles who was a natural gossip. It was he who tipped off the *Gazette* about the body at the Bathurst Arms with a phone call in the middle of Wednesday morning. All he knew was that a man was dead in one of the bedrooms, and that Thornhill and Kirby were there with a team of SOCOs. But that was enough.

A murder could mean lucrative business for a local paper, with the nationals and the bigger provincials queuing up for information and photographs. Philip was bogged in a meeting with one of the *Gazette*'s main advertisers, but Jill and a photographer drove down to the Bathurst Arms in the Ford Anglia belonging to the *Gazette*.

Two police cars were parked outside the pub. Bayswater usually acted as police surgeon but there was no sign of his Wolseley yet. There was a constable at the door but he flatly refused to give any information.

'Might as well shoot a roll of film while I'm here,' said the photographer. 'At least it's not bloody raining.'

'Try the back,' Jill suggested.

He nodded. 'If there's a body, that's where they'll take the ambulance.' He raised the camera and pointed it at the constable. 'Smile, please.'

Jill wandered round the outside of the pub, noting down details she might be able to use. The Bathurst Arms was a well-known establishment, but it catered mainly for men so she knew little about it apart from the fact that it had a dining room which did a good trade at lunchtime. It was a substantial Victorian building at the bottom of Lyd Street, separated from the river by the towpath and a grassy bank. The gates to the yard were closed. The windows gave nothing away. Apart from the smoke curling from two of the chimneys, the place might have been deserted. She thought she saw movement behind the window of a first floor room at the back and wondered whether that was where the body was.

The police car had attracted the attention of a couple of men with nothing better to do. The pub would be closed at lunchtime, and soon the news would be all over town. Jill tried the nearby shops — a newsagent's, a small ironmonger's, a barber's and a tobacconist's — but gleaned nothing of value.

'I wouldn't know what's going on, would I?' the ironmonger said. 'Why don't you ask that nice bobby over there?'

In situations like this, Jill knew, she was handicapped by her accent and by the fact she had not been born and bred in Lydmouth. She walked down to the Lyd and strolled slowly along the towpath, lifting her face to the spring sunshine. There were now several benches along the river between the Bathurst Arms and the New Bridge beyond the railway station. The council had recently made an attempt to smarten up the riverside, in the hope of attracting more tourists to the town. But they needed to do something about the grass, which was long, lank and speckled with dandelions and daisies. Apart from an old man on the nearest bench, the path was deserted. At the end of the bench were more weeds — something tall and green, with small purple flowers. Beyond the river, the hills rose up to the Forest.

Jill glanced back at the pub. There was definitely movement at that first-floor window. She glimpsed a shoulder and an arm

– and something that might possibly be a camera. Richard was in that pub, but she tried not to think of that.

The old man was trying to stand up. As she glanced at him, he began to cough, a bubbling, retching sound that shook his entire body. Jill walked on a few paces, hoping he would stop. But he didn't. Reluctantly she turned round and walked down to the bench. The dew would soak the fine leather of her shoes, and because of the length of the grass, her ankles were wet within a few seconds. The man was arched forward now, and every few seconds a spasm of coughing shook his body.

'Can I help?'

He glanced up at her and wiped his lips with a bloodstained handkerchief. He shook his head, which brought on another spasm. Jill waited for it to subside. The man was tall, grey-faced and unshaven. He wore a heavy overcoat and a muffler. She guessed he was in his sixties, though he looked older.

'Shall I fetch someone?'

'No,' he muttered.

'Do you live near?'

He jerked his thumb at the pub.

'At the Bathurst?'

He nodded.

Jill stopped feeling like a busybody and started feeling guilty; good Samaritans weren't supposed to have selfish motives. 'Then why don't I fetch someone, or help you back?'

'I don't need help.'

The old man tried to stand up. But when she held out her arm, he took it and used it to pull himself to his feet.

'I'm all right now,' he muttered, and began to cough again.

'Not with that cough.'

'It's this bloody fresh air.'

Leaning on Jill, he staggered slowly up the gentle slope of the bank to the towpath, where he paused to cough. His fingers tightened on her arm as the cough racked his body. Gradually the grip relaxed.

'Shall we move on?' Jill wished she had left him on the bench. 'It's not far.'

He nodded, his face gaunt and grim. Jill glanced up at the first-floor window at the back of the Bathurst Arms and wished that one of those policemen would come and help. She and the old man plodded towards the pub, both of them staring at the ground. Below them flowed the tarmac of the path, so slowly they seemed hardly to be moving. Side by side went the man's old black boots, unlaced and scuffed, and Jill's shoes, neat blue leather, now stained perhaps irreparably with damp. There was no more coughing, though the man's breathing was laboured.

'Alvington! What the hell are you doing?'

Jill looked up. Dr Bayswater strode towards them. She noticed that his flies were undone, and looked away. The old man stopped and stared.

'You shouldn't be out.'

'Needed some air. All those police.'

'If there's any more of this nonsense, I'm packing you off to hospital.'

'No. I won't go.'

Alvington glared at Bayswater, who took his other arm. The three of them walked towards the door.

'Ah, Miss Francis,' Bayswater said and bent forward so that he could leer at her. 'Prettier than ever, eh? I wonder what brings you to this part of the world?'

He chuckled knowingly as he spoke. Jill did not reply. She preferred Bayswater when he was being brusque. They rounded the corner and reached the door of the pub, where the constable was waiting. She knew her time was running out, that soon the men would vanish into the building. Damn the good Samaritan. It was time to be ruthless.

'I know someone's died, and the police are there,' she said to Alvington. 'But who is it?'

He glanced at her with a face so full of pain that

she wished she had not spoken. 'Man called Rowse,' he said.

Alvington began to cough again as he was saying something else. Jill wasn't sure, but she thought it might have been: 'The poor bloody bastard.'

Chapter Twelve

A room changes when there is a body in it. The dead take precedence over the living.

When Thornhill stopped in the doorway of the bedroom, he did not look at any of the three police officers who were already there, and he took no notice of Brian Kirby, who was standing at his shoulder. He wanted to see the body, and for the moment nothing else interested him. The main reason for this, the only one he was happy to acknowledge openly to himself, was that he had a professional obligation to do so. But there were other, more personal reasons – a prurient curiosity, a fearful fascination, a simple determination not to look away from death, because that would be to give death another small victory.

The room was silent. The Scene-of-Crime Officers had been chattering away a few seconds earlier. Now they stood silent, their faces turned towards the door but their bodies angled in such a way that Thornhill could look directly at what he had come to see. Cameron Rowse lay on his left side, with his left knee drawn up towards his body. He appeared to be dressed in the clothes Thornhill had seen the previous evening, including the tweed jacket with the hound's-tooth check.

Behind Thornhill, Kirby let out a low whistle. 'Quite a jacket, isn't it? Give you a migraine at fifty paces.'

The photographer began to laugh, glanced at Thornhill, and stifled his amusement. Thornhill caught the glance and knew it for what it was: people were wary of him, a situation which had both advantages and disadvantages. Thornhill, born and bred on the other side of the country, was still considered an unknown quantity, possibly dangerous, by many of his colleagues at Lydmouth Police Headquarters. But it wasn't simply because he was what they called a foreigner. Though Brian Kirby was a Londoner, people weren't wary of him. Thornhill looked away from the body and glanced back at the door. The key was in the lock, on the outside.

Kirby interpreted the glance and said, 'According to Jane, it was there this morning.'

Thornhill nodded, storing the fact away in his memory. He wished there were fewer people here – it was a small room, almost a third of it filled by a double bed. Directly opposite the door was a dressing table with a large oval mirror. To the left was the bed, and beyond it the window. On the right was a wardrobe, a table and chair, and a towel rail. The carpet was worn, especially near the door. There was an electric fire, unplugged. The walls were papered with a pattern of improbable flowers. Framed colour reproductions of local beauty spots hung on the walls. The castle ruins. Bluebells in the Forest. The river Lyd on a snowy day. Tintern Abbey. It looked as if the Alvingtons had furnished the room with a job lot from an auction.

Among the litter on the table was a typewriter, a pencil with a chewed end, the spool from a roll of film and a copy of the *Empire Lion*. An army-surplus haversack had been upended over the bed. Searched? Not necessarily. Rowse might have been an untidy man with an uncomplicated idea of unpacking. Shaving tackle, a sponge bag, a pair of socks. Odd how shabby the possessions of a dead person looked, as though they suddenly decayed when their owner died.

His eyes went back to the corpse. Thornhill's daughter

Elizabeth often slept in the position that Rowse was in; and it looked as though Rowse was sucking his thumb too.

Feet pounded up the stairs. Dr Bayswater erupted on to the little landing. His hair was awry and his flies were undone.

'Well?' he demanded. 'Where is it?'

Thornhill took a step towards him. 'May I have a word, Doctor?'

'All right. But don't take all day.'

Thornhill murmured, 'Your dress needs – ah – adjusting.'

Bayswater laughed. 'My dear chap, you sound like a notice in a public lavatory.' He put down his bag and buttoned his flies. 'Still, much obliged. One doesn't want to frighten the horses, eh?'

Behind Thornhill, someone smothered another laugh.

'In here, Doctor.' Thornhill led Bayswater into the bedroom. 'As far as we know, he's not been moved.'

'Have you taken your snapshots?'

Thornhill looked at the photographer, a man named Flack, who nodded. 'Yes.'

Bayswater knelt beside the body and began to examine it. As he explored it, he grunted like a pig investigating a trough with exceptionally promising contents. After a moment, he beckoned to Kirby, and the two men gently rolled over the body, which was stiff with rigor mortis.

'Get out of the bloody light,' Bayswater roared at Flack, who had strayed in front of the window. 'You can take your wretched pictures in a moment.' He stared down at Rowse. 'It doesn't look as if we're dealing with blowpipe-wielding pygmies, does it? Well, that's something.'

No one said anything. Thornhill had a theory that Bayswater's sense of humour had been formed at medical school and had not changed in essentials since then. He stared at the three stab wounds in Rowse's chest, the entry holes rimmed with blood. All three punctures were on the left-hand side of his torso, piercing the jersey which he had worn under his jacket. Two were in the chest and one in the abdomen. There was a small dry, brown puddle on the floor.

'Not much blood,' Thornhill said at last.

Bayswater shrugged. 'Very considerate in the circumstances. Less mess for all concerned. But internal bleeding's a different matter.' He pointed at Rowse's right hand. There were cuts across the flexor surface of the finer joints and between index finger and thumb. 'Looks like he tried to grab the blade.'

'What sort of knife, do you think?' Thornhill asked.

'Judging by the entry holes it might well have been a blade with only one edge. But the skin contracts around the wound, so it's not necessarily an accurate guide. The blade was probably wider than it looks, and of course not as thick in the middle.'

Post-mortem lividity had drained the blood to the lowest points of Rowse's body, so that a bluish-pink stain like a large bruise marked the left-hand side of his face. In the centre of the discoloured area was a white patch where the side of the face had actually been in contact with the floor. Bayswater touched the lividity with a fingertip, but the stain did not temporarily fade under the pressure. He glanced up at Thornhill, to see if he needed to spell out the significance of this, but Thornhill nodded to show that he already understood: lividity reached this point only after the victim had been dead for ten or twelve hours, when the blood had had time to coagulate in the vessels.

'How much force would you think was needed?' Thornhill said.

Bayswater shrugged. 'Depends how sharp the knife was, the speed of the blow. The hardest part would be getting the tip through the skin.' He pointed to the floor. 'Hey – what's that?'

Thornhill bent closer to look. Half hidden by the fold of the jacket was the glint of silver. He knelt beside Bayswater, took out a propelling pencil and used it to slide the object across the carpet into the open. It was a silver cigarette lighter.

'Ah,' said Bayswater, and grinned. 'Can it be a clue?'

Chapter Thirteen

'West London.' Brian Kirby flicked open his notebook and checked the address he had copied from the register of the Bathurst Arms. 'Kestrel Road, Shepherd's Bush.'

The police car drew away from the kerb. Thornhill glanced at the pub. Gloria's face bobbed in the gloom behind the window of the lounge bar.

'You'd better get on to the Yard,' he told Kirby. 'Ask them to take a look.' He raised his voice so their driver could hear. 'Porter, I want to go to Vance's Garage. Do you know the owner?'

'Joe Vance, sir. I used to sit next to his brother Jack at school.'

Thornhill was not surprised. You could usually rely on Porter to claim some sort of acquaintance with almost anyone who lived in or near Lydmouth.

'Not short of a bob or two,' Porter went on. 'Him and his brother.'

'The Vances?' Kirby leaned forward so he could see himself in the rearview mirror and fiddled with the knot of his tie. 'You wouldn't think it, to look at that garage of theirs.'

'They do all right,' said Porter with oracular certainty. 'Joe especially. There's a lot of women wouldn't mind being Mrs Joe Vance.'

They found Joe underneath a ten-ton lorry in his workshop. He wriggled out to talk to them, not bothering to conceal his reluctance. But when Kirby revealed the reason for their visit, his attitude changed.

'Dead? Bloody hell. How?'

'We'll have to wait and see what they say at the inquest,' Kirby said.

Joe glanced at Thornhill. 'A sergeant, an inspector *and* Peter Porter, eh?'

'When did Rowse get here?' Thornhill asked.

'Between three and half past yesterday afternoon.'

'And what did he want?'

'A new front wheel and a new front fork.' Vance took a half-smoked cigarette from behind his ear. He took his time lighting it. 'It's over there.' He pointed with the spent match towards the back of his workshop. 'See? The Triumph.'

The four of them gathered in a semi-circle round the motorbike. Kirby made a note of the registration number. Thornhill peered into each of the panniers in turn. They were empty.

'I was going to start work on it this afternoon,' Vance said.

Kirby shrugged. 'No point now.'

Thornhill crouched to examine the bent fork. 'So where did the accident happen? I assume it was an accident?'

'Out on the Gloucester road a couple of miles beyond Ashbridge. Said he swerved to avoid some sheep.'

'And how did he get here?'

'I didn't ask. He just walked in off the street.'

Thornhill straightened up. 'What was he carrying?'

'A haversack.' Vance's close-set eyes gave him a shifty appearance, perhaps misleadingly.

'Was that all?'

'He had a little typewriter in a metal case. Maybe a camera, too.'

Thornhill turned to go. 'We'll send someone round to collect the bike.'

Kirby began to follow, and then hesitated. 'What did you think of him, Mr Vance?'

The mechanic rubbed his cheek, leaving a smear of oil on his pale, freckled face. 'Wouldn't trust him an inch. Not that it mattered.'

'Why didn't it matter?' Thornhill said.

'I had the bike, didn't I? If he wouldn't pay, I could always sell it and I'd make a profit on that. Either way, I couldn't lose.'

'If you didn't trust him, why did you send him to the Bathurst Arms?'

'I — I knew the Alvingtons could do with the trade.'

'But you didn't trust him. Weren't you afraid he might skip without paying them what he owed?'

Vance shook his head. 'If he'd done that, he wouldn't have got his bike back.'

They said goodbye and picked their way among the abandoned vehicles to the road.

'He got a bit rattled at the end,' Kirby murmured to Thornhill.

'I noticed.'

'It was when the Bathurst Arms came up.'

'And the Alvingtons.'

Kirby grinned at Thornhill as he opened the door of the car. 'Joe Vance, eh? Don't say he's smitten.'

'He wouldn't be the first,' Thornhill said, 'and he won't be the last.'

'Mr Thornhill?'

He turned. Vance was coming towards them. 'What is it?'

'I just wondered, look. Will they be open this dinnertime? At the Bathurst, I mean.'

*   *   *

The police allowed the Alvingtons to open the public bar at one o'clock. The Scene-of-Crime Officers were still on the premises, but Cameron Rowse had not gone into the public bar and Thornhill accepted the Alvingtons had to make a living. The dining room and the lounge bar remained closed.

The Alvingtons did more than merely make a living at lunchtime. News of Rowse's death had spread rapidly through Lydmouth. Drawn by disaster, people flocked to gawp. But they could hardly gawp without buying a drink. Even Harold made one of his rare appearances behind the bar, though only for a few seconds. At the sight of the crowded room, something resembling a smile crept over his wan face. Then Jane saw him, abandoned her customers and took her father back to the sitting room where he spent most of his time.

'Your lord and master looks pleased with himself,' Ivor Fuggle said to Gloria as he watched her pouring his second large whisky. He turned up the volume of his new hearing aid. 'And so he should be. I've never seen so many people in here.'

'My feet are killing me. Haven't sat down since breakfast.' Gloria put his whisky on the counter of the public bar and allowed his eyes to linger on her cleavage. 'The poor man – Mr Rowse, I mean. To think I was chatting to him only last night.'

Ivor Fuggle laid a pound note beside the glass but kept his fingers on it. 'I wonder what you talked about.'

She rested her index finger on one end of the pound note. Fuggle did not move his hand. Their eyes met.

'He was a journalist,' Gloria said at last. 'Like you.'

Ivor Fuggle chuckled. 'Forty years on the *Post* – man and boy.' His voice oozed out of his plump carcass like a stream of dark treacle. 'Naturally I'm interested in the fate of a fellow wielder of the pen. Why was he down here? Do you know?'

Gloria dropped her eyes to the pound note. Fuggle smiled

and lifted his hand. She slid the note towards her in a swift, flowing movement and tucked it into a half-pint pot under the counter.

'He'd come down from London to write about the squatters at Farnock Camp. He went over there yesterday afternoon to talk to them.'

'Who did he work for, my dear?'

'He was a freelance. He thought the *Picture Post* might like it.'

'Sounds rather a long shot to me.'

Spurred by the scepticism, Gloria said, 'He wasn't worried, though. If no one else would have it, he said the *Empire Lion* would take it. Him and the editor were like this.' She held out her hand, forefinger and middle finger squeezed together.

'The *Empire Lion*, eh?' Fuggle's eyebrows arched. 'Let me guess: he wasn't on the squatters' side?'

Gloria nodded. 'He'd have hanged the lot of them if he had his way. Next best thing to traitors.'

'Quite right. Half of them up there are probably as red as ...' He chuckled. 'As red as your lovely lips, my dear.'

Gloria smiled, secure in both her beauty and her knowledge. 'And if the truth were told, them squatters aren't the only ones.'

'What do you mean by that?' Fuggle said, his voice suddenly sharp.

She patted her shining hair. 'I don't know if I should betray a confidence.'

'But Rowse is dead. Poor chap.'

She looked up at him through her eyelashes. 'Doesn't that make it even more important?'

Fuggle sighed and reached for his wallet. A ten-shilling note went the way of the pound.

Gloria glanced around, slipping the note into the tankard and noting that Jane was busy with a large order. She leant across the counter and lowered her voice.

'Mr Rowse was up at the Bull earlier in the evening. He told me he had a bit of an argy-bargy when he was up there. Guess who with?'

Fuggle said nothing. He smiled at her with his brilliant white false teeth, and waited.

'Another person in your line of work,' Gloria went on. 'Wemyss-Brown.'

For an instant, Fuggle's eyes went blank. Then he said softly: 'You're saying he's a Communist?'

'I'm not saying anything,' Gloria replied with a flagrant disregard for the truth. 'But that's what Mr Rowse told me last night. He said Wemyss-Brown had fought in the Spanish Civil War.'

'That would certainly explain the line the *Gazette* has been taking with Farnock Camp.' Fuggle beamed at her. 'So he and Rowse had a difference of opinion, eh?'

'Nearly came to blows, they did. But Inspector Thornhill and Mrs Wemyss-Brown turned up.'

'Dear me. It sounds most unpleasant.' Fuggle's voice took on an unctuous tone. 'Let us be thankful it was no worse. Nearly came to blows, eh? Tut, tut. Who would have thought it of Mr Wemyss-Brown?'

'Like a raging bull, according to Mr Rowse.' Gloria giggled. 'Talk about red rags.'

'Have you told all this to the police?'

'Well, by all accounts Mr Thornhill was there for some of the time. Anyway, they haven't asked.'

'They will, my dear, they will.' Fuggle swallowed the last of his whisky. 'And now if there's nothing else, I really must tear myself away.'

The street door opened. Gloria watched Joe Vance coming into the bar. She smiled.

Chapter Fourteen

———◆———

Jill Francis's lunch was an orange washed down with a cup of stewed tea. She ate the orange while she was typing up her notes on the Rowse story, such as they were. She had just finished the typing when there was a phone call for her.

'Jill? It's Oliver. I need to see you.'

'I'm working.'

'You don't understand. Something's happened.'

'What?'

'I don't want to talk about it over the phone.'

'Can't it wait until this evening?'

'Please, Jill.'

It was the note of pleading in Oliver Yateley's voice that made her change her mind. Oliver cajoled, he blustered, he argued with the appearance of overwhelming logic; but he rarely pleaded. He was a proud man, and pleading was a confession of failure.

'I can manage five minutes.'

'Thank you. I'll buy you a cup of coffee. Isn't there a café near your office? We could meet there.'

'No.' The Gardenia would be crowded with people she knew. But she did not want to take Oliver back to Church Cottage.

'Damn it.' His irritation was an almost palpable force at

the other end of the phone line. 'I'll pick you up in the car, then. In five minutes?'

'All right.'

Jill spent most of those five minutes making herself presentable and wondering at her own vanity. She reached the front office just as Yateley's Humber pulled up outside. He did not look at her as she climbed into the car. He let out the clutch and the car glided into the traffic that flowed along the High Street. A moment later, they were driving down the Chepstow Road.

'Can't you pull up?' Jill demanded. 'I really have got to be back at work soon.'

He glanced at her, his face tight-lipped. 'This is important. Really important.'

'So is my job.'

He braked sharply, jerking her forward in her seat, and pulled the car over to the kerb. They were opposite the driveway to the RAF Hospital on the outskirts of town.

'Now what is all this?' Jill went on.

He gave her the rueful, little boy smile which she remembered so well from the Dolphin Square days. 'I'm sorry to be such a pest. The thing is, when I last saw you, things were bad enough. But since then they've become even worse. Have you heard about the murder?'

'Are they sure it's murder?'

'What else can it be? The victim's a man called Cameron Rowse. He was some sort of journalist.'

'I know. I met him yesterday afternoon.'

There was no mistaking the alarm in Oliver's face. 'Where?'

'At Farnock Camp. He claimed to be researching a feature on the squatters.'

'He didn't mention me?'

'No.'

Oliver let out his breath. 'I'd given him a lift an hour or so earlier. His motorbike had broken down.'

'Very nice of you, I'm sure. But what's it got to do with me?'

'He recognised me. Not right away, I think — later. He came up to the Bull in the evening so he could have seen the register. Or perhaps he knew my face.'

'It's probably the voice.' Jill opened her handbag and took out her cigarettes so she did not have to look at his face. 'It's very recognisable.'

'Maybe.' He took one of the cigarettes she offered him and fumbled for a lighter. 'The point is, he started wondering why I was down here. And he followed me when I called on you.'

'Oh Lord.'

'It's not just us. He phoned Virginia last night.'

'So she knows?' Jill bent forward as Oliver clicked his lighter.

'About you and me? I'm not sure — I don't think so. But that's not what worries me.'

'It worries *me*.'

'The real problem is that Rowse managed to finesse the — the other thing out of her. And the next thing he did was turn up in the Bull and try to blackmail me.'

'What did you do?'

'I gave him fifteen pounds — just to buy time to think.'

'When was this exactly?'

'I told you — yesterday evening.'

'Why didn't you phone me?'

Oliver inhaled and made a fuss of winding down the window. Then he said, 'Because I didn't want to worry you. I needed time to think about it.'

'You were scared.'

'I beg your pardon?'

'You were scared. Scared of how I'd react if you threw this one on my lap as well. But now Rowse is dead you've got no choice. Because if he was killed, you had a very good motive for murdering him.'

'Don't be absurd.'

'I don't think I'm the one who's being absurd.'

'You never used to talk like this. You're so – so abrasive.'

'Why do you think that is?'

There was a silence. The car filled with smoke. Jill coughed. Oliver's air of unshakable self-confidence was one of the things she used to like about him; she had hoped that some of it would rub off on her. But the self-confidence was not unassailable after all: it was a bubble, easily pricked. And once that was gone what was left except a weak man with a habit of expecting others to help him out of his scrapes?

'Look, Jill – I know I've been a fool, and I know I've made it worse in the last few hours.' Like all good politicians, he was expert at responding immediately to changes in those he was talking to, at reading the infinitesimal signals and reacting appropriately. 'What more can I say except I'm sorry? But the fact of the matter is, this is a mess, and it affects us both. And—'

'How does Rowse's death affect us both?'

'Because if it gets about that you and I had an affair, it's not going to do your reputation any good. Especially in a place like this. We went through all that yesterday. And if they find out about the abortion as well, then God help you.'

Jill glared at him and bit the inside of her cheek to hold back the tears. She could smell the shaving cream Oliver used, and for an instant she was back in the bathroom of the Dolphin Square flat: looking at her own face in a mirror framed in sea-green incorruptible tiles, and mouthing the words, *I'm pregnant.* He had always called it the abortion. But it had been a baby. It could have been a person.

'We agreed to get rid of it,' Oliver went on. 'It was your choice as well as mine. And in order to get rid of it, we had to commit a crime.'

She was silent, fighting to keep her head above the rising

tide of memory: the back bedroom with stained wallpaper in Earls Court, the nurse who smelled of sherry and the man with the soft hands and the rubbery face who had once been a doctor.

'I'm just trying to be realistic,' he murmured. 'I know this must sound brutal, but we must face up to the situation.'

'The first thing to face up to,' Jill said in a tight little voice, 'is that your situation is about a million times worse than mine.'

There was a silence in the car. Jill watched tendrils of smoke curling from the tip of her cigarette and rising to the crack of the open window. She did not look at Oliver. His breathing sounded very loud in this confined space.

'Look, Jill.' He rested a hand on her sleeve, but she pulled her arm away. 'Should I go to the police about giving Rowse a lift? Or would it be better to let sleeping dogs lie? After all, the police will be interested in what Rowse did when he got to Lydmouth, rather than how he got there.'

'One of the things he did in Lydmouth,' said Jill, astonished at how self-interest could blind someone to the obvious, 'is blackmail a Member of Parliament, who therefore had a very good motive for murdering him.'

'If I said nothing, no one need ever know.'

'I wouldn't bank on it. You don't know what this town is like. Someone will have noticed you together in the Bull. And the police will want to trace Rowse's movements on the day before he died. That includes finding out who gave him a lift.'

'But I don't know what to do.' Oliver's tone made it clear that he was inclined to blame Jill for this undesirable state of uncertainty. 'What do you think?'

'Frankly, I don't care what you do.' Jill reached for the door handle, knowing that what she had said was not entirely true, but it was nevertheless a satisfying remark to have made. She opened the door, dropped her cigarette in the gutter and

got out of the car. She stooped so her face was level with his.
'I'm not your mother. I'm not your wife.'

'Get back in.'

'No.' She began to close the door.

'You're just being childish. Let me run you back and
we can—'

'No, we can't,' Jill said. 'I'm walking.'

She slammed the door. As she walked with her head high
down the Chepstow Road, the anger swiftly evaporated. It left
behind a sense of relief, as if an irksome job, long postponed,
had at last been completed.

Chapter Fifteen

At Police Headquarters, there was an influential school of thought that held that PC Peter Porter was one of those divine jokes on a par with Sunday licensing hours, the activities of the Ministry of Agriculture and the Special Theory of Relativity.

Had there not been the post-war shortage of applicants for the force, it was unlikely that Porter would have been taken on. Big, red-faced and clumsy, he was widely believed to have the largest pair of feet in Lydmouth. Apart from his time in the army, he had always lived with his mother and grandmother, first in Templefields and later in a little house on the council estate at Edge Hill. Once he was in the police force, he had rapidly become the butt of the canteen.

Porter was accustomed to being at the wrong end of other people's jokes: he had been mocked during his service in the South Wales Borderers, just as he had been persecuted from his first day at elementary school. To make matters worse, he was a bastard, a fact which had been made clear to him all his life. No one knew who his father was. In 1926, his mother had been raped in one of the back alleys of Templefields after she had drunk herself into a stupor while celebrating New Year's Eve.

Peter Porter ambushed Thornhill outside the CID office

on the first floor of Headquarters. Thornhill was already late for a meeting with Superintendent Williamson and the Chief Constable about the Rowse case. But Porter was a human barrier in the middle of the corridor. At present, Porter was loosely attached to Divisional CID as a sort of universal dogsbody because Thornhill had unwisely expressed a desire for a driver with local knowledge.

'Sir,' Porter said. '*Sir.*'

He reminded Thornhill of a boy with an urgent need to request permission to go to the lavatory from his teacher. 'Yes?'

'The lighter, sir. The Richelieu lighter.'

'What about it?'

'It might have come from Mr Crawley — you know, down by the war memorial.'

'Why there? We've got plenty of other tobacconists. Or it's the sort of thing a jeweller might stock.'

Porter looked depressed. 'It's just that I was in there before Christmas, looking for a present for — for someone, and I heard him talking to another customer. He was saying he'd decided to try stocking some Richelieu lighters because nobody else in Lydmouth carried them.'

Thornhill looked up at the moist face, hovering like an airborne jellyfish several inches above his. 'Shouldn't you be off-duty? It's after two.'

'I thought you might need me, sir. You might want me to drive you somewhere or something.'

It was the last two words — *or something* — that made Thornhill say, 'Do you know Mr Crawley?'

'Oh, yes. My gran used to do cleaning for Mrs Crawley's parents. When they were alive, that is.'

'Since you're here, I want you to have a look at that lighter — go downstairs and get them to show it to you; say I sent you — and then go and talk to Mr Crawley. See if he's sold that particular model to anyone. And if so, who.'

Pinker and moister than ever, Porter's face hung over him. 'Yes, sir,' he breathed.

It was only when Porter was gone, when Thornhill was hurrying to his meeting with Superintendent Williamson and Mr Hendry, that he realised he had forgotten to ask the obvious question – and Porter had not thought to answer it unprompted.

Had the customer whom Porter had overheard talking with Crawley actually bought one of those Richelieu lighters? And if so, who had it been?

Chapter Sixteen

—◆—

'Edith, my dear,' Bernard Broadbent said when Edith Thornhill opened the door. He was standing in the tiled porch of the Thornhills' house, his head hunched forward, beaming, holding out a bunch of daffodils like an Olympic torch. 'Are you going to take pity on an old man and give him a cup of tea?'

'Come in, Uncle Bernard.' Edith knew he liked to be called Uncle, though she was in fact his first cousin once removed. 'What lovely daffodils. You can have a whole pot for those.'

She tried to edge him into the sitting room, but he slipped down the hall towards the kitchen, the room where the Thornhills spent most of their time. As he stretched out his hand to the door, there was a burst of shrieking on the other side. Edith hurried after him. David was trying, perhaps for fun, to tie his sister with a piece of string to the cast-iron frame that supported the sewing machine. When they saw Uncle Bernard, the children froze.

'Hello, kiddies. How's tricks?'

The children said nothing. Uncle Bernard padded round the table towards them. He was a large, stooping man with narrow shoulders, greying hair, a long face and a heavy lower jaw. David said that Uncle Bernard looked like a badger.

'What's this? Can't let a young lady be tied up.' He patted

David on the head, and the boy ducked away. 'You untie that wrist, and I'll do the other. OK?'

He talked to the children while she made the tea and found a vase for the daffodils. The kitchen was a mess, with dirty plates on the table and washing draped around and above the boiler.

'I got a favour to ask,' Uncle Bernard said as she was clearing the table. 'Another one.'

'Of course.' Edith wondered whether there was any fruit cake left in the tin, or only crumbs.

'Are you doing anything on Friday evening?'

'I don't think so. But I don't know about Richard.' She glanced distractedly at the children. 'Why don't you go and tidy your rooms before Daddy gets home?'

Obviously relieved, the children left the room, beginning to squabble again as soon as they had closed the door.

'It's you I mean,' Uncle Bernard said. 'There's this concert at the High School. Madrigals or some such. You know me: about as musical as this table. I wondered if you could come and prod me if I doze off. And stop me if I put my foot in it with the teachers.'

'I'd love to come.' Edith's mind was already running ahead like a sprinter: Richard's possible reactions, which babysitter, who else might be there and — above all — what on earth would she wear? 'Of course, I'll have to check with Richard.'

'Of course.'

The kettle boiled, and she left him for a moment to make the tea. Fortunately the tin contained enough for three slices of cake. One of the slices was more crumbs than slice, but she arranged the cake to conceal this.

'It should be quite an occasion,' he said when she returned. 'They want to raise funds for a music room. It's a sort of memorial to Heather Parry.'

'Who?'

'I was forgetting. Before your time. Sad story.' He told

Edith about the disappearance of the schoolgirl three years before. 'The Parrys live in my ward, you see, and when I was elected they wrote to me to see if there was anything I could do. As far as they're concerned, the worst thing is they don't know what's happened, one way or the other. Even knowing she was dead would be easier to cope with than the uncertainty.'

'It must be terrible.' Edith put herself in the place of Mrs Parry and shivered. 'Can't the police —?'

'I've had a word with them. Tried to ginger them up a bit. No reflection on your Richard, of course, but I don't think they ever treated the case as urgent.'

She offered him the cake, keeping the damaged slice away from him. He took a piece and demolished it in two mouthfuls. For all his money, Edith thought, Uncle Bernard ate like a child afraid that if he let food linger on his plate, someone might snatch it from him.

'This music room idea,' he went on. 'It's something the Parrys and the headmistress have cooked up between them. School needs a music room, and the Parrys are prepared to put up a fair amount of the money.'

'As a sort of memorial to Heather?'

'A memorial without a body.' Uncle Bernard stared grimly across the table. 'She may be alive still.'

'It's a way of trying to say goodbye,' Edith said. 'That's what it is.'

'Maybe. This concert should raise a bit more towards the music room. I've made a little donation myself as well. All in a good cause.'

Edith nodded.

'It'll be nice to have a lady on my arm,' he said, smiling. 'Concert's at seven-thirty, by the way. Shall I pick you up in the car at about quarter-past?'

'Yes — that should be fine.' She held up the teapot and looked enquiringly at him.

'Who knows — maybe one day we'll be going there to listen to Lizzie.' Bernard held out his cup. 'And then there's David. He's a fine lad.'

'Thank you,' murmured Edith.

'Not so long now and he'll be ready for his eleven plus. Have you thought about what happens then?'

'Well, there's the grammar school, of course,' Edith said carefully. 'Though I sometimes wonder if Ashbridge School might be a better choice in the long run.'

Uncle Bernard dropped sugar lumps into his teacup. 'They've had their troubles lately.'

'Yes, but that's in the past. Anyway, if David went there, it would be some time in the future.'

'You get some rough kids at that grammar school now, worse than we were.' He gave her a wide grin. 'And that's saying something. What does Richard think?'

Edith shifted uneasily on her chair. 'He prefers the grammar school.'

'Why?'

'Mainly the cost, I think. Though if David went to Ashbridge as a day boy ...'

'It's another expense, there's no denying it.' Uncle Bernard took out his pipe and pouch and began to stuff tobacco into the bowl with stubby but deft fingers. 'However you look at it. But I sometimes wonder where I would have ended up if my mam and dad could have sent me to the grammar school. Let alone to Ashbridge.' He struck a match and, shielding the bowl with the palm of one hand, lit the pipe. Even that he did with efficiency and deliberation. He blew out a mouthful of smoke. 'I don't approve of these public schools. If I had my way I'd shut the lot of them tomorrow. But there's no denying they do something for a boy. The way I see it, while the system's there, you might as well make the best use of it you can.'

'I agree.'

There was a silence. Uncle Bernard puffed his pipe and stared at the vase of daffodils on the windowsill. Upstairs the children were banging about in David's bedroom, which was immediately over the kitchen. Edith wished they would be quieter.

'I'm not being nosy, mind,' he said at last. 'But I know you got something when your mother died. That could help with school fees.'

Edith said hesitantly, 'Our landlord's thinking of selling this house. He's given us first refusal.' She felt a twinge of disloyalty, moral rheumatism. 'Richard's very much in favour.'

She knew how much he would hate the thought of her discussing their finances with Uncle Bernard. But there was no help for it. She had to think of the children.

Chapter Seventeen

PC Peter Porter sidled into the CID office with the air of a dog who expects a reprimand for taking liberties. He knocked over a wastepaper basket, sending the grey metal cylinder rolling over the floor, disgorging its contents as it went, until it collided with the leg of a desk. Someone tittered. Someone else said, 'Oh Christ!' Porter flushed.

'Are you looking for someone?' Brian Kirby asked.

'Mr Thornhill, Sarge. He's not in his office.'

'He's not in the wastepaper basket either,' remarked DC Flack.

'What shall I do, Sarge?' Porter asked, spreading wide a pair of hands like T-bone steaks. 'He sent me out to interview someone.'

Kirby looked blankly at him. One of the first things a policeman learns is never to show surprise.

'And it's urgent,' Porter went on. 'The Rowse case.'

'You better tell me then.' Kirby pushed back his chair and stood up. 'Come on. I want a brew. You can tell me while the kettle's boiling.'

The kitchen was a small, thin room with a barred window overlooking the car park behind Headquarters. Kirby filled the kettle, put it on the ring and lit the gas. Standing in the doorway and frowning with concentration, Porter watched every movement.

Kirby opened the tea caddy. 'Aren't you meant to be off-duty?'

'Yes, Sarge, but I thought I'd better stay in case Mr Thornhill needed me.' Porter's face brightened perceptibly. 'It was that lighter they found under the body. The Richelieu. I'd heard that Crawley's was the only place in town you could buy Richelieus. Mr Thornhill wanted me to go and talk to him. So I did. That was just after dinner.'

Kirby glanced up at the clock on the wall. 'You took your time.'

Porter shook his head violently. 'Mr Crawley was out, look. There was only the girl in the shop, so I had to wait till he came back.'

Kirby took a couple of mugs from the draining board. 'You want some tea?'

'What?' Porter frowned again, grappling with the necessity of thinking of two things at the same time. 'Yes, please, Sarge.'

'So does he stock Richelieu lighters?'

'What – ah, yes, Sarge. And he's sure he's the only shop in Lydmouth that does.'

'And he's got that particular model?'

Porter nodded. He took out his notebook, opened it and peered anxiously at his own writing. 'The lighter's called Royale. He ordered three of them just before Christmas.' Porter licked his lips. 'He's had them in stock since the eighth of December.'

'Yes, but has he sold any of them?'

'Oh yes. I should have said. Sorry. But he's got one left – and it's just like the one we found at the Bathurst. Mr Crawley says it's quite a popular line because gents and ladies can have them. Small enough for the handbag, he said, and large enough—'

Kirby rapped a teaspoon against the side of the kettle. 'Who bought the other two?'

Porter blinked, licked his lips and looked down at his notebook. 'Mr and Mrs Wemyss-Brown.'

Kirby whistled.

'It was ever so funny, Mr Crawley said, because they got them separately. Mrs Wemyss-Brown bought one for Mr Wemyss-Brown as a Christmas present. And then two days later, Mr Wemyss-Brown came into the shop for his special mixture — he has a regular order, look, once a week — and he saw one of these lighters in the display case and said, ooh, he'd have one too — for Mrs Wemyss-Brown.' Porter smiled happily. 'I'd like to have seen their faces on Christmas morning. Talk about coincidence. What a laugh!'

'And I'd like to see their faces,' Kirby said, 'if it turns out that it was one of their lighters we found under Cameron Rowse's body.'

Chapter Eighteen

When he awoke, Howard knew at once that he had been asleep for hours. The light had changed. He felt cold and weak but clearer-headed than he had been earlier in the day.

With his fingers he explored his immediate surroundings, inch by inch. An earth floor, which felt like demerara sugar beneath his fingertips. Logs with fissured bark on their sides. Sacks below him and above him — those he remembered. On top, however, there was something softer and warmer — a wool blanket.

Phyllis, he thought. *Can't do enough for me — some things never change.*

The knowledge made Howard tingle. Optimism trickled through him like brandy. Everything was going to be all right. He knew that there was much he needed to do, but at present he was too tired even to think. He allowed himself to drift back towards sleep.

Soon afterwards, he awoke again. This time, however, he awoke with a jolt rather than gradually. A noise outside. For an instant panic leapt to his throat and he gasped for air. Heels were thudding on tarmac. They had found out. They were coming for him. They would never believe that it hadn't been his fault, that—

Then there was Phyllis staring down at him. She was wrapped

in a shapeless brown raincoat and her hair was tightly confined in a headscarf.

'You're awake,' she said.

The relief made him feel giddy. Howard wanted to say, *Of course I am, you silly cow — can't you see?* but talking was more trouble than it was worth. Anyway, she knew what he thought of her — had done for years. The silly bitch needed to be disciplined. *A woman, a wife, and a walnut tree, the more you beat them the better they be.*

'I've brought you some soup.'

She crouched down and put a Thermos flask on the ground within his reach. He noticed with a little thrill of pleasure that she was careful not to come too close to him.

'Shall I pour some?'

He cleared his throat and nodded. He watched Phyllis unscrewing the flask and pouring a little soup into the cup. She put the cup on the ground beside the flask and straightened up.

'You'll have to help me,' he whispered.

For once he did not mind making a confession of weakness. He watched her hesitate, glance back at the doorway and finally — slowly — draw nearer to him. What did physical weakness matter when he had such a demonstration of his power?

Phyllis knelt beside him and, supporting his shoulders with one arm, held the cup to his lips. He sipped, and his tastebuds felt as if they had exploded. The richness of the soup was almost painful. He jerked back his head and felt a drop of soup trickling down his chin. *Stupid bint.*

'More,' he muttered.

Sip by sip, mouthful by mouthful, the soup slipped down his throat. A tide of wellbeing spread through him. Greedily he sucked the soup until the cup was empty.

Phyllis said, 'You got the address from Mother, didn't you?'

Howard stared up at her. Her arm was still around his

shoulders. They were as close as lovers, as close as they used to be. He had never liked Phyllis's mother. He had traced the old bag's address through the vicar of the church she used to go to. It turned out to be a little rented flat in Golders Green, two rooms on the second floor with the use of a kitchen and bathroom. When he had appeared without warning on the doorstep, he had thought she would faint.

It had taken him only a moment to persuade her to take him upstairs. She had been afraid that he would make a scene in front of the landlady. He had known she would give nothing away to him willingly, so he had asked for a glass of water. Her address book was in plain sight on top of the bureau. It had been the work of a few seconds to find where Phyllis was living. Then her mother had come back with the glass of water, but by that time he was sitting in the armchair by the gas fire, as innocent as could be. She had refused to give him Phyllis's address of her own free will, naturally, and soon after he had left, swearing at the old woman, partly because it gave him satisfaction to see her wince, and partly because he wanted her to think that she had fooled him.

'You won't be able to bother her again,' Phyllis said.

'Done a bunk, has she? I wonder why.'

'So she wouldn't have to run the risk of you pestering her again.'

Howard snorted with genuine amusement. Phyllis's defiance was new – or if not new, then long-suppressed. He would have to tame her all over again. It was a challenge. He felt almost affectionate towards her, as a sculptor feels towards a formless block of marble that contains, somewhere inside it, the shape he wants. Perhaps it was because he was running a temperature, but he suddenly saw himself in a new light: he was an artist, an artist of the mind and heart, and his raw material was other people.

Phyllis withdrew her arm and stood up. 'Anyway, you'll have to go. You can't stay here.'

'Why not?'

She fiddled with the Thermos flask, pretending to tighten the cap. 'For one thing, my employer wouldn't like it. And for another, I don't want you.'

'I'm not well.'

'I can't help that.' Phyllis glanced nervously towards the doorway. 'Go to a doctor. How you had the nerve to come here—'

'That's why *you* came here, isn't it?' he interrupted. 'Because you thought I'd never dare come back.'

She said nothing. She was still looking towards the doorway, her face gaunt.

'Not everyone's as yellow as you, Phyllis,' he went on in a voice that was little more than a whisper. 'But I like it here. Something about the air, perhaps – believe me, it's nice to breathe fresh air for a change. No, I think I'll stay for a while.'

'You can't!'

'How can you stop me?'

'I'll call the police.'

'Will you?' He hesitated, savouring his control of the situation, despite his illness. 'Do you know what I did when I was leaving your mother's? I took a little souvenir. You remember – the gold snuffbox? The one that belonged to your grandpa?' He had pawned it within an hour. 'Now why didn't she stop me?'

Phyllis turned to look at him. Still she said nothing.

'Because she was scared.' Howard smiled at her. 'And why do you suppose she was scared?'

'She's had plenty of reason to be scared of you.'

'She could have called the police. She could have accused me of theft. She could have screamed so her landlady heard.' He smiled again. 'But do you know what she really did? She said, "Oh for God's sake take it, but don't come back." So in a manner of speaking she gave it to me. Now why would she do that?'

'I wish you were dead,' Phyllis said. 'I've never felt like that about anyone before.'

Howard chose to ignore that, for now; but she would pay for it later. 'Your mother gave me the snuffbox for the same reason that you won't go to the police. Because you're scared. Because she's scared. Your mother didn't go to the police, either – she moved. Now, what does that tell us?' He arched his eyebrows, pretending to wait for her answer as a teacher waits for a pupil's reply. 'What it means, logically, Phyllis, is that you and your mama are frightened of the police. You're calling yourself Richards, down here, aren't you?'

'It's my name.'

'Johnnie Richards died in nineteen forty-two, Phyllis. Face it. You're married to me. But how do you think Mrs Portleigh would feel if she found out you weren't really a war widow, if she found out you were using a false name?' He paused before tightening the screw one more time. 'If she found out that someone like me was your husband?'

'It's not against the law to change your name. In the circumstances, it's only natural.'

'I'm not sure Mrs Portleigh would see it like that. In any case, there's the little question of false pretences. When you applied for this job, I'm afraid you can't have told the whole truth and nothing but the truth. Naughty, naughty.'

She drew her mackintosh more tightly round her, as if trying to guard against infection. 'I'm going now.'

'Have you paid your debts yet?'

'What do you mean?'

Howard heard the panic in her voice and drew strength from it. 'Getting on for fifteen hundred quid, wasn't it?'

'They were your debts. Nothing to do with me. I trusted you.'

'The house was in your name, Phyllis dear. All that unpaid rent. And you really shouldn't have run up those bills with tradesmen. Still, you never were a very good manager, were you?'

With great pleasure, he saw tears trickling down her cheeks. He felt tired, but knew he could not yet afford to sleep. He studied her face as if it were a chessboard, planning his next move. He had learned from experience that the most effective way to exert control in these cases was to do it gradually.

'What I'd really like,' Howard said sweetly, 'is a cigarette.'

Chapter Nineteen

'There's a gentleman asking for Mr Thornhill,' Sergeant Fowles said. A hissing, like water pouring through a sluice, followed the words down the phone line, the sound of Fowles sucking his dentures.

'He's in a meeting,' Kirby replied. More than half his attention was on the reflection of his cheek in the small mirror lying on his desk.

'Gent's in a hurry.'

Kirby was convinced that that small pink mark just below his left eye was developing into a spot. 'So are we all. What does he want?'

More hissing. 'Won't say.'

'Ask him to wait. If he wants to play silly buggers, it's his problem and not ours.'

Fowles lowered his voice to a throaty whisper: 'He gave me his card. Name's Yateley. He's an MP – I heard him on the wireless the other night.'

Kirby reluctantly abandoned the putative spot. He knew that everyone was equal in the eyes of the law, but it was no use pretending that some were not more equal than others. 'All right, I'll come down.'

The MP was a big, well-dressed man, with the air of one used to having his own way. Kirby took him into the conference room, which was slightly less shabby and considerably more spacious than any of the interview rooms. He pulled out a chair for the visitor. Yateley laid his black Homberg and gloves on the scarred mahogany table. His fingers fiddled with the brim of the hat.

'I was hoping to see Detective Inspector Thornhill.'

Kirby spread wide his hands. 'I'm sorry, sir. He's not available.'

'Then where is he?'

'He's out of the building, sir. Is there any reason why you can't talk to me instead?'

'I've met Inspector Thornhill before.'

Kirby was surprised, but didn't show it. Perhaps the two men had met before Thornhill's arrival at Lydmouth. 'I can pass on a message to him as soon as he comes out of the meeting, sir. Or maybe you'd like to leave a note? Or I could ask him to come and see you. Where are you staying?'

'The Bull. Look, Sergeant, I suppose there's no reason I shouldn't tell you. The thing is, I don't particularly want to get involved with all this. A man in my position can't be too careful, you know. I know Mr Thornhill is a sensible man, and I wondered if he could advise me.'

'Perhaps it would help if you said what it was about, sir.'

'It's to do with this man who was killed last night.'

'You knew him?'

Yateley shook his head. 'I met him yesterday for the first time. His motorbike had broken down between here and Gloucester. He'd smashed the front wheel against a rock, I think. I gave him a lift into Lydmouth.' Yateley produced a cigarette case and took out a cigarette, which he rolled with an air of concentration between finger and thumb as though attempting to assess diameter and circumference. 'And I bumped into him during the evening, oddly enough. Just for a moment or two. It was at the Bull. In the bar.'

Kirby was making notes. He looked up. 'Did he say why he was coming to Lydmouth, sir?'

'For a short holiday, I think that's what he said. Oh yes, he said he was a freelance journalist. I guessed he was something of the sort – he had a camera and a portable typewriter with him. He told me he might have a chance to do some work while he was down here.'

'What do you think he meant? That he was following up a story?'

'I've no idea. He could have meant that, or he could have meant he had some writing to do, or he could have simply meant that if some work turned up, he wouldn't be averse to doing it.'

'Where did you drop him?'

'On this side of the station.'

Yateley put the cigarette in his mouth at last and fumbled for a light. Kirby found his lighter and offered the man a flame.

'And you met Mr Rowse again?'

'Yes – I was having a drink before going out to dinner. He saw me in the bar and came over for a moment.'

'What did you talk about?'

'Oh – I don't know. He thanked me for the lift, I remember that, and he asked me if he could buy me a drink, but I was on the verge of going out, and to be honest I didn't want to encourage the acquaintanceship.'

'What time was this, sir?'

Yateley shrugged. 'A quarter past seven? Half past seven? I didn't look.'

'Did he mention his name?'

'No, I don't think he did.'

'Then how did you know that the man who died was the man you'd given a lift to?'

'Because that porter chap at the Bull told me. You know him? Quale, is it? He said that someone called Rowse had been killed at the Bathurst Arms, that he was a journalist from London, and that he'd been drinking in the Bull last night. Quale asked if I'd seen him — Rowse was wearing rather a loud tweed jacket — you simply couldn't miss it. Once seen, never forgotten.' Yateley pushed back his chair and stood up. 'Well, Sergeant, that's all I can tell you, I'm afraid.'

Kirby stood up as well. 'I'm sure Mr Thornhill will want to be in touch with you, sir. We may need a statement.'

'Sergeant, I'd appreciate it if we could keep my name out of the papers. You understand that a man in my position needs to be careful ... Of course, if you need a statement from me, that's another matter. I'm only too delighted to do anything I can to help. All things being equal, however, I'd rather not publicise the fact that I'm in Lydmouth.'

Kirby stared across the table. 'I see, sir. Don't mind my asking, but is there any particular reason for that?'

Yateley stared gravely back at him. 'I'm afraid that's confidential.'

Pound to a penny it's something to do with Farnock Camp.

The MP cocked an eyebrow, and Kirby suddenly felt the man's charm. 'You know how it is,' Yateley said. 'No names, no packdrill.' He took a step towards the door, then stopped. 'Perhaps you'd let Inspector Thornhill know that I called. Tell him I'll be at the Bull for another night. I'd like to see him. But I realise he has a lot on his plate at present.'

'It's an ill wind,' Superintendent Williamson observed, 'that blows nobody good.' With his pipe sticking like a Churchillian cigar from the corner of his mouth, he turned to Thornhill, who was sitting beside him in the rear seat of the first police car. 'By the time we've finished, it won't seem quite so like Home Sweet Bloody Home.'

Williamson had to raise his voice to make himself heard over the clanging of the police car's bell. He was looking better than he had done for days. The procession roared down the hill towards the river. There was another car behind, and behind that a van. In total, Thornhill calculated, there were eleven uniformed officers and four detectives.

'Do we need the bell, sir?'

'Oh yes. Just to make the point quite clear. Or the next thing we know, someone else will move in.'

The Superintendent had proposed the raid, but Thornhill was almost sure that he had been acting on a suggestion from the Chief Constable, James Hendry. And behind Hendry there would be other suggestions, other hints, impossible to prove. Hendry played golf with the Lord Lieutenant of the county, who still had a great many friends at the War Office. Or perhaps someone at the Home Office had picked up the phone this morning. Over the whole business hung a spurious urgency, so much so that Thornhill had not even been able to talk to Kirby before leaving Police Headquarters.

He stared out of the window, wondering whether he would miss his six-thirty appointment with Jill Francis. The Cardiff train was pulling into the station, smoke rising to join the few white clouds high in the blue April sky. Cars pulled over to allow the police procession to pass. On a corner of the station approach road, a small boy in shorts and a torn jersey pointed at them, his face filled with an uncomplicated joy. If only, Thornhill thought, life were always that simple.

They roared over the bridge. A pair of moorhens rose from the water, and flew upstream, their panic obvious from the ragged beat of their wings. The road ahead curved and climbed towards the green smudge of the Forest. Their driver, Porter, turned into Farnock Lane.

'Right,' said Williamson. 'We're going to go through this place like a dose of salts.' He turned his head and murmured in a voice that only Thornhill would be able to hear, 'We've got *carte blanche*, Mr Hendry says. He'll back us all the way.'

'Yes, sir.'

Williamson stared challengingly at him. 'If only life were always this simple, eh?'

Life was always simple for small boys, Thornhill thought. Or at least simpler.

When they had turned into Farnock Lane, the van had followed; but the second police car behind them continued up the hill towards the Forest. According to the map, the camp had a second entrance, which could be reached by a farm track running parallel to the lane.

'Just in case any of them try to make a bolt for it, sir,' Williamson had told Hendry. 'Classic pincer movement. We'll squeeze them like a pair of nutcrackers.'

Williamson had served in the county regiment during World War I, and Thornhill suspected that the Superintendent relished the opportunity to live out a military fantasy. It was unfortunate that the occupants of the camp would not be able to conform to it.

Porter swung the car into the entrance of the camp, braked hard and brought them to a swaying halt in front of the group of Nissen huts nearest to the lane. The van followed, but stopped just inside the gateway, effectively blocking it. Doors opened, and policemen tumbled out.

Two mud-smeared children were sitting in what had once been a flower-bed, nursing equally grubby teddy bears. They stared open-mouthed at the intruders. A woman appeared in the doorway of one of the Nissen huts. She shouted at the children, and they reluctantly scrambled to their feet and went towards her.

'What the hell are you doing?' she yelled at the two constables who strode towards her.

One of the children turned round, saw the advancing policemen and screamed. She turned to run, tripped and fell full-length on the cracked concrete of the roadway. There was a moment of silence, of waiting. Then she burst into fear-fuelled howls of pain. The woman darted towards the fallen child. So did one of the constables.

The officer reached the little girl first and bent down to pick her up. The woman launched herself at him crying, 'You bastard!' Caught off balance, the policeman keeled over. His colleague seized the woman from behind. She hacked at his shins with her heels. More women and a couple of men came running from other Nissen huts and from the recesses of the camp. Somewhere in the distance, there was more shouting. Thornhill guessed that the occupants of the second police car were now invading the camp by the other entrance.

Williamson grasped the arm of Inspector Jackson, the head of the Division's uniformed branch. 'Right!' he bellowed, his face flushing a dangerous shade of purple. 'I want this lot under lock and key. And I want it now.'

'Yes, sir.'

'And radio for reinforcements.'

It was an ugly battle, and Thornhill watched it from the sidelines. When Jackson grabbed one of the toddlers, probably to keep it out of harm's way, he was attacked by a woman wielding a knife. They got the knife off her in seconds, but Jackson suffered a cut on his hand. Another uniformed officer received a bloody nose. A male squatter kicked Porter in the crotch and then punched him in the face.

Not that the outcome was ever in doubt. Most of the prisoners were herded into the van. A second van arrived, bringing unnecessary reinforcements and taking away the rest of the squatters, including the children.

Williamson rubbed his hands together as he watched the last of them being herded aboard. 'No better than animals, if you ask me. Look at the way they went for young Porter.'

Thornhill bent down and picked up one of the toddlers' teddy bears.

'Scum,' Williamson went on. 'No other word for it. Impeding a murder enquiry. Resisting arrest. Attacking police officers.

And then just look at the mess they've made of this place. Makes you sick, doesn't it?'

As they were talking, two other squatters, both male, arrived from work. They lost their tempers and soon joined their friends in the van. The vans left, and the remaining police officers began to search the camp under Williamson's supervision.

Thornhill was nominally in charge of a group of men investigating the part of the camp that had not been used by the squatters. He did not take part in the search himself, and he did not give the men any orders. He wandered to and fro among the ruined huts, hands in pockets, the teddy bear tucked in the crook of his arm. The spring sunshine was surprisingly warm. He looked at ruined buildings and piles of rubbish. Sheep bleated on the hillside above the camp. Beyond it was the darker green of the forest, cool and mysterious. High in the sky was a bird that might have been a swallow, the first one of the year. Surely it was too early for swallows?

He rounded the corner of the ruined guardhouse near the second entrance to the camp and found himself face to face with the Superintendent.

'For Christ's sake, Thornhill,' Williamson said. 'What are you doing with that bloody teddy bear?'

Chapter Twenty

In the drawing room at Troy House, a wood fire was burning brightly in the fireplace to counteract the growing chill as the evening approached. The tea tray had been removed and Charlotte was knitting. She heard footsteps outside and her husband's voice in the hall. She looked at the clock. Usually he dropped in at the Bull for a drink after work. Smiling, because it always pleased her when he came home early, she gathered up her knitting.

The door opened and Philip came into the room. She knew at once that something was wrong. He came over to her chair and bent down to kiss her.

'What's happened, dear?'

'The police went up to Farnock Camp this afternoon. In force.'

'And about time too,' said Charlotte, who strongly disapproved of those who put their own needs before those of their country.

'I had a tip-off from Sergeant Fowles. Too late to do anything about it, unfortunately. They went in like a gang of commandos. There was a pitched battle.'

'I'm sure the police didn't start it. Have the troops moved back?'

'I'm not sure.' Philip leaned on the mantel and stared at

the flames. 'Jill went down there and tried to get in. There were police on both gates, but no sign of the Army.'

'Isn't that rather odd?'

'Not necessarily. There's a connection with the Rowse case, you see. When Jill was there yesterday afternoon, she found him ferreting around.'

'Nasty little man.'

'I suppose someone must have liked him – though personally I find it hard to believe.' He took a cigarette from the box on the mantelpiece. 'By the way, have you seen my lighter? The one you gave me?'

Before Charlotte had time to answer, the telephone began to ring. Philip went to answer it. He shut the door of the drawing room behind him. At first Charlotte heard nothing, but then Philip's voice became audible, which meant he must almost be shouting. A moment later, he came back into the room and veered towards the drinks tray.

'It was that bloody man Fuggle from the *Post*,' he said over his shoulder. Whisky glugged into his glass. 'Do you know what? He said he'd heard that I'd once been a member of the Communist Party, and would I like to confirm or deny this.'

'Philip – calm down. Getting upset won't help.'

He turned. 'Then what will?'

Charlotte opened her mouth and then closed it. She had known about Philip's youthful fling in Spain long before they married. During their courtship it had given him a romantic aura. But there was a long gap between then and now, and in the interval the world had changed. She was well aware that there were people in Lydmouth who considered Communism to be a form of secular Satanism.

Philip sat down heavily on the sofa. 'I don't know what to do.'

Nor did Charlotte. But she stretched out her hand and rested it, plump and beringed, on her husband's knee. 'We'll think of something,' she said grimly. 'Don't worry.'

It was almost seven o'clock when the doorbell rang. Jill put down her notebook and went to answer the door. Richard Thornhill was standing on the pavement, hands deep in the pockets of his coat. He refused to meet her eyes. Alice waddled between Jill and the door jamb and rubbed her distended body against Thornhill's ankles, purring loudly.

'You'd better come in,' Jill said.

He was careful to avoid brushing against her as he came into the hall. Alice retreated to the cupboard under the stairs to examine the cardboard box Jill had put there earlier in the day. Nursing her anger – how dare he? – Jill followed Thornhill into the sitting room.

'This business at the camp,' she said. 'It's terrible. And they told me you were actually there.'

'It was not my choice.'

'Yes, but you went along with it.'

He was turning his hat round and round in his hands as though steering a car through an endless bend. He said nothing. His silence infuriated her still further.

'I know some policemen enjoy that sort of thing.' To her horror she felt tears pricking at her eyelids. 'But I thought you were different.'

'If I could have stopped it, I would have done.'

'Did you even try?'

He looked at her. 'No.' He took a step towards her, then stopped. 'I've been wondering if I should resign. What do you think?'

The nakedness of his appeal caught her off guard. She had been prepared for silence, for excuses or even for anger. But not for this.

'The whole thing was set up,' he went on, speaking in a thick, stumbling voice. 'Hendry must have talked to Williamson, and probably to Jackson as well. God knows who's been talking to Hendry. The Rowse case gave them the excuse they needed. They used it – and they used me, too. I had to be brought along to show we were there as part of the murder investigation.'

'What do you mean?'

'Rowse was up at the camp on the day he was killed. You know about that. There's every reason to believe that he was murdered. So that gave Williamson a cast-iron reason to go into the camp to ask questions.'

'But Williamson *didn't* do that. He—'

'He went in like an invading army,' Thornhill interrupted. '*We* went in. We were looking for a fight, and he and Jackson made sure we damn well got one. Well, that was it – all the excuse we needed. Williamson and Hendry are happy. So's the Army, because we've done their dirty work for them. Half the people at Headquarters are acting as if it's a re-run of VE day. And in the middle of it all, I'm trying to run a murder enquiry.'

'What will you do?'

'I don't know.' He laughed, a harsh sound like the whine of car's starter motor. 'Williamson would be delighted if I chucked it in. There must be something else I can do to earn a living. Become a debt collector, perhaps.'

She stretched out her hand and took his hat. He glanced down at it, his face surprised as though he had forgotten he was holding it.

'Take your coat off, Richard, and sit down.'

He obeyed her. 'Do you remember when I phoned this morning? Before all this blew up?'

'Yes.' She draped the coat and hat over the back of the sofa.

'I was going to say that I'd made up my mind not to come and see you again. Not – not like this. As friends, I mean. Because it wasn't fair to you, or to Edith.'

'I see.' She turned away and decided that the fire needed more coal. When she straightened up, she said, 'You must do as you think best. But I don't think you should resign. It would just give people like Williamson a field day.'

He looked up at her from his chair. 'Then there's something I need to know.'

'What?'

'Is Oliver Yateley something to do with this?'

She folded her arms in case her hands were shaking. 'I don't understand.'

'I think you do. I wouldn't ask if it weren't relevant to the case. But first — there's something I should tell you. I've met Yateley before. Just after you first came to Lydmouth. Do you remember?'

'I didn't realise you'd met him, if that's what you mean. But of course I remember the first time I came to Lydmouth.'

Their eyes met. She and Richard had been involved in another case, and she still felt he had pursued justice on that occasion at the expense of mercy. For the moment, though, the only thing that mattered was that Richard knew something about herself and Oliver.

'You see, when he was here last time, he got very drunk,' Richard went on, his voice gentle but remorseless, just as he must speak to his suspects. 'I helped him up to his room. He had a photograph of you. He didn't realise I'd seen it.'

'I used to know him quite well.'

He ignored her attempt to stop him with a half-truth. 'Yateley was desperate to talk. He talked to me because he didn't know me from Adam. He told me about his — his friendship with you. And about how it ended.'

'He had no right,' Jill said.

'He did his best to be discreet. He didn't mention any names. If I hadn't seen that photograph, I wouldn't have made the connection.' Richard hesitated. 'I'm sorry I have to mention this. It's your business, yours and his, nothing to do with me.'

Of course it's your business, you silly man.

'But I need to know why Yateley's here.' He held up his hand like a policeman on point duty to prevent her interrupting. 'The thing is, he's involved whether he likes it or not. It turns out that he gave Rowse a lift into Lydmouth yesterday afternoon. Rowse's motorbike broke down the other side of Ashbridge. And then Rowse was hanging round the Bull yesterday evening – I saw him there myself – and Yateley's staying at the Bull. The barman saw them talking. And isn't Yateley on a Parliamentary sub-committee for defence? I couldn't help wondering if one reason why he'd come down was to have a quiet word with Henchry about Farnock Camp.'

Jill shook her head. She sat down in the armchair on the opposite side of the hearthrug because her legs felt weak. This business at Farnock Camp had stirred everything up. Her emotions were in such a tangle. One disturbance created another, in defiance of logic. The evictions had made her furious. But would she have been quite so angry if Richard Thornhill had not been involved?

'As far as I know,' she said crisply, 'Oliver Yateley came to Lydmouth to see me. I certainly don't know of any other reason.'

'I see.'

'It's not what you think.'

He was already on his feet. 'I'm sorry I've taken up so much of your time. And I hope I haven't upset you.'

Suddenly Jill was standing as well. 'It's true that Oliver came to see me, but he's not in love with me. And I'm not in love with him. Not now. But there was something he needed to talk about, and I'm afraid I can't tell you what it is.'

'Has it anything to do with Rowse's murder?'

'I don't see how it can have. But if you like, I'll try to get Oliver to talk to you.'

Richard nodded. 'That would be useful. In a case like this, half the problem is knowing what's relevant and what isn't.' He scooped up his hat and coat from the sofa. 'By the way – you must have seen Rowse's camera at Farnock Camp. Have you any idea what make it was?'

'A Contax, I think. Thirty-five millimetre.'

'Thank you.' He smiled awkwardly at her. 'I must go.'

Jill held out her hand, an absurdly formal gesture. He took it, but neither of them tried to shake hands. He brought up his other hand and clasped it round hers. A clock ticked. Seconds passed. Alice, stretched against the arm of the sofa and wantonly displaying her bellyful of babies, watched them with unblinking eyes.

'Thank you,' he said. 'Thank you for listening to me. And thank you for putting up with my questions.'

Swiftly he raised her hand and took a step forward. She felt his lips brush the back of her hand and heard the minute explosion of a kiss. And then, before she had time even to register surprise, he was gone, leaving behind him nothing but a current of moving air, a faint, masculine smell of hair oil and a sense of absence. There were footsteps in the hall and the front door closed. Jill and Alice were alone in the house with the long evening before them.

Chapter Twenty-One

He had a full belly after the night's hunting.

The young fox surveyed the field from the shelter of the hedge. The hummocky grass was studded with rocks and incurious sheep. His nose twitched, drawing in the rich flood of smells. There were lambs among the sheep, but none it would be safe to approach. He was not hungry enough to run risks.

Keeping in the lee of the hedge, he trotted up the slope towards the Forest and home. His brush floated like a feather duster after his skinny body. The trees in front of him were still a mass of blue shadow. On the skyline was a brilliant smear of yellow and orange. Above that was the dome of the sky, a clean and almost transparent colour that was neither blue nor green.

At the edge of the Forest the fox stopped. He turned to view the world he was leaving behind. A pair of rabbits were bobbing on spring-loaded legs among the sheep. At the bottom of the field was another hedge, and beyond that a muddy lane with fencing topped with barbed wire running along the other side. There were many ways through that fence, and he had often explored the man-made territory beyond.

The further downhill he looked, the more mist there was. Lydmouth was still shrouded in a grey darkness beside the river.

Only the spire of St John's was visible, poking into the sky as though probing for something that might be concealed there.

Something was not quite as it normally was. The fox's brain registered the minor anomaly without identifying it. There were fewer smells in the air. No smoke came from the chimneys attached to some of the huts. Nothing for him to worry about, nothing that mattered.

His nose twitched once more. Then he turned, slipped through the stone stile and vanished into the darkness of the Forest, sliding deeper and deeper among the trees. His own smell guided him like a thread through a labyrinth as he pattered purposefully towards the warmth and safety of his earth.

At last he was safely underground. Near the entrance, he paused. There was a smell here that needed to be sniffed. It was part of his routine when he entered or left the earth. The smell was very faint, but still delightful. There had been food here once, good food, and a ghostly trace of it lingered.

As he moved away, his left hind paw snagged in a fragment of rotting cloth. Instantly he pulled it free. The rotting cotton tore. The sound it made was like a faint, ragged gasp. The fox ignored it.

The red disc of the sun pushed itself from the jagged row of black treetops along the skyline. Light poured into the valley of the Lyd like water into a bowl. Its warmth melted the mist that clung to the town, the river and the lower slopes of the valley. Buildings appeared, ghostly at first and then increasingly substantial. At the Bull Hotel, light touched the upper windows of the façade overlooking the High Street. The rooms behind the windows were still dark.

In Room 9, Oliver Yateley lay in bed and stared at the vertical crack of light near the top of the window where the two curtains failed to meet. The crack reminded him of the blade of a dagger, point downwards.

His body ached. Over the years the bed's horsehair mattress had sagged into the shape of a hammock. His head had worn a dent in the pillows. At one point in the night, he had thrown off most of the bedclothes, but then the cold had reached him instead.

The light grew stronger. Yateley gave up the pretence of trying to sleep, sat up in bed and felt for his dressing gown. A moment later, he padded across the draughty floor to the window and drew back the curtains. The High Street was a pale grey canyon, empty of visible life. Birds chattered, an incontinent flow of chirrups and squeaks.

He needed the lavatory. Unlocking his door, he slipped on to the landing. The long corridor had the ghostly quality of a place seen at the wrong time. The shoes he had left outside his room for cleaning were still there, still dirty. Even the maids were asleep. He hurried to the lavatory.

Afterwards he could not bear to go back to bed. He settled himself in the armchair by the window, with the eiderdown on top of him and the overflowing ashtray on the windowsill at his elbow. On the opposite pavement, a constable strolled in the direction of the police station. Yateley watched the man peering up the steps to the library and checking the handle of the newsagent's door. A milkfloat trundled along the road, and its driver exchanged greetings with the policeman.

Yateley lit his last cigarette. To the east, the sky was drenched in colour, and the sight of it reminded him of a Turner painting in the National Gallery whose name he could not remember. It struck him as bizarre — only one step removed from madness — that at a time like this his mind should be thinking about a painting. He rubbed his eyes, which felt as though someone had lined their sockets with sand.

Then he heard the footsteps. They were firm and regular — and certainly not trying to be quiet, despite the time —

the footsteps of someone who had a right to be walking along the landing. Yateley shivered under the eiderdown. He remembered a friend who had served in military intelligence telling him that the early morning was the favoured time for arrests. People were at their most vulnerable then. Both their bodies and their minds operated with reduced efficiency.

The unheeded cigarette burnt down to his fingers. He yelped with pain, dropped the butt on the eiderdown and leapt to his feet. The cigarette rolled down the eiderdown and fell to the linoleum under the window. He ground it out under his slipper.

The footsteps had passed his room and were descending the main staircase. Feeling foolish, he sat down again, drawing the eiderdown round him, and rubbed the stubble on his chin. He could not stay here for ever, a prisoner in this ghastly hotel in this tinpot little town in the middle of nowhere. He would have to do something soon – but what? He was like a man in a quicksand: activity of any sort would merely hasten the end.

It occurred to him then that there was more than one way of ending. There at least he had a choice. They could not take that away from him.

Something nasty in the woodshed.

Before the war Howard had read a novel in which those words were a recurring phrase. Everyone except him had seemed to find the book very funny. He had never had much time for reading, or for pretending to laugh at stupid jokes. Anyway, here he was in the woodshed, but he wasn't nasty. And it wasn't funny, either.

The light was growing round the edge of the door frame, and filtering through the cobwebs and glass of the window. But it was the dream that had woken him, not the dawn. As usual the dream had left his heart pounding. The dream was one reason why he had come back to Lydmouth. He was convinced that when he had tidied up, when there was no longer any danger of discovery, the dream would leave him.

The panic subsided. Howard twisted his head on the pillow, but the little travel clock Phyllis had brought him was just beyond his range of vision, and he couldn't be bothered to reach out a hand for it. He was surprisingly warm. She had also brought him a ground sheet and an armful of blankets. There were cigarettes, too, a bottle of beer (now empty) and an untouched Thermos flask of soup. He had slept better than he had since leaving London – if the truth were known, better than he had for weeks. He felt safe here in a way he had not felt in London, not since the cheques began to bounce. He had Phyllis to look after him, Phyllis to guard him.

Now the dream had receded, his mind was clearer than it had been for days. The fever – 'flu or whatever it had been – was at last subsiding. There was much to do, but he knew he must not hurry. He needed to build up his strength and settle himself into his new life.

His eyelids were heavy. Nothing wrong with a bit more shut-eye. As he drifted back to sleep, his wrist began to itch again and without thinking he scratched it.

'You're always doing that,' Phyllis had once said in the few months they had lived together as man and wife. 'It's as if you're trying to scratch the tattoo off your skin.'

Chapter Twenty-Two

Edith Thornhill put her husband's breakfast on the table. 'Richard? There's something we should talk about.'

He glanced up at her. 'Can't it wait?'

'I know this isn't a good time. But somehow it never is.'

Above their heads came a series of thuds followed by a wail from Elizabeth: the children were making their beds and getting ready for school.

'I know,' Richard said, his mouth already full of fried egg. 'And it's likely to get worse at work.'

She hated it when Richard was involved in a murder case, or in those that involved any sort of violence and danger. 'I wish you had a proper job,' she heard herself saying, and knew at once she'd made a mistake.

'It is a proper job. And someone has to do it.'

'Yes, but why does it have to be you?'

He shrugged. Suddenly he surprised her by dropping his fork on his plate and stretching out his hand to touch her arm. It was an oddly tentative caress, as if he expected a rebuff. Perhaps he did, Edith thought, feeling a twinge of the familiar guilt. Since Elizabeth's birth, she had not enjoyed that side of their life together.

'I'm sorry,' Richard said. 'Why don't you sit down and have some tea? What did you want to talk about?'

She sat down reluctantly, aware that there were a hundred and one things she should be doing before she walked the children to school, and quite capable of doing at least some of them and talking to Richard at the same time; why could men think of only one thing at a time?

'It's about Mother's money.' She glimpsed the wariness in his face, before he dropped his eyes and began to saw at the rasher of bacon. 'And David's school fees.'

'I thought we'd agreed that it's more important to use the money as a deposit for the house.'

'Yes, but—'

'The chance won't come again,' Richard said. 'In any case, I've already told Shipston that we'd like to make an offer.'

Shipston, a local solicitor, was their landlord.

'But I do wonder if we should put aside the money for David's school fees instead.'

'He'll do very well at the grammar school, assuming he gets in. We've been through all this. In any case, there's no great rush.'

Edith shook her head. 'It's important to plan ahead.' She stared at him, willing him to agree with her. 'David's education is the most important thing we can give him.'

'Perhaps I'll be made up to Chief Inspector. Give it a couple of years, and it might happen. Then we could think again.' He mopped up egg yolk with a square of fried bread. 'Perhaps.'

'You know Uncle Bernard came to tea yesterday?'

He nodded. 'To ask you to the madrigal concert?'

'Yes, that was one thing we talked about. But we got on to schools for the children. He might be able to help.' She hesitated. 'One way or another.'

'What do you mean by that?'

'He was talking about how important education was. How important a good school can be in later life. He meant a public school.'

'That's rich – coming from a Labour councillor.'

'He doesn't like public schools any more than you do, Richard. But he thinks while they're there, we might as well use them.'

'That's the sort of thing politicians are always saying. Besides, David's not Uncle Bernard's child. He's ours.'

'Yes, but he has a point. The important thing is that the children get a good education.' She stared at Richard, watching him align his knife and fork precisely in the middle of his empty plate. 'He's quite a wealthy man, now. He as good as hinted—'

'I'm sorry, Edith, I don't want charity.'

'But it's not charity – it's family.'

His face had that tight, closed look. 'Charity's still charity. The problem is, it confers obligations.'

'And there's another possibility.' Edith smiled at Richard and picked her words with even greater care: 'Now Uncle Bernard's on the Council. Apparently there's some sub-committee he may be asked to join . . .' She began to gather up the dirty crockery from the table. 'It can't do any harm having a friendly face on it. There's nothing wrong in it. It's all quite open and above board.'

'No. I don't want that sort of favour.' He pushed back his chair. 'I really must be going. I'm not sure what time I'll be back. I'll—'

'Mother's money is mine.' Edith thought of David, and felt her determination harden. 'I don't think we should use it for the house. I'm going to put it aside for his education.'

While Alice ate a hearty breakfast, preparing herself for the ordeal to come, Jill found that she could manage no more than half a cup of coffee and a slither of toast.

She knew why. She was too excited and too apprehensive. She had felt like this when at the age of ten she had first succeeded in balancing on a bicycle: euphoria mixed with the depressing knowledge of impending disaster. It was all Richard Thornhill's fault. There were no two ways about it: she had enjoyed having him kiss her hand; a corny gesture, true, but undeniably a romantic one. On the other hand, Richard was a married man, with children, and Jill had had quite enough of married men. He was a senior police officer. They both lived in Lydmouth, which, as far as privacy was concerned, was rather like a large goldfish bowl. In fact, now she came to think of it, if she was going to fall in love with someone, she could hardly have made a worse choice.

The mood clung to her as she walked to work. On the landing outside the reporters' room she met Philip, who was looking depressed.

'Why are you looking so cheerful?' he demanded.

'It's spring,' said Jill, and felt foolish.

'Don't expect it to last. By the way, we've just had a call from the police. Williamson's throwing a press conference at half past ten. I thought I'd wander along. Do you want to come?'

Jill repressed a shiver of anticipation. 'All right.'

'Watching Williamson in full cry is always good for a laugh.'

When she and Philip were walking up the High Street to the police station. Jill glanced at the Bull and wondered if Yateley was still there. That problem was still there, rumbling away in the back of her mind.

'A penny for them,' said Philip, who could be disconcertingly sensitive at times. 'You look as if someone has just walked over your grave.'

She smiled at him. 'Just thinking of ghosts.'

At Police Headquarters, the Conference Room was already full of familiar faces and thick with smoke. Though it was relatively early in the day, there were people from Birmingham, Cardiff and Bristol. Jill recognised several stringers for national newspapers. Like policemen, journalists took the murder of one of their own very seriously.

Jill and Philip were among the last to arrive. They had just sat down when there was a flurry at the door and Superintendent Williamson and Richard Thornhill came in, with Ivor Fuggle of the *Post* at their heels. Thornhill's eyes met Jill's for an instant. She thought that he looked tired. Then Ivor Fuggle sat down next to her and Thornhill looked away.

Fuggle leant across her and said in a phlegm-laden whisper to Philip, 'Heard the latest on Farnock Camp, old man? There's a rumour they're going to charge the squatters.'

The press conference itself was an anti-climax. As usual on these occasions, Williamson enjoyed himself enormously. What he actually said, however, was disappointing. He ran over the bare facts of the case: Rowse had come to Lydmouth on a working holiday and on his first night had been stabbed to death in his room at the Bathurst Arms. Yes, he had visited Farnock Camp on the day before he died, and there was every reason to believe that he had planned to write a story on the squatters. The inquest had been adjourned. The police were investigating several possibilities and at present they had no intention of calling in the Yard.

At question time, Philip was one of the first to raise his hand. 'Do you think there's a connection between the murder and Farnock Camp, Superintendent?'

'At this stage it's too early to say, Mr Wemyss-Brown.'

'We understand you searched the camp yesterday and also evicted the squatters.'

'That is correct.'

'Will the one's you arrested be charged?'

Williamson frowned. 'I'm afraid I can't comment on that at present.'

'What about the rest of them? Where are they living, now they're homeless?'

'That's not my department, sir. You'll need to talk to the Council.'

A man from Bristol chipped in with questions about the number of stab wounds and the time of death. The briefing took another direction.

Afterwards Fuggle nudged Philip's shoulder as they were leaving Police Headquarters. 'Looks like it won't take them too long to sort this one out, eh?'

'What makes you say that?'

'It's obvious they've got something on the squatters.' Fuggle chuckled. 'I hope I'm not treading on any toes, old man, but Communists have a habit of thinking the end justifies the means. Still, I expect you've grown out of all that now.'

Fuggle slipped into the sunlit High Street. Jill turned, sensing someone behind them. It was Richard Thornhill. He was looking not at her but at Philip.

After the press conference and the photographs, Williamson's bonhomie evaporated. He called Thornhill into his office, waved him to a chair and sat down behind his desk.

'You know Oliver Yateley is staying at the Bull?'

Thornhill nodded.

'You've met him, of course. Mr Hendry feels that having him on the doorstep is all the more reason why this investigation should be a credit to the Force. Do I make myself clear?'

'Yes, sir.'

'He's also pleased that we've sorted out this Farnock Camp business. We'll be keeping a guard on the place until the army move back in.'

'When will that be?'

'Tomorrow evening, probably. Then we can wash our hands of the whole business – apart from the four we've got in custody.'

'I wasn't happy with what happened yesterday afternoon, sir. I felt we used unreasonable force.'

There was a moment's silence. Williamson poked a paperclip into his left ear and dug out a piece of wax which he deposited on his blotter. Thornhill waited for the explosion. To his consternation, it failed to come.

'There's a lot of things I'm not happy about,' Williamson said with a yawn. 'And people, come to that.' He pulled a file towards him and opened it. 'Be that as it may, we've still got jobs to do. Now – this Rowse business. The post mortem's not much use. Three stab wounds. Probably administered with a large penknife or kitchen knife – almost certainly it's a blade with only one cutting edge.' He ran his finger down the typed report. 'The assailant was probably a right-hander. No great force needed so it could have been a man or a woman. At the time of his death, Rowse had recently eaten a large meal and drunk a large amount of alcohol – that's all confirmed by the Alvingtons, of course. May have been too drunk to put up a fight. Now what about access?'

'Anyone could have slipped into the room via the door to the yard during the evening,' Thornhill said. 'I need to talk to the Alvingtons again about when they locked up.'

Williamson shut the file. 'Has Kirby got anything out of the Yard?'

'Not much. They sent someone round to look at Rowse's lodgings. He was a freelance photojournalist, not doing too well. He owed money to his landlady and to several tradesmen.' Thornhill hesitated. 'He seems to have done a lot of work for the *Empire Lion*. So if he had done a piece on Farnock Camp, he would probably have attacked the squatters.'

'Whereas while he was there, while he was talking to them, he was all sweetness and light?'

Thornhill nodded. 'We're still not certain what's missing from his room at the Bathurst. His landlady had no idea about his possessions. There's also the possibility that the robbery was interrupted. His wallet was in his jacket, and his cheque book was lying on the bed. But his camera and his notebook had gone. He used them both up at the camp, and we know he took his notebook when he went to the Bull in the evening.'

'He was taking photographs up at the camp.' Williamson stared out of the window. Despite his vigorous performance at the press conference, he looked ill. 'So – for the sake of argument, let's say that the squatters talked a little too openly to him, thinking he was on their side. Maybe he took photographs of them all. Then they realised their mistake.'

'How?' Thornhill said.

Williamson waved aside the interruption. 'Easy enough – maybe someone saw his name in the *Empire Lion*. They're all local people, so they know their way around – they find out where he's staying, and try and get his notebook and his camera. They don't want the bad publicity. Then he wanders upstairs and catches them red-handed. They panic, and Bob's your uncle.' He looked at Thornhill. 'That Coalway woman seems to be the ringleader. I want you to have a go at her.'

'Has she said anything yet?'

'Nothing that was worth hearing. She just swore at me when I tried to talk to her, but maybe you'll have more luck. Just as well she's in custody.' Williamson permitted himself a smile. 'Makes it so much more convenient.'

'Do we really have to keep her locked up?'

'Are you questioning my judgement?'

'No, sir. But –'

'Good.' Williamson's eyes darted to another file on his desk. 'Oh – and what about the Parry case? Any news on that? Mr Broadbent was on the phone earlier this morning.'

'We've drawn a blank so far.' Thornhill suppressed his surprise. They were in the middle of a murder investigation and the Superintendent was chasing up a three-year-old missing person case.

'Keep it moving. I know we've got other things on our mind at present, but I don't want us to lose sight of this. You'd better go and talk to that Coalway woman.'

'One other thing, sir. You remember the lighter that was under Rowse's body?'

'Yes — what about it?'

'Rather a good lighter for a man who was having money problems. Young Porter has been making some enquiries on his own initiative.'

'Porter? *Initiative?*'

'It's a Richelieu lighter, and apparently Crawley's is the only stockist in Lydmouth. He's sold only two of that model — to the Wemyss-Browns.'

Williamson sat up sharply. 'Are you sure?'

'Sergeant Kirby went round and confirmed it.'

'The *Gazette* has been very much on the squatters' side.' Williamson sucked his teeth. 'And we know Rowse and Wemyss-Brown had words at the Bull. Nearly came to blows, didn't you say?'

'Yes, sir.'

'Christ.' Williamson's face was suddenly wary. 'This could be very interesting.'

Chapter Twenty-Three

Brian Kirby watched Williamson and Thornhill coming down the stairs to the ground floor of Police Headquarters. A partition of plywood and frosted glass separated them from the area behind the reception counter. Neither of them looked well. Williamson was clinging to the rail of the banisters, his face grey and exhausted. Kirby thought the Superintendent should have retired after the last illness. Thornhill looked haggard. Maybe it was because of work. Or maybe Edith Thornhill had kept him busy last night.

Kirby rather fancied the inspector's wife. He quite liked an older woman – preferably on the plump side and blonde, a woman who knew how to please a man, and who didn't get silly ideas about where it might all lead. Once or twice he had caught Edith looking at him, and he had wondered whether the feeling might be reciprocated. Not that he would do anything about it, even if it were. Only a fool would mess around with the old man's wife; and Kirby prided himself on not being a fool. But there was just a possibility that the old man himself might find other distractions. Kirby had sometimes wondered if Thornhill might be sweet on Jill Francis.

Williamson ignored Kirby and stretched out his hand towards the door in the partition. Simultaneously the door swung violently towards him. Porter blundered through, not looking where he was going because his eyes were on Sergeant Fowles behind the reception counter. First the door banged into Williamson's arm and then all sixteen stone of Peter Porter. The impact swung Williamson backwards. Thornhill grabbed him, preventing him from falling. Williamson snarled at Porter, who opened his mouth to say sorry but couldn't find the precise word. The Superintendent pulled himself away from Thornhill. Sergeant Fowles lifted the flap in the counter to allow Williamson through. The four of them watched in silence as Williamson stalked out of the building. On the way through the outer doorway, he passed a woman coming in.

'Porter,' Thornhill said. 'Good work with that lighter.' He turned to Kirby. 'By the way, were there any prints on it?'

'No, sir. Just Rowse's. Which reminds me: the CRO have got nothing on Rowse. In theory he's as clean as a whistle.'

The spring-loaded door in the glass partition was still ajar. Kirby was facing the gap. As he was speaking to Thornhill, he saw the woman advancing on Fowles. She wore a long, brown coat and an elderly hat decorated with artificial flowers. Her face was as round as a bun, with tiny features.

'It just won't do,' she said as she neared the counter. 'It's robbery, and it's got to stop.'

'Yes, Madam,' said Fowles. 'How can we help?'

'Brian,' Thornhill said quietly, 'I'm going to the Bathurst Arms now. Would you phone Mr Yateley, give him my compliments, and ask if it would be convenient for me to call on him at the Bull after lunch. Two-thirty, say.'

The voice was growing louder on the other side of the glass partition. 'That's the third day in a row. My hens are layers. Someone's stealing the eggs – there's no other answer. And last night, they put a hand through my larder window and took half a pound of cheese. I told the constable, and he did nothing at all about it. What can you expect – the boy's still got his mother's milk wet on his lips. What do we pay our rates for, that's what I want to know?'

'Will you be needing a driver today, sir?' Porter asked Thornhill.

'No, I don't think I will. If need be I'll drive myself.'

Kirby saw the despondency flickering on Porter's face. He glanced at Thornhill, and guessed that the inspector had seen it too.

'I want someone from the CID,' Mrs Veale was saying. 'A proper detective.'

Thornhill smiled. 'But there is something else you can do.'

Mrs Norah Coalway was waiting in the interview room under the watchful eyes of a policewoman called Joan Ailsmore, one of a handful who had recently joined the force. The barred window framed a view of the police car park. Mrs Coalway did not look up when Thornhill came in. He sat down opposite her at the scarred metal table, and waited. At last she raised her eyes. Her face was bleak and implacable. She blinked.

'It was you who had our Marge's teddy, wasn't it?'

'Yes. She's got it back.'

There was a silence. Then: 'They were like animals.' She glanced at Thornhill. 'Some of them.'

'Tell me,' he said, 'do you know the Bathurst Arms?'

Her eyebrows shot up. 'Course I do. I used to work in the kitchen there. That was when the first Mrs Alvington was alive.'

'Did you know that Cameron Rowse was staying there?'

She hesitated. 'No.'

Thornhill thought she was lying but he didn't press it. 'Tell me about Mr Rowse — what was he like?'

'That's what all this is about, isn't it?'

Thornhill was silent.

'You think one of us topped him,' she went on. 'That's why I'm here.'

'I don't think anything.' Thornhill heard himself place a slight emphasis on the pronoun. 'I'm just trying to find out what happened.'

'He kept going on about how he wanted to help.' Norah Coalway poked her tongue through the gap in her front teeth. 'He talked to us for a while, look, then some of the men came back from work and he talked to them. Then he went off round the camp, taking photographs.' Again the tongue poked through the gap in the teeth. 'You can see what he took on the film. Then Miss Francis turned up. You'd better talk to her.'

'I shall.'

'I don't think she liked him much. He left soon after she came. Just checked he had our names right and walked off. That was one thing that made me think he wasn't on our side, after all. In fact I even wondered if he wasn't a reporter. A Nosy Parker from the government, maybe, or the Army.'

'Is there anything else you can remember about him? Anything else that struck you as odd?'

She stared at him. 'You're asking a lot, aren't you, mister? You lock me up in here, take my kids and my man away, and then you expect me to tell you everything you want to know.'

'The sooner we sort this out, Mrs Coalway, the sooner you'll be with your family again.'

She laughed, scornfully. 'I won't bank on it. Anyway, I can't think of anything else.'

Thornhill pushed back his chair and stood up. 'You've been very helpful. Thank you.'

'You're a funny bugger, aren't you?'

The policewoman sucked in her breath.

Mrs Coalway stared up at him. 'We were making the camp really nice, you know, the part where we lived. Like a little village.'

Thornhill said, 'Were there any strangers around there on Tuesday? Apart from Cameron Rowse.'

'Not as far as I know.' Her face cracked into a smile. 'Not unless you count the man with the fish.'

Chapter Twenty-Four

Miss Gwyn-Thomas, Philip's secretary, poked her long, thin head into the reporters' room. 'Councillor Broadbent is in the front office,' she hissed. There was a drop of clear moisture on the end of her long, wandering nose. 'He wants to see Mr Wemyss-Brown, but he's gone to lunch.' Her eyes carefully avoided Jill. 'So he said he'd see whoever was in charge.'

Miss Gwyn-Thomas had not found it easy to accept Jill's recent appointment as deputy editor of the *Gazette*. It would not have mattered if Jill had been a man. Miss Gwyn-Thomas was in love with her employer and had considered Jill a rival since the day she joined the staff of the *Gazette*.

'What does he want?' Jill asked.

'He didn't say.' Miss Gwyn-Thomas clamped her lips shut, conveying the impression that, even if he had, she might think twice about passing on the information to someone as lowly as the deputy editor.

On her way downstairs, Jill checked her face in the mirror in the ladies' lavatory. In the front office, Bernard Broadbent was standing by the window, holding his hat in his hands and watching the traffic in the High Street. He heard Jill's footsteps and turned as she approached, holding out his hand and running his eyes over her.

'Miss Francis? Pleased to meet you.'

The first thing that struck her was his size. He wasn't tall but he was bulky, with the physique of an aging wrestler. He spoke with a Lydmouth accent. She knew he was related in some way to Edith Thornhill.

'Philip Wemyss-Brown told me all about you,' he went on. 'I hope I haven't come at a bad time?'

'Not at all,' Jill lied. 'How can I help?'

'I suppose I could have phoned, but I happened to be passing. The thing is, Mr Wemyss-Brown came to see me on Tuesday evening – we had a long chat – a sort of interview, really. And I also had a word with him about the Heather Parry case.' Broadbent came a step nearer, and Jill was suddenly aware of his bulk, and of the force of his personality. 'You've heard about that?'

'The girl who vanished – yes.'

'He was going to put something in the paper about her – see if we could jog people's memories.' Broadbent rubbed his lower jaw, which projected from his face like the prow of a ship. 'Then I thought, why not mention it in the interview itself? Actually quote me as making an appeal for information. It could add a bit of colour to the piece. See what I mean?'

Jill did. 'That shouldn't be a problem at all. I'll have a word with Mr Wemyss-Brown when he comes back from lunch. He's hoping to put it in tomorrow's edition, as you probably know.'

Broadbent nodded. 'One other thing. Do you know who you'll be sending along to cover the madrigal concert at the High School?'

'Tomorrow evening? I'm not sure what Mr Wemyss-Brown has decided. He may want to go himself, of course.'

'Give him this, will you?' Broadbent produced a small brown envelope and gave it to her. 'A couple of tickets.'

'I'll see that he gets them.'

'I won't keep you, then. Glad to have met you, Miss Francis.'

Wasting no more time, he left the office, leaving Jill wondering at her own confused reaction to the man. Broadbent was clearly using the missing girl as a means of providing favourable publicity for himself. There was something ruthless, almost animal, about him, like a great, grey bear in relentless pursuit of a pot of honey. All that was quite straightforward. The confusion sprang from the fact that Jill had liked him.

Since the murder, Jane Alvington had lived in a nightmare world where everything was almost the same as in the everyday waking world, but not quite. The differences, some obvious and some half glimpsed and some merely suspected, were full of menace. She had no appetite for food and was sleeping badly. Fear had taken up residence. It squatted inside her like a toad, feeding on her distress. Even her period, which had begun on the Tuesday afternoon just before Rowse's arrival, had mysteriously stopped.

The business carried on. Gloria had insisted, and despite his illness Jane's father had encouraged this. By Thursday morning, the Bathurst Arms had almost returned to normality, at least on the surface. The annexe with the guestroom was still under police control, but the dining room and the bars were open.

'At least it's good for trade,' Harold Alvington said at breakfast time on Thursday. 'It's an ill wind.'

'Then I wish it would blow somewhere else,' Gloria snapped. 'It's not nice having police on the premises.'

Harold stared at her, his face was expressionless. They were in the living room, and he was in his reclining chair near the fire, his eyes half closed. It had never been easy to tell what he was thinking, but since his illness Jane had found it even harder. When you looked at him now, you saw the illness not the man. Gloria stabbed her fork into her fried egg. Yolk spurted out, the egg's blood. Jane watched, and wondered.

'The car should have been serviced last month,' Harold said.

Gloria shrugged. 'Not much point, is there? You haven't driven it since the summer.'

'Maybe you could drive it.'

'Me? You joking?'

'Why not?' His eyes were shut. He was putting all his energy into speaking. 'Plenty of women drive cars, don't they? You could have a few lessons.'

'I'd like to learn,' Jane said.

'Later,' Harold said. 'You're too young. What about it, Gloria?'

'All right. If you want.'

He nodded. 'Have a word with Joe Vance next time he's in.'

Harold drifted into a doze. The two women finished their meal in silence and then began the morning jobs. One advantage about working in a pub was that it left little time for thinking. Jane lost herself in the usual blur of activity: dealing with the cook, the cleaner, the tradesmen and the men from the brewery. A few minutes before opening time there was a ring at the door. Jane went to answer it. Inspector Thornhill was waiting outside, hat in hand.

'May I come in? Just a few more questions.'

Jane held open the door. 'We're a bit rushed, sir.'

'Not to worry – this won't take long.'

She showed him into the living room. She was surprised to find that her father wasn't there. In the last year it had gradually become Harold's domain. The room smelled of medicines, Gloria's cigarettes and stale air. Sometimes Harold spent the night here in the reclining chair, and Gloria and Dr Bayswater had talked of moving down a bed. The heavy curtains and the dark furniture, both inherited from Jane's grandparents, made the room feel as if it were closing in on you.

Jane left Thornhill there and went to fetch Harold and

Gloria. She found them in the lounge bar: Harold sitting by the fireplace watching Gloria laying out ashtrays on the tables.

'Bloody copper,' Gloria muttered. 'Picks his times, doesn't he?'

She and Jane helped Harold along the hall to the living room and settled him in his chair. Thornhill sat down opposite in an armchair, notebook in hand. Gloria lit a cigarette and stood smoking by the window. Jane sat near her father.

'Just a thought,' Thornhill said. 'When Mr Rowse was up in his room, during the afternoon and the evening, did any of you hear anything?'

'What do you mean?' Gloria said, her voice louder than usual. 'Like talking?'

'Anything.'

'He was moving around in the afternoon, just after he got here.' Harold ran his fingers through his thinning hair. 'I was in here trying to have a nap, and the door was open. He must have had his door open too.' As he spoke, his voice faded in volume. 'That's all I remember.'

Thornhill looked at Gloria, who shook her head.

Jane said, 'I heard him typing. It was in the evening.'

'When?'

'I don't know exactly. Between six and half past?'

'I thought he'd gone out before half past five.'

'He did.'

'When he asked about the Bull? You're sure he went out just after that?'

'Oh yes, sir. I saw him go.'

Thornhill tapped the tip of his pencil against his notebook. 'So it looks as if he came back for a while, and then went out again?'

'I suppose so. I—'

'If it *was* him coming back,' Gloria interrupted, moving away from the window and grinding her cigarette into an ashtray. 'Could have been someone else up there. Anyone could have walked in.'

'Could they?'

'It's possible,' Harold said slowly. 'If we didn't see Mr Rowse coming in, he probably came through the back door from the yard.' He paused to gather the strength to continue. 'And if we didn't see him, we wouldn't have seen anyone else, either.'

Thornhill nodded. 'Did he lock his room when he went out?'

'Don't know,' Gloria said. 'Some do, some don't.'

'Didn't leave the key with us if he did,' Jane said. 'What about the typing? Wouldn't that give you an idea?'

'There's no sign that Rowse or anyone else typed anything on Tuesday afternoon or Tuesday evening.'

'But he must have done. Or someone must. I heard the typing.'

'To go back to the door,' Thornhill said. 'The door to the yard. When was it locked on Tuesday evening?'

There was a silence, then Harold stirred. 'We usually lock up when the bars shut. We leave the back door open till then, because the lavvies are across the yard.'

'That's when I locked up on Tuesday,' Gloria said quickly. 'About a quarter to eleven, I reckon.'

Harold frowned. 'Are you sure?'

'I think so.'

'You put the Yale down and the bolts across? Sure?'

'I suppose I must have done.' Gloria shook her golden head as though trying to get rid of a cloud of gnats. 'That's what I always do.'

Jane glanced at Thornhill, who was watching this conversation and sitting very still in his chair.

'It's just that when I came down on Wednesday morning,' Harold went on, 'the Yale was down but the bolts weren't across.'

'Are you sure of that, Mr Alvington?' Thornhill said sharply.

He nodded once, then his chin sunk down on his chest.

Gloria looked up at the clock. 'Oh my God. Is that the time? Inspector, if you've nothing more to ask Jane, maybe she could open up?'

Thornhill had no objection. There were people waiting outside when Jane opened the doors. For a few minutes she covered both bars. Then Gloria joined her.

'Thornhill's gone,' Gloria murmured, eyeing the crowd in the lounge bar. 'Him and his bloody questions.'

Gloria served in the lounge bar, Jane the public; both of them kept an eye on the little snug and on the women who worked in the kitchen and waited at tables in the dining room. There had been a press conference at the police station during the morning, and there was an influx of journalists from outside town. Most of them crowded into the lounge bar, and Jane watched how her stepmother blossomed under their attention. The lines seemed to vanish from her face, the smiles returned, and soon Jane heard the irritating trill of Gloria's laugh.

At half past twelve, Joe Vance arrived. Jane had been waiting and hoping for this. Her eyes had a miraculous ability to pick out his carrot-coloured hair in a crowd, just as her ears could distinguish his low drawl among a babble of raised voices.

Empty glass in hand, Jane stepped back to get a better view of him, ignoring the customer she was supposed to be serving. She wanted to cry. Joe had come to the saloon bar, not the public, even though that must have meant changing his clothes and washing because they didn't allow people in work clothes in the lounge bar. She watched him pushing his way through the crowd towards the bar. From here she also had a good view of her stepmother: the too-short skirt, the too-bright colours, the shiny material stretched tightly to show the curves of the body beneath. Joe looked really smart in a sports jacket and tie, as if he were going out for the evening, as if he worked in an office not a garage.

He leant on the counter. Gloria moved towards him.

'Hello, Gloria. Hello, Jane.'

Jane smiled at him and wished she could think of something witty to say.

Gloria reached for a clean tankard. 'Usual?'

He nodded. 'How's it going?'

Gloria shrugged. 'We're coping. But it'll be a while before we're out of the woods.'

Joe leant closer to her. 'If there's anything I can do, Gloria, you just need to say.'

'There is something.'

Joe licked his lips. 'What?'

'Harold wants the car serviced.'

'No problem.' He looked at her, hungry for more.

'Actually, I'm thinking of learning to drive.' Gloria leaned across the counter, perching like a stork on one leg; a stork in stockings and stiletto shoes. 'Maybe you could spare the time to give me a lesson or two. Sort of show me the ropes.'

There was a movement in the hall that led to the private part of the house. Jane swung round. Her father shuffled towards her, the soles of his slippers whispering along the linoleum. A grey spectre in a stained grey cardigan, he put out a hand to prop himself against the wall.

'Come on, Jane,' he said. 'There's customers waiting to be served.'

'You shouldn't be here, Dad.'

Harold scowled, not at her but at his weakness. Gloria laughed at something Joe said. Jane helped her father back into the living room.

'Going to need more bar staff if this keeps up,' he wheezed as she lowered him into his chair. 'I feel so bloody useless, girl.'

She smiled brightly. 'You just stay there, Dad. See if you

can have a little snooze. If you have a rest now, maybe you can help this evening.'

'I'll do that. Tell Gloria I'll look after the public tonight.'

She knew he did not believe that any more than she did.

Chapter Twenty-Five

'Mrs Nipper!' the children chanted in the playground of the Edge Hill Mixed Infants on Thursday afternoon, clapping as they danced round the one of their number who had been selected to represent this figure of terror. 'Mrs Yipper! Mrs Slapper! Mrs Crapper!'

Mrs Veale heard the singing as she watched PC Peter Porter cycling slowly towards her, but she barely registered it. Almost every playtime, unless it was raining, the pattern was the same. On and on the children sang until the current Mrs Nipper, Yipper, Slapper or Crapper pounced on her chosen victim, while the rest of the circle fled squealing to the safety of the lavatories.

Mrs Veale was far too well informed not to know that the children were singing about her. The children believed her to be a witch on the grounds that she lived on her own and had a sharp tongue in her head. They neither knew nor cared that the body of Bert, her only child, had never been recovered from a Blenheim bomber which crashed into the North Sea in 1943. Her husband had lingered on until the previous winter and then slipped quietly out of her life. Mrs Veale had never quite forgiven him for losing an arm at Gallipoli, but the desertion of the rest of his body had hit her harder than she cared to admit. His last words – spoken not to her but to their dog – had been, 'Thank God it's nearly over.'

The little white dog was the next to go. Its name was Freddy, but the children of Edge Hill affected to believe that dog and mistress were interchangeable, and therefore called it Nipper or Yapper, Slapper or Crapper. Mrs Veale knew that there had been considerable rejoicing among the Mixed Infants when the witch's familiar collapsed with heart failure on the green while chasing the vicar's cocker spaniel, a week to the day after John Veale's funeral. She brought the body home in a wheelbarrow and buried it in the vegetable patch. If she mourned, she told no one.

Now she lived alone in the little cottage at the end of a terrace that faced north across the green at Edge Hill. Hers was the house closest to the church, and she had often complained about the noise of the bells. She kept hens in a run at the bottom of the garden. They were important as sources of food and income. Even if they hadn't been, she would not have taken kindly to the discovery that someone was filching the eggs. There was no doubt about it – she found a bootprint in the muck by the door of the run. If Freddy had been alive, it would never have happened.

The hens were the reason why Porter was here. Edge Hill's resident police officer had recently retired. Once a day, a beat officer came over from Lydmouth on his bicycle, but he was never there when Mrs Veale needed him. Hence her decision to visit police headquarters and demand protection for herself and retribution for the criminal.

When Peter Porter was assigned to the case, Mrs Veale's feelings were mixed. True, he was a genuine detective, in the sense that he was attached to the CID, a circumstance which lent her distinction in her own eyes and in those of her neighbours. But he was also Evie Porter's son: in other words he was a bastard, scum washed up from Templefields to the Edge Hill council estate. Not much distinction there. The boy was widely known to be several pence short of a shilling. On the whole, this was a point in his favour. Mrs Veale, who was secretly a woman who liked a flutter, considered it a sporting certainty that Peter Porter would do as she told him.

'Now, Peter,' she told him when she was ushering him down the long, thin garden to the scene of the crime. 'You want to catch this crook. So do I. And I've got a plan.'

'Well, Mrs Veale, we got procedures for—'

'He knows I'm a widow, look, all on my own, not even a dog for company. He thinks he's on to a good thing, eh? So that's why he'll be back.'

The path took them through a group of fruit trees, sprouting with new life, and through a vegetable patch which was already beginning to show signs of neglect. There was a pigsty here, used for compost since the departure of the last pig in 1939.

'He's chancing his luck,' Mrs Veale went on, skewering Porter with her eyes, a technique she found invaluable when dealing with the weak-minded of any age. 'Look at the way he put his arm through my larder window last night. Bold as brass. Next thing we know, he'll be murdering me in my bed.'

'You do lock up, Mrs Veale?'

She ignored this. They approached the coop at the bottom of the garden. Chickens flocked to greet them, poking their beaks through the wire in the hope of food.

'Stupid buggers,' Mrs Veale said.

Her husband and son had built the coop from chicken wire, corrugated iron and scraps of timber. It leaned against the gable wall of a sturdy little stone barn. There was a row of nesting boxes just inside the wire. The henhouse stood in one corner of the coop, its door open in the daytime.

'Do you lock their door at night?' Porter asked, frowning.

'Of course I do. Wouldn't have any chickens, if I didn't. I'm not *stupid*, Peter Porter.' She skewered him once again. 'Unlike some I could mention.'

She watched him start to blush and then walked to the

door of the barn. The door was made of oak planks and the padlock was the size of Mrs Veale's fist. Beside it was a small window with two vertical bars.

Mrs Veale touched the padlock in what was almost a caress. 'You'd need a crowbar to get that off. And some muscles.'

'Oh, aye?'

'Look through the window.'

Porter took a step forward, tripped over a length of guttering half concealed in the grass and collided with the wall of the barn. He peered through the window. Mrs Veale waited, knowing what he would see: the workbench, with tools ranged neatly above them, just beneath the big skylight on the far side of the roof; and the wireless sets that John used to build – with Bert before the war and by himself, with less enthusiasm, afterwards. Bolted to the bench were several vices, John's largely unsuccessful method of compensating for his missing hand and his missing son. Two elderly deckchairs leaned against the wall between the bench and a rusty hand-lawnmower.

'That's money, look,' Mrs Veale told him. 'Take them down the King's Head in Mincing Lane on Friday night, and you got cash in your hand.'

'Aye. Very nice. Now, about these hens—'

'Look at the window.'

'Eh? No one could get through that with them bars. And it's fixed shut.'

'The glass, boy. Look at the glass.'

He frowned at it. 'Needs a bit of a clean. If you don't mind me saying so.'

'Not all of it does.' She pointed at the spot between the two bars, about five feet from the ground, where there was a roughly circular clearing in the grime that covered the rest of the pane.

'Oh,' Porter said. 'Ah.'

'He's got a torch,' Mrs Veale said. 'Stands to reason, don't it? He needs it to see the eggs. And he stood here, rubbed the glass with his hand, because he wanted to have a look inside. He sees all that stuff.'

'It's all right, Mrs Veale. He couldn't get in there, not without a crowbar, like you said. And any road, he wouldn't want to make a noise. But if you're worried, we—'

'Me? Worried? It's that bugger ought to be worrying. Because we *want* him to go in there, Peter.'

'Why?'

For a moment, she considered him with the dispassionate interest of a potter contemplating a shapeless mass of wet clay. Then she answered his question.

Chapter Twenty-Six

Jill yawned as she turned into Church Street. It had been a long day and a short night. With a pang of nostalgia she longed for nursery pleasures: a boiled egg with toast cut into soldiers on a tray by the fire; a long bath; a cup of cocoa, followed by the refreshing, dreamless sleep one thought one had had as a child but probably hadn't. At the back of her mind was the hope, barely recognised, that Richard might phone or even visit her. Oddly enough, at this moment it barely mattered whether he was present in actuality or not. Part of Jill wanted merely to be left alone, so she could hug her secret to herself, feel its shape and texture, and gloat.

She was inserting her key into the door of Church Cottage when she heard a car door slam behind her. She bent down to stroke Alice, her tail high, overflowing with her own kind of love and the anticipation of food. There were hurried footsteps crossing the road behind her. She turned, already knowing whose face she would see.

'Jill,' Oliver said. 'I need to talk to you.'

Oliver had always taken his needs very seriously, Jill thought, and they were always more important than one's own.

'I suppose you'd better come in.'

'Thanks.' He added perfunctorily, 'It's very good of you.'

Alice miaowed, perhaps sensing the possibility of a deferred mealtime.

Jill led the way into the hall. 'Come in the kitchen. I need to feed Alice.'

Usually she would have gone upstairs to take off her hat and coat and probably change. But she had no intention of prolonging Oliver's visit unnecessarily. She left her coat and hat in the hall and went into the kitchen. Oliver followed her. For a moment he watched in silence as she opened the refrigerator and began to prepare Alice's supper.

'Can I help myself to a drink?' he said abruptly.

'Of course. There's some beer in the larder. Otherwise try the sideboard in the dining room.'

'Would you like one?'

'No, thanks.'

By the time he returned with an inch of whisky in a glass, Alice was already gobbling her food. Oliver added a drop of water from the tap. Jill sat down at the table and waited for him to sit opposite her. This was not a social call, and party manners did not apply. Oliver evidently felt the same. He sat down and pulled out his cigarettes.

'That cat food stinks,' he said. His eyes met Jill's. 'Sorry – didn't mean to be rude. I thought you'd never come home. I've been waiting there for nearly an hour.'

Oliver had the ability to make the simplest statement of fact sound like a complaint. The Humber had been parked outside the almshouses – and Jill wondered, perhaps uncharitably, whether Oliver had chosen that spot so that Jill would not see the car when she turned into Church Street from the High Street. There had always been a devious side to him.

'What have you been doing?' she asked.

'I went for a drive. Up to Hereford and beyond. I don't know what to do with myself, you see – I'm in limbo until you make up your mind.' He sipped his whisky. 'Look, I know I'm asking a great deal of you, and I'm sorry. But I'm sure you can see it from my point of view, too. I've been thinking. There's a very good chance we can keep this under wraps.'

The words tumbled out of him. Jill stopped listening. She went to the sink and poured herself a glass of water and returned to the table.

'And there was a message from the police when I got back to the Bull,' Oliver was saying. 'Thornhill wanted to see me this afternoon, but of course I wasn't there.' He glanced at Jill. 'He seems quite a decent chap. Did I tell you I bumped into him that other time I came to Lydmouth?'

Jill shook her head and took one of Oliver's cigarettes.

Automatically he clicked his lighter and leant across the table. 'It was just after you'd given me my marching orders. To be honest, I'd been drowning my sorrows, and he more or less put me to bed.'

'You didn't tell him —' Jill began.

'Of course not. What do you take me for?'

Jill smiled. 'I don't think you want to hear the answer to that question.'

He flushed. After a pause, he said, 'You've every right to feel bitter. But — will you help me?'

He stared across the table at her. Once, in their early days, Jill had told him that he had speaking eyes. The memory embarrassed her now. She didn't want to hear anything that Oliver's eyes might be trying to say. The smoke from their cigarettes curled up towards the ceiling, meeting each other and intertwining. Alice finished her meal and padded over towards Jill, licking her lips. She remembered seeing a pregnant dog in the Bois de Boulogne when Oliver had taken her to Paris, and remembered Oliver saying that there was something obscene about a pregnant animal; it looked so unnatural.

Jill sighed. 'All right.'

He stretched out his hands towards hers. She pulled away.

'I don't want to do this, Oliver. If I'm doing it for

anyone, it's for your poor bloody wife and your poor bloody children.'

'I say—'

The ringing of the telephone interrupted him. Without a word, Jill got up and left the kitchen. Alice followed and stalked into the cupboard under the stairs.

Oh God. Please don't let the kittens come this evening.

Jill shut the door of the dining room behind her, a barrier between herself and Oliver. Her hand trembled as she picked up the phone.

'Jill, dear, is that you?' Charlotte's voice thundered down the line; she worked on the principle that telephones worked better if you shouted at them. 'I'm sorry to disturb you, but I've got a favour to ask.'

Chapter Twenty-Seven

When Charlotte returned to the drawing room. Philip was where she had left him – hunched in his armchair, staring at the fire. He was doing nothing, not even smoking or drinking. He did not look up as she came in.

'Jill's coming,' Charlotte said brightly. 'Isn't that nice?'

Philip did not react.

'I said I'd run over and fetch her,' Charlotte pressed on. 'I won't be a moment. You'll be all right?'

He looked across the room at her. 'It won't do any good.'

'Neither will sitting there feeling sorry for yourself.'

He turned away, resuming his inspection of the fireplace. Charlotte gazed at him for a moment, her lips pursed, but realised that she was not going to get anywhere with him at present. She went along the hall and into the kitchen, where Susan was preparing supper.

'There may be three of us this evening,' Charlotte said.

Susan looked up from the potatoes she was peeling. 'It's only corned-beef hash. Too late to change that now. I doubt if it'll stretch to three.'

'It's Jill.'

The grim expression vanished from Susan's face. 'Oh, that's all right. I'll just peel a couple more potatoes.'

'I'm not sure whether she will be staying. Just a possibility.'

Susan nodded and went back to her peeling. Charlotte picked up her handbag and left the house. Old servants could be such a trial. Susan was becoming increasingly cantankerous. It was partly due to age, Charlotte suspected, and partly because Susan had realised that she was to all intents and purposes irreplaceable and behaved accordingly. Fortunately she liked Jill, who had stayed at Troy House for several months while she was looking for lodgings in Lydmouth. Susan even called Jill by her Christian name, a privilege she reserved for the Wemyss-Browns and then only in private, a mark of esteem in this topsy-turvy world.

The Rover was still parked outside the house. A moment later, Charlotte was turning into Church Street. A dark-green Humber was coming towards her, right in the middle of the road. Charlotte leant on the horn, and after a long blast the oncoming car pulled over to the kerb to let her by. She smiled with satisfaction; she enjoyed the combative side of motoring.

When the Rover drew up outside Church Cottage, Jill was waiting in the doorway, still in the clothes that she wore for work. She walked round to the passenger side of the car and climbed in. Charlotte let out the clutch and pulled away.

'It's frightfully kind of you, and at such short notice. You will stay for supper, won't you? That's the least we can do for ruining your evening. It's nothing much, I'm afraid, but we can make Philip find a decent bottle of wine. You hadn't anything planned for this evening, had you?'

'No – not really.'

'I wondered if you might be seeing that nice Mr Yateley.'

'The only really important thing was feeding Alice, and I've done that.'

Charlotte noted the change of subject. 'What are you going to do with all those kittens?'

'Heaven knows.' Jill glanced at Charlotte. 'How's Philip?'

'It's very strange, dear. He's really quite shaken. People don't realise, but he's very sensitive. And when you're used to everyone liking you, this sort of thing can have a disproportionate effect.' Her hands tightened on the steering wheel. 'If it were me, I'd react very differently.'

They turned off the main road at the war memorial. In a moment they would be at Troy House.

'I want to help, of course,' Jill said. 'But I'm not sure there's a lot I can do.'

'The very fact you're there will help.' Charlotte changed gear with unnecessary violence, and the car jerked forward. Before meeting Charlotte, Philip had been in love with Jill; the old jealousy still had power to hurt, as did the unsettling possibility that Philip might still be a little in love with her. 'He respects your judgement.'

They drew up outside the house. Though it was growing dark, Philip had not drawn the curtains. The big bay window was like a proscenium framing a stage set before the actors come on.

In silence, the two women went inside. Philip emerged from the little room beside the dining room, which he used as a study. He had a small, red notebook in his hand. He looked perfectly normal. Charlotte felt a rush of irrational exasperation. Philip had no right to look perfectly normal.

'Hello, Jill. Good of you to come.'

'Anything to avoid cooking. So it's a council of war?'

'Let's have a drink first,' Philip said, opening the door of the drawing room. 'Sherry? Gin?'

It was growing chilly. Jill warmed her hands by the fire. Philip bustled over to the drinks trolley. Charlotte felt her exasperation increasing.

'You might have drawn the curtains, Philip.' She tugged them viciously across the bay window. 'You know how nosy people are. And what have you been doing? Your jacket is simply covered with dust and cobwebs.'

'I wanted to jog my memory.' He poured sherry for the women. 'When I was in Spain, I kept a sort of diary.'

Charlotte nodded, realising that she had misjudged her husband. 'That might be useful if it comes to court.'

'I don't want that.'

She glared at him. 'We shall have to see. We shan't let them get away with libel.'

Charlotte dropped into a chair on the other side of the fireplace from Jill. Philip brought them their glasses.

'What exactly are they going to do?' Jill asked.

'We don't know. Not exactly.' Charlotte watched her husband pouring himself a large gin. 'It's just that a friend of a friend works on the *Empire Lion*, and they'd heard that there's going to be a big feature on the Rowse case in this week's edition.'

'As far as they're concerned, it's like manna from heaven,' Philip said. 'Murder of our gallant correspondent while he was investigating unpatriotic scroungers at Farnock Camp. Was he killed to prevent him from revealing the truth? Et cetera.'

'Surely the truth had already been revealed?' Jill objected. 'That article in the *People*, remember?'

'That won't stop them.' Philip sat down on the sofa. 'You know what the *Empire Lion* is like. They'll drop dark hints about nests of Communist spies and saboteurs. Fifth columnists all over the—'

'The point is,' Charlotte interrupted, 'they've decided to make Philip into the villain of the piece.'

'The *Empire Lion* likes to have a villain,' Philip said. 'And in this case, it's going to be me. The Communist editor of the local paper. The enemy in our midst who abuses his position to support traitors. This man is known to have quarrelled with our gallant correspondent hours before he was murdered.'

Charlotte spilled a drop of sherry on her skirt. 'Darling, really—'

'Do you know if they've found out about the quarrel?' Jill asked.

'They can hardly have failed to. The odds are the story's all over town.'

'But you're not a Communist,' Jill said. 'Were you ever?'

Philip shook his head. 'But they won't let a little thing like that stop them.'

Charlotte's exasperation boiled over into anger. 'Then we'll sue them for every penny they're worth.'

'They won't say it outright,' Philip said. 'They've got a nice line in innuendo.'

Jill said, 'Do they know about Spain?'

'I've never made any secret of that.'

'Perhaps you should have done,' Charlotte said, and immediately wished that she had not.

Philip glanced at her, and she tried to ignore the anger in his face. Then he turned back to Jill: 'I was only there for ten days. And most of that time I was down with dysentery. They shipped me home before I got anywhere near the fighting. Comical, really. I was probably more of a hindrance than a help. But I don't regret it.'

Charlotte snorted. 'Even now?'

'Things were very different. The Fascists were the enemy. As far as I was concerned, anyway. We weren't to know that Stalin himself was a Fascist in all but name. We weren't to—'

'Philip, I don't think a sermon on the rise of the police state in the twentieth century is going to help.' Charlotte's irritation suddenly collapsed. 'Oh dear – I'm sorry. It's just that I feel that we've got to be practical.'

Philip levered himself away from the sofa and padded over to her. He stroked her arm. 'It's OK, old girl. Now – who's ready for a refill?'

Before anyone could answer the doorbell rang. Philip went to answer it. Charlotte's eyes met Jill's.

'Damn,' Charlotte whispered across the hearthrug. 'I really don't want to talk to anyone.'

There were male voices in the hall and a moment later Philip ushered in Richard Thornhill.

'*An Inspector Calls*,' Philip announced, his mood having swung from despair to moral indignation to roguish fun in the space of thirty minutes. 'I suppose we can't offer you a drink?'

Thornhill greeted the two women and declined the drink. Charlotte noticed that he avoided looking at Jill.

'I'm sorry to bother you so late,' he said. 'Just one or two questions.'

Jill made as if to stand up. 'Perhaps I should leave.'

'Not for our sake,' Charlotte said. 'I'm sure you don't mind taking us as you find us, Mr Thornhill. We have no secrets from Miss Francis.'

'It's entirely up to you.' After a pause, Thornhill looked from Charlotte to Philip. 'I believe you both have Richelieu cigarette lighters. May I see them?'

'Of course you may,' Charlotte said. 'But may one ask why?'

'It's a question of elimination, Mrs Wemyss-Brown.'

Charlotte waited for him to expand, but he did not go on. She stood up. 'Mine is in my handbag. I'll go and get it.'

'In fact, I've not seen mine for a day or two,' Philip said.

'When did you last have it, sir?'

'Let me see – it would have been Tuesday evening. I remember having it in the Bull. But I couldn't find it later on that evening when I was at Mr Broadbent's.'

'It might have slipped into the lining of your jacket,' Charlotte said, a chilly suspicion beginning to sprout in her mind. 'That happened with your propelling pencil once. Do you remember?'

'I'll see if it's there,' Philip said. 'Won't be a moment.'

Philip and Charlotte left the room. Charlotte wanted to say to him: '*Be careful, be careful.*' He smiled at her and went upstairs. Charlotte crossed the hall to the breakfast room, where she had left her handbag on the bureau. Returning to the drawing room with the lighter in her hand, her footsteps noiseless on the carpet, she heard the sound of Thornhill's voice.

'I called at Church Cottage on my way, but you weren't there.'

Jill said something indistinguishable in return. Charlotte paused at the open door, shielded from the two people inside the room.

'I had to see you anyway,' Thornhill went on. 'Officially, I mean.'

Charlotte frowned. What on earth could the man mean?

'Jill, what's all this about the man with the fish?'

'Who?'

'I was talking to Norah Coalway about Rowse's visit to Farnock Camp. She said that when you were there, he asked who the man with the fish was.'

Charlotte glanced at the pewter vase on the dark oak chest which stood in the hall beside her. The wood gleamed from decades of Susan's polishing but the daffodils in the vase looked as though they had been dragged through a haystack. She began to rearrange them. She wasn't eavesdropping. Anyway, if the conversation in the drawing room were private, they would not be talking so near to a half-open door.

'That's right,' Jill was saying. 'I'd forgotten. Rowse was checking the names of the squatters. He said he'd met the man near the other gate, the one near the Forest. Small and dark: because Norah said in that case it couldn't be her Sid because he's got fair hair.'

'So who's the small, dark man with the fish? Did he say?'

'No – I'm afraid I interrupted. I didn't believe the *Picture Post* had commissioned Rowse, you see, and I didn't believe he was on the squatters' side, either. So I started asking him awkward questions. He couldn't wait to get away, which rather confirmed what I thought.'

'The man with the fish? A fisherman?'

Thornhill's voice trailed way. There was a silence. Charlotte was about to leave the daffodils to their own devices when Jill began to speak again, but in quite a different voice.

'Richard – you mustn't. Not here.'

Charlotte hesitated, her hand on her bosom, holding her breath. She heard Jill sigh, and then a barely audible noise, a sort of squelching click, that might almost have been – surely not? – the sound of a kiss.

Howard stood in the doorway of the woodshed, leaning against the jamb. That bloody tune was still going round his head.

Mrs Nipper! Mrs Yipper! Mrs Slapper! Mrs Crapper!

It's time, he thought, to make it quite clear to Phyllis where she stood, time to show her who's in charge. There was no danger. It was almost dark now. At present, Mrs Portleigh went to bed at seven o'clock; Phyllis had told him. There was no reason why he should not have the run of the ground floor. After a couple of nights lying on sacks in the woodshed, the idea of sleeping on a sofa in a warm room seemed the next best thing to heaven. Besides, he wanted to have a look around. Now he was feeling better, there was no point in letting the grass grow under his feet.

The yard was a tarmac square with two dustbins near the gate. The back door was painted black. Swaying slightly, Howard crossed the yard, turned the handle and pushed the door inwards. He found himself in a scullery with a stone sink, a twin-tub washing machine and a mangle. The light was on. A further door was ajar, leading, he presumed, to the kitchen itself. He opened it.

Sitting at the table was an elderly woman in a pale blue, quilted dressing gown with her hair in curlers. For a long moment they looked at each other. His skin tingled. Her mouth opened but she said nothing. He almost burst out laughing — she looked so like a fish.

Instead he smiled, and took a step towards her.

Chapter Twenty-Eight

The maternal instincts of Mrs Edie Porter did much to shape the course of events in Edge Hill during the early hours of Friday morning. High up on the list of duties she imposed on herself was the necessity of feeding her son Peter until he could eat no more. On Thursday evening, this had seemed even more imperative than usual – after all, he was going to stay awake all night in a freezing cold barn to ambush a dangerous criminal. She gave him a substantial tea. A few hours later she followed this with an even more substantial supper.

'Whatever you do,' Mrs Porter said to her son as he was putting on his overcoat, 'don't catch cold. Do you think a hot-water bottle would help?'

'No, Mam. Don't *fuss*.'

'You'd think Mr Thornhill would have told someone to come with you.'

'He doesn't know. Not yet.'

Mrs Porter eyed her son and wisely said nothing. But she clung to him for a moment when he kissed her goodbye. At last he slipped into the night with a knapsack containing a blanket, a packet of sandwiches and a flask of cocoa.

The church clock was striking midnight as Porter opened the gate of Mrs Veale's cottage. The windows were dark. He walked slowly down the path, his torch sending a pallid beam swooping before him. The yellow eyes of a cat blazed with reflected light from the shelter of an overgrown buddleia.

When he reached the bottom of the garden, he inspected the hen coop by the light of the torch. Several eggs glowed palely in the nesting boxes. The hens were silent. Breathing heavily through his mouth, Porter unlocked the padlock on the barn door. Mrs Veale had given him detailed instructions on this point: leave the lock dangling from the hasp, and the door a few inches ajar.

He flashed the torch round the barn. Nothing had changed since the afternoon. He opened one of the deckchairs and positioned it behind the door. Finally he sat down – gingerly, in case the fabric was rotten, draped the blanket over himself and switched off the torch.

Then he waited. And waited.

The night was full of noises – the rustle of leaves and the movements of small animals. A lorry rumbled north on the main road. A little later there was the distant drone of an aeroplane. The sound of his own breathing seemed to grow louder and louder. When Porter shifted his weight, the deckchair emitted a deafening creak. The cold crept slowly over him, inexorable as an incoming tide.

Time rolled onwards. The church clock failed to strike one. Perhaps it was faulty. Worst of all was the fear that he might not succeed in arresting the thief. Porter was not frightened of violence – he was a big man, and in a fight he usually found his weight and his strength were enough to immobilise an opponent. But his arrests had a habit of going wrong for other reasons, usually because criminals tended to react in ways he had not predicted.

When he could bear the waiting no longer, Porter switched on his torch and examined the dial of his watch. It was thirteen minutes after midnight. He reminded himself sternly that he was a detective, that Mr Thornhill had trusted him with this job. He switched off the torch and yawned. Mr Thornhill was the only senior officer who had ever trusted him with anything. It was a matter of pride to Porter that he had been selected from all the officers in Lydmouth to be Thornhill's driver, on the basis of his skill and local knowledge. And now Thornhill had given him a chance to prove his competence in another area.

Porter drifted into a reverie in which he coolly stepped in front of an armed bank robber and received a bullet that would otherwise have mown down Inspector Thornhill. He – Porter – was mortally wounded, but lingered long enough to hear Mr Thornhill express his gratitude and sorrow in a few, well-chosen words.

'Don't die, Porter. We can't manage without you.'

Even this fantasy could not sustain Porter indefinitely. After another age had passed, he switched on the torch once more. It was now twenty-two minutes after midnight. He opened the knapsack and found the sandwiches and the Thermos. A snack would help to keep him awake.

He spun out the meal for as long as he could, and then sipped a cup of cocoa. When that was finished he felt much warmer and much more optimistic. Another reverie slipped into his mind, and another visit from Mr Thornhill.

'Brilliant work, Porter. So he's asking for fifteen other offences to be taken into consideration as well? Superintendent Williamson will be delighted.'

The last thing Porter remembered was the church clock striking one. The last thing, that is, until he woke with a start to hear the scrape of the door closing and the click of the padlock snapping shut.

Fortunately Mrs Portleigh had not been a heavy woman.

'Take her legs,' Howard told Phyllis.

He pushed aside the blanket and hooked his hands under the old woman's armpits. Several hours earlier, they had moved Mrs Portleigh from the kitchen floor to the sofa in the drawing room. The eyes were shut, thanks to Phyllis, but the mouth had dropped open. Would he dream about this one, as he did about the other?

'Come on. Take the legs.'

Phyllis still didn't move. 'What are you going to do?'

'We can't just leave her here.'

'She should go in her bed.'

'I've explained all that.' Howard made himself sound patient. 'I know it seems wrong, but it's too warm in the house. The cellar's the best place. It's only for twenty-four hours.'

It was cold down there, a penetrating chilliness that seeped into the bones. He suspected the cellar might have belonged to an older house on the site — the floor was covered in cracked flagstones, and the walls were rough masonry, damp to the touch.

He looked down at the body. Step by step, he thought, that was the way; and once more he felt the excitement of creation. He felt much better than he had for days — fully alive. This new crisis seemed to have cleared his mind. But his body was still weak from the fever and from lack of food.

Phyllis rubbed her eyes, which were red with weeping. 'I still think I should ring the doctor.'

'What's the point? It won't bring her back to life. But if you do that maybe the police will come. And you'd have to phone the daughter in Chepstow, too. She'll come over right away. Tomorrow morning there'll be the son from Birmingham. People aren't stupid. They'll want to keep an eye on things. Make sure the servants don't pinch the jewellery.'

'I — I could hide you.'

Howard shook his head. 'Wouldn't work. I'm not well enough to go anywhere. And they'd want to poke around their inheritance. Once they find me, the whole business gets out. Your false name. Your debts. *Me*.'

'But if someone finds out . . . ?'

'I've explained all that. If she's kept cold, she won't . . . It won't look as if she's been dead for as long as she has.'

'But won't they be able to tell?'

'Tell what?' Howard heard the hint of exasperation in his voice and forced himself to smile reassuringly at her. He let go of the body and stood up. 'No one's going to be looking for problems. Why should they? The old lady had a history of heart failure. She had another heart attack, and this one killed her. *And that's exactly what happened.* If we keep her cold for twenty-four hours, you can find her in bed and ring the doctor. What's today?'

She blinked, disconcerted. 'Thursday. Well, Friday, I suppose.'

'OK. So it's only till Saturday morning. And that'll give me time to get a bit stronger and sort out what I'm going to do next.' He stared at her. 'And then I'll be out of your hair. End of problem, eh?' He nodded at Mrs Portleigh. 'It's not going to make much odds to *her*, is it?'

Phyllis glanced at the clock on the mantel: almost two o'clock. Like a chess-player, he watched her, calculating her next move before she did. If she didn't do what he wanted, he thought, then disgrace loomed for her. If she did, then she had him on the premises. Better the devil you know. How fortunate that she did not know the full story: about the bouncing cheques in London and the unpleasant errand which made it so important for him to return to Lydmouth.

'Come on, Phylly.'

She was staring at her employer's face, which was rubbery and pale, with a faint blue tinge; the pallor of death had the effect of accentuating the old lady's grey, wiry moustache. For an instant he was on the verge of making a joke about needing a shave. The silence went on too long and he knew he had to break it, to stop Phyllis thinking.

'Best to get it over with. Then we can get some sleep. Things will seem better in the morning. You wait and see.'

She dragged her eyes away from Mrs Portleigh. 'But what about Mrs Forbes?'

'Who?'

'The cleaner. She'll be here in the morning.'

'What's she like?'

'Nosy.'

'Does she need to go in the cellar?'

'Not usually. Anyway, there's a key. But she changes Mrs Portleigh's bed on Fridays.'

He smiled. 'Not this Friday.'

'But what shall I say?' Phyllis wailed.

'Mrs Portleigh's not feeling well and doesn't want to be disturbed. And that's good, isn't it, because it prepares the way for what happens next. For the heart attack.'

He watched relief spreading over her face. It was one of the things he had always liked about Phyllis: that he could read her like a book. Then her expression changed.

'But what will you do? She sometimes goes into the woodshed. She goes everywhere. You'll have to hide in the cellar while she's here, or in the spinney.'

'No. I've got a better idea.' Howard bent down and once again hooked his hands under Mrs Portleigh's armpits. 'Come on. Let's get the old lady into the cellar. We need our beauty sleep. It's probably best if you hold her round the knees.'

For a moment emotions chased across Phyllis's face. Then she gave a quiet little moan and at last did as he wanted.

Chapter Twenty-Nine

The Chief Constable did not normally call at the Bull Hotel before breakfast, but Members of Parliament are not normal people. To his chagrin, Yateley refused to see him. Hendry phoned Thornhill at home from the manager's office and explained what had happened.

'He wants *you* for some reason,' Hendry said, a peevish note in his high voice. 'Any idea why?'

'I need to see him in connection with the Rowse case, sir. I tried to make an appointment yesterday.'

'Oh yes. Perhaps that explains it. He gave Rowse a lift into town, didn't he? Let's hope he didn't murder him – then the fat really would be in the fire ...' Hendry allowed a snicker of laughter to escape him. 'But – but I gather Yateley said he *knew* you.'

'I've met him before, sir.'

'Eh? When?'

'He was in Lydmouth just after I moved here. We talked a little.'

Hendry grunted, a sound that emerged as a squeak. 'Well, get over there right away. And be discreet, for God's sake. We've got enough problems without having this splashed all over the papers.'

Thornhill decided that 'right away' was an elastic term which could be stretched to allow him to finish his breakfast. He went back to the kitchen and told Edith what had happened. They had quarrelled the previous evening, ostensibly about money and the children, and up to now their conversation this morning had consisted of monosyllables. The news fascinated her, as he had known it would. This was the one part of his job that Edith loved: gathering scraps of information which were not generally known; and if news concerned well-known people, so much the better.

'But *why?*' she said. 'You'd think he was the last person. It just doesn't make sense.'

'I don't know.' He pushed his cup across the table and watched as she poured him another cup of tea. 'Maybe he's going to tell me.'

David rushed into the kitchen and seized his satchel. 'Where's my cap?'

'Try the hall cupboard,' Edith suggested. She waited until her son had gone. 'And why does Hendry want you to deal with it? Haven't you enough on your plate?'

'Yateley asked for me by name.' Thornhill tried not to think about Jill Francis, and about Yateley's reason for coming here. 'You remember I met him when he was in Lydmouth?'

'It's quite a compliment.'

'Hendry didn't like it.'

Edith shrugged. 'But it's not going to do you any harm, is it?'

Her face had acquired a dreamy look. He guessed that she was thinking of possible promotions, of a life for them both in which Members of Parliament were frequent visitors.

'This is all hush-hush, by the way,' he said gently. 'It really mustn't get out.'

She nodded. 'Of course.'

He knew he could trust her. Edith instinctively under-stood the rules of this sort of game. In many ways she was the perfect wife for an ambitious policeman.

The problem was that he didn't have the right sort of ambitions.

'You haven't forgotten I'm going out this evening?' she said. 'The madrigal concert?'

'No.' He sipped his tea. 'I hope I can get back in time.'

'I've nothing to wear. Nothing suitable. I might have to buy myself something.'

He nodded, and left all the words unspoken: *Are you sure you need to buy something? Surely you've got a wardrobe full of clothes? Money's rather tight at present* ... Now that Edith had a little money of her own, none of the formulae were appropriate.

After breakfast, Thornhill drove to the Bull Hotel and parked the little Austin between Yateley's gleaming Humber and Dr Bayswater's grubby Wolseley. He met the doctor himself on the stairs. Bayswater beckoned him into the little smoking room opposite reception. At this time of day the room was empty.

'Damn fool thing to do.' Bayswater ran long, elegant fingers through the greasy tangle of his hair. 'Wasting everyone's time like this. Meanwhile I've got patients waiting who really need me.'

'So it wasn't too serious?'

'Serious? A child could have done better. He had no more intention of killing himself than I have. Tell you one thing, he's not getting my services on the NHS. I'm going to send him a whacking great bill.'

'So what exactly happened?'

'Maid brought him his early-morning tea at about seven-thirty. Room was empty. But she could hear water running in one of the bathrooms. Then she saw water coming under the door, so she got the manager. Frinton and Quale broke the door down, and there he was. Still conscious. Silly ass.'

'So it wasn't a genuine suicide attempt? More of a – what do you call it? – a cry for help?'

'Cry for attention, more likely.' Bayswater took out a

cigarette and tapped it on the packet. 'Politicians — bunch of spoilt kids if you ask me. If you want to kill yourself, I told him, you'll have to do better than a few shallow cuts with a blunt penknife. Nowhere near the arteries, of course — he's no fool. Then he left the water running and just lay back and waited for someone to come and rescue him.'

Thornhill passed the doctor an ashtray. 'Did he say what was bothering him?'

'No. And I didn't ask. Bloody irresponsible — think of the effect on this place. Can't you have him prosecuted for wasting police time, or something? No, don't answer. No one's going to prosecute a man like Yateley, are they?'

When Bayswater had left in a cloud of exasperation, Thornhill went upstairs to the manager's office. Frinton was clearly apprehensive about the effect of the attempted suicide on his hotel and almost as angry about it as Bayswater was, though he hid it better.

'Any idea why he did it?' Thornhill asked.

'None at all.' Frinton's eyes were brown and cloudy. 'Quale tells me he spent a lot of time on the telephone last night. He used the booth in the hall. Apparently one of the other guests complained because he was taking so long.'

The manager had nothing else to add to Bayswater's account. He took Thornhill to Yateley's room, performed a brusque introduction and left without asking how the patient was. Yateley was sitting up in bed with a breakfast tray on the table beside him. He was smoking and reading *The Times*. White bandages peeped like shirtcuffs from his pyjama jacket. His briefcase was on the bed.

'How are you?' Thornhill said.

'Better than I deserve. Why don't you bring that chair over from the window? I'm sorry to be such a nuisance.'

Thornhill brought the chair and sat down. He refused a cup of tea and a cigarette.

'Listen,' Yateley said. 'You did me a favour once before, and I want you to do me a favour once again.'

Thornhill said nothing.

'I've got myself in quite a mess, you see. The final straw was last night: I rang my wife, and she told me she wanted to divorce me. Quite out of the blue.' He spread out his hands, exposing the bandages and wincing, perhaps a little theatrically. 'That's what tipped me over. But they found me in time, thank God. And it's not too late to try to sort this out.' He smiled wistfully, and his charm slithered towards Thornhill like an invisible snake. 'If you help me, perhaps I can.' He paused, cocking his eyebrows.

'I'm listening, sir.'

'I'm not asking you to do anything you shouldn't. I need to talk to a police officer, you see, and I'd rather it was you than someone I don't know.'

'Does this relate to the Rowse case?'

Yateley nodded. 'When I talked to your sergeant on Wednesday, I'm afraid I wasn't entirely frank.'

Thornhill waited.

'What I told him was quite true, so far as it went. I did give Rowse a lift into Lydmouth on Tuesday, just as I said. And I'd never met him before, either. I didn't tell Rowse who I was, but somehow he must have guessed. Just my luck to give a lift to a journalist.' Another smile, this one inviting sympathy. 'The upshot was, he traced me to here. And then he followed me when I went out that evening.' He hesitated, his fingers plucking the coverlet on the bed. 'Look, Thornhill – can I tell you something in confidence?'

'I can't guarantee anything, sir. For obvious reasons.'

'Of course not. I do understand. But – well, a lady's reputation is at stake.'

Thornhill was filled with a powerful urge to throw the teapot at Yateley.

'I'm a married man, but a year or two back I had an affair.

I make no excuses for what I did. My wife was in Yorkshire, you see, and I was spending most of my life in London ... Damn it, I fell in love. I was a fool, but there it is. I offered to marry the lady, of course, but she said no: she felt my first duty must be to Virginia – that's my wife – and to the children. I suppose she was right. I think you know the lady in question – she's a journalist, and she works for the *Lydmouth Gazette*: Miss Francis.'

'Yes, sir.'

'So you see why this is such a delicate business?'

Thornhill nodded, and struggled to conceal his disgust. But was he himself any better? Yesterday evening, he had kissed Jill at Troy House, a fact he remembered with a mixture of surprise, breathless excitement and incredulous shame. His disgust had more to do with jealousy than moral superiority.

'Do you think Rowse got hold of this – this friendship?'

Yateley pulled a face. 'Not exactly. He wasn't sure why I was down here – whether I had – ah – personal reasons for seeing Miss Francis, or whether it was something to do with that business at Farnock Camp. So he was really rather clever: he rang my wife. He gave a false name but there's no doubt about it. She described his voice. Rowse had a London accent, and as you've probably heard, he had a rather distinctive lisp. She was already in a bit of a state.'

'Why? Because you'd come to see Miss Francis?'

'No – she knew nothing about that. Not then. Anyway, Virginia thought I was in London until Rowse telephoned her. The point is, she was already in a state. Then Rowse said I wasn't in London, and asked if I was in trouble ... Not to put too fine a point on it, she lost her head and blurted out what was worrying her. And me.' Yateley licked his lips and reached for his cigarette case. 'Which also happened to be the reason why I needed to come down here to see Miss Francis.'

'Is all this relevant, Mr Yateley?' Thornhill felt his self-control slipping. 'I'm a police officer, not a psychologist.'

For an instant, Yateley's eyes widened. 'I'm so sorry, Inspector. I don't mean to bore you. But this does have a point.' His lips twisted. 'You might even say it concerns national security. In fact some people *do* say it concerns that. Which is the real problem.'

Chapter Thirty

'Sergeant?' Superintendent Williamson was on the threshold of the CID office. 'In my room, if you please.'

Kirby followed the Superintendent down the corridor and into his room. Williamson sank into the chair behind the desk with an audible sigh of relief; he did not ask Kirby to sit down.

'Where's Mr Thornhill?' he said.

'Still at the Bull, sir.'

Williamson pulled out a pipe and reamed it with sharp, vicious jabs from a blackened penknife. Kirby didn't know why Thornhill was at the Bull, but he knew the Chief Constable had sent him there, bypassing Williamson to do so. Now he also knew that Williamson's nose was out of joint.

'We have just – been made – to look – ridiculous.' The knife blade stabbed deeper into the pipe with each burst of speech. 'If the *Gazette* – gets hold of this – they'll have – a field day.' He blew through the pipe, sending a plume into the air above his desk; the plume disintegrated and fluttered like volcanic ash on to Williamson's blotter, which was densely populated with doodles of cats. 'When I say *we*, Kirby, I mean this force in general and the CID in particular. An officer nominally under my command has made a bloody fool of himself. And of us.'

As he was talking, Williamson's face had flushed a dusky red, tinged with grey. Kirby felt a stirring of alarm. Maybe the old man was on the verge of a heart attack. How bloody awkward that would be, especially if he, Kirby, had to deal with it.

'It couldn't have happened at a worse time,' Williamson went on, patting his pockets violently, searching for his tobacco pouch. 'We've got the eyes of the country on us, thanks to Rowse and Farnock Camp.' He paused and glared at Kirby, as though holding him personally responsible. 'Well? What do you say to that?'

'But what's happened, sir?'

'Young Porter's happened, that's what. I've just had Inspector Jackson on the blower. It seems that Porter – on *temporary* secondment to the CID – and working with *you* and Mr Thornhill – has been investigating the theft of some eggs. *Eggs*, Kirby. And on his own initiative, if that's the word I want, he set an ambush for the thief last night and lay in wait for him. Unfortunately, Porter dozed off. So the thief locked him in the bloody henhouse, pinched some eggs and a few tools for good measure, and made off into the night.'

Kirby stared at the head of a snarling cat on Williamson's blotter. Laughter welled up inside him.

'When Porter deigns to put in an appearance, I want to seen him right away. Off you go.'

'Yes, sir.' Kirby turned and opened the door, allowing himself the relief of a smile.

'Sergeant – one moment.'

'Sir?'

'Mr Thornhill tells me you're co-ordinating the search for Heather Parry. What have you got?'

'Not a lot, I'm afraid, sir. We're still waiting to hear from Birmingham, but we've drawn a blank elsewhere. I heard from the Yard this morning.'

'That's the problems with these girls.' Williamson drummed his fingers on the blotter. 'Could be anywhere. Might have changed her name. Could be married. Could have emigrated. Could be living with some man. But she must have gone somewhere.'

'Not necessarily, sir. She might still be here.'

'I hope you're wrong, Kirby. For everyone's sake.' Williamson flapped a hand like a jellyfish. 'Go away. Oh, and when Mr Thornhill comes in, I want to see him, too.'

The news of Porter's nocturnal escapade had already reached the CID office: Porter himself, red-faced and on the verge of tears, was explaining what had happened to an audience that wanted to mock rather than listen.

Kirby perched on the corner of his desk while Porter stumbled through his story. It wouldn't hurt Williamson to wait five minutes before he flayed Porter alive. It might even improve the superintendent's temper. There was something comic, Kirby considered, in the spectacle of so large a man so close to tears.

'He even took my Thermos, Sarge,' Porter wailed, having fixed on Kirby in Thornhill's absence as the person in authority least likely to be unkind to him. 'Finished off my cocoa.' He swallowed. 'And then – and then he *peed* in it.'

A wave of laughter filled the room. Porter stood with his head bowed. It occurred to Kirby that perhaps this wasn't so funny after all. How would Thornhill look at it? Somewhere out there was a joker who thought he could get away with taking the piss – all right, an unfortunate phrase – out of a police officer. It was the sort of story that would spread through the town by midday. It didn't matter whether the *Gazette* carried it or not: the tale of Porter's Thermos would circulate invisibly under its own power.

Kirby raised his voice to carry over the sniggers. 'Where's the flask?'

'In my locker. I—'

'Have you washed it yet?'

'No, Sarge. Shall I do it now?'

Kirby shook his head. 'Take it downstairs and see if they can get any useable prints off it.'

The laughter redoubled. Porter edged towards the door.

'And after that,' Kirby went on, 'Superintendent Williamson wants to see you in his office.'

Chapter Thirty-One

'By the way, Joe's coming this afternoon,' said Gloria Alvington as she plumped up a cushion and placed it behind her husband's head.

He looked up. 'Good.'

She had been particularly nice to Harold during breakfast. Afterwards, she fussed over him – taking him to the lavatory, settling him in the chair, finding him the newspaper he lacked the energy to read. Nursing was not one of her talents – she tended to treat Harold as if illness had made him both deaf and stupid – but on this occasion she could not be faulted for effort. Meanwhile Jane spun out the dusting of the living room in order to keep an eye on her stepmother.

'I told him you wanted the car serviced,' Gloria went on. 'And I mentioned your idea about driving lessons and he said he'd take me out for a run this afternoon. Isn't that kind?'

Harold glanced up at her, his face suddenly alert. Then his forehead corrugated with worry. 'You haven't got a driving licence. And I'll have to look into the insurance. Pass me the folder in the—'

'It's all right, dear. He won't take me on the open road, not this time.' Gloria patted her husband's head as though he were a dog which might bite. 'Don't worry. He taught his mother to drive last year – he's very experienced. Mrs Vance drove to Gloucester the other day, all by herself.'

Unable to bear any more, Jane threw the duster in the wastepaper basket and left the room. She went upstairs to her bedroom and flung herself on the bed. In the distance she heard the familiar sounds of the Bathurst Arms. Everyone except herself and her father would be working. She knew she should feel guilty. Instead she felt anger pulsing like a pain through her. She would have liked to open the window and howl as loud as her lungs could manage.

'What you doing?'

Jane looked up. Gloria was standing in the doorway.

'There's work to do, my girl. I wouldn't like your father to see you like this.'

'I don't feel well.'

'I know what's wrong with you.' Gloria smiled, and it was not a nice smile. 'But don't worry, you'll get over it.'

Jane sat up on the bed. She struggled to look dignified. She was uncomfortably aware of the difference between herself and her stepmother — how could she blame Joe? She didn't want to blame him: she wanted to blame Gloria. The worst thing about all this was she couldn't attack Gloria without admitting her own failure.

Joe would rather have you than me.

'What you mean — I'll get over it?'

'I think you know exactly what I mean, young lady, and it don't do you no credit.'

Jane tossed her head in a fair imitation of the stepmother. 'You're wrong. There is something worrying me — and maybe it's something to do with you. But it's not what you think.'

'Really?'

'It's not fair what you're doing to Dad.'

'You want to keep your nose out of other people's business, young lady.'

'My dad is my business.'

'I hope you're not trying to say there's something between me and Joe Vance. Because if you are——'

'Joe? What's he got to do with it?'

'More or less everything as far as you're concerned. I've seen you mooning after him. Now – enough of that: there's work to be done. You can get off your backside and come downstairs. Otherwise, I'm going to have to tell your dad. If you really cared about him, you wouldn't be worrying him at a time like this.'

Jane stood up and faced Gloria. Her stepmother towered over her, largely because of her heels.

'And if you want to get a man like Joe to like you, you've got to do something with yourself,' Gloria said. 'No man wants a suet dumpling.'

Suet dumpling, suet dumpling, suet dumpling.

'I'm going out now,' Jane said in a low voice.

'You can't just walk out in the middle of the morning.'

'Who's going to stop me?'

Jane pushed past Gloria and ran down the stairs. She went out of the back door. It was cold, but she did not bother to find her hat and coat. She walked blindly up Lyd Street, her eyes fixed ahead, ignoring everyone she met. The words filled her like an undigested meal, heavy and painful: *No man wants a suet dumpling.* Tears ran down her cheeks and blurred her vision.

When she reached the High Street, she turned left. Somewhere inside her was the idea that, if she walked far enough, she could walk away from herself: away from the suet dumpling. She saw Inspector Thornhill coming out of the Bull Hotel, his lean face distorted like everything else by her tears. If the suet dumpling couldn't have Joe Vance, then nor could Gloria.

She ran across the road, ignoring the traffic. Brakes squealed. Someone swore at her.

'Mr Thornhill?'

'Hello, Jane.'

'Can I have a word, sir?'

He was already moving away. 'I'm afraid I'm in a bit of a rush.'

'I'll walk with you.' She clutched his sleeve. 'I've got something to tell you.'

He glanced first at her hand, then at her face. He took her arm and steered her into the shelter of a shop doorway. 'Now what is this?'

She stared at him, and suddenly there were no more choices. 'I saw her,' she whispered.

'Saw who?'

'Gloria. She was going up the stairs.'

Thornhill patted her shoulder. 'Take your time. Which stairs?'

'The stairs to the guest bedroom.'

'This morning?'

She shook her head. 'Tuesday evening. Tuesday night, really. I don't know when, exactly – it was after midnight, though. I couldn't sleep. So I came down to collect a magazine from the living room. There was still quite a good fire in there, so I curled up on the sofa. I think I must have fallen asleep. Next thing I remember was the footsteps. And when I looked, I saw Gloria walking down the hall towards the back door. But she didn't go out – she went upstairs. Up the stairs to Mr Rowse's room.'

Thornhill bent down so his head was very close to hers. 'And what did you do then?'

She looked up at him. 'I went back to bed.'

'Did you hear or see anything else that night?'

For a moment, she hesitated. Then: 'No, sir. I just fell asleep.'

'Why didn't you tell us before?'

'I couldn't,' Jane wailed. 'It'll kill my dad. I shouldn't have done it now. I wish I hadn't.'

Chapter Thirty-Two

On Friday morning, Howard woke late. It took him a moment to realise where he was. It had been his first night in a proper bed for more than a week. He had gone to sleep late, with a third of the bottle of Mrs Portleigh's whisky inside him. For once he could not remember dreaming.

In the distance he heard the sound of a Hoover. The cleaning woman — Mrs Forbes — must be hard at work. He stretched luxuriously, relishing the knowledge that he was safe as well as comfortable. The window was slightly open and he heard the cries of children in the playground of the nearby school. Some of them were singing.

'Mrs Nipper! Mrs Yipper! Mrs Slapper! Mrs Crapper!'

Phyllis had made up a bed for him in the dressing room which opened off Mrs Portleigh's bedroom. It was a small, spartan room which contained little beside the bed, a chest of drawers and a wardrobe full of the late Mr Portleigh's clothes. He had already glanced at the clothes and discovered that Mr Portleigh had been a very small man and as plump as his name suggested.

He stretched once more. He would have liked some tea, but knew he would have to make do with the water in the carafe until Mrs Forbes had gone. Never mind. This was luxury after the woodshed. He groped for his cigarettes. He could use the time to make plans.

Suddenly he heard a sound on the landing: footsteps, moving quickly. The door of Mrs Portleigh's room opened and the footsteps hurried across the floor. The knob of the dressing-room door rattled.

'Open the door,' Phyllis hissed.

Howard was already out of bed, padding across the floor in Mr Portleigh's pyjamas. Cold air eddied around his ankles. He turned the key in the lock. Phyllis pushed past him into the room.

'What the hell are you doing here?' he whispered.

For a moment, she could not speak. Panic often had that effect on her. She stood there in her flowered housecoat, clutching her arms beneath her breasts; her face twitched.

He took her shoulders and shook her. 'Come on – pull yourself together.'

'It's Mrs Forbes.' Phyllis stared up at him with faded blue eyes. 'She says she has to come in here. In the dressing room.'

'Well, tell her she can't. Didn't you say that Mrs Portleigh wasn't feeling well, and wasn't to be disturbed.'

'She says Mrs Portleigh told her to take down the curtains in the dressing room. They need cleaning.'

'Things have changed. Mrs Portleigh is ill. Surely she understands that Mrs Portleigh doesn't want to be disturbed.'

'Mrs Forbes says that Mrs Portleigh won't mind, that she'll tiptoe across the room.' Phyllis swallowed. 'She's a very difficult woman to argue with.'

'You don't have to argue with her. She's just a bloody charwoman. You *tell* her.'

Phyllis shook her head. 'You don't understand. No one tells Mrs Forbes what to do. Even Mrs Portleigh.'

'For God's sake,' Howard muttered. 'You still haven't learned how to say boo to a goose, have you? Why can't *you* take the curtains down?'

'Because Mrs Forbes has got to hang up the summer curtains in their place, and I don't know where they are ... If I try to stop her, it's going to look terribly odd.' Phyllis looked around the small room. 'Perhaps there's somewhere you could hide? Under the bed?'

'Lock the door and be done with it.'

'There's no key. Besides, if I did that, she'd probably call the police ... She's always trying to get me in trouble with Mrs Portleigh.' Her voice rose suddenly. 'Oh my God! She'll see the bed's empty! I—'

He held up his hand for silence, suddenly aware that the sound of the Hoover had stopped some time ago. 'Where is she now?'

'Having her elevenses.' Phyllis clapped her hand over her mouth, as though trying to prevent the panic from dribbling out. 'I should be with her. She'll think it odd ...'

'Put my things in the knapsack,' he ordered.

'But there's no point. As soon she comes in, she'll realise that Mrs Portleigh's not in bed. She'll know that—'

Howard was already opening the door of the dressing room. 'Mrs Portleigh *will* be in bed.'

'I don't understand.'

'Don't talk. Bring the whisky, you stupid woman. And the glass.'

He moved soundlessly across the room to Mrs Portleigh's bed. Everything was how its owner had left it, from the carafe of water on the bedside table to the coverlet turned down, ready for her to come to bed. The curtains were drawn across the window and there was no other light in the room. He peeled off his pyjama jacket and slid into the bed, burrowing down under the eiderdown.

'What does she wear in bed?'

Phyllis gaped at him. 'What?'

'A nightie?' He arranged the pillows so they would partially shield him from any one coming through the door from the landing. 'Come *on*.'

She blinked. At last the urgency of the situation seemed

to reach her. She slipped his knapsack under the bed, opened a drawer and took out a white cotton nightdress. 'She usually wears a cap, too – over the curlers.'

'Good. Find one.'

The cap had an elasticated brim and was made of cotton, a lively Liberty print. Howard pulled it over his head and snuggled under the bedclothes, turning away from the door. He wasn't much taller than Mrs Portleigh, and certainly no fatter.

'Tell her I'm sleeping – that I had a bad night.'

'But I already have. What happens if –?'

'Shut up, and just do as you're told.'

He heard the footsteps receding, the click of the closing door and then fainter footsteps on the landing and the stairs. His heart was pumping. He began to hum, almost soundlessly, in time with the beating of his heart. *Mrs Nipper! Mrs Yipper! Mrs Slapper! Mrs Crapper!*

It was too warm in Mrs Portleigh's bed. Sweat prickled against his skin. The elastic around the cap was too tight for comfort. He wanted to use the lavatory. The pillow smelt of fading perfume and fading health. Nausea stirred inside him. He must look absurd in Mrs Portleigh's cap and nightgown, with Mr Portleigh's pyjama trousers below. He did not like the idea that he looked ridiculous.

At last Howard heard Mrs Forbes coming up the stairs. Her footsteps were rapid and assured, like the taps of a hammer. He held his breath and fought the urge to scratch his forehead, where the elastic was irritating the skin. The footsteps became quieter as they drew nearer, Mrs Forbes' token attempt not to disturb the slumbering invalid. He clenched his fists. Only one set of footsteps: that was typical of Phyllis; if she could run away from trouble, she would. He imagined her cowering in the kitchen with her hands over her ears and her eyes squeezed shut.

There was silence. He guessed that Mrs Forbes was standing

in the doorway, looking towards the bed, looking at him. If she only knew ... Laughter welled up inside him.

'Mrs P?' Mrs Forbes came a step nearer, then another. 'Mrs P?'

He heard the footsteps again – moving into the dressing room. Then the scrape of curtains moving along the brass rail. He let out his breath as quietly as he could. His hands were wet. How long would it take Mrs Forbes to change the curtains? Would she be able to resist the temptation to peep at her employer on the way out?

Even if he survived this crisis, what then? Without warning, his mood swung towards despair. But as he lay there in a warm, moist darkness, waiting for discovery at any moment, an idea came to him, flashing like cheerful lightning over his gloomy mental landscape. Suddenly he saw the way not only to escape his immediate problems, but also to make the most of the opportunities with which fate had presented him.

Sheer bloody genius, Howard told himself, and all thanks to Mrs Portleigh.

Chapter Thirty-Three

On Friday, Jill Francis found it hard to sit still, let alone to work. She invented excuses to leave her chair; and usually, when she was on her feet, she drifted to the window and looked down on the High Street beneath. She knew why: it was just possible that Richard Thornhill might be passing. She had behaved in much the same way when at the age of thirteen she had fallen in love with the son of her father's bank manager. She had made a fool of herself on that occasion, too.

Halfway through the afternoon, she could contain her restlessness no longer. She needed exercise and distraction. The new issue of the *Empire Lion* should have arrived by now. She put on her hat and went out. It was a grey, windy day, much cooler than it had been earlier in the week. She walked along the High Street to the newsagent's opposite the Bull Hotel. There was a stack of red, white and blue *Empire Lions* on the counter. The cover sported a British lion which was ogling a bilious-looking Britannia. The shop's owner was reading a copy. Jill noticed that he was wearing a regimental tie.

'Terrible business,' he said as he handed her change from a ten-shilling note. 'Traitors in our midst, look.'

'Really?'

'It's all in there. You'll see.'

She tucked the magazine under her arm and left. Instead

of going back to the office, she turned into the Gardenia Café. She did not want to read the *Empire Lion* with *Gazette* employees peering over her shoulder; it would have seemed somehow unfair to Philip. The café was crowded, and she was lucky to find a vacant table near the back. She sat down and ordered a pot of tea and a scone. While she waited for tea, she reluctantly unfolded the magazine.

It did not take Jill long to find what she was looking for. Rowse's murder and the associated business of the unpatriotic squatters at Farnock Camp formed the main story and also the subject of the editorial.

The treatment was worse than she had feared. The *Empire Lion* presented Rowse as a fearless patriot. He had been murdered — in a vicious and cowardly manner — while trying to expose a foul scandal that threatened Britain's war effort. The *Empire Lion*, which was equally fearless and equally patriotic, would not be silenced: come what may, it would present the facts to its readers. The squatters were Communist sympathisers, it went on to suggest, who were probably in direct communication with Moscow. There was clearly a substantial fifth column in the apparently sleepy and conservative town of Lydmouth. Far be it from the *Empire Lion* to point the finger of blame at a fellow organ of the Press, but the *Empire Lion*'s overriding duty was to the Great British Public. The *Empire Lion* could not honourably conceal from the Great British Public that a local newspaper, the *Lydmouth Gazette*, had been sympathetic to the squatters from the start. At this point, the *Empire Lion* included several selective quotations from the *Gazette*, illustrating its apparent bias in favour of the squatters.

Floating on an ever-swelling cloud of indignation, the *Empire Lion* moved up to a higher level of innuendo. Might the *Gazette*'s apparently inexplicable stance have something to do with the political sympathies of the editor? Few townsfolk in Lydmouth realised that Philip Wemyss-Brown had fought for the Communists on the Republican side in the Spanish

Civil War. The *Empire Lion* thought it only fair to its readers to point out that, despite his military experience in Spain, Mr Wemyss-Brown had not served in the British armed forces during World War II. Perhaps Mr Wemyss-Brown was not aware that, even at this moment, thousands of British lads were risking their lives in Korea so that we might live in freedom. Perhaps Mr Wemyss-Brown did not realise that the bullets that killed our gallant boys were fired by Communist soldiers.

So it went on. In its way, the *Empire Lion* had done a masterly job. It blended sarcasm, hints, and facts to create an impression of solid information. The editor roguishly suggested that patriotic members of the Great British Public should write to the proprietor of the *Gazette* — Mrs Philip Wemyss-Brown — and demand that she sack the editor. There was a glowing obituary of Cameron Rowse with a blurred snapshot showing him in uniform. On the opposite page was a photograph of Philip among the crowd during a Remembrance Day parade; his face was glum and frowning; and — as the caption-writer pointed out — he was not wearing a poppy. (Knowing Philip, Jill thought, it had simply fallen out.)

Jill sipped her tea and nibbled her scone. Someone had primed the *Empire Lion*, and done it with great efficiency. It was someone who knew a great deal about both Philip and Lydmouth. The real give-away was the photograph, which was of professional quality and almost certainly had come from a newspaper backfile; few people in Lydmouth would take photographs of a parade on Remembrance Sunday.

The most likely culprit was Ivor Fuggle. He had even had the cheek to phone Philip to ask if he was — or had been — a Communist. In the last few years, the *Evening Post* had been slowly but surely losing ground to the *Lydmouth Gazette*. Neither Fuggle nor the *Post* would risk openly publishing such an attack on Philip; their motive would be too obvious. But feeding the story to a third party would be another matter.

Jill pushed aside her plate and opened her handbag, looking

for cigarettes. She was furious – and what made it even worse was the knowledge that there was little she could do about it. She tried not to think of the effect the article would have on Charlotte and Philip. The timing could not be worse. There had been more casualties in Korea during the last twenty-four hours, lavishly reported in both the *Gazette* and the *Post*.

'May I join you?'

Startled, Jill looked up, knocking her cup and spilling tea in the saucer.

'Sorry – I didn't mean to surprise you,' said Edith Thornhill.

'My fault. I was miles away. Won't you sit down?'

'I'm not disturbing you?'

'Of course not.'

Jill signalled to the waitress and folded the magazine, concealing the garish front cover. Edith peeled off a pair of carefully darned gloves. As she sat down, the chair creaked beneath her. Edith had put on weight recently, Jill thought, but it suited her. Many men liked generously-built women with a warm smile and the appearance of placidity.

'How are the children?' Jill asked, instinctively groping for the safest topic available.

'Fine, thanks. They're having tea with friends today. That's why I'm on my own.' Edith grinned at Jill. 'It feels wonderfully wicked. I've just been shopping at Madame Ghislaine's.'

'Did you buy anything?'

Edith leant closer. 'A silk blouse – cream, with a navy-blue piping on the collar.'

'How lovely.'

'I wanted the sort of thing you can wear in the evening as well as in the day. We are *lucky*.'

'Oh?'

'Having a dress shop in Lydmouth. Madame Ghislaine is very up to date. We might almost be in London.'

Jill smiled politely. Fortunately the arrival of the waitress made it unnecessary for her to reply. Anyway, why shouldn't Edith Thornhill believe that Madame Ghislaine offered the height of metropolitan chic? It was a benign illusion which hurt no one and benefited both Madame Ghislaine and her customers. The only regrettable part of it was Jill's own reaction: the unthinking condescension of a Londoner towards a provincial assumption of sophistication. And she wasn't even a Londoner any more.

'The only trouble is,' Edith went on when the waitress had left, 'that it makes me feel so guilty.'

'But why?'

'Spending all that money on myself, on clothes.'

'But one has to wear *something*.' Jill produced the comforting rationale she had so often used to herself. 'Besides, buying quality usually turns out to be an economy in the long run.'

'Oh yes. That's what I always say.'

The two women exchanged glances of understanding. Damn, thought Jill: I don't want to like this woman. Edith's tea arrived. Jill refilled her own cup, putting off her return to the *Gazette*.

'Do smoke,' Edith said, noticing the cigarette packet on top of the *Empire Lion*. She demolished half a teacake. 'I sometimes think I should start smoking again. So nice to have something to do with the hands.'

'So you used to?'

'Oh yes – and so did Richard. But we decided to give up when David was on the way. It's quite an expense, isn't it, and when you've got children . . .' Edith took another mouthful of teacake. 'Not that Richard ever smoked much. Unlike me.'

Jill lit a cigarette. Hearing his wife talk about Richard had much in common with picking scabs. For a moment, neither woman spoke. Seeing us here, Jill thought, people would assume that here were two friends having tea together.

'Are you going to the madrigal concert at the High School?' Edith asked.

'Probably. Are you?'

'Yes — Uncle Bernard asked me.'

'Uncle —? Of course.' So that was why Edith had needed the blouse. Jill wondered whether Richard had been included in the invitation. 'Have you seen the interview with Mr Broadbent in the *Gazette*?'

'I've got it here.' Edith gestured at the shopping bag on the floor by the table. 'He mentions that poor girl, Heather Parry. The one the concert's for. Are you going to be writing it up for the paper?'

'If I go, yes. But my cat's on the verge of producing kittens. If she decides that tonight's the night, I'll have to stay at home and ask someone else to cover the concert.'

'What will you do with the kittens?'

'I don't know. Mary Sutton says she'll put a notice in the parish magazine.'

'We might be interested, actually. It would be good for the children to have a pet. They certainly want one. Perhaps they should have one each. Otherwise they'll squabble.'

'I'll let you know when they're born. Then you can see if any of them appeal to you. I should warn you that the father's probably a tom who lives in the almshouses over the road. Rather a bruiser.'

'I shall have to see what Richard thinks, of course. He's not too fond of cats.'

'Oh?' Jill passed the bowl of sugar lumps across the table to Edith, glimpsing Richard's hinterland, largely unknown to her but familiar territory to Edith. 'I really should get back to the office.' She looked up, trying to attract the attention of the waitress.

'I should have been home five minutes ago.' Smiling placidly, Edith wiped buttery fingers on her table napkin. 'Tell me — I know this is rather a change of subject — do you think going to a public school is good for a boy?'

'Morally? Or in practical terms?'

'I was wondering whether it might be useful in later life. Knowing the right people, and so on.'

'I suppose it depends what the boy wants to do.' At last Jill succeeded in attracting the attention of the waitress; she mimed her request for the bill. 'You're thinking of sending David?'

'Well, yes. Just a thought – my mother left me a little money.'

Jill said, 'I heard she'd died – I'm so sorry.'

The waitress arrived with Jill's bill. A moment later, Jill said goodbye to Edith. She was aware that Edith would have liked to say more, that there was something on her mind; but Jill was relieved to get away. If there is a possibility that you are going to cheat someone in the near future, then in one sense the less you know about them the better. If you get to know them well, there's always the danger you might start liking them.

Chapter Thirty-Four

Thornhill recognised the woman who opened the private door of the Bathurst Arms: she worked in the kitchen and occasionally waited in the dining room.

'Is Mrs Alvington in?' he asked.

'No, sir. But Mr Alvington and Jane—'

'It was Mrs Alvington I wanted. Did she say when she'd be back?'

'I'm sure I couldn't say. She's having a driving lesson, look. Joe Vance took her out in Mr Alvington's car. Shall I ask her to phone you when she gets in?'

'Don't bother. I'll call again.'

Thornhill drove back to Police Headquarters, wondering whether Gloria Alvington's driving lesson had something to do with Jane Alvington's sudden desire to reveal what she had seen on Tuesday night. Which begged the question: *reveal* or *invent*?

In the police car park, two men were waxing Williamson's car. Sergeant Fowles flagged Thornhill down as soon as he went inside.

'The Super would like a word, sir.'

Thornhill climbed the stairs, preparing himself mentally for another inquisition about Yateley, a sequel to the lengthy interrogation which had followed his interview at the Bull that morning. When he reached the Superintendent's office, the first thing he noticed was that Williamson had changed his suit. He was now wearing a funereal pinstripe, with a clean collar and his regimental tie. All this — including the sparkling car outside — was in honour of an impending visit by an official from the Ministry of Defence, in order to see Oliver Yateley. The Chief Constable was unable to meet him, and had delegated the job to Williamson. No one was meant to know where Williamson was going, let alone whom he was meeting, but word had seeped out.

'Have you seen this?' Williamson demanded, waving the *Empire Lion* in a red-white-and-blue blur in front of Thornhill's face. 'I don't know what this bloody town is coming to.'

'No, sir. Something to do with Rowse?'

'The entire magazine is practically devoted to him.' Williamson tossed it on the desk and stood up. 'Him and Wemyss-Brown. You'd better read it. The bastards give the impression we're either incompetent or corrupt or most probably both. I'd like your comments, in writing.' He shrugged his heavy shoulders into a lightweight overcoat that Thornhill had never seen before. 'After all, you were actually there when Wemyss-Brown was going hammer and tongs with Rowse on Tuesday evening.' Suddenly his voice sharpened: 'Where exactly did Wemyss-Brown go after he left the Bull on Tuesday?'

'Mrs Wemyss-Brown drove him home. They had supper, and then Mr Wemyss-Brown left at about nine o'clock to talk to Councillor Broadbent. They're doing a piece on him in the *Gazette*.'

'Drive or walk?'

'He walked, sir.'

'Quite a step from Troy House to Narth Road.'

'Mr Wemyss-Brown said he wanted to stretch his legs. Almost certainly he needed to clear his head as well — he'd had a few drinks.'

'And Counsellor Broadbent gave him a few more.'

Thornhill nodded.

'So it's the end of the evening,' Williamson said, settling his trilby on his head and adjusting the angle in the mirror over his fireplace. 'He's as drunk as a lord and he's walking home. How does he say he walked home? By the High Street?'

'No, sir. He says he cut down to Nutholt Lane, then into Church Street and through St John's Passage.'

'I don't suppose anyone saw him?'

'None of the beat constables, sir. I don't know about anyone else. We haven't asked.'

'Yet. Has it struck you that it wouldn't have taken him much longer to walk home by the river? And if he went back that way, he'd have passed within spitting distance of the Bathurst Arms. Ten to one he's nursing a grievance about Rowse. After all, quite apart from politics, Rowse wasn't being very nice about Mrs Wemyss-Brown, was she? And we don't know what else was said. Maybe Rowse was threatening to splash his Commie past all over the *Empire Lion*. More than likely. So Wemyss-Brown decides to pop into the Bathurst Arms on his way home. Have it out with Rowse once and for all.' Williamson's pale eyes stared at Thornhill. 'Well?'

Thornhill concentrated on a framed photograph of the Superintendent shaking hands with the Lord Lieutenant of the county. 'It's possible, sir.'

'You can't argue that lighter away, Thornhill. And I tell you another thing: a great many people in this town are going to think twice about Philip Wemyss-Brown once they've read the *Empire Lion*.'

'Sir, he's not the only possibility. We still haven't identified the "man with the fish" that Rowse saw.'

Williamson paused with his hand on the doorknob. 'The man with the fish probably didn't exist. Rowse had a lisp, didn't he? So "fish" would be "fith". God knows what he meant, if anything. But it's hardly likely to be relevant to us.'

'What about Yateley?'

'Yateley didn't leave his lighter underneath the body. Anyway, keep your mouth shut about Yateley. He's nothing to do with us.'

'But sir—'

'You heard. There are reasons.' Williamson glowed with the comforting consciousness of inner knowledge, his pride restored. 'Mr Hendry and I have discussed the question of Mr Yateley in some detail. I can't tell you any more.' He flung open the door but stopped so sharply on the threshold that Thornhill almost bumped into him. 'I'm not sure when I'll be back. Oh, and Thornhill: one thing you mustn't do is talk to Miss Francis.'

'I – I beg your pardon, sir?'

'What's the matter with you? Perfectly straightforward. As part of this Yateley business – ah – I may want to talk to her, and we don't want to give her time to think about what she's going to say.'

'Yes, sir. I see what you mean.'

'In this sort of case, you have to think out the implications.' Secure in his superiority, Williamson sounded almost benign. 'It's not like ordinary police work. Needs a different approach. Altogether subtler. Some people understand that more readily than others. Anyway, in the meantime, I want you to talk to Wemyss-Brown. Make him go over his route home. Find out if anyone saw him where he said he was. And get on to Uniformed again: see if he was spotted elsewhere.'

Williamson strode away down the corridor and a moment later his footsteps thundered down the stairs. He was looking better than he had done for months: the prospect of meeting a senior civil servant had acted like a tonic on him.

Thornhill went back to his own office. His in-tray was stacked with folders, letters and internal memoranda. This Yateley business had pushed everything else to the bottom of the heap. He opened the *Empire Lion* and began to skim through its contents. He read quickly, unwilling to prolong the experience longer than necessary. Before he had finished, there was a knock on his door and Sergeant Kirby came in with a sheet of paper in his hand.

'What is it, Brian?'

'We've just finished the house-to-house around the Bathurst Arms.'

'Anything?'

'Not a thing. Most people were asleep by that time on Tuesday night. Still, I thought you'd like to know.'

'It doesn't mean much. Anyway, the attacker could have come along the towpath, from either direction.'

'Not much lighting down there. And if he did come that way, he didn't leave any traces. We've searched for a quarter-mile upstream and downstream. Do you want us to drag the river?'

'Not yet. But Rowse's camera and his notebook must be somewhere. And so must the knife.'

'In theory.' Kirby shrugged. 'Funny sort of case, isn't it? The more you look at it, the less you see.' He nodded at the magazine. 'Didn't know you read that, sir.'

'I don't if I can help it. But this is a sort of memorial issue for Rowse: all about him and Farnock Camp.' He paused. 'And all about Philip Wemyss-Brown and the inexplicable inefficiency of the police investigation into Rowse's murder.'

'Nasty.' Unexpectedly Kirby grinned. 'But we have had one success. They gave me this on my way upstairs.' He handed Thornhill a report from the Fingerprint Department. 'They found a positive match for Porter's egg-snatcher. And the only reason we had the prints on file was because of the Farnock Camp business. Turns out they belong to Sid Coalway.'

Thornhill glanced at the report. Then he looked up and snapped, 'Get Uniformed to pull Coalway in. Go with them yourself and take two cars. If you get there before the pubs open, you'll probably find him at home. Make sure the neighbours know about it.'

'You sure, sir?' Kirby looked puzzled. 'Isn't it like swatting a fly with a hammer? All he did was nick a few eggs and stuff, and play a joke on Porter.'

'That's just the point: I don't want people to think they can get away with playing jokes on my officers.'

Kirby began to smile but thought better of it. 'Yes, sir. What about the kids, though? Someone will have to look after them if their dad's down the cells as well as their mum.'

'Norah Coalway's back home,' Thornhill said. 'Haven't you heard?'

Kirby raised his eyebrows. 'I've been out all day.'

'Ruispidge went to see the Chief Constable and persuaded him that it would be wise to drop the charges against her and the others. Bad publicity.' He paused. 'It turns out that Norah's dad used to work as a cowman on Home Farm.'

The two men were silent for a moment, contemplating the enigma of Sir Anthony Ruispidge, whose notion of justice was a disconcerting combination of feudalism and philanthropy.

'Another thing, Brian: make sure Coalway's lodgings are searched. Send someone up to Farnock Camp and poke around there again.'

'If you say so ...'

'He's been pinching eggs very methodically. So perhaps he steals other things as well.' Thornhill pushed aside the thought of Norah Coalway and her two little girls. 'Besides, it'll show Coalway we mean business.'

'Yes, sir.'

Thornhill sent Kirby away. He wrestled for a moment with the uncomfortable thought that Kirby might find his behaviour as irrational and inconvenient as he found Williamson's. Too bad. He stared morosely at his in-tray. He knew what he should be thinking about: the Rowse case; that was the real job he had to do. He did not think it likely that Philip Wemyss-Brown had killed Cameron Rowse. But he was too experienced not to know that a man could behave out of character on occasions, particularly when he was drunk and felt under threat. He ran his forefinger down the pile of folders and papers. At least two-thirds of the pile was no more than a series of distractions – that fool Yateley, Porter's egg-snatcher with the misplaced sense of humour, and the three-year-old search for a missing teenage girl.

What really worried him was Jill Francis. How would she react if Superintendent Williamson and a high-ranking civil servant suddenly arrived on her doorstep, full of awkward questions about her private life? He wished he could have warned her. He weighed the pros and cons of disobeying Williamson, finally deciding that the arguments for disobedience were not quite strong enough.

Would Jill blame him for that, he wondered? And how would she react to the news that Lydmouth CID were proposing to investigate the possibility that her friend and employer, Philip Wemyss-Brown, might be responsible for the murder of Cameron Rowse? Whichever way he turned, Thornhill found problems, and whichever way he looked, he saw Jill Francis's face.

He stood up and stepped away from his desk, trying literally to step away from the thoughts that filled his mind, clamouring for attention. It was all a matter of perspective, he told himself. Somewhere on the other side of the world was a war whose shadow was touching their lives even in Lydmouth. In a few days that shadow could darken until it enveloped everything in a night without stars. He shivered, knowing that the thought was too immense for his mind to hold. Better to concentrate on the here and now: on finding the murderer of an unpleasant little journalist, and on trying to make sense of falling in love with a woman who was not his wife.

The phone began to ring. He grabbed the handset. 'Thornhill.'

'Get yourself over here,' Williamson snarled. 'To the Bull.'

Thornhill cleared his throat. 'Is there —?'

'Just get here.' Williamson slammed down the phone.

A moment later, Thornhill left Police Headquarters and walked briskly along the High Street. MORE CASUALTIES shrieked a placard outside the newsagent's on the other side of the road. He turned into the Bull. Quale was sitting behind the reception counter, apparently engaged in scraping dried porridge from his striped waistcoat. When the old man saw Thornhill, he unhurriedly stood up and leant across the counter.

'You'll find them in Mr Yateley's room, sir,' he confided, managing to convey the impression that he was parting with privileged information and should be rewarded accordingly.

Thornhill groped in his pocket and put a shilling on the counter. 'Who's up there?'

'Mr Yateley, Mr Williamson and a ... gentleman — from London, I understand.'

Thornhill nodded. By now he was expert at translating the complex vocabulary of Quale's insinuations, many of which were a matter of facial twitches and tactical silences rather than words. The man from London was not a gentleman and, worse, Quale had not taken to him.

'One other thing: on Tuesday evening, did you happen to notice where Mr Yateley was?'

'He went out to dinner at the Walnut Tree in Trenart, sir. He asked me to book a table for him.'

'What about afterwards?'

Quale smiled. 'He must have got back at about ten-thirty. A little unsteady on his feet, if I may say so. He had a few more drinks in the bar, and then I helped him upstairs just before I went off duty.' The old man paused. 'He didn't ask for a pass key, and the night porter didn't see him go out.'

'You checked?'

'Yes, sir.' Quale's eyes met Thornhill's. 'Just in case it

might be useful. Though in my humble opinion, Mr Yateley wasn't in a fit state to go anywhere.'

'Thank you, Mr Quale.' Thornhill found a half-crown in his pocket and slipped it discreetly on the counter. 'You've been most helpful.'

'Thank *you*, sir. And by the way . . .'

'What?'

'The gentleman from London asked me just the same question.'

Thornhill nodded his thanks and went upstairs. There was still a uniformed constable outside Yateley's room. This precaution had been Williamson's idea. Thornhill tapped on the door and a voice he did not recognise told him to come in.

There were three men in the room. Yateley was in bed smoking a cigarette, with the remains of a substantial tea around him. He looked irritated, but he nodded at Thornhill. Williamson, still in his new overcoat, was sitting on a hard chair near the door. Standing near the bed was the man from the Ministry of Defence. The first thing Thornhill noticed was how young he was.

'Inspector Thornhill,' Williamson muttered. 'Mr Blaines.'

Blaines pointed to the chair by the window. 'You sit there.' His eyes flicked across the room to Williamson. 'As for you, I don't think we need you any more. One copper's company, two's a crowd, eh?'

Williamson flushed. 'Are you sure that's a good idea, Mr Blaines? There may be—'

'Of course I'm sure it's a good idea! Just go away, will you?'

The door shut behind Williamson. Thornhill glanced surreptitiously at Blaines. He was plump and powerfully-built, with a turnip-shaped head and curly yellow hair to which oil had given a corrugated sheen. He wore baggy grey flannels, scuffed black shoes and a tweed jacket whose pattern made Rowse's seem a model of sobriety.

Blaines swung round and caught Thornhill watching him. 'Before you make yourself too comfortable, tell the man on the door to run away and play.'

When that was done, he told Thornhill to sit down again.

'We need to get one thing straight,' he said. 'If a word of any of this gets out, I'll throw the Official Secrets Act at you. You don't talk to the wife about this, you don't talk to the mistress. You don't talk to your mates, either.' Blaines stretched, as unselfconsciously as though he were alone, and then farted, a long, solemn sound that rose in pitch at the end to signal its completion. All the while he stared at Thornhill. 'What I don't want is people making a fuss. I do not want constables guarding the door and making it quite clear that something is going on. Is that clear?'

'Yes, sir.'

'Your boss seemed to think I'd like to be met at the station by a civic reception and an escort from the Household Cavalry.' Blaines tired abruptly of the subject and glanced at the man on the bed. 'You stay there – OK, Mr Yateley? Me and Mr Thornhill are going for a little walk.'

Yateley stirred on the bed. 'Look here, we need to discuss what happens next.'

'As far as you're concerned, not much is going to happen in the immediate future. Just stay where you are. You've caused quite enough trouble as it is.' Blaines glanced at Thornhill and jerked his head at the door. 'Come on.'

Thornhill followed Blaines out of the room. As he closed the door he looked at the man in bed. Yateley seemed literally to have shrunk. He smiled apologetically at Thornhill, and his shoulders twitched in the ghost of a shrug.

Blaines paused at the head of the stairs. 'Yateley's mistress – I've arranged to see her at her house. You know where it is?'

Thornhill nodded. His left hand, which was shielded by

his body from Blaines's eyes, fiddled compulsively with the seam of his trousers. 'What about Mr Yateley? Do you want me to get someone to sit with him?'

Blaines shook his head. 'No point. He's not going anywhere. Not since this morning.'

'Since the suicide attempt?'

'Not just an attempt. It wasn't all a failure. He managed to kill something.' Blaines grinned, exposing irregular teeth. 'But not quite what he intended.'

'I don't follow, sir.'

'Just my little joke, Thornhill. What I mean is, all the stuffing's gone out of him. He's no more likely to make a break for it than I am.'

They went downstairs and passed Quale, who pretended not to see them. Blaines stopped under the portico of the Bull and glanced up and down the High Street.

'Besides, he wouldn't get far even if he tried,' Blaines went on, lighting a cigarette. 'I've got his car keys and his wallet, and I've sent his trousers to be pressed.' He looked at Thornhill. 'How far to this house?'

'Five minutes' walk. But Miss Francis may well be at work still. Shouldn't we —?'

'She'll be at home. I told Williamson to phone her.' Blaines sauntered down the High Street. 'And that gives you and me a nice opportunity to have a little chat on the way. I want to know what Yateley's told you — every damned last detail. And why did he want to talk to you? Why an inspector when he could have had the Chief Constable if he needed a copper?'

'We've met before, sir.' Thornhill wondered if Blaines already knew the answer to these questions, if he were merely testing Thornhill's willingness to answer accurately.

'Did he mention the affair on that occasion?'

'Yes, sir. He didn't mention Miss Francis by name, but he told me about the affair, and said she had recently ended it. I happened to see a photograph of her.'

Blaines sniffed. 'So it's not just something he and Miss Francis cooked up to suit the occasion?'

'I doubt it.'

'But why the hell did he choose you for his heart to heart?'

'Miss Francis had just made it quite clear she had had enough of him. He was in quite a state. He'd had a few drinks.'

'Pissed as a rat in a brewery. That's what I heard. Just like he was on Tuesday night, eh? Which at least should mean he's in the clear with this Rowse business. All right: what did Yateley tell you this morning?'

'He said he had come to Lydmouth because the security services were investigating him.'

'Too right. And how do you think it looked when he vanished off the face of the earth on Tuesday? Bloody fool. Go on.'

'He told me that when he was an undergraduate at Jerusalem College, Cambridge, he'd joined the Communist Party. He claimed that it was just a youthful fling – that he stopped going to meetings after a couple of weeks. He said that he'd forgotten all about it until the last few months.'

'Did you believe him?' Blaines asked.

'I didn't believe he'd forgotten all about it. As for the rest, I kept an open mind. No reason why it shouldn't be true.'

Blaines stopped outside Woolworth's, apparently to examine the window display. 'So on Tuesday afternoon he turned up in Lydmouth. Did he tell you why?'

'I understood from him that the security services were investigating the possibility that he might be a Communist agent.' Thornhill watched Blaines's eyes, wondering if the man were using the plate glass as a mirror. 'They'd uncovered what he called his flirtation with Communism at Cambridge. He told me that there had been leaks, and that he was under suspicion because he was aware of a good deal of classified information through a Parliamentary Committee he serves on. He also told me that there were a number of gaps in his diary

– times when he'd met Miss Francis, gone away with her. He said your people had found traces of the affair but did not know who the woman was. Or whether the relationship was sexual. They thought she might be a Soviet agent. And Yateley made it worse by refusing to say anything.'

'So why exactly does he come to Lydmouth?'

'To find out if Miss Francis would be willing to support his story if he gave your people her name.'

'Odd.' Blaines turned his head and looked directly at Thornhill, who realised for the first time how unlined the man's face was. 'Why didn't he just phone? Why did he feel he had to ask her at all?'

'He said he felt he owed it to her: that there was a danger he'd ruin her reputation by saving his.'

'Pish!' said Blaines. 'Folks like Yateley only have gentlemanly scruples when it suits them. What was the real reason?'

'I don't know.'

'Then tell me what you think. This ain't a court of law.'

'I think there was a good deal of ill feeling when Yateley and Miss Francis parted. I think he was afraid she might refuse to support him. And if she did refuse, he'd be in a worse position than when he started, because it would look like he was trying to cook up an alibi.'

'Hell hath no fury like a woman scorned,' Blaines said. 'Something like that. We learnt it at school.'

'But according to Yateley, it was she who ended the affair.'

'The one sensible thing she's done.'

'Does her connection to Yateley have to be public knowledge?' Thornhill said.

Blaines turned and flicked the butt of his cigarette in an arc across the pavement to the gutter. 'What's it to you?'

'In a town like this everyone knows everyone else. People have old-fashioned views.'

Blaines snorted again, this time with what sounded like

genuine amusement. 'Having a fling with a married man –
and a Communist to boot. She'd be tarred and feathered,
would she? Is that how you do things in Lydmouth?'

Thornhill said nothing.

'Are you a local man?'

'No, sir.'

'Thought not. And Miss Francis ain't local, either, is she?
You read the *Empire Lion*?'

Thornhill licked his lips. 'Not usually.'

'But you've seen today's issue?' Blaines waited for Thornhill's
nod before he went on: 'Miss Francis's lover – her *former* lover
– was once a Communist. She works for, and is very friendly
with, another man who fought on the Republican side in the
Spanish Civil War. Maybe "fought" ain't quite the word I
want, but it's the thought that counts. So probably he's as red
as a tomato too.' He spun to face Thornhill and prodded him
in the chest with a nicotine-stained forefinger. 'Coincidence or
conspiracy?'

'As far as I know, it's pure coincidence, sir. Yateley and
Wemyss-Brown must be roughly the same age. In the Thirties
they both went through a left-wing period. So did a lot of
young men. I don't even think they've met.'

'That's not the point. The point is that the *Empire
Lion* doesn't believe in coincidence. Conspiracy sells more
copies.'

Thornhill swallowed. 'And what do you believe?'

Blaines stared at him for a long moment. Then he shrugged
and began to walk along the High Street. Thornhill followed,
soon catching up so the two men were walking side by side.
They turned right into Church Street.

'After you've introduced us, I want you to wait outside,'
Blaines said. 'Is it far?'

'It's the cottage on the right-hand side. Next to that set
of gates.'

They walked in silence for the rest of the way. When they

reached Church Cottage, Blaines waved at Thornhill to ring the doorbell.

'The trouble with this sort of business is that a lot of people tend to get hurt.' Blaines stared straight ahead at the closed door, but his voice was gentler than before; perhaps he thought Jill Francis might be crouching on the other side of the door with her ear to the letterbox. 'It's got nothing to do with whether they're innocent or guilty.'

'Just one of those things?'

'It's like they catch an illness. Happen to get in the way of a germ.' Blaines broke wind again, but this time he produced a deep, thundering sound. 'The Crack of Doom,' he added without a smile.

Chapter Thirty-Five

Mincing Lane was one of the few survivors of the warren of decayed streets that had once filled the Templefields area near the station. The arrival of two police cars, one with a clanging bell, brought the neighbours to the windows and the Coalways' landlady to the front door.

'Police,' Kirby told her, flashing his warrant card for form's sake. 'I'm looking for Sidney Coalway.'

'In there,' she said, pointing a finger like a dead twig at one of the doors which opened into the hall. 'I knew they was trouble the moment I saw them.'

When Kirby arrived, the newly reunited family was in the middle of high tea. Sid Coalway, still unshaven, was eating a boiled egg and drinking pale ale from the bottle. The two little girls were feeding toast to their teddies, and Norah Coalway was rushing around seeing to everybody's needs except her own. The room was not large, and with five police officers it seemed even smaller. Kirby had brought a detective constable and three uniformed officers, including Joan Ailsmore.

'Is this all they've got?' he said.

The landlady pouted, as if she took the question as a criticism. 'They share the kitchen with the other tenants. Lovely big room, with a bath and everything. And there's a nice outside toilet.'

'Bloody busies,' Sid drawled in a manner that suggested he had had several pale ales before this one. 'Can't you leave a chap alone, hey?'

'Vermin,' muttered the landlady. 'Them kiddies are full of lice.'

'You keep them out of it, you old cow,' roared Sid. 'And while we were talking about vermin, what about the bedbugs? I found three last night. You want me to show you the bites on my bum?'

'All right, all right,' Kirby said, herding the landlady out of the room and closing the door on her. 'Now, Sid, we're going to have a look round. OK?'

While the police searched, the children continued to feed their teddies, for all the world as though such invasions were a common occurrence in their lives. Norah Coalway said nothing: she stood there scowling, giving nothing away. Her husband did enough talking for all of them.

'You know what this is, Mr Kirby? Persecution. You're hounding a poor honest working man. And his wife and nippers. I shall be writing to my MP about this. Don't think I don't know what it's all about. It's political, look. Of course, I don't blame you personally, sergeant. You and me, we're both working men. But I just hope you can look yourself in the face after this.'

The landlady poked her head back into the room and informed no one in particular that this was a respectable house, and that no one else had ever complained of bedbugs before. Everyone ignored her. A small crowd had gathered on the pavement outside the house. They tried to peer through the window, which was covered in grubby net curtains.

In the alcove nearer the window there was a wardrobe which was used partly as a larder. On one shelf was a straw-lined basket containing seven eggs which almost certainly came from Mrs Veale's hens.

'Where did you get these, Mrs Coalway?'

She shrugged. 'Sid got them.'

'The eggs?' Sid scratched his head ostentatiously. 'Now let me see. I remember! I went for my constitutional this morning and I met this old gypsy woman down by the river. She asked if I'd like to buy twelve new-laid eggs, and I said—'

'Enough of your lip,' Kirby interrupted. 'Save it for your memoirs.'

'Sarge?' Joan Ailsmore was standing on a chair and examining the top of the wardrobe. 'Take a look at this.'

Bundled in a sack was a selection of tools. They included a chisel sharpener in a box. When Kirby turned the box over he found the pencilled initials JV underneath. John Veale?

He held up the box. 'Where did you get this, Sid?'

'Let me see. There was a man in the King's Head the other night. Never seen him before. Birmingham accent. He had a beard, I remember. Asked if I'd like to buy a few tools that used to belong to his old dad.'

Norah took the little girls to the corner of the room furthest from the window. She settled them on her lap and told them a story about a fairy godmother. The magic failed to work. The girls' eyes remained fixed on the strange men moving about the narrow confines of their home.

Having finished his egg, Sid lit a cigarette. 'Bloody police state, that's what this is.'

Joan had found something else on top of the wardrobe, right at the back. She glanced across the room at Kirby and beckoned him with her eyes. He went over to her. She stepped down from the chair and handed him a bundle of dirty rag. Inside was a cheap clasp knife with a handle of dark wood and dull metal. Wordlessly, the police woman pointed to rust-coloured stains on the handle, the apparent source of similar stains on the rag.

'First you turn up like a bunch of storm troopers and throw us out of our homes,' Sid was saying, 'then you throw my missus in jail for no good reason, leaving these poor motherless kiddies to fend for themselves. Then you turn up here and tear the place apart. I wouldn't be surprised if you're planting evidence. Norah! Remember I said that. I think they're planting evidence. They think they can grind me down, just because I'm a working man. They've got another thought coming. They're not going to make *me* a bloody victim of the class war.'

'Class war, is it?' Kirby said softly. 'Then I reckon you're on the losing side, mate.'

The room filled with a brief, inexplicable silence. The only sound was the monotonous murmur of Norah's voice as she continued with the exploits of the fairy godmother. But both she and the children were staring at Sidney Coalway, who was still sprawling, apparently at his ease, at the table where the family had been eating high tea. Blurred faces were still pressed against the window. Joan smoothed her skirt. She looked pleased with herself. Taking care not to touch the knife, Kirby wrapped the rag around it.

'Get your hat and coat, Sid,' he said. 'You're nicked.'

Chapter Thirty-Six

The Madrigal Society of the Lydmouth High School for Girls was in exceptionally fine voice that evening. This might have had something to do with the fact that a dozen boys from the choir of nearby Ashbridge School had been drafted in to sing the tenor and bass parts. During the clapping that followed an impassioned rendition of Morley's 'Springtime mantleth every bough', Charlotte Wemyss-Brown leant towards her husband.

'Try not to look so glum,' she whispered.

'I'm not looking glum,' Philip snapped, and continued to clap at a pace suitable for a funeral. 'How much longer does this go on for?'

'Hush, dear.'

Jill, who was sitting on the other side of Philip, turned over another page of her notebook. The applause petered away. The music mistress, who was seated at the grand piano, raised her hand and then brought it down upon the keyboard. The adolescents on the stage burst into song. They would go no more a-roving with thee, fair maid, and they spent the next five minutes explaining and reiterating their decision. Meanwhile the covert glances that flashed across the stage suggested that at least some of the singers meant the opposite of what they were singing.

'Enough hormonal energy,' Jill noted in her neat shorthand, 'to light Piccadilly Circus.'

In theory she was here to cover the concert for the *Gazette*; in practice she was also lending support to the Wemyss-Browns. To tell the truth, she was glad of the excuse to get away from Church Cottage. The memory of Blaines's visit was still uncomfortably fresh. The sitting room smelled of his cigarettes, and worse. She had felt physically threatened by him – he was a big, bulky man who by accident or design had sidled close to her whenever he could. Even worse had been his questions: he had fumbled his way methodically through the story of her affair with Oliver Yateley.

'Don't mind me asking,' he'd said. 'We need all the details, for confirmation. Can't be too careful, can we?'

As a journalist, she had a professional appreciation of his technique: the same questions, asked again and again in slightly different ways, in a lengthy process of eliciting answers and then testing them. She had told him the truth, as far as she could; given him precise dates dredged up from old letters and diaries. Slowly she had charted the painful course of her affair with Oliver Yateley: and one consequence had been that she came to realise how few and how short their meetings had been. So much heartache had sprung from such little cause. The real worry was what Blaines would do with his knowledge. He had made no promises. She had no doubt that if it suited his purposes, he would feed information about the affair to the press. There was still the possibility that the *Empire Lion* would brand her as the scarlet woman of Lydmouth. The publicity could force her out of her home and her job.

Even worse than this was the sense that she was now defiled. Now the secret was out in the open, it was revealed for what it really was. What once had seemed romantic was now made sordid. Jill felt as though she had given Blaines permission to rummage through her underwear, and had then stood by, watching him do it. She imagined him pawing through the information with his colleagues, chuckling over her gullibility. 'Poor girl thought Yateley was going to leave his wife for her! Can you beat it?'

Was she now on the verge of making the same mistake, this time with Richard Thornhill? Surely not, she thought, surely she had learned from experience? Besides, had she ever loved Oliver Yateley? She had been flattered and aroused by his attentions. But Richard was different. How different? The questions scuttled round her mind like rats in a maze with no exits.

Philip's problems were a distraction, and by contrast with hers a welcome one. He had been understandably depressed since she showed him the *Empire Lion*. He had wanted to stay at home this evening, Charlotte had told Jill, but Charlotte wouldn't let him. Charlotte was a prominent figure in the school's Old Girls' Association and her absence from the concert would have been noted; so would Philip's, in the circumstances. On this occasion Jill agreed with Charlotte: Philip would have to meet people sooner or later, and in any case moping at home was bad for morale. Jill glanced along the row. Philip was staring straight in front of him, his face expressionless; his hands were twisting the concert programme. Beyond him, Charlotte was smiling fixedly at the stage and beating time to the music.

The song came to an end. Next the programme took a religious turn with a number of Negro spirituals. Joshua fought the battle of Jericho, Peter was told to ring those bells, and then there were soulful versions of 'Nobody knows' and 'Steal Away'. After an excursion to Middle Europe for three or four Kodaly and Seiber arrangements, it was back to Merry England with 'The Ash Grove' and 'Be gone, dull care'. Finally, there was a rousing rendition of 'The Mermaid', and the concert was over.

'Storm of applause,' Jill scribbled on her pad, suppressing a yawn.

Dr Margaret Hilly, the headmistress of the High School, left her seat in the front row and mounted the stairs to the stage. She was a small, round woman with a carrying voice and a well-deserved reputation for ruthlessness. She proceeded to thank everyone who had helped in whatever capacity with the concert. She produced appropriate quotations, one in Latin, one in Greek, in praise of music. She outlined the projected benefits that the new Parry Music Room would bring to the school as a whole and to future generations of pupils.

'Let us not forget the reason why we are here today.' Dr Hilly swept her eyes from one side of the hall to the other. 'Heather Parry was one of the best singers the Madrigal Society has ever had. She was a soloist in the Choral Society and the leader of the School Choir. If she were in Lydmouth today, almost certainly she would be here with us, enjoying the splendid music we've heard this evening. Her absence is a tragedy that touches us all, and especially, of course, her family. We hope and pray that somewhere she is alive and well, and that soon we shall see her bright, smiling face among us again. In the meantime, let us be positive – just as Heather is herself – and keep her memory green. I cannot think of a better way to do this, or a way that she would have approved of more, than the Parry Music Room, with the splendid facilities it will have. All the proceeds from this concert will go towards it. Mr and Mrs Parry have already given us a most generous donation to set the ball rolling, and Councillor Broadbent has promised to match it.' She stared round the audience as if making a mental note of who was there. 'Further donations will be most welcome.'

Dr Hilly glanced towards the wings on stage right. The youngest member of the Madrigal Society seized a bouquet from the waiting music mistress, ran down the steps and presented it to Mrs Parry. More applause broke out.

'Surely it's over now?' Philip muttered to Charlotte. 'Oh God, Broadbent wants to put his ha'porth in.'

Charlotte shushed her husband by jabbing his arm with her elbow. Broadbent mounted the stairs to the stage and repeated the substance of what Dr Hilly had said but in different words and with rather more of them. Afterwards, the youngest member of the Madrigal Society descended once again from the stage with a bouquet clutched in both hands. Jill craned her head to see Edith Thornhill receiving it. She was sitting in the front row.

Charlotte had seen her, too. 'You know she's related to Bernard Broadbent?' she whispered across her husband to Jill.

Jill nodded.

'Do you know how?'

'Some sort of cousin, I think. But she calls him Uncle Bernard.'

'Really? I wonder if he's planning to use Edith Thornhill as his official escort. It must be so difficult if you haven't got a wife – all those functions to go to. Much easier if you have a woman on your arm.'

The clapping faltered, diminished and stopped. Jill made another note: *Bouquet for Mrs Richard Thornhill.*

People were beginning to move from their seats. Philip picked up Charlotte's handbag and gave it to her. Charlotte took his arm and, followed by Jill, they joined the crush of people filing out of the hall.

'According to the programme, they're serving coffee and biscuits in the library,' Charlotte said.

'Not to us.' Philip sounded desperate. 'I want a proper drink.'

'Yes, dear, perhaps we should be getting back. It's later than I thought.'

Near the door, the flow of the crowd brought Jill and Edith Thornhill together. They smiled at each other.

'Lovely concert,' said Edith. 'And weren't the little ones sweet?'

'Weren't they? Is that the new blouse? It's lovely.'

'Yes. Luckily Richard likes it too.'

'He must be very busy at present.'

'I certainly hope not,' Edith said with a grin. 'He's meant to be looking after the children, and they should have been asleep hours ago.'

The current pushed them into the foyer. Broadbent reclaimed Edith, and said a few words to Jill before he was claimed in his turn by a summons to Dr Hilly.

Jill followed the Wemyss-Browns outside.

'There!' Charlotte said to Philip as they walked down the short drive to the school gates. 'That wasn't too bad, was it?'

'It was awful. And I don't mean the music.' Philip glanced at Jill who was walking on the other side of him and added gruffly, 'Thanks for coming.'

She smiled up at him. 'It'll blow over. Anyway, most people know better than to take much notice of the rubbish in the *Empire Lion*.'

'Just what I said,' Charlotte pointed out. 'Things will seem much better in the morning.'

The three of them turned out of the drive. There were lines of cars on both sides of the Narth Road. The Wemyss-Browns had been among the latecomers, and had been unable to park in the school grounds. They walked up the road to where the Rover was parked. Philip unlocked the doors on the passenger side.

'You've got a flat tyre,' Jill said, pointing to the rear nearside wheel.

'Damn.' Philip went round to the boot. 'I'd better change it. It'll take a while — you two could walk home, if you want, or perhaps someone will give you a lift.'

'Philip,' Charlotte said quietly. 'I think the tyre at the front is flat as well.'

Like children playing a following game, the three of them walked in silence round the car. All four tyres were flat. Wavering capitals straggled across the Rover's windscreen, clearly visible in the light from the streetlamp. KILL RED BASTARD.

Charlotte touched one of the letters and examined her fingertip. 'I think it's lipstick,' she said, taking her husband's hand. 'How very vulgar.'

Chapter Thirty-Seven

In the dream she was singing. Howard wasn't sure what. In the dream, he had tried not to listen, just as in life. But now, edging towards consciousness, he tried to remember the song, because if he thought about that he couldn't think about the rest of the dream.

Something from one of those shows she was always going on about. Probably *Oklahoma*, her favourite. She had been the sort of girl who thought that life should imitate the plot of a musical. In a sense, that was where the trouble started.

In the dream, he was trying to kiss her, but she kept turning away her head because she didn't want to stop singing. Her body twisted and turned in his arms, slippery as a fish. Why wouldn't she stay still? Why wouldn't she stop singing? It was an insult to him, an insult to the urgency of his desire. In the end, he'd lost his temper, but that led to a different problem, and somehow the insult had turned to humiliation. And then—

Now Howard was wide awake, sweating in Mr Portleigh's pyjamas, buried under Mrs Portleigh's bedclothes. When he groped for the light switch, his hand knocked over the glass that had held whisky. He heard it shatter on the floor. The light blinded him, and for a moment he cowered under the eiderdown. Cautiously he pushed his head into the light and squinted at the clock. Not yet three. He hated this time of morning when the world was asleep. It was the time when nothing made sense.

Howard sat up in bed and reached for his dressing gown. He wasn't a weakling, not like most people who let despair roll over them like a regiment of tanks. He flung off the bedclothes and climbed out of bed. He wondered whether to wake Phyllis and make her sweep up the broken glass. The only thing that stopped him was the knowledge that she would need to have it all explained to her at least five times before she understood what he wanted her to do. She could do it in the morning.

He draped Mr Portleigh's dressing gown over his shoulders, padded downstairs and went into the sitting room. There was a faint red glow from the fire. He switched on the lights — Mrs Portleigh had been a thrifty soul and had left the blackout curtains across the window, so there was no fear of the light being seen by nosy neighbours. He dropped a few lumps of coal on the fire, lit a cigarette and poured himself a small whisky.

Things could be worse. All the necessities of life were to hand. Not bad for a chap who a day or two ago hadn't even a roof over his head. He rolled the whisky round his mouth and imagined it scouring away everything he did not want to have. A flame flickered in the fireplace. He reached for a newspaper which was folded open on the table by the chair.

Idly he scanned the page. More casualties. Bloody fools. Nobody wanted another war. So why didn't we just drop a few bombs on them and leave it at that? That would teach them a lesson they wouldn't forget and then the rest of the world could get on with their lives. He yawned, rested the paper on the arm of the chair and took another sip of whisky. His eyes brushed across the newspaper and a name leapt off the page. He blinked and took another sip of whisky. The name was still there, in the middle of a dense column of black type.

Heather Parry, Heather Parry, Heather Parry.

He seized the paper. The name was mentioned in an interview with a local bigwig who'd just become a county councillor. The man was called Broadbent, and he droned on about what a terrible loss it had been for Heather's family, and how awful it was for them not to know whether she was alive or dead.

Awful for them? What about him?

The newspaper mentioned a madrigal concert at Heather's old school. The money it raised would be going towards a new music room for the school, together with donations from Heather's parents and old Broadbent. With sweat trickling down his neck, Howard read the rest of the article. They made Heather out to be some kind of saint. The police had re-opened the case and were making enquiries all over the country.

He lit another cigarette. He had assumed that by now Heather would be forgotten, and that he could therefore take his time over making the arrangements. Two more days here, and he would be fighting fit, ready for anything the world had to offer. He had planned to slip away on Sunday night, when Phyllis was asleep. He had already worked out most of what he was going to take with him — jewellery, mainly, and also cheque books and deposit books. There was other valuable stuff in the house, but most of it was too large and too heavy. He had considered getting Phyllis to hire a car for him so he could take more, but had discarded the idea as too risky. He had congratulated himself on his wisdom: most people in his position would be greedy, and that would be their downfall. Not him though: he was going to leave while the going was good.

That had been the plan — but now?

He looked at the clock — a quarter past three — and sat up sharply in the chair. Great generals adapted their tactics to suit the occasion. Who was it who said that? Napoleon? It was quite simple: he'd divide the operation into two. He *would* leave

Lydmouth on Sunday, just as planned, catching the milk train with a suitcase full of souvenirs. Phyllis wouldn't dare report him and he could start a new life with an easy conscience.

But he would handle Heather tonight. Now he came to think of it, that would be a much better idea, because dealing with Heather might be a messy job and he'd need to tidy himself up afterwards. Maybe that article in the *Gazette* had been a blessing in disguise.

Howard finished the whisky and went upstairs to get dressed. Mr Portleigh provided him with shirt, jersey and underwear; he wore his own trousers. In Mrs Portleigh's wardrobe he found a hat with a half-veil stretching below his nose. He tried it on and admired himself in the mirror. He chuckled: no two ways about it, the hat was a stroke of genius.

He went downstairs and assembled what he wanted to take with him in a canvas bag which would go over his shoulder: cigarettes and matches, an Ordnance Survey map of the area from Mr Portleigh's study, a torch, candles, matches, a penknife and a trowel. He examined the coats, which were kept in a lobby by the side door and settled on a tweed overcoat which must have belonged to Mrs Portleigh. It would go with the hat. He wanted the coat for warmth, and he reasoned that the hat would mislead anyone who might see him from a distance. His fingers fumbled as he did up the buttons on the unfamiliar left-hand side. Finally he pulled on a pair of Wellington boots.

He left the house by the back door. Apart from a brief reconnaissance before going to bed, it was the first time he'd been outside since leaving the woodshed and meeting Mrs Portleigh. The night was still but the air had a cutting chill. Stars glittered in a black sky. He shivered, and only partly from cold.

He skirted the house and walked down the grass verge of the drive towards the open gates. He had calculated that at this time of night it would be safe to walk directly to the building site on the other side of the main road rather than trek through the spinney and over the fields as he had done when he arrived on Wednesday morning. Feeling uncomfortably exposed, Howard walked rapidly along the green. A lorry travelling north forced him to dive into a neighbour's drive. Standing there in the darkness, his heart pounding with exercise and adrenaline, he wondered if he should turn back. He fought the temptation, knowing that his logic was sound. Only a coward would stop now and he was not a coward.

The rumble of the lorry died away. Howard scurried across the main road and into the shelter of the building site. A moment later he reached the footpath that had brought him up from the river. Here he felt justified in using the torch, though he was careful to keep the beam down. The path was lower than the surrounding fields and further enclosed by high hedges. He followed it downhill, stumbling occasionally and listening intently for other sounds. His footsteps and his breathing sounded unnaturally loud. Once he glanced up at the sky but quickly looked away, diminished by the cold, remote brilliance of the stars.

Gradually the path levelled out. The exercise was making him sweat. He was approaching the outskirts of Lydmouth. On the right the fields had given way to allotments. Suddenly – before he expected – he reached the towpath along the river. He stood still for a moment, listening to the silence. The only way he could cross the river was by the New Bridge. That meant streetlamps and a far higher risk of running into a patrolling constable.

Howard slid like a shadow along the towpath. On his left, the Lyd ran black and gleaming towards the sea. Near the bridge, puddles of light were reflected in the water. There were lights in the station and in the coal yard beside it. The important thing was that nobody was in sight. Nothing moved – not even a cat, not even a car. He sucked in a mouthful of air and left the shelter of the towpath. He scuttled over the bridge, the heavy bag banging against his hip, towards the welcoming darkness on the far side of the river.

Once across the bridge, he breathed more easily. But he was still on the main road, and traffic was always a possibility, even at this time of night. He forced his weary legs into a shambling run. He trotted past Farnock Lane and dived into the next opening on the left, the farm track that led behind Farnock Camp. Ten minutes later, he reached the ruined guardhouse where – in what seemed like another life – he had encountered that damned nosy parker.

He pushed aside the memory. But other memories forced their way into his mind. This was the way he had brought Heather on that last afternoon. It had been a warm spring, that year, and in his memory there was money in his pocket, the girl hanging on to his arm, and the sun shone from dawn to dusk. For a while, everything had been perfect.

They had crossed the stile opposite the guardhouse and followed the path up a field strewn with stones and sheep. Heather ran ahead towards the forest, her skirt floating and swinging in the air. He followed, with her bag slung over his shoulder. She looked back, smiling.

Just you wait, you little tease.

As they reached the shade of the trees she had started singing, looking at him, expecting applause. He had forced himself to smile and say, 'When we get to London, this friend of mine just won't be able to believe his ears.' He had been rather proud of this invention: the friend was a theatrical impresario planning to put on a new musical. The girl danced in the dappled sunshine under the leaves. They were going to say goodbye to their special place and then, in the evening, they would leave for London. They would travel separately, to avoid problems, and meet in the buffet at Paddington Station. That was what Heather thought, anyway.

Bye, bye, Heather.

Now it was night. The trees closed around him. So did

the darkness, thick and suffocating. It was not long before he realised that he had not made enough allowance for the darkness and for the passage of time. In his memory, the little clearing where they used to meet had only been a matter of twenty or thirty yards from the field. The ground rose steadily upwards, and the clearing was a shallow bowl scooped into the slope. On the upper rim of the bowl stood a great beech tree whose leaves sheltered the bowl like a green canopy.

Howard stumbled among the trees, pausing to listen to the sound of his breathing and the rustle of invisible leaves, and to peer into the blackness around him. At last he stopped, crouched and lit a cigarette. Soon it would be dawn. He couldn't afford to take too long. He tried to empty his mind of everything except the warm harsh flavour of the cigarette. When he had finished, he tossed away the butt, watching its glowing tip drop away into the darkness.

Dropping and dropping, disappearing into darkness below his feet ...

Suddenly galvanised, Howard scrambled up. His feet crunched on a soft carpet of husks from the beech nuts. The tree itself was a huge shadow a few yards to his left, towering over the clearing. Awkward in coat and boots, he scrambled down to the place where they had been together. Suddenly he did not know whether to be glad or afraid.

His breath was coming in shallow gasps. He turned on the torch, its beam yellow and puny in the immensity of the surrounding darkness. There was the green-grey trunk of the beech – the roots that splayed out from the base like arthritic serpents – and, to the left of the tree a jumble of irregular stones, perhaps the spoil from an abandoned quarry. He took a few steps to the left. The torchlight slithered across the ground and into a recess not much larger than a double bed. At the bottom of the recess was a thick layer of leaves left over from the previous autumn. Just as there had been before.

'Look!' Heather had said. 'Aren't the colours pretty? It's like a fairy carpet.'

At the back of the recess was the opening, narrower than he had remembered, a diagonal slit between two rocks with its upper end masked by one of the trailing roots of the beech. Inside was a narrow passageway between two layers of rock. Heather — showing off her education, as usual — had said it was probably a small mine, hundreds of years old, where men with candlesticks in their mouths had scrabbled for iron ore and prayed that the hill would not collapse on top of them. Howard swallowed, his mouth dry, remembering how difficult it had been to drag her suddenly heavy but still warm body into the tiny gap between the rocks. Then he had to go back with her bag and throw that on top of her.

He bent down and shone the torch inside. All he could see was grey-pink rock and a layer of fine dry earth. How far had he dragged her in? At the time he had been in the grip of an emotion so powerful that his memory of what had actually happened was warped and patchy. What he remembered most clearly was how angry he had been with that stupid girl, and how scared.

He removed his hat and coat. He crawled inside, taking his weight mainly on his knees and his elbows. The torchlight wavered in front of him. The air was cool and smelled foul. Then he saw her.

Her? In one sense it was no more Heather Parry than he was. What he had assumed was a knob of rock half buried in the earth was a bone. Beside it was the remains of a sandal, the buckle rusted, the leather coated with dust. Howard forced himself to crawl further, round a bulge in the rock. Before he realised it, he was on top of her, just as he had been before. History was repeating itself and he wanted to scream. Something shifted beneath his weight. For an instant he expected cold arms to circle his neck. He screamed, and the sound emerged as a sob.

He had spread his coat over the bed of leaves and they had been lying in the sunshine, kissing and talking about what she would do when they reached London. It was his last chance because he could not risk staying longer in Lydmouth. He had been determined that this was the day when he would break down her defences. In a way, he had succeeded, though not in the way he had expected. She had drawn away a few inches, wanting to hum a melody — one of her more irritating features was that she believed herself to be capable of writing for musicals, as well as starring in them.

'Listen, Johnny, listen.'

He had pinned her down, half playfully, half as a show of force. Sometimes you had to be firm with women, sometimes you had to show them who was boss.

'*Johnny* — stop it ...'

He had squeezed her breasts but then she had started crying out and he had to use that hand to cover her mouth. Her struggles excited him. With his other hand, he pushed up her thin cotton dress. He had his knees between her legs now, forcing them apart. He unbuttoned himself, and then — then the worst had happened. His penis was flabby and shrivelled, though a moment earlier it had been pressing urgently against his trousers. It was all the fault of the girl and her bloody singing.

Heather couldn't say anything because his hand was still over her mouth. But he knew that she would tell everyone. They'd throw him in prison and laugh at him because he couldn't even do it to her properly. His anger at the unfairness bubbled over. The blood thundered in his head. He knelt on Heather's thighs, just below the pelvis, grabbed her throat with his free hand and shook her, trying to punish her for what she had done and what she would do. She made matters worse by fighting him. The silly bitch writhed like a landed fish, almost dislodging him. He squeezed her throat and banged her head against the rocks.

Have to teach her a lesson, teach her a lesson.

And then there had been nothing more to do except try to

hide her, and to get back to town and pray that no one had seen them together. He left Lydmouth that evening, just as he had planned. Ever since that day he had worried about Heather's body in the crack in the rocks. Anyone might stumble on her. Worse still, anyone might find her bag.

In his hurry to get away, he had made a mistake that might still prove fatal: he had not searched her bag. He was almost sure that she would have brought the two notes he had written her on the Bull Hotel's letterhead. They would be as good as a signed confession.

It was time to do what was necessary. He examined his surroundings with the torch. There was so little room in this crack in the rock that now he was as close to Heather Parry as he had ever been. Except it was hardly Heather Parry any more. Time and animals had seen to that. The dress was now brown, rotted and torn. There were bones – larger ones mainly – and a dusty mound that must be the bag. But there was little else, apart from an unpleasant smell which might or might not relate to what had once been Heather Parry. Howard reached out a hand and with a sense of wonder touched the dome of the skull. How could so much have gone so quickly? It was like magic.

He stirred, and there was the chink of metal on rock. He pointed the torch in the direction of the sound. Heather's wristwatch – a present on her last birthday; she had been absurdly proud of it. He'd been a fool to leave it on her wrist. The wrist had gone now, but the watch was still there, and still might help someone identify the bones. He picked it up and thrust it deep in the pocket of his trousers. He would bury it somewhere else in the Forest.

He seized the handle of her bag and crawled backwards into the fresh air. The zip had rusted shut. He used the penknife to rip a hole in the side. Inside he found clothes, a sponge bag, a pair of shoes and a towel. At the bottom was a small leather folder. Inside were his letters, a ration book, a Post Office Savings Book containing more than £27, and a gold bracelet he had given her. Smiling, he stuffed the folder and its contents in the pocket of Mrs Portleigh's overcoat.

But there was still work to be done. Carrying the trowel, Howard forced himself back into the hole. For a while time lost its meaning. With the help of the trowel, he gathered all that remained of Heather Parry into an untidy heap and pushed it deeper and deeper into the rocky passage.

He lit a candle to supplement the torch and the flame burned steadily which at least meant there was a supply of fresh air. Deeper and deeper he pushed his bundle into the rock. The further she went in, the safer he would be. The only sounds were his breathing and the scrape of bones and rock and metal. One more push would do it, one more shove: with a grunt, Howard thrust himself forward as if into a woman and found that he could not move.

He was wedged in the rock, a filling in a stone sandwich. He tried to tug himself back but the rocks seemed to clamp down on him. It was as though he were trapped in a vast mouth whose jaws were closing. Sweat streamed off him. He wanted to scream. He fought panic as hard as he'd ever fought anything in his life. He would not die here with Heather Parry. He was worth more than this.

Sobbing, Howard concentrated all his strength into trying to slither backwards. He wriggled to his left, then to his right, then to his left again. Something feathery brushed against his face. A cobweb? A lock of Heather's hair? He lay still. Tears ran down his cheeks, tasting of salt and childhood. It was so unfair. He had come so far, done so much, and now he was dying.

With a spasm of rage, he tensed his body and twisted it like a cork in the neck of a bottle. His jersey caught on something and he heard it rip. Rock scraped the knuckles of his right hand and he squealed with pain.

But he was moving.

He felt cooler air on the skin of his exposed ankles. Part of him was outside. A moment later, he was safe, gulping down lungfuls of night air, huddled against the roots of the beech.

The cow can't hurt me now.

To the east, the sky was perceptibly less black than elsewhere. Howard foraged for his cigarettes.

Safe at last.

Suddenly he stopped, a cigarette halfway to his mouth. He could hear something. The sounds grew steadily louder. Somewhere beyond the trees, headlights pricked the darkness. Along the road below came the rumble of many engines. A man was shouting orders, the words unintelligible.

Howard stood still, listening and shivering. So he wasn't safe at all. The army had cut off his retreat.

Chapter Thirty-Eight

Richard Thornhill lay in bed listening to the ticking of the alarm clock and watching the darkness fading as dawn approached. He turned his head on the pillow, trying to read the time.

Edith stirred. 'Are you all right?'

'Fine, thanks.' He glanced at her face, a pale blur.

'Can't you sleep? Is it the case?'

'Yes,' he lied. 'I'll just go to the lavatory.'

When he returned to their bedroom, Edith turned towards him as he slid into bed. 'I've not been sleeping very well, either. Too excited, I suppose. Isn't it silly?'

'Not at all.'

'It was going out with Uncle Bernard. We don't get out much, do we? It was a nice concert, too. And those lovely flowers they gave me. So sweet.'

He knew she was smiling from the tone of her voice. 'I hope it won't be a problem.'

'Why should it be?'

'Since Bernard's a councillor and I'm a police officer. Do you think he might ask you again?'

'I should think it's quite likely. Anyway, there's no need to worry. Mr Hendry was at the concert, too, and he came over and had quite a chat with us. He's very nice, isn't he?'

She sounded so cheerful that Thornhill bit back the obvious

comment: that the Chief Constable was always nice to county councillors. The bed creaked as she edged closer to him. He felt her hand come to rest on his leg.

'You've been very good to me, Richard. I know it's not easy, with Uncle Bernard being a councillor, and then you've had to deal with me and Mother's money, and on top of that you've got this horrible case.' The hand stroked his leg and moved higher. 'I do love you.'

Edith wrapped her arms around him and drew him towards her. They kissed. He stroked her back and then her breasts. She gave his thigh a perfunctory pat and then rolled on to her back, waiting for him. She preferred sex to be brief, and Richard to take the active role. But his body refused to cooperate. He kissed her again and ran his hands over her body and between her legs. Still nothing. After a moment or two, he pulled away from her.

'I'm sorry,' he muttered.

'Never mind. It's the wrong time – what with the case and everything. It doesn't matter. It's nice just to have a cuddle.'

'You're right, darling.' The endearment sounded strange to him, like a word from a foreign language. 'I can't get this wretched case out of my mind. I think it's on the verge of breaking.'

She drew herself closer to him again, her arms warm and heavy. Why did she have to be so nice about it? She stroked him as though he were a fretful child and he tried not to feel irritated by her touch. A blackbird sang outside the window.

'I think I might as well get up.' He kissed her cheek and slipped out of bed. 'Try and go back to sleep.'

'What are you going to do?'

'Go down to the station.'

Edith sat up and switched on her bedside light. 'You're not going out without a proper breakfast.'

'There's no need.'

'Yes there is.'

He would have preferred to be alone, but he could not find a way to say this without hurting her feelings. He shaved while his bath was running, listening to the clatter of the frying pan in the kitchen below. Perhaps Edith had her own guilt to expiate – for enjoying her brief role as a VIP yesterday evening, for buying herself a new blouse, for insisting she had a right to decide how to spend the money her mother had left her. Perhaps she wanted to cook his breakfast at this godforsaken hour of the morning out of simple love for him and that was even worse.

She cooked him bacon and eggs, fried tomatoes and fried bread. While he ate, she brushed his hat and coat, and then returned to refill his cup and pass him the butter and the marmalade. He would have liked to make conversation but could think of nothing to say. It was a relief to say goodbye with a peck on the cheek.

Outside it was a gleaming spring morning, green and cold. Thornhill drove slowly through the town, seeing no one but a milkman. On impulse, he made a diversion which took him past St John's and then down Church Street. The windows of Jill's cottage were curtained. What had he expected? To see her waving at him as he passed?

A few minutes later, he left the Austin in the car park behind the Police Headquarters. He found Brian Kirby yawning at his desk in the CID office. His tie was loose and the ashtray in front of him was full to overflowing. Thornhill pulled over a chair and sat down.

'What's the verdict? Have we got him or not?'

Kirby winced, shaking out yet another cigarette from his packet. 'We have and we haven't, if you know what I mean.' He ran his fingers through his hair, usually well-greased and gleaming but now spiky and furrowed after a night full of head-scratching. 'He's a slippery bastard, that one.'

'So he's not admitting anything?'

Kirby shook his head. 'Nothing important. He admits

stealing the eggs and locking Porter in Mrs Veale's barn. But that's about as far as it goes. He didn't have any choice on that – because of the fingerprint evidence. But he's not giving away anything else. He even denies nicking the tools. He still says he bought them in good faith in the King's Head.'

'All right then. What about his movements on Tuesday night?'

'He left the camp at about six o'clock. He admits that his wife told him about Rowse's visit. He's vague about his movements. Says he just walked around for an hour or so. Can't remember where. But somewhere between eight and nine, he turned up in the King's Head. I talked to Mrs Halleran – she remembers seeing him there, but can't remember him talking to anyone.'

'And then?'

'Coalway says he went home to bed. Didn't see anyone, didn't talk to anyone, either on the way home or at the camp.'

'Apart from Norah?'

'For what it's worth. I've not talked to her yet.' He yawned. 'We drew a blank at Farnock Camp as well – if he was hiding stolen goods there, we couldn't find them. But I've asked the army to let us know if anything turns up.'

'Have they moved back in?'

'During the night.' Kirby pulled a sheet of paper on to the blotter. 'Talking of the army, I did manage to trace Coalway's former CO – man named Hallboy, lives near Cirencester. Coalway was in the Glosters at the tail end of the war and the beginning of the peace. He spent a lot of his time in the glasshouse.' Kirby hesitated, licking his lips. 'It seems he was fond of using his fists when he'd had a drink or two.'

'What about his politics?'

'Hallboy didn't know he had any.' Kirby grimaced. 'I got the impression he rather liked Coalway.' His voice became an upper-class parody: 'Bit of a rogue, cheeky blighter, too, but one's seen worse.'

Thornhill sighed. 'It comes down to the knife.'

'That's the trouble. The lab's just phoned through the report. It could have been the knife tha was killed Rowse. But there are no useable prints apart from Coalway's. The handle's not a particularly good surface. There were smudges, yes, and fragments of old prints, but nothing else they could identify.'

'And the blood?'

'It's human. That's something, I suppose. And it's O Rhesus Positive, just like Rowse's. But it's also just like half the bloody human race's.'

'How does Coalway explain having the knife?'

'Said he'd found it on the river bank.' Kirby scowled. 'He was having a stroll, he says, on Thursday morning. And there it was: wrapped in the rag, in a bit of long grass by the riverside.' The scowl intensified. 'About fifty yards from the Bathurst Arms.'

'What do you think happened?'

'I reckon he did it,' Kirby said harshly. 'Maybe he didn't mean to kill Rowse, but I think he meant to frighten him. Maybe Norah put him up to it. Then it all went wrong — there was a struggle — and the next thing he knows Rowse is lying dead at his feet. So he grabs the camera and the notebook and gets out.'

'What did he do with the notebook and the camera?'

'Burns the notebook, buries the camera, maybe? He had plenty of opportunity to do that.'

'In that case, why didn't he get rid of the knife as well?'

'People don't act logically. Not if they're full of beer and they've just killed someone.'

Thornhill stood up. 'It's not enough.'

'Means, motive and opportunity, sir. Record of past violence.'

'It's all circumstantial. We need someone to have seen him

at the Bathurst Arms late on Tuesday night. Something to tie him in with the time and place.'

'The knife ties him in with the place. It's got to be him, sir. If it isn't him, who is it?'

Thornhill hesitated. 'You could make out a pretty strong case against Wemyss-Brown. His cigarette lighter was there, after all. Or even against Norah Coalway.'

'If Sid Coalway confessed,' Kirby said slowly. 'Well . . .'

'That would be different,' Thornhill said. He stared at his sergeant, wondering just how far Brian Kirby would go to secure a conviction if he believed it was well deserved. 'It would have to satisfy me,' he added softly, 'as well as the court.'

Chapter Thirty-Nine

Thornhill went into his office and made a start on the mound of paperwork in his in-tray. He worked steadily for a couple of hours. There was a tap on the door and Kirby came in.

'Still here?' Thornhill said.

'I thought I'd better let you know, sir. Norah Coalway's downstairs. Making a nuisance of herself. I'll go and—'

'No. I will.' Thornhill capped his fountain pen and stood up. 'Go and have a few hours' sleep, Brian.'

Kirby looked at him and then rubbed red-rimmed eyes. 'You're the boss.'

Thornhill heard Norah Coalway before he saw her. '. . . he's only in here because he hasn't got any money. You can say what you like, Jim Fowles, there's one law for the rich and another for the poor. Do you know what I heard? They found a cigarette lighter under that man Rowse's body. And the lighter belongs to a very important person in Lydmouth. But has he been charged? Has he bloody hell. But my Sid, well – he's a different—'

She broke off as Thornhill appeared. His face pink, Fowles glanced at him with imploring eyes. Norah was leaning on the counter. On either side of her she had placed her daughters, with a fine eye to effect. The girls were sitting on the counter with their backs to

Fowles, apparently oblivious to what was going on around them.

'You, there,' Norah said, catching sight of Thornhill. 'Mr What's-your-name. It's all your fault. Couldn't even do the dirty work yourself, could you?'

'I'm glad to see you, Mrs Coalway.' Thornhill smiled at her and opened the flap of the counter. 'I wanted to have a word so you've saved me a journey. You'll have a cup of tea now you're here, won't you?'

She frowned at him, and one of the little girls – Marge? – peered over her shoulder at him, two fingers of her right hand deep in her mouth and the grubby teddy bear clutched to her chest.

'I'm sure we can find someone to look after the children while we talk. Sergeant, would you see if WPC Ailsmore is –?'

'No one's taking the kids away from me. They go where I go.'

Thornhill nodded. 'Of course.'

Fowles cleared his throat. 'There's no one in the interview rooms at present, sir.'

An interview room had bars on the window, a smell of sweat and old cigarettes, a scarred metal table bolted to the floor and a Judas hole in the door. Thornhill said: 'Let's go to the Gardenia, Mrs Coalway. It's a little further, but they do a much nicer cup of tea than we can manage. And perhaps the children might like something to eat?'

Norah opened her mouth, then closed it again. Thornhill was already on her side of the counter. Beside Norah stood a rusty pushchair of antique design with a shopping bag full of potatoes attached to it.

Norah found her voice at last. 'I've got a lot to do this morning. I—'

'So have I,' Thornhill said. 'Now, which of these young ladies is going to ride in the pushchair?'

Norah shrugged and gave way. A moment later, she and

Thornhill were walking down the High Street, with Thornhill in charge of the pushchair containing the smaller child, while Norah towed Marge along rather more quickly than Marge wanted. In the Gardenia, which had just opened, Thornhill tactfully ascertained that none of the Coalways had had any breakfast. He encouraged them to order what they wanted.

'And who's paying for all this? That's what I want to know.'

'We are, Mrs Coalway.' Thornhill wondered how this item was going to look on his expenses claim.

Norah sniffed, her face was bleak. They were attracting one or two curious glances in the café – particularly from two women at the window table; Thornhill was almost sure they worked at the *Gazette*. The waitress had been ready to be awkward about the pushchair – 'I'm not leaving it outside,' Norah had said. 'There's a lot of light-fingered people in this town' – but then the waitress had recognised Thornhill, and her opposition had melted away. Thornhill had noticed that their order arrived with remarkable promptness, and wondered whether this was because of the Coalways or himself.

When the children were deep in buttered toast, Thornhill said, 'Mr Coalway's fine. Or so my sergeant says. I've not seen him yet this morning.'

Her eyes flashed at him over her teacup. 'What's he charged with, then?'

'We don't know yet.'

'And all for nicking a few eggs to feed your kiddies?'

Thornhill said nothing.

'Have you got kids, Mr Thornhill?'

'Two. A little older than yours.'

'And if they were going hungry, would you steal for them?'

'This won't get us anywhere, Mrs Coalway.'

'Yes, but would you?'

He looked across the table at her. She was about the same

age as Jill. He tried to imagine what she might have looked like if she had had the same sort of life as Jill. He said: 'Yes.'

She waited for him to qualify what he had said, but when he didn't, she gave him the hint of a smile. She glanced at the children, and then said, choosing her words with care, 'Sid didn't do it, you know – that man Rowse I mean.'

'How do you know?'

'I know him.'

'I understand that when he was in the army—'

She stopped him with a wave of her hand. 'Yes, he had a few fights. He gets that way when he has a few drinks.' Unconsciously, she rubbed her cheek. 'He used to, anyway, when he was younger, but he's settled down now. He's a family man.'

'He had a few drinks on Tuesday night.'

'Yes,' she shot back, 'and then he came straight home to me.'

'And what time was this?'

She dropped another spoonful of sugar into her tea and stirred it slowly. 'I don't know. Somewhere between eleven and half past, probably.'

Thornhill said gently, 'A jury would think you were naturally biased.'

'You mean they wouldn't take my word. Just because I can't afford—'

'No, not because of that. Because you're married to Sidney. There'd be just the same problem if your husband happened to be the Prime Minister.'

Her mouth twisted in disbelief. 'Or Mr Wemyss-Brown, I suppose?'

Thornhill nodded, refusing to be drawn. 'There's the knife.'

'It's not Sid's,' she hissed. 'I've never seen it before.'

'He says he found it on the river bank near the Bathurst Arms. While you were – with us.'

Her weather-beaten face darkened. 'So it wasn't a plant?'

'Who would do that?'

Her lips twisted. 'Who do you think? One of your lot, of course.'

Thornhill stared at her for a moment, long enough to make her feel uncomfortable, to make her look away from his eyes. 'None of my officers would do a thing like that.'

'How can you be sure?'

'Because they wouldn't have a job if they tried anything like that.'

'You expect me to believe that?'

Thornhill shrugged. The children, alerted by the change of tone in the two adult voices, stared at their mother and, more warily, at Thornhill. Norah pushed a forkful of scrambled egg into her mouth.

'All right,' she said with her mouth full, 'perhaps I'm wrong. But you don't know what it can be like. And I bet there's a lot going on that you know nothing about.'

After a pause, Thornhill said, 'When your husband went out on Tuesday night, was he looking for Rowse?'

'Of course he wasn't. Why should he want to do that?' Norah's voice was rising in volume. 'What's this country coming to? Can't a man go out for a pint without—'

She broke off. The waitress was hovering beside Thornhill's chair. He glanced up at her.

'Mr Thornhill? There's a phone call for you.'

Thornhill excused himself and followed the waitress through the archway at the back of the café. The telephone was in a small office whose walls were covered with pictures of kittens. Thornhill picked up the phone.

'Sir?' It was Brian Kirby, who was meant to be off-duty. 'We've got a witness who saw Rowse and Coalway together on Tuesday night.'

Thornhill glanced at the door, making sure it was closed. 'Who?'

'His name's Henry Plantin. He works in the Reference Library. Hasn't been in since Tuesday evening, though – been at some librarians' conference in London. He'd heard there'd been a murder in Lydmouth, but this was the first time he'd seen a photograph of Rowse. And he recognised him: he came in the Reference Library on Tuesday evening. Wanted to see *Who's Who*. He probably wanted to look up Yateley. And that must be how he got Mrs Yateley's phone number.'

'Hold on – what time was this?'

'About six o'clock. Mr Plantin's fairly sure of that, because he'd just come back from his tea break.'

'And where does Coalway fit in?'

'He came in just after Rowse. Sat near him, too.'

'How did Plantin know it was Coalway?'

'The library had a problem with him last year. The kids took out some library books and didn't bring them back. So the library wrote to Mrs Coalway. Next thing they knew, Sid turned up drunk as a lord one afternoon and told them what they could do with their books.'

'Why haven't we heard of that before?'

'We weren't called in. The library sorted him out.' Kirby's disdain was evident from his voice. 'Soft-hearted lot.'

'And what happened on Tuesday evening?'

'Well, nothing actually *happened*, sir.' Kirby's tone had now become almost apologetic. 'Mr Plantin thought that Coalway might have been trying to see what Rowse was doing. Then Rowse left, and a moment later Coalway did too.'

'And was Coalway doing anything besides peeping at Rowse?'

'Reading a newspaper.' Kirby hesitated. 'It's another nail in his coffin, sir – whichever way you look at it.'

'Don't talk to Coalway about it yet.'

'But, sir—'

'I'll be back in five or ten minutes.'

Thornhill rang off and went back to the café. The children

had finished eating and were crouching beside the pushchair, feeding raw potatoes to their teddies; the carpet around the pushchair was now speckled with earth. Norah had poured herself another cup of tea and lit another cigarette. He sat down opposite her.

'And Sid wouldn't use a knife,' she said, as though there had been no interruption to their conversation. 'He'd punch someone in the gob, maybe, if he was drunk and he'd been provoked, but that's about it.'

Thornhill ignored this. 'When your husband got back on Tuesday afternoon, you must have told him about Rowse.'

She nodded. 'Everybody was talking about it.'

'Did you tell him that you weren't sure whether to trust him – that Miss Francis wasn't sure whether to trust him?'

She shrugged. 'I don't remember.'

'It would be strange if you hadn't.'

She glanced at him and her eyes flickered. 'Then maybe I did.'

'This isn't helping either of us, Mrs Coalway. Listen, for the sake of argument, let's say you did tell your husband about Rowse, and that you thought he might not be trustworthy. I think it's possible that you or Mr Coalway might have thought that it was a good idea to investigate Cameron Rowse. So perhaps your husband trailed him, found out something that confirmed your suspicions. Then he had a few drinks; we all need a bit of liquid courage, sometimes. Then he thought he'd go and talk to Rowse – and that's when it all went wrong. You used to work at the Bathurst Arms, so I expect Mr Coalway knew his way around. Maybe he slipped in the back door and went upstairs to the guest bedroom. Then Rowse comes upstairs, and he's had a few drinks too. And there's some sort of a quarrel, some sort of an accident, and then Rowse is lying on the floor.' Thornhill stared at Norah, who said nothing. 'So maybe he grabbed Rowse's camera and notebook – just in case they contained something which might cause you problems later. Did you know they were the only items we know were stolen from Rowse?'

'You sodding bastard,' she whispered, so faintly you could hardly hear the words.

'Someone saw your husband follow Rowse into the library earlier in the evening. And when Rowse left, your husband left, too.'

'I knew I shouldn't have trusted you.'

'Mrs Coalway, I'm not saying this is what happened. I'm only saying it could have happened like this, and that some people will believe it did.'

'But it didn't. For God's sake, I know Sid.'

Thornhill looked at her, and thought that if either of the Coalways had killed Rowse, it was far more likely to have been her. Norah had a determination, perhaps a ruthlessness, that her husband lacked, especially when the welfare of her family was concerned.

'If your husband didn't kill Rowse,' he said gently, 'the best way to defend him is to find out who did.'

'I don't know nothing.'

'Perhaps you don't. But at this stage we've no idea what's important and what isn't.'

She pulled the packet of Woodbines towards her, only to find that it was empty. 'There's nothing I can say,' she said with finality.

'Yes, there is. For a start, you can tell me about the man with the fish.'

Chapter Forty

Jane Alvington thought of the time before Gloria had come to the Bathurst Arms as a golden age, an Eden without the serpent. Jane's stepmother had always been inclined to flirt with the customers, particularly if they were rich or good looking or preferably both. Now Harold was dying, she was much worse. Gloria was like a bitch on heat, Jane thought; but it was more than that: she had her eye on securing a comfortable future for herself when Harold was dead.

Yesterday afternoon Gloria had returned from her driving lesson with Joe Vance in a state of ill-concealed excitement. Joe himself had come into the lounge bar later in the evening. Jane, in the intervals of serving in the public bar, had caught sight of them talking together, their heads very close; and every now and then Gloria threw back her head and laughed girlishly; and on other occasions she leant forward, her elbows on the bar counter to give Joe a better view of the wares in the shop window.

Jane hated Gloria. And now she hated Joe as well.

Last night, a tube of lipstick had had something to do with the laughter. Joe put it on the counter and Gloria opened it, laughed even harder and lobbed the tube into the wastepaper basket. Perhaps Gloria had dropped it in the car during her driving lesson (or whatever she called it). In that case why did the lipstick make Gloria laugh until the tears ran down her powdered cheeks, until her nose gleamed, until she was forced to retire to repair her make-up?

Love and hate are both obsessive. Jane had retrieved the lipstick when she was tidying up the bars before bed and examined it in the privacy of her room. It was Gloria's usual shade, scarlet, and it had been worn down almost as far as it would go. The stub had been flattened, and there was grime on it, as though it had been used to mark a dirty surface. Before she went to bed on Friday evening, Jane concealed the lipstick in the toe of an old sock and hid it at the back of her chest of drawers.

On Saturday morning, the mystery was solved by the woman who did most of the cooking at the Bathurst Arms. Her eldest boy was a police constable, and he had been on duty in Narth Road last night. Which was where he'd found Mr Wemyss-Brown standing beside his Rover after the concert at the High School. All the Rover's tyres had been slashed, and someone had written something very rude indeed across the windscreen in red lipstick.

Jane held Joe Vance's future in the palm of her hand, and she didn't know what to do with it. Then, just after ten o'clock on Saturday morning, Inspector Thornhill arrived. At the time, Jane was in the dining room sorting out cutlery. Gloria answered the door herself. Harold was dozing in the living room, which since last night had become his bedroom as well; they had moved his bed downstairs yesterday afternoon.

Jane heard Gloria and Thornhill talking as they passed the half-open door of the dining room. They went into the office near the kitchen, and the door closed behind them. Jane gave herself no time to think. She put down her handful of knives, left the room and slipped out of the back door. The office looked out into the yard but its window was closed. She slipped across the yard and into the outside lavatory. Suet dumpling, she thought, and felt tears pricking against her eyelids.

A few minutes later, when she had the tears under control, she went back into the dining room. She found Gloria standing by the window.

'I want a word with you, young lady.'

Jane felt herself blush, but she said nothing. She gathered up the knives and began to lay place settings.

'You've been telling tales out of school.' Gloria had drawn closer, and was standing almost at Jane's shoulder; her voice was low, but hard and cutting, very unlike the languorous drawl she used when she was speaking to men. 'Trying to make out I was in Rowse's room on Tuesday night, eh? Now listen, you fat little pudding, you'd better watch your step. If you're not careful, you're going to end up with nothing at all. And how do you think your dad's going to feel about all this? But you don't care about that, do you? Just looking after number one — that's you.'

Goaded, Jane swung round. 'I did see you.'

'Rubbish. You dreamed it. Anyway, who's going to believe you? You've never liked me since I married your pa. And now you're getting yourself all worked up about Joe Vance, not that he gives a toss about you.' Suddenly her eyes widened and slid away from Jane towards the doorway. 'Harold! You should be in your chair.'

Jane stared at her father, who was leaning against the jamb of the door. He looked from her to Gloria. 'I've had enough of you two squabbling,' he mumbled. 'I just came to tell you — I'm expecting a visitor at ten-thirty.'

Gloria stared at him. 'You never said. Who?'

'Shipston.'

'Shipston?' All the confidence and anger had drained from Gloria's face. Suddenly she looked fragile, almost ugly. 'The solicitor? Why's he coming?'

'He's bringing something for me to sign,' Harold said. 'My new will.'

Chapter Forty-One

Judging by the crumbs that had lodged in the folds of his bright yellow waistcoat, Mr Blaines had had quite a struggle with his breakfast. He took Jill into the coffee room, which as usual was empty.

'Thanks for dropping by, Miss Francis,' he said, waving to one of the sagging leather armchairs. 'Makes less fuss, you see. The last thing we want to do is make a fuss, eh? We've had quite enough of that already.'

Jill stared at the civil servant, wondering how someone could look and sound so unpleasant and yet radiate such unshakeable self-confidence. 'What will happen? Can you tell me?'

Blaines shrugged. 'It's not up to me. I'm just the messenger.'

'But you must be able to make an educated guess.'

Blaines shrugged again. Podgy fingers played with the creases of his trousers. 'You have to ask what's best, don't you? In general — not just for you or me or Mr Yateley.'

'Well, what is best?'

'One thing for sure: a scandal involving a member of the House of Commons isn't going to do anyone much good.' Blaines stared at the empty fireplace. 'All right, Yateley was a Communist when he was eighteen, but we all did things we'd like to forget when we were eighteen. From our point of view, the big question mark was all those holes in his life – and you've explained what he was up to then.'

'He's – he's good at his job.'

Blaines glanced at her. 'As an MP?'

She nodded.

'Public life, private life,' he went on, 'you can't always separate them, much as we'd like to.' He scratched his thigh. 'At least he's patched things up with his wife. They had a long telephone call last night. That'll please everyone. Communism's one thing, you know, but Communism and adultery leading to a messy divorce – well, that's quite another.'

'So you think it's all going to be hushed up?'

'Did I say that? I don't think, Miss Francis – I just do what I'm told. Put it this way: if anyone asks my opinion, I'll say I can't see any point in dragging all this out into the open. And that means what you and he were up to, as well as everything else.'

For a few seconds the room was silent apart from the scritch-scratch of Blaines's fingernails on his twill trousers.

Then Jill said: 'Thank you.'

Blaines stood up. 'He's driving me back to town. He's got someone to see in Whitehall. Then he'll be catching the train up to Yorkshire: see his missus. Do you want to say goodbye?'

'Not particularly.' Jill stood up. 'I must get back to the office.'

Blaines opened the door. Instead of holding it open for her, he went through first; he was that sort of man. Jill followed him into the hall. To her horror, Oliver Yateley was standing by the reception counter watching Quale, who was staggering down the stairs with a suitcase in either hand. She wondered whether Blaines had somehow arranged this meeting, for sinister purposes of his own.

Yateley saw Jill and smiled. 'Come to say goodbye? That's kind.'

Jill held out her hand. 'I hope everything goes well with you.'

They shook hands, and then stood back to allow Quale to pass between them on his way to the Humber, which was still parked in the yard. Blaines leant against the wall and lit a cigarette, blatantly eavesdropping.

'Thanks for everything,' Oliver said in the voice she associated with intimate murmurs across candlelit tables.

She shook her head, rejecting the thanks, rejecting everything that Oliver had to offer, past, present and future. 'Goodbye.'

The saddest thing of all was that they had nothing left to say to each other. Why on earth had she been willing to sacrifice her job and her reputation for a man to whom she had nothing to say?

She shook hands with Blaines. The two men followed Quale into the yard. As Oliver disappeared, Jill felt suddenly weak, one burden had been lifted, one problem solved. But it wasn't simply relief: it was also fatigue. She glanced at the clock behind the reception counter: nearly eleven. The *Gazette* could do without her for twenty minutes. She went into the lounge, rang the bell and ordered coffee. It was a big room, but no one else was there; it was rather like having coffee in one corner of a field. She sat in a chair by the window, smoking a cigarette and leafing through a magazine. Afterwards she couldn't even remember which magazine. Now Oliver was out of the way, there was leisure to consider the Rowse case – or, more exactly, the effect the Rowse case was likely to have on Philip. She wondered whether the police could really think that Philip might have killed Rowse. To anyone who knew Philip the idea was absurd. But she knew that the police were not particularly interested in the slippery uncertainties of psychology and motive: they preferred hard evidence: fingerprints and eye witness testimony, handmade Turkish cigarettes and confessions that would stand up in court.

It was time to go back to the office. On the way she would

go home and find out if Alice was any nearer to becoming a mother. She paid her bill and went into the hall, drawing on her gloves. Quale leant over the counter towards her.

'Mr Broadbent and Mr Wemyss-Brown have just gone into the bar for a drink,' he murmured in a throaty whisper that brought to mind fetid bubbles emerging from the noisome depths of a black bog. Then, with great deliberation, Quale winked.

Jill smiled at him. 'Thank you for telling me.'

'Will you be joining them, Miss?'

'I wish I could.' Jill thought she knew what was happening: Quale and Broadbent were rallying behind Philip in his hour of need.

'You heard about what happened to Mr Wemyss-Brown's car?' Quale went on.

'I was with the Wemyss-Browns when they found out.'

'Terrible business.' Quale shook his head, suddenly as grim as a hanging judge. 'Mr Wemyss-Brown is such a nice gentleman too. Unlike some I could name.'

Quale's standards of gentility were as exacting as those of the College of Arms, though not identical in nature. Quale's criteria were a subtle blend of snobbery, moral judgement and self-interest. An excess in one department would often compensate for a shortfall in another. He was ruthless in applying his verdicts, but was often willing to revise them; circumstances, he was wont to say, altered cases. The circumstances in question were usually financial.

'Take that man from London,' Quale said, warming to his theme. 'As soon as I clapped eyes on him, that civil servant, I said to myself that's not the sort of guest that's going to reflect any credit to this establishment. Unlike Mr Yateley, I might say – very nice gentleman, indeed. With Mr Blaines, though, it was all do this and do that, and never a word of thanks.'

Nor, Jill guessed, a tip.

'That man Rowse – just the same. I took one look at his jacket, and I knew. Just like I knew with that man Simcox.'

'Who?'

'Before your time, Miss.' Quale propped himself on his elbows, settling down for what might be a long haul.

'Oh my goodness,' Jill said quickly, looking wildly at the clock behind Quale. 'Is that the time? I must fly.'

'I knew he was a wrong 'un. As soon as I saw the fish,' Quale was saying.

'I'd love to hear all about it,' Jill said. 'But—'

'Said he was a major, that's what he'd signed in as.'

At that moment, the telephone began to ring in the office behind the reception desk. Quale produced a sound from the back of his throat that sounded remarkably like a growl. Slowly, he turned away to answer it.

'What a pity. You must tell me next time, Mr Quale.'

Jill walked quickly out of the hotel, in case it proved to be a wrong number, and emerged into the sunlit High Street. It was not until she had almost reached the *Gazette* that what Quale had said sunk in.

As soon as I saw the fish . . .

She went upstairs. Because it was Saturday, few people were in the office. But she found Miss Gwyn-Thomas filing assiduously in her cubby hole outside Philip's room; even filing could be a form of love. She looked up as Jill came in.

'Mr Wemyss-Brown isn't here.' Miss Gwyn-Thomas added with calculated ambiguity, 'I'm afraid I can't tell you where he is.'

'Actually, it was you I was hoping to see. I wonder if you could tell me something.'

Miss Gwyn-Thomas fiddled with the protuberance on the end of her long thin nose, an unconscious gesture that usually denoted indecision, emotional turmoil or both. 'Well, Miss Francis — I'm not sure — what exactly did you want to know?'

'Does the name Simcox mean anything to you? A criminal of some sort, perhaps? Quale mentioned he'd been in Lydmouth about three years ago.'

'He was some sort of confidence trickster,' Miss Gwyn-Thomas admitted reluctantly. 'I think he put up at the Bull. Yes, it was about three years ago, now I come to think of it.' She shrugged. 'Anyway, you'll find all the details in the backfile.'

'I wondered if you knew when – a little more precisely, perhaps?'

'No.' Miss Gwyn-Thomas bowed her head over the filing cabinet once more. 'I'm afraid I can't help you there.'

Jill thanked her with the excessive politeness one used to those one disliked and went back downstairs. At the back of the building was another flight of stairs going down to the basement. This in all but name was a series of cellars with concrete floors. The largest of them had three walls lined with scuffed metal shelving, on which rested the only complete run of the *Lydmouth Gazette* in existence.

She switched on the unshaded light bulb. It was cold down here, and she was glad she had not yet taken off her coat. She glanced round the room. Mounds of yellowing paper surrounded her, stretching back to 1886 in the far left corner. People occasionally came down here to check a fact. But no one had tidied the place for decades. Many of the piles were askew, shreds of torn paper lay on the floor, and it looked as if an extended family of mice had been nesting in the decade before World War I.

Jill put her handbag on the scuffed deal table in the middle of the room and pushed back her cuffs. She worked back through the mounds to three years earlier, began with April, went back to March and finally found what she was looking for near the end of May. By this time, her hands were filthy and her fingers left smudges of old ink on whatever she touched, including the cuffs of her cream blouse and her pale beige skirt.

The first item was a short piece at the bottom left-hand corner of the front page. It mentioned that Major John Howard-Simcox had been arrested in Cardiff and charged with various offences committed during a visit to Lydmouth. The next day there was a report that police had successfully opposed an application for bail. Simcox had apparently stayed at the Bull Hotel for several weeks, run up a huge bill, and then decamped without paying for it. He had also left a number of other unpaid bills in the town.

Jill skimmed forward through the weeks until she came to the report of his trial.

'OFFICER' JAILED FOR FRAUDS

Howard John Simcox, of Bristol, was sentenced to three years' imprisonment at the County Quarter Sessions today for offences committed in Lydmouth earlier this year.

He was arrested in Cardiff, having left the Bull Hotel, Lydmouth, without paying his bill. He claimed to be suffering from amnesia, the result of a wartime wound.

Detective Sergeant Kirby told the court that Simcox had also run up large bills with several Lydmouth tradesmen. In total his debts amounted to over £250.

During his stay in Lydmouth, Simcox posed as 'Major John Howard-Simcox' and told stories of active service in the Commandos. It transpired that during the war he had been an army cook who had never risen above the rank of Lance Corporal and had never served outside the United Kingdom.

While sentencing Simcox, Mr Justice Rowlands commented, 'It is clear that you incurred these debts in the knowledge that you would not be able to pay them, and that you had no intention of ever doing so. A particularly despicable feature of your behaviour is your assumption of a military rank and record to which you are not entitled.'

No mention of the fish.

Jill's training reasserted itself. She took her notepad from her bag, turned back to the earlier reports and began to note down their dates and what they said. When she reached the first report, recording Simcox's arrest in Cardiff, her eye was caught by another item on the same page.

NO NEWS OF MISSING GIRL

There is still no news of Heather Parry (18), daughter of Mr and Mrs George Parry of Narth Road, Lydmouth, who has not been seen since 6 May. A police spokesman says that they are pursuing a number of leads, including the possibility that Heather may have gone to London.

Heather is in the Sixth Form at the Lydmouth High School for Girls and has won several awards for her singing. She hopes to train to be a teacher.

Mr Parry said, 'All we want is for our darling daughter to come back home. We think she may be staying away because she thinks that her mother and I will be cross with her. But we will welcome her back with open arms.

The stiff words rose from the dry paper and made Jill's eyes smart. She glimpsed the Parry parents across a chasm of three years: waiting and hoping, still believing in the possibility of a happy ending. She had seen Mr and Mrs Parry at the madrigal concert last night: two grey people with lined faces, wearing clothes that seemed slightly too large for them. Grief shrinks people.

Jill sat back in her chair, stretched and reached for her cigarettes. Heather Parry must have vanished at about the same time that Simcox decamped from Lydmouth. Coincidence? Simcox had been sentenced to three years in prison. It was possible that by now he had been released, assuming he hadn't got into further trouble while he was in prison.

It all came down to the fish. Could Quale's fish be the same as the fish that Rowse had mentioned at Farnock Camp? But in that case, you would have thought that Lydmouth was the last place that Simcox would return to. Even if Simcox had returned, though, he would hardly have killed Rowse to prevent the fact from being publicised. After all, he had been tried and convicted for his crimes; he had paid his debt to society. On the other hand, perhaps Rowse's death had not been murder, but some sort of violent accident.

An accident? Three stab wounds?

The possibilities collided with each other like a shower of meteors. Jill turned over another page on her pad and wrote: *ask Quale re fish.* She considered this for a moment, then added, *Ring Richard.* She stared at the words she had just written, aware that she was oddly reluctant to do either of these things. Both of them might open doors into the unknown. In the last few years she had had more than her fill of excitement and uncertainty.

Jill put the newspapers away and went upstairs into the reporters' room. As she had expected, it was empty. Her colleagues had either gone home or to the pub. She consulted the directory and dialled the number of the Bull Hotel. You couldn't spend your life shivering beside a closed door, afraid of what might lie on the other side.

'The Bull Hotel.'

'Mr Quale? This is Miss Francis. I wonder if you could help me.'

'Always glad to oblige, Miss.' In Quale's dictionary, help was loosely defined as a service for which one expected to be paid, either now or in the near future. 'Do you want a word with Mr Wemyss-Brown? Him and Mr Broadbent are still in the bar.'

'No, it's not that. When I was at the Bull this morning, you began to tell me about Simcox – the con man who stayed at the Bull a few years ago.'

'Ah yes, Miss. It's funny, though.'

'What is?'

'I don't recall mentioning he was a con-man.'

'I asked someone at the *Gazette*.' Jill was aware it was never wise to underestimate the power of Quale's native intelligence when his own interests were concerned. 'You said you knew he wasn't a gentleman as soon as you saw the fish. I just wondered what exactly you meant.'

There was a silence on the other end of the line. Then Quale said slowly, as though rationing his words: 'He had a tattoo of a fish on his right wrist. His jackets had long sleeves to cover it. I noticed it when he was signing the register. Why?'

'I'm not sure,' said Jill, which was true, though disingenuous. 'But I'm very grateful. Thank you, Mr Quale.'

She rang off and made a note about the fish tattoo on her pad. *The man with the fish.* She thought it was difficult, perhaps impossible, to remove a tattoo. She remembered the stories of those who had suffered in concentration camps during the war, the fortunate survivors left with a permanent memento of their experiences tattooed on their arms. Then she sighed, picked up the phone and rang Police Headquarters.

Chapter Forty-Two

Phyllis knew that Howard had gone to bed later than her, and with the bottle of whisky, so she was not surprised when he did not appear by nine o'clock.

She forced herself to eat a slice of toast and made another pot of tea, just to occupy her mind and her hands. One way or another, she knew, the situation could not endure. Friends and tradesmen would call at the house. There would be bills to be paid, cheques to be signed. People would wonder why she and Mrs Portleigh were not in church tomorrow. Mrs Portleigh's children might telephone at any moment and demand to talk to their mother.

There was also the point that nature itself was at this very moment adding another sort of urgency: Mrs Portleigh had been dead for over twenty-four hours. Even in the cool of the cellar, she would not stay as she was for much longer. Phyllis remembered a rat she had found decomposing in the woodshed a few weeks earlier and winced. Maggots – where on earth did they come from? She pushed aside her teacup.

Mechanically Phyllis followed her morning routine, so oddly altered now that Mrs Portleigh was no more and Howard had come back into her life. She relaid the fire in the sitting room, emptied ashtrays, tidied a newspaper which had been left on the floor and flicked a duster over the furniture. All the time, she strained her ears to hear the click of Mrs Portleigh's bedroom door.

Later, she tiptoed upstairs to make her bed and clean the bathroom. Then it was time to peel the potatoes for lunch. Howard was fond of potatoes. She was about to start when she heard the doorbell. She held on to the sink for support. With one hand over her heart, as though trying to prevent it from leaping out of her chest, she slipped into the hall. She could see a blurred silhouette through the stained glass that filled the upper half of the front door. She knew from experience that she would not be visible from the outside. The doorbell rang again. She felt a spurt of anger: the noise would wake Howard, and Howard was always nasty when he woke unexpectedly from a deep sleep.

Phyllis darted into the little morning room on the left. Suppose it was the police? Or Mrs Portleigh's son, who had his own key to the door? The morning room had a bay window and Phyllis sunk on her knees beside it and pushed the curtain just an inch away from the wall. The vicar was standing on the gravel path outside the front door and looking up at the house. As Phyllis watched, he turned and walked slowly down the drive, leaning heavily on his stick.

Shaking with relief, Phyllis went back into the kitchen. She expected Howard to emerge at any moment, probably in a foul temper. She peeled another potato, then another, and another. Soon the saucepan was full.

Still no Howard. How very odd.

She gathered up the potato peelings into a colander and went through the scullery to the back door. It was sunny outside, but surprisingly cold. She gulped the fresh air experimentally, as though it belonged to a strange planet on which she had just landed. It was only as she was returning from the compost heap that an anomaly, subconsciously registered, forced its way into her conscious mind: the back door had been neither locked nor bolted.

Phyllis sat down at the kitchen table. It might mean nothing at all. Though she was sure she had locked up before she went to bed, it was perfectly possible that Howard had gone out for a breath of fresh air. She had taken one of the sleeping pills, and fallen almost at once into a dark hole of sleep. If Howard had gone out, she would not have heard him. When he came back, he might well have forgotten to lock up. When he was drunk, his confidence in himself grew and his actual powers tended to decline. She did not think it likely that he would have stayed out – she knew that he was scared of being recognised, all the more so because of what had happened to Mrs Portleigh. What puzzled her more, however, was that he had still not come downstairs to find out who had been at the door.

Another quarter of an hour crawled by. It was now eleven o'clock. Phyllis went into the lobby by the side door where the coats, hats and boots were kept. It did not take her long to realise that Mrs Portleigh's tweed coat, the one she used to wear for winter gardening in times gone by, was no longer hanging on its usual peg.

So perhaps he *had* gone out. Even so, the absence of the coat didn't necessarily mean he was still outside.

Phyllis tiptoed upstairs again and paused to listen outside the door of Mrs Portleigh's room. Howard was now using Mrs Portleigh's bed, not the one in the dressing room next door, because he claimed that Mrs Portleigh's was much more comfortable. She bent down. The key was still in the lock. She examined the gap between door and jamb: the door was not locked. She rested her right ear against the crack and listened. No sound – only the chilly tickle of the draught against the delicate skin of the ear.

She straightened up and tried very hard to think logically about the situation. Either Howard was inside, but so fast asleep that he wouldn't hear if she opened the door, or he wasn't there at all, in which case there was no risk of him being cross if she disturbed him. She shut her eyes, screwing them tightly closed, took a deep breath and opened the door.

When she opened her eyes, Howard wasn't there. The bed looked as if he had slept in it at some point. The window was closed and the room smelled of stale cigarettes and whisky, and underlying those a sour masculine smell. There was a broken glass on the rug by the bed. Phyllis slipped like a ghost across the room to the open door of the dressing room beyond. That was empty, too.

He's gone.

She felt a stab of relief, as intense as a shooting pain. But the relief did not last. Her eyes lingered on the pile of clothes on a chair in front of the dressing table: most of them had belonged to Mr Portleigh, as had the razor which was on the dressing table, but Howard obviously intended to take them. She looked for the canvas knapsack Howard had brought from London and found it under the bed in the dressing room. He was coming back.

Phyllis looked up, suddenly afraid that she would find him looking at her from the doorway. It would be just like him to sneak back into the house and catch her here. She almost ran on to the landing and down the stairs. In the sitting room, she stood at the window staring down the drive at the green and the cottages beyond, sparkling in the spring sunshine. This was her chance, she felt, if only she knew what to do with it. With Howard gone, she had an opportunity to slip away from his control. Mrs Portleigh was waiting as patiently as a time bomb in the cellar. Howard would find a way to blame her for that, both for the death and for the fact they had not reported it. She began to walk round the sitting room, circumnavigating the sofa again and again, desperately hoping that if she walked far enough she might reach the answer to her problems.

At last she came to a decision: the one thing she couldn't do was stay here and wait for Howard. Nothing could be worse than that, even if they hanged her for killing Mrs Portleigh. She put on her coat and hat and went upstairs for her handbag. She looked around her bedroom, at her possessions, at the wardrobe that contained her clothes, at the chest of drawers. There was nothing here that she wanted to take with her. She didn't want anything in the world except not to be with Howard.

Phyllis went back downstairs. The front door was still locked and bolted. She left the house by the back door and locked it behind her. Why should she make things easy for Howard? She walked down the drive, across the green, and began to walk down the main road towards Lydmouth.

At first she walked quickly, but gradually her pace slowed. Tears were running down her cheeks, but they no longer seemed to matter. She had not troubled to do up her coat. Why bother? She thought of what might lie ahead, rather as one might try to guess what was going to happen in a film in which one was not particularly interested.

She might walk into the police station and sit there until someone asked her what she was doing. Or she might go to the station and catch a train. She could go to London and see Mother. Not that she wanted to – but it would be somewhere to go. Or she could simply walk and walk until something happened or failed to happen. Or she could find a bench and sit down. In theory these were choices which she could make, but in practice she knew that she had no control over anything, least of all her own life.

'I am thirty-eight,' Phyllis said aloud, 'and I don't care any more.'

Two women, chatting at the gate of one of the semi-detached houses along the road, looked oddly at her as she passed. She ignored them.

In the distance she saw the spire of St John's. On the left, beyond the river, the hills rose up to the forest. A train whistled. In the clear air, a plume of smoke was visible along the floor of the valley, marking the progress of the train.

There was a jolt. She had not been looking where she was going — she had stepped from the pavement down to the road itself. She walked on. A car hooted and a bicycle bell jangled. Then suddenly she had to stop.

A maroon car was in front of her. It formed a barrier. She could have walked round it, but she lacked the energy. So she stood there, staring down at the dusty bonnet, her arms dangling by her side. A door slammed. There were footsteps.

Ah well, so it's all over now. Phyllis wasn't sure what was over, but she knew that something was.

'What the bloody hell do you think you're doing?' Dr Bayswater said. 'Trying to kill yourself?'

Chapter Forty-Three

Sidney Coalway's misery was as obvious as an open wound.
The man was sitting in Interview Room No 2, leaning forward
with his elbows on the table, staring fixedly at the scarred metal
surface as though waiting for it to do something. He had not
combed his hair or shaved since yesterday. If humans and apes
were not separate species but simply different points on the
same continuum, then Sidney Coalway had crept a little closer
to the ape – and to a depressed ape at that.

Kirby got up as Thornhill came in and backed away from
the table so Thornhill could take his chair. Thornhill sat down
and pushed aside Kirby's ashtray. Kirby leant against the wall
behind Coalway's chair. Thornhill glanced at him and Kirby
gave an almost imperceptible nod. They were doing a variant
on the old double-act routine: Kirby had opened proceedings
as the hard man.

'It's looking bad, Sid,' Thornhill said gently. 'Don't
you agree?'

Coalway said nothing. The skin wrinkled round his eyes
as if he were trying not to cry.

'Let's look at what we've got, shall we? Mrs Coalway
admits that she told you about Cameron Rowse, and
about her suspicions that he wasn't quite what he said he
was. And—'

'She's lying,' Sidney interrupted, raising his head. 'No, she ain't – you've made her say that. Tricked her.'

Thornhill sighed. 'Just pretend I'm a jury, Sid. Pretend you're on the jury too. Do you think it's likely Norah *wouldn't* have told you? The whole camp must have been buzzing with the news. Rowse was going to do an article about you all – in the *Picture Post*, remember? – that's what he said. You'd have heard all about Rowse taking lots of photographs, making lots of notes, so he had the names and the faces of everyone at the camp. Everyone at the camp, Sid, except you.'

For the first time Coalway lifted his head and stared at Thornhill with bloodshot eyes. 'So? Maybe I did hear something. It's not a crime, is it?'

'Let's carry on with how the jury will see it. Next thing they'll hear is that you went out.'

'Is that a crime too?'

'During the early evening, Rowse went into the library. You followed him. You sat near him. Tried to see what he was doing.'

'I did not.'

'Come off it. You were recognised by a witness of very high standing – completely independent. The sort of witness that juries tend to believe. Then Rowse left, and you left soon after. We don't yet know what you did immediately after that. It's most likely that the jury will think you followed Rowse back to the Bathurst Arms, just to make sure that was where he was staying. Perhaps you were able to work out which was his room. You knew the layout, of course, because Norah used to work there when you were courting. Anyway, we know for sure you were in the King's Head in Mincing Lane for most of the rest of the evening. You drank quite a lot, we're told, and you didn't talk much. And then you left at closing time – half ten, in theory, almost certainly more like eleven, or even a little later. Where did you go then?'

'I went home.'

'Anyone see you?'

'Norah. She was awake when I got back to the camp. She'd swear to the time, can't have been later than —' Coalway's eyes flickered, as he made calculations with unaccustomed speed '— than a quarter-past eleven. Almost certainly earlier.'

'Shame no one else saw you. Because juries tend not to take too much note of what wives say about their husbands. You know that as well as I do.'

Thornhill paused, calculating that here was a good moment to allow Coalway to come to grips with the reality of his position. He was aware — and rather ashamed — of the fact that the phone call from Jill Francis was occupying far more of his thoughts than was proper. Nor was he thinking of what she had said for professional reasons. He was in unfamiliar territory, where private inclinations mingled unpredictably with professional obligations. He forced himself back to the job in hand.

'It's not an alibi that's going to cut much ice with our jury, Sid. All they know for sure is that you'd been following Rowse, you've got reason to suspect that he's not what he says he is, and that you've had a few drinks. And you know and I know what you're like when you've had a few drinks, Sid. We talked to your commanding officer. Remember him? Colonel Hallboy.'

Coalway shook his head slowly from side to side, a gesture that had more to do with despair than disagreement.

'The next thing the jury will hear is that Rowse is found stabbed in his room the following morning. It would have been easy for an outsider to gain access to that room late in the evening, via the back door from the yard at the Bathurst. The only things that appear to be missing are his camera and his notebook. I wonder what construction the jury will put on that. Finally, when police officers searched your room on Friday, what should they find but a knife wrapped in a blood-stained rag hidden on top of a wardrobe? The blood matches Rowse's blood group. As far as our forensic laboratory can judge, the blade could well have been the one that stabbed Rowse to death. And the only identifiable fingerprints on the knife are yours.'

Thornhill sat back and watched Coalway. Kirby rubbed the stubble on his chin and grinned; he had resisted Thornhill's attempts to send him home. Coalway ran grimy fingers through his hair, twisting and tugging the strands as though he were trying to pull them out. After a while he looked up at Thornhill.

'That's all very fine and dandy, Mr Inspector,' he said with a flash of his old swagger. 'The only problem is, that's not what happened. But you don't give a sod about that, do you? You're trying to fit me up. You think that because I'm—'

'That's enough, Coalway,' Thornhill said. 'What did you do with the camera and the notebook?'

'I never saw the bloody camera or the bloody notebook.'

'You certainly saw the notebook in the library – we know that.' It was a debating point, designed merely to throw Coalway a little further off-balance.

'But I didn't kill him.' Suddenly Coalway was on his feet, his arms flailing. 'I didn't kill him. Do I have to beat that into your bloody heads?'

Coalway advanced round the table, his arms flailing at the air as though he were trying to repel an attack of midges from all sides. Kirby put an armlock on him and Porter blundered into the room with the handcuffs. Coalway stared helplessly at Thornhill. His face puckered and flushed. He looked like a child when excitement proved too much and turned into a tantrum, a child in collision with grim-faced adult authority.

Like a child, Sidney Coalway glared at Thornhill. And like a child, his lip trembled and his eyes filled with tears.

Chapter Forty-Four

With a sigh of pure pleasure, Charlotte Wemyss-Brown closed the front door of Troy House and smiled at her reflection in the hall mirror. She hurried back to the drawing room and peered through the window, keeping well back so she could not be seen by anyone outside. She was just in time to see Lady Ruispidge and Mrs Sutton climbing into the Ruispidges' majestic pre-war Bentley, almost certainly the best known car in Lydmouth. It had been standing outside Troy House for the better part of an hour.

A butcher's boy cycled past. A curtain twitched on the other side of the road. A neighbour, towed along by his Airedale in the direction of Jubilee Park, stared at the car. It was all very satisfactory.

The Bentley drew away from the kerb. Charlotte loaded coffee cups on the tray. Philip had telephoned just before her guests left, to tell her that he would be lunching at the Bull with Bernard Broadbent; he also mentioned that he'd agreed to make a donation to the fund for the Heather Parry music room.

Charlotte hummed as she worked. Unlike Philip, she had lived in Lydmouth all her life. It was a place which made its own judgements. Yesterday, after the contents of the *Empire Lion* had become public knowledge, had been one of the most unpleasant times of her life, though she had been careful to conceal this from her husband. Today, however, she felt that Lydmouth had rallied round them in their time of trouble – not everyone, it was true, but people who counted.

Susan came in to collect the tray. 'How many for lunch?' she demanded.

'Just me. That was Philip on the phone – he's lunching at the Bull with Councillor Broadbent.'

'Now you tell me.' Susan paused at the door. 'Waste of a roast, isn't it? Still, there'll be a nice bit of ham for you to cut at for your supper. By the way, I got some more of that chutney Philip's so fond of.'

The doorbell rang.

'I'll answer it,' Charlotte said. 'You get rid of the tray.'

She followed Susan into the hall, waited until she was out of sight and opened the front door. On the doorstep was a young woman, rather plump, whom she had never seen before.

'Yes?' Charlotte said, noting the cheap shoes, the wrinkled stockings and the grubby coat that had clearly been made for someone else. Then she noticed that the woman – hardly more than a girl, really – had eyes which were swollen from weeping. Charlotte added, in what for her was a gentle voice, 'What do you want?'

'Mrs Wemyss-Brown . . . it's about your car . . .'

Charlotte frowned. 'What about it?'

'I know who did it.'

'You'd better come in.'

She held open the door. Once the girl was in the hall, Charlotte's instincts as a hostess revived themselves. She took her guest's coat and showed her into the drawing room.

'Who are you, dear?'

'Jane – Jane Alvington.'

Charlotte nodded. 'Of course. Your parents keep the Bathurst Arms, don't they?' The scene of Rowse's murder. Mental alarm bells were jangling; Charlotte was not the daughter and wife of newspaper editors for nothing. 'Do sit down.'

Jane perched on a chair. Charlotte sat opposite and looked expectantly at her visitor.

'The car?' Charlotte prompted. The memory of last night's outrage was still fresh in her mind.

The girl nodded dumbly. She started to say something, stopped and then fumbled at the catch of her handbag. Her lips and her hands were trembling. She produced a cheap lipstick and held it out to Charlotte.

'What's this?' Charlotte opened the lipstick. It was worn down to the base, and the stub was covered with a smear of dirt. But you could still make out the colour – rather a bright shade of red. She looked up at Jane. 'Was this the lipstick that was used –?'

'Yes,' Jane muttered. 'I – I heard them talking about it, afterwards. I . . .' Her voice trailed away and two tears ran down her cheeks. She sniffed moistly.

'Now, now, dear.' Charlotte handed her a clean handkerchief. 'Blow your nose.'

Jane obeyed. Charlotte lit a cigarette and waited for the girl to regain control of herself.

'If you tell me all about it,' Charlotte said, 'you'll feel much better.'

Jane's fingers tried to smooth out the damp handkerchief. 'I just don't know what to do, or who to tell, because they'll just say I'm lying, so what's the point. But I thought maybe you—'

'Quite right, dear,' Charlotte said. 'After all, it is our car. Now, you're obviously a sensible girl, and I want you to tell me exactly what happened, from the beginning.'

'I heard them talking in the bar last night,' Jane said slowly. 'Gloria, my stepmother, and – and Joe Vance.'

'Vance? The man who runs the garage?'

'Yes. He gave Gloria a driving lesson yesterday afternoon in my dad's car. And then he took the car back for servicing.'

Gloria Alvington, Charlotte thought, swiftly searching her memory for scraps of information: no better than she should be, by all accounts. Used to be the barmaid at the Bathurst Arms, and married the landlord when the first wife died.

'Joe came in for a drink late last night, and I heard him and Gloria laughing about something. He gave the lipstick back to her – I thought maybe she'd left it in Dad's car – but she looked inside the tube, and laughed even more. Then she threw it away. I didn't know what to think till this morning, when I heard what had happened to your car.'

Charlotte stared at the girl. 'But – but Vance always seemed such an obliging man. The car's at his garage now – he's replacing the tyres for us.'

Jane's mouth tightened. Then she said, 'Joe's not one to miss an opportunity, ma'am. Business is business with Joe.'

'It's outrageous,' Charlotte said rather mechanically, because she was concentrating on working out the implications. 'So he vandalises our car *and* makes a profit out of it. Well, he's not going to get away with this.'

Jane shook her head. 'It's no good. It'll be my word against theirs. Besides, that's what happened before.'

'Before?, What do you mean?'

'I saw Gloria going up to Mr Rowse's room on Tuesday night.'

'After he'd gone to bed?'

She nodded, and Charlotte thought that underneath the puppy fat in the girl's face there was character and determination. 'I didn't tell anyone, at first – I knew it would kill my dad if he heard. But then yesterday – yesterday, I changed my mind, and I told Mr Thornhill. He came to see Gloria this morning and she denied it. Just flat out. Her word against mine. And – and she's the sort of person who can make people believe she's telling the truth.'

Especially, Charlotte thought, if the people in question were male. She wondered why Jane had changed her mind about telling the police.

'You're sure about all this?'

'Of course I'm sure,' Jane said, glaring at her.

'In that case, I want you to stay here while I telephone Mr Thornhill myself. I won't be long.'

Glowing with indignation, Charlotte went into the hall, closing the door behind her. Now she thought about it, that Vance man had always seemed a bit too good to be true. He was very obliging, yes, but his bills were a little steep, and his eyes were very close together. Besides Charlotte disliked carrot-coloured hair, particularly on a man.

She looked up the number of the police station, dialled and, when the phone was answered, asked for Mr Thornhill. But the Inspector was out; he was expected back at about two o'clock. Charlotte said she would phone back later and put the phone down. She didn't want to talk to any old Tom, Dick or Harry. Thornhill was in charge of the Rowse investigation, and he would be able to confirm that Jane had talked to him, and that he had talked to Gloria. Besides, Charlotte was increasingly curious about the man, especially since she had overheard that interesting exchange between him and Jill on Thursday evening.

She went back into the drawing room. Jane was snuffling inelegantly into the handkerchief.

'Mr Thornhill wasn't in,' Charlotte said. 'Listen, my dear, I know everything must seem ghastly at present, but things will get better.'

Jane looked up. 'How?'

'Because I shall make sure that they do. Does your father know anything about all this?'

'I'm not sure. I don't think so. I don't want him to be hurt.'

The tears began to flow again. At that moment the door opened and Susan appeared.

'Lunch is ready, ma'am,' she announced, contriving to make four innocent words carry a heavy load of accusation.

'I've got to go out,' Charlotte said. 'I'm not sure how long I'll be.'

'It'll spoil. It's no good trying to re-heat roast potatoes.'

'Then you and Jane must have lunch in my place.'

Jane and Susan stared at Charlotte in surprise. This pleased her, because she liked to catch people off-balance. It took her ten minutes to deal with their objections, get herself ready and leave the house.

Usually she would have taken the car but of course the Rover was languishing in Joe Vance's garage. In a way, Charlotte was glad to walk. All the worry about Philip over the last few days had coalesced and converted itself into anger. Here at last was something she could do; and by God she was going to do it. She stormed down to the High Street, passed the offices of the *Gazette* with barely a glance, and walked almost the whole length of the town to Joe Vance's garage near the railway station. To her fury, the door of the workshop was closed and padlocked. The Wemyss-Browns' Rover was standing forlornly outside. She banged on the door of the house behind the workshop, where Joe Vance lived. In the end, a neighbour poked her head out of an upstairs window and stared with interest at Charlotte.

'You won't find him there, my love,' the neighbour said calmly, clearly enjoying the spectacle.

'Well, where is he?'

'He's down at the Bathurst Arms, I shouldn't wonder.'

'Is he, indeed?'

Charlotte snorted her thanks and strode away. She knew Lydmouth, as she was fond of telling friends, like the back of her hand. She knew its alleys and paths, its shortcuts and its cul-de-sacs. She walked down to the river, cutting through a coal merchant's yard because that was the shortest route, and followed the towpath to the Bathurst Arms. Both banks of the river were covered with spring flowers, but she barely noticed them. The walk did nothing to calm her down. She cultivated her anger like a rose.

When she reached the Bathurst Arms, she did not hesitate but went straight into the low-ceilinged lounge bar. Charlotte thrust her way through the crowd, occasionally murmuring, '*If* you please' like an engine emitting puffs of smoke as it forced its way up a steep gradient. Conversations withered and died. Charlotte noticed Ivor Fuggle, that vile reporter from the *Evening Post* who had been responsible for feeding information about Philip to the *Empire Lion*, at a table in the window. He was staring at her and fiddling with his hearing aid. Let him listen, she thought, let them all listen.

By now the room was almost silent. Joe Vance was leaning on the counter, freshly shaved, his hair slicked back. Gloria stood with her hands on her hips, her face grim, knowing that Charlotte's arrival meant trouble, though not exactly what.

'Mr Vance,' Charlotte said in a carrying voice, 'Mrs Alvington: I've got a bone to pick with you two.'

Apart from Joe, the drinkers near the counter backed away, leaving Charlotte in the middle of a small semi-circular clearing in front of the bar.

'I don't have to put up with this,' Gloria said, 'not in my own house, look. You can bloody well—'

'Are you going to throw me out?' Charlotte placed her hands palms down on the counter and glared first at Gloria and then at Joe. 'Or are *you* going to do the dirty work, Mr Vance? After all, you're quite used to doing that, aren't you? Now, I've no objection at all to doing this in public. The more the merrier. I've got nothing to be ashamed of. But I imagine you two would prefer to talk about what you've done somewhere more private. It's entirely up to you.'

'I'm sure I don't know what you're talking about,' said Gloria, making a quick recovery. 'But in any case, we're busy, we're short-staffed, and if there's something you want to talk about, you'll have to do it later.'

'I take it that means you'd prefer an audience. In that case—'

'No,' said a new voice. 'In private.'

Startled, Charlotte looked past Gloria. Standing in the doorway at the back of the bar was Harold Alvington. She had not seen him for at least a year, and for an instant she did not know who he was. He was clutching the jamb of the door and looked like death on two legs.

'I should be very glad to do that, Mr Alvington.' She felt annoyed, because the appearance of Harold Alvington had thrown her to some extent off her stride; one could not be quite as emphatic as one might wish in the presence of a man who was so obviously ill.

'I can't leave the bar, Harold, especially since Jane's gone off without so much as a by your leave. Enid can't handle both bars and the snug by herself.'

'She'll have to,' Harold said. 'Let Mrs Wemyss-Brown come through.'

She stared at her husband for an instant and then obeyed.

'And Mr Vance,' Charlotte said.

Harold nodded. Charlotte followed him into the hall behind the bars. He moved slowly, leaning heavily on a stick. Charlotte followed, with Joe Vance and Gloria bringing up the rear.

Charlotte cleared her throat. 'Are you sure you're up to this, Mr Alvington?'

'Yes,' he said without turning round.

He led them into a room furnished as a living room, apart from the bed against one wall with an invalid table beside it. Near the window was a jumble of furniture – a sideboard, two tables and an easy chair – pushed aside to make way for the bed. Harold sat down in a high-backed armchair. He was finding it hard to breathe. Charlotte sat down. Gloria and Vance remained on their feet, murmuring to each other near the door.

'I shall begin by saying that your daughter Jane is at present at my house,' Charlotte said. 'Now, I know she is young and I know she has been under a great deal of strain lately. But she made two very serious accusations and since one of them directly concerns me, I have come here to find out the truth. And I should say that I will also be in touch with the police.'

'You can't believe anything that girl says,' Gloria put in. 'I don't mean to be unkind, Harold, but she's never liked me, and that's the truth. And this business with the murder has upset her, look – thrown her off balance, and—'

'Your daughter, Mr Alvington,' Charlotte went on, 'came to see me this morning in a state of some distress. She brought me a lipstick which she said belonged to Mrs Alvington here. According to her, she saw Mrs Alvington throw it away last night. Mr Vance had just brought it to her. He and Mrs Alvington found something excruciatingly funny. When Jane retrieved the lipstick she discovered it had been used on something grubby. Like a car windscreen, perhaps. Then this morning she discovered that yesterday evening my motor car was vandalised. Someone had slashed the tyres and scrawled a vulgar insult on the windscreen. In lipstick. How very amusing, eh? All the more so because my husband asked Mr Vance to repair the car.'

'It's lies,' Joe Vance muttered, 'all lies. I never touched your car last night, I—'

'Prove it,' Gloria said. 'That girl's done it all out of spite, I—'

'I'm quite determined to get to the bottom of this, Mr Alvington,' Charlotte said, staring at the grey face in the armchair opposite hers. 'I shall make sure that the police examine this lipstick very carefully in one of their laboratories. They can tell a great deal with forensic evidence these days.' Charlotte was not quite sure what they could or could not find out from the lipstick, but she was fairly sure that none of her listeners would have a better idea than she did. 'I shall pursue this with the full rigour of the law.

I hope you won't mind if I use your telephone to ring the police.'

He held up a hand that trembled. 'One moment. You said Jane made two accusations.'

Charlotte hesitated before answering. She was not a cruel woman, but this was war, and in war the ordinary rules of life were suspended. She and Philip had suffered much in the last few days, and she was certain that Joe Vance and Gloria Alvington had wantonly made things worse. She said, with a harshness she would later regret, 'Jane tells me that she saw Mrs Alvington go upstairs to the room occupied by Cameron Rowse on Tuesday night – after Rowse had gone to bed.'

'It's a lie, a bloody lie,' put in Gloria.

Charlotte overrode the interruption. 'After much heart searching, Jane very properly told Inspector Thornhill, who came here to talk to Mrs Alvington about it. I understand that she denied everything. In other words, once again it was her word against Jane's. But I wonder if this business with Mr Vance and my car may mean that Mrs Alvington's word no longer carries the weight that it used to do. Especially when the police confirm that the lipstick is the one that was used.'

'You bitch,' Gloria said. 'I'm going to—'

'Jane was right,' Harold whispered. He began to cough, and waved an arm feebly.

Gloria brought him a glass of water from the table by the bed. She put her arm round him and held the glass to his lips. 'It's all lies, Harry. You know me.'

He sipped the water, staring up at her. Then he sighed and pushed the glass away. He looked across the room at Charlotte. 'There's no point in keeping quiet any longer. God knows I've tried to forget. But I'm not going to see my Jane called a liar. Not when she's telling the truth.'

Gloria took a step forward. Her skin had paled beneath her make-up. Her lips seemed twice their normal size and twice as bright. 'Harry, love, *please*. Harry.'

'I was awake on Tuesday night, too,' her husband went on. 'Light was off, but the door was open. I saw you walking across the landing, Gloria. Must have been about half-past twelve. You were wearing that negligée thing of yours. You went downstairs, and I heard your footsteps in the hall. I don't know where you went after that, though.' His lips twisted into a smile. 'But I can guess, Gloria. I can guess.'

Chapter Forty-Five

Because it was both Saturday and lunchtime, the *Gazette* office was deserted. Like all normally busy places, the absence of people gave it a ghostly feel. Echoes bounced through empty rooms. Divorced from their owners, objects took on an extra significance. Jill looked at her typewriter squatting on her desk and thought that she'd never realised before how much it resembled a black toad.

While she was waiting for Richard Thornhill, she spent longer than she would normally have done in front of the mirror in the ladies' lavatory. There were no rules for this sort of meeting. Well, she thought, dabbing powder on her cheeks, perhaps that was appropriate.

The doorbell rang and she went to answer it. The front office was closed, and she had told him to come round to the side door in the yard. The yard had the advantage of not being overlooked. One wouldn't like to cause gossip.

When she opened the door, Richard smiled at her. She stood back so he could come inside. For a moment, his face was caught in sunlight and with a pang of concern she noticed the dark smudges beneath his eyes. When he was tired, Richard's face acquired a haggard quality that made him look more like a starving artist in a garret than a prosaic policeman. Neither of them spoke until she had shut the door.

'We've got the building to ourselves,' Jill said in what she hoped was a neutral voice. 'I've brought the relevant issues up to the reporters' room.'

He followed her up the stairs. 'I've checked Simcox's file. And I had a word with Brian Kirby. Simcox definitely has a tattoo of a fish on his right wrist. Apparently he tried the Merchant Navy for a few weeks before the war. It's a relic of that time.'

She had spread out the newspapers on the big table in the centre of the room. He sat down and began to leaf through them.

'Have you had lunch?' she asked.

'No.'

'Nor have I. I bought some bread and some ham on my way to work — would you like a sandwich?' She didn't quite know what to do with herself; playing at being a hostess would solve at least that problem. 'There are some apples, as well.'

'I couldn't possibly—'

'It's no trouble. As I say, I was going to have something myself.'

She gathered together the materials for lunch. As she was now officially the deputy editor, Philip had given her a key to the office safe, which stood in one corner of his room. On the bottom shelf was an emergency supply of pale ale. She borrowed two bottles and carried the laden tray into the reporters' room. Richard sprang up to help her, almost knocking over his chair.

'Don't let me interrupt you.' She opened one of the bottles of beer. 'I'll just carry on.'

While she nibbled an apple, Richard skimmed through the reports of Simcox's arrest and trial. Afterwards, he sat back and took a long swallow of beer.

'That's interesting. You're right about the timing: Heather Parry definitely vanished on the same day that Simcox left the Bull. At the time they assumed that Simcox left Lydmouth because he realised his financial bubble was about to burst. But it could have been for an entirely different reason.'

'What's his history? Can you tell me?'

'There's nothing confidential about it. Howard John Simcox, born in Croydon in nineteen twenty. Father was a milkman. He went to a grammar school but when he was fourteen the father died and he had to leave school. Found a job in an office in the City; dismissed for petty thieving. They didn't prosecute, and he got another job. In nineteen thirty-eight, he altered a cheque, and this time the employers weren't so lenient. He got six months that time. After he came out, he tried the Merchant Navy, but that wasn't a success. He's been married at least once.'

'What about affairs?'

Thornhill's eyes met Jill's. 'He seems to be attractive to a certain type of woman. By all accounts, there's a streak of sadism in him. He was nearly charged with rape early in the war, but the case was dropped for lack of evidence.'

Poor little Heather Parry.

'Then there was the army,' Thornhill was saying. 'Simcox turned out to be quite a good cook, so he spent most of his time attached to an officers' mess in a base in Leicestershire. There was a problem with the mess accounts but nothing was ever proved. After the war, he started posing as an officer – travelled round the country, stayed at reasonable hotels and got credit wherever he could. He married a war widow called Phyllis Richards in Bristol in forty-six. She had a little money but he soon got through that. Then he ran up debts in her name for much more. After a few months, he left her and started travelling round the country again. That's when he ended up in Lydmouth.'

'He must have known he'd get caught.'

'Not necessarily. People can be incredibly stupid. They think they're invulnerable. There was a psychologist's report in the file. The man thought Simcox almost believed his own fantasies, all that stuff about being a war hero. He fooled a lot of people — he learned a lot while he was working at the officers' mess. Certainly enough to put up a plausible impression.'

'But where is he now?'

Thornhill looked at her and smiled. 'That's where it begins to get interesting. He was released a few weeks ago. And almost at once he went back to London and up to his old game with bouncing cheques. I went through the *Police Gazette*, and there he was. Scotland Yard would very much like to talk to him. But there's been no sign of him for about ten days. It's as if he's vanished off the face of the earth.'

'The man with the fish,' Jill said slowly. 'Why would he come back here? You'd think it's the last place he'd choose. What about the wife?'

'They can't trace her, which is odd. She left her address in Bristol soon after Simcox was sentenced.'

'Hardly surprising, really.'

'She owed a lot of money.'

'Or he did.'

He nodded and took another long swallow of his beer. 'It's possible that Simcox is looking for her. When the Yard were trying to find him, they turned up an address in London for his wife's mother. But mother-in-law had left in a hurry two days earlier, with no forwarding address. Her landlady thought it rather odd — after all, the old lady had been there for years, and furnished rooms aren't easy to find in London. It was just after a man called round to see the old lady. They showed her a photograph of Simcox and got a positive identification.'

He took out an envelope from his inside jacket pocket, removed a black-and-white print from it and slid it across the table to Jill. It was an unflattering, harshly-lit shot. Simcox had a thin face with a suggestion of hollow cheeks, in some ways not unlike Thornhill's. His hair, which looked the next best thing to black, was swept back from a widow's peak. In his way, he was a good-looking man. He had the type of face that can be perversely attractive to some women because it hints at danger and unreliability. He was staring straight at the camera, expressionless. Jill pushed the photograph back to Richard, taking care not to touch his hand. Thornhill looked at the photograph for a moment. Jill wondered whether he saw the likeness to himself. He slipped the print back in the envelope.

'He has a record of violence towards women.' Thornhill rubbed his eyes. 'He's clearly a psychopath, or the next best thing to it. He was in Lydmouth at the time that Heather Parry vanished.' He looked across the table, shaking his head. 'But it's all circumstantial.'

'He left Lydmouth on the very day that Heather disappeared,' Jill pointed out.

'It's certainly suggestive, but no more than that. And would he be likely to come back here if he had killed Heather?'

'If we're right about the fish, he has come back.' Jill hesitated, collecting her thoughts. 'In a sense, it's equally unlikely that he would come back to a place where he'd defrauded a lot of people. It's a difference in degree, not in kind.'

'Murder's something different.'

'Yes,' Jill said. 'I don't dispute that. Not to you and me, or to most people. But what about Simcox? You called him a psychopath.'

He nodded, conceding the point. 'But that doesn't answer the question of why he came back.'

'Perhaps he left something behind.' She tried to think of reasons she might go back to her house after leaving it in the morning. To turn off the gas? To feed Alice? 'Or perhaps he remembered something which he ought to have done, something important.' She noticed that he was looking at the ham on the plate between them. 'Shall we eat now? Would you like some more beer?'

For a moment they ate in silence. No, Jill thought, not

silence, because her chewing sounded abnormally loud, as did her breathing. She glanced up. Richard was staring at the shelf of reference books, as though his job depended on his memorising the titles.

It was not just the fact that they were together that made her feel strange, but also the setting: this room was where she worked, and there, opposite her, was Richard Thornhill, working his way steadily through a ham sandwich. It was as if one of the fundamental laws of physics had been shown to have an exception where no exception should exist, a tiny anomaly which, if you allowed yourself to dwell on its implications for too long, would undermine not only the law in question but also the entire conceptual framework of which it was a part.

Best not to think too hard. Jill forced herself to swallow the mouthful she had been chewing for what seemed like half a century, and washed it down with pale ale.

'Jill?'

She looked across the table, glad to have such a broad mahogany barrier between them. 'Yes?'

He pushed aside his plate, the sandwich half eaten. 'There's such a lot to say. I know this isn't a good time—'

'No time is a good time.'

In the silence, the words lay between them, their meaning shifting and shimmering like a reflection in moving water. Richard stood up and walked to the window. He stared down at the yard.

'I didn't plan this,' he said. 'I didn't *want* this to happen.' He glanced over his shoulder, as though needing to reassure himself she was still there, and then shrugged. 'I'm sorry. Nothing *has* happened, really, has it?'

'Hasn't it?'

He looked sharply at her, as though she were a suspect. 'What I mean is, I've no right to impose my — my problems on you.'

'For God's sake.' Jill stood up because she needed to do something. '*Your* problems?'

There was a flash of what might have been anger in his eyes. He walked swiftly round the table towards her. 'I don't make a habit of this,' he snapped. 'I don't know how it's done.'

'How what is done?'

'This – this sort of friendship.'

'But I do know, I suppose? Apply here for lessons in adultery?'

He stopped as if she had slapped him, spreading his hands wide. 'Jill, I didn't mean that, I promise.'

'You've known all about Oliver and me from the start.' She was dismayed by the bitterness in her own voice: *I had not known I cared so much.* 'Is that why you thought I might be suitable? Or would amenable be a better word?'

'That's nonsense.' He moved closer, but did not touch her. 'You must never think that. I don't care what else you think, but not that. It simply isn't true.'

She glared up at him. 'Then what is true, Richard?'

Vertical worry lines appeared between his eyebrows and darted up his forehead. 'It's true that I love you.'

For an instant they stared at each other. Then he turned and left the room. She listened to his footsteps on the stairs and the slam of the door to the yard.

Chapter Forty-Six

At some point Howard lost track of time and drifted into an unpleasant sort of eternity.

The bloody army was everywhere. By dawn, he had realised almost at once that it wasn't just a convoy of trucks passing through Lydmouth and over the bridge. No, these trucks had come to stay. He had crept out to the edge of the Forest and stared down the field at Farnock Camp. The headlights were inside the camp, along the lanes to the front and back gates, on the road up to the Forest and coming over the new bridge. Not one convoy, but two, arriving from opposite directions. Since this was the army, the convoys had arrived at the same time, and the net result was a Godawful mess that would keep them busy for hours.

The trouble was, the army had cut off his line of retreat. There was no way he could get back to Edge Hill before daylight. Even now, the darkness was growing steadily paler behind him. He would have to lie low in the Forest during the day: there was nothing else he could do. It was going to be bloody uncomfortable. He had no food and only two cigarettes. He was also increasingly cold. In the enclosed space of the little mine, he had worked up a fine sweat. But now he was finding it hard to stop his teeth chattering.

He walked slowly back the way he had come, towards the

little clearing with the beech tree and the mine. The best thing
to do would be to climb further up the hill, deeper into the
Forest. He had not gone very far, however, when he received
the second shock of the morning – and this one was even
worse than the first.

Somewhere ahead of him, higher up the hill, there were
footsteps – many footsteps. He stopped to listen, cocking
his head. The footsteps weren't just ahead of him, they were
everywhere. It was hard to be sure in the near darkness under
the trees, but it seemed to him that men were advancing on
the left and the right as well. And behind him lay the field
and the headlights and Farnock Camp.

He darted up to the clearing with the beech tree. The
footsteps were nearer. A man laughed. There was a clank of
metal, and someone swore, the word clearly audible in the
night air. If he could hear them so easily, they would be
able to hear him. Howard dropped to his hands and knees,
slipped among the roots of the beech and crawled back into
the mine.

The decision was not a conscious one. Once inside, though,
Howard realised that it had been a wise one. He knew of no
other hiding places, and he had no time whatsoever to find
them. Unpleasant though it was to be back here, at least it
was warmer. He tried to ignore the smell.

The drumming of his heart began to subside. If the
convoy coming down from the Forest was at a standstill,
they were obviously getting the men out of the trucks and
making them cut through the trees to the camp. They had
probably gone by now. He wondered if he dared light one
of his last cigarettes.

'What about here, Sarge? It's out of the wind.'

Howard's heartbeat abruptly accelerated. It sounded as
though the speaker were a couple of feet away from the
opening of the mine. There were more voices, a brief conference,
and then a series of sounds that Howard recognised only too

well from his own career in the army. The clearing was full of soldiers, and they were doing what soldiers always did when they had a spare five minutes: brewing tea, smoking cigarettes, and slandering their officers. One of them actually emptied his bladder against the roots of the beech tree. As Howard heard the rustle of urine, it reminded him that his own bladder was uncomfortably full.

He had forgotten to wind his watch the previous evening. A little light filtered through the opening of the mine, but not enough for him to be able to use it to estimate the time of day. He was very uncomfortable. Sometimes it seemed to him that the rocks below and the rocks above were moving imperceptibly closer together, and that sooner or later he would be squeezed to death, flattened like an ant squashed beneath a human heel.

Later there was another hazard: cramp shot through his left leg. As the day crawled on, he began to wonder if someone or something deeper in the mine was watching him malevolently. He thought it might be Heather's ghost. Because if Heather had left a ghost behind her, this was where it would be. Once he stretched his hand into the darkness, trying to relieve the strain of being in one place for too long, and his fingertips touched something smooth and rounded. Rock or bone?

Go away, Heather, go away.

It was the thought of Heather waiting in the darkness that finally drove him outside. By now, he was fairly sure the soldiers had moved on. He had heard nothing of them for some time. He would be more at risk outside, but anywhere seemed preferable to this crack in the rock with Heather Parry for company.

Gradually, pausing to listen after each movement, he wriggled backwards out of the slit. The light was so intense it hurt his eyes. He stood up in the recess underneath the beech tree and stretched. He was still wearing Mrs Portleigh's coat. He made an ineffectual attempt to brush off some of the mud and dead leaves that now clung to it. He straightened the felt of the hat and settled it on his head. The world, seen through the thick gauze of the veil, suddenly rippled as though underwater. With trembling fingers, he unbuttoned himself and urinated against the roots of the beech tree in the place the soldiers had used. The relief was so great it was almost painful.

Afterwards, he buttoned up his trousers and then the coat. To judge by the sun, it must be at least midday. He had pins and needles in one of his legs.

What now? He would have to wait until the evening before crossing the river and returning to Edge Hill. He would have to go deeper into the Forest. Find some water, perhaps. It wouldn't be much fun, but almost anything was preferable to spending the day in the mine.

He turned to go, feeling in the pocket of the coat for one of the precious cigarettes. He stepped away from the shelter of the beech.

Then he saw the soldiers.

They were lying in a patch of sunlight on the other side of the clearing. Two of them were asleep. But the third, though he was lying on his side, had his eyes open, and he was staring straight at Howard.

The veil swayed in the breeze. Howard wanted to run, but his legs would not obey him. His knees trembled.

The soldier stood up. He was very young, little more than a teenager. He had fair hair and a pale, bony face.

'Hello, missus. Where did you spring from?'

He moved closer.

'Don't you touch me,' Howard squealed. He started to run as fast as Mr Portleigh's Wellington boots would allow him. As he ran, he sobbed.

Chapter Forty-Seven

'They've got a room free at Brook House,' Dr Bayswater said to Thornhill. 'I'd like to take her over there now.'

'Who'll pay?' asked Thornhill. Brook House was a private nursing home, a few miles south of Lydmouth.

'We'll worry about the money later.'

'But we'll need to talk to her again. Soon.'

'Then you can do it there, Thornhill. The woman's at the end of her tether. She needs proper care and attention, and that's all there is to it.'

'There's no chance she'll run off?'

'In her present state, I doubt if she could blow her own nose. Don't worry – she's my patient, and I'll take full responsibility.'

Thornhill nodded, privately relieved. The arrangement would be irregular, but at this stage of the investigation, he wasn't sure whether they would have to charge Phyllis Richards, and, if so, with what. They had to put her somewhere in the meantime, and her state of health made supervision essential.

The two men had been talking in the corridor outside the interview room. They went back inside. WPC Joan Ailsmore was trying to persuade Phyllis to drink a cup of tea, without success. As the door opened, Phyllis's eyes fastened on Dr Bayswater.

'We're going now,' he announced. 'I'm going to take you to a nice nursing home where you'll be perfectly safe. Come along.'

Joan led them down the corridor to the door which led directly to the car park at the back of Police Headquarters. Phyllis clung to Bayswater's arm as they walked. Her head was bowed and she looked ten or twenty years older than her real age. At the door, Thornhill said goodbye and went up to Williamson's office. The Superintendent had just returned from briefing the Chief Constable on the latest developments.

'Well, Thornhill, this is a pretty kettle of fish. First there's this Portleigh woman, another body to muddy the waters. And then Gloria Alvington. Fine-looking woman, mind.' Williamson eased the waistband of his trousers surreptitiously, as if the thought of her was making him uncomfortable. 'Too many unanswered questions for my liking. Too many bloody suspects, as well.'

'There's another thing, sir. Howard Simcox left Lydmouth on the day that Heather Parry disappeared.'

Williamson sat down suddenly, the chair creaking beneath his weight. 'Are you saying they went together?'

'It's possible, sir.'

'You're not a local man, Thornhill, so you may not understand how people around here feel about Heather Parry. We want this sorted out, and we want it done quickly.'

Thornhill said, 'There might be another explanation. That Simcox left Lydmouth but Heather Parry didn't.'

'You think she's dead?'

Thornhill nodded. 'If I had to lay money on it.'

'Damn. I know her father.' Williamson groped automatically for his pipe, his usual solace in times of stress. He looked agitated, as if the case was taking its toll on him. 'Who've you sent over with the SOCOs to Edge Hill?'

'Sergeant Kirby, sir. And Porter.'

'Oh my God.'

'He lives there. Local knowledge might be useful.'

'Let's just hope he doesn't leave his Thermos anywhere.' Williamson snorted with irritation. 'To go back to Rowse. Anyone could have got into his room from the outside before they locked up the Bathurst Arms. We know Gloria Alvington went to see him in the early hours. All right, she said he was on the floor when she got there, but we needn't necessarily believe that. Wemyss-Brown's lighter was under the body, and Rowse and Wemyss-Brown certainly quarrelled a few hours earlier. Rowse was blackmailing Yateley, but Yateley couldn't have left the Bull on Tuesday evening. Anyway, then we've got Sid Coalway, who's probably our best bet, if only because of the knife. The odds are, he'll hang because of that knife.'

'Just as likely to have been Norah.'

'Possible.' Williamson sniffed. 'More like a man than a woman, isn't she? Why doesn't she smarten herself up? Or then there's Simcox himself. Maybe Rowse took a photo of him, maybe Simcox wanted it back. Maybe Rowse went upstairs to his room and found Simcox stealing the film from his camera.'

Thornhill nodded. He kept seeing Jill's face frozen with shock when he told her that he loved her. How could he have been so stupid? He tried to concentrate on Williamson's rasping voice.

'No, you mark my words, it's Sid Coalway who deserves to hang for this. Nasty bit of work, in my opinion, and it's about time he got what he deserved. Don't you agree?'

Thornhill lifted his head. 'Yes, sir,' he said wearily. 'I suppose he's the ideal candidate.'

Unlike Howard Simcox, Sidney Coalway was already in police custody. Unlike Gloria Alvington, he had something that could pass muster as a motive. Unlike either Gloria or Norah, he was a man, and his plight was therefore unlikely to touch the sentimental hearts of a jury and the British public. Unlike Philip Wemyss-Brown, his wife was not a newspaper proprietor, and he lacked the money to buy the best legal help available. There was no doubt about it: of all the available suspects, Sid Coalway would be a popular choice of murderer.

If only detection were always that simple. Well, Thornhill thought, perhaps it often was.

Chapter Forty-Eight

Something about Mrs Portleigh's bedroom turned Brian Kirby's stomach. Desperate for fresh air, he opened the window and leant out, as if examining the wall beneath the sill. Perhaps lack of sleep was catching up with him at last. Children were playing on the green – four girls of nine or ten, and two much younger boys. They were singing and dancing round one of the boys who, trapped in the middle of the whirling circle, kept turning and twisting as though looking for a way out.

Kirby turned back into the room. The SOCOs had finished in here and were now at work next door in the dressing room. Mrs Portleigh's bedroom was all frills and flowers, with pink shades on the wall lights and a pink eiderdown on the bed. She had taken her religion seriously, by the look of it – the Bible on the dressing table, a Palm Sunday cross tucked in the mirror, on the wall reproductions of wishy-washy paintings of Jesus, shown with a flowing beard and a winsome smile and often equipped with a gaggle of adoring children.

He wouldn't have liked the room at the best of times. What made it worse was the way in which Howard Simcox had filled it with traces of his personality, not obliterating the evidence of Mrs Portleigh, but overwhelming it by force. A full ashtray stood on the Bible. The wardrobe door and the drawers were partly open. Broken glass glittered on the rug by the bed. Simcox's smell, stale and sweaty, overlaid the rosy, sickly perfume of Mrs Portleigh. If the room had been a woman, Kirby thought, you'd have said it had been raped.

'Sarge?'

One of the SOCOs, Flack the photographer, was standing in the doorway of the dressing room. 'You'll want to have a look at this.'

Kirby went into the dressing room.

Flack pointed at a grubby khaki knapsack on the rug beside the narrow bed. 'It was underneath the bed.'

Kirby crouched beside it. The knapsack's flap was open. He tugged at the canvas to enlarge the opening, taking care not to touch the contents. Using his pencil, he hooked out a maroon cashmere jersey that smelled of mothballs. Underneath were at least three leather cases of the type designed to hold jewellery. He prodded them with the pencil and something rattled. There was also a bundle of papers, including a cheque book, held together with a thick elastic band. Silver glinted at the bottom of the bag.

'Blimey,' said Flack. 'Regular magpie's hoard.'

Kirby didn't answer. Delicate as a fly-fisher, he hooked the pencil through a loop of leather beside a silver box and pulled gently upwards. A leather strap lengthened. He met an obstruction and gradually increased the pressure. With a jerk, a camera rose out of the bag.

'It's a Contax,' Flack said.

Kirby looked up him. 'Same kind as Rowse's.'

'Rowse? I didn't know Simcox was in the frame for that.'

'He is now.' Kirby stood up. 'You carry on. I'd better report this.'

'Bloody nutcase, Sarge. Why would he want to kill Rowse?'

Kirby shrugged. 'He's the only one who can tell us that.' He nodded at the camera. 'If we're lucky, we'll find the film still in there.'

'He wouldn't be that stupid.'

'What makes you think that? I know Simcox, remember. It was my evidence that helped send him down. Take it from me, he's no genius. Otherwise he wouldn't have got caught.'

Flack frowned; he was a thin young man whose obsessive attention to detail was his main qualification for the job he now did. 'Killing someone because they took a snapshot of you? Doesn't seem much of a motive.'

'What's new?' Kirby glanced at Flack, a comparative rookie with less than two years' experience, and that in a county force. 'No need to worry about that.'

'But—'

'Listen, when I was up in the Smoke, I was on a case where an old lady got her throat slit. Know why? A tramp asked her for sixpence, she said no, so he whipped out his penknife. So bugger motive.' Kirby pointed at the camera. 'That's what I like. Hard evidence. A good brief can argue about motives till the cows come home. But you can't argue with a stolen camera, can you?'

He went downstairs, feeling more cheerful than he had for several hours. Finding the camera had put a different complexion on this job. He had felt sidelined when Thornhill had packed him off to Edge Hill, though it was true that Kirby was the best person to deal with Howard Simcox because he actually knew the man.

But the camera had brought the two cases together. Kirby wondered briefly what sort of a man would be capable of killing Rowse and then, a few days later, killing an old lady and leaving her body to rot in her own cellar. But only briefly: he had long since decided that trying to solve the mystery of other people's motives was a waste of time and effort.

At the foot of the stairs he glanced at the door that led to the cellar. They had taken away Mrs Portleigh's body before Kirby arrived but Flack had said she was already beginning to smell.

He found the telephone in a small room furnished in a dour, masculine style – leather armchairs, glass-fronted bookcases and a desk with a reading lamp, a pristine blotter and a tobacco jar beside a rack of dusty pipes. The telephone was on the broad windowsill. As Kirby stretched out a hand for it, he glanced outside. PC Porter was walking up the drive towards the police cars parked by the front door. Kirby had sent him to talk to the neighbours on either side of Rochester House; the job was simple enough even for Porter, and it got him out of Kirby's hair.

Oh Christ—

An old woman was pursuing Porter up the drive, moving in a swift ungainly waddle. 'Peter!' she called, the shrill voice audible through the closed window. 'Peter!'

Porter turned. The woman seized him by the arm. It was the old bag who had turned up at Headquarters to complain about the theft of her eggs, Kirby realised, the old bag who was therefore indirectly responsible for Sidney Coalway's arrest. He went swiftly into the hall. The front door was opening. He was just in time to place himself in the path of the woman as she bypassed Porter and tried to invade the house.

'Yes, madam?'

'What's going on, young man? Where's Mrs Portleigh?'

'Sarge,' Porter put in, 'I tried to stop her.'

'It's Mrs Veale, isn't it?' Kirby said.

'It's not nice, having police cars all over the place. This is a respectable village. Has something happened to Mrs Portleigh?'

Kirby fell back on officialese. 'No doubt you'll be informed in due course.'

'And what about Mrs Richards? Where's she?'

Kirby smiled and took Mrs Veale's arm.

'What are you doing?'

'I'm afraid I shall have to ask you to leave, madam.' He pushed her gently out of the house and began to walk with her down the drive. 'A crime has been committed, but we can't tell you any more at present.'

'She's dead, isn't she?'

Kirby smiled blandly at her.

'Or are they *both* dead?'

He did not reply. Mrs Veale's round face reddened with frustration. She murmured something about it being her rates that paid his wages, and that in her day old folk were treated with respect and he could take his hands off her, thank you very much, she wasn't some dangerous criminal. Not that the police seemed to be very good at laying their hands on dangerous criminals. Maybe that was why they terrorised old ladies instead.

At the gates, Kirby stopped and abandoned officialese: 'OK, love, you go home now and have a nice cup of tea, eh?'

'You haven't heard the last of this, young man.'

'No,' Kirby agreed cheerfully, 'I don't suppose I have. Ta for now.'

He watched her waddling slowly across the green. The children were still playing there. When they saw her, they abandoned their game and scattered across the grass. But they were still singing, Kirby noticed — some nursery rhyme, he supposed, though he did not recognise the words. Their thin, reedy voices carried over the grass towards him.

'Mrs Nipper! Mrs Yipper! Mrs Slapper! Mrs Crapper!'

Chapter Forty-Nine

The CID took over the office beside the kitchen at the Bathurst Arms. Thornhill called Dr Bayswater, who packed Harold Alvington off to bed and read Thornhill a short lecture about what he, Bayswater, would like to do to those who harassed people dying of cancer.

When Thornhill interviewed Gloria Alvington, he took care to have Joan Ailsmore taking notes in the corner. Gloria was quite capable of claiming that he had tried to make a pass at her, if it suited her. At first she denied everything, insisting that Harold and Jane must have been mistaken. Harold, she said, was too ill to know what he was saying, half the time, and in any case Dr Bayswater was giving him morphine and everyone knew that made you imagine things. As for Jane, Gloria didn't like to speak ill of her own stepdaughter, but the girl had always been a nasty piece of work.

'She never wanted me to marry Harold, and that's the gospel truth. That girl's always hated me. She'd say black was white if she thought it would do me harm.'

Thornhill persevered, taking Gloria over the ground again and again. At the start of the interview, Gloria sat upright in the chair, rarely looking at Thornhill, with her legs close together. As time went by, however, her body relaxed. She smoothed her dress against her thighs with fingertips adorned with bright red nails and allowed her knees to drift apart. She tossed her head once or twice, and the strawberry-blonde hair glinted like a field of corn.

Thornhill took her back to her conversation in the bar with Rowse, just before he went to bed. 'After all, Mrs Alvington, you were the last person to see him. Did he have a nightcap?'

'Yes, he did – a large brandy.'

'And you?'

Gloria stared abstractedly at the window. 'I think I might have joined him. I find a glass of something helps me sleep.'

'What did he smoke?'

Momentarily disconcerted, she stared at him. 'I don't know. Wait a minute, it was Woodbines. Odd, really. I would have thought he'd smoke something posher. You know, he had that nice lighter and he was going on about all these important people he knew in London. But—'

'A lighter? You never mentioned that before.'

'Nobody asked me, did they?'

'What sort of lighter?'

She shrugged, a languorous movement that somehow contrived to make her bosom tremble. 'How should I know, Mr Thornhill? But I do know quality when I see it. It was silver, I tell you that, the real thing.' Her eyes were shrewd. 'I'd recognise it if I saw it again.'

Thornhill nodded, and from long practice kept his face looking impassive, even slightly bored. The discovery of the Richelieu lighter was a piece of information which the police had kept to themselves. If Gloria identified it as the one Rowse had been using in the hours before his murder, then the case against Philip Wemyss-Brown became much weaker. But there was always the possibility that information about the lighter had leaked out. If that were so, he wouldn't put it past Gloria to be playing some devious game of her own.

'Let's go back to exactly what Mr Rowse had to drink,' Thornhill suggested, bringing them back to a subject they'd already covered exhaustively once before this afternoon, and covered on previous occasions as well. Gradually he worked his way round to the subject of Rowse's bedroom.

'There's just the one light, isn't there?'

She nodded.

'Hanging over the bed, and coming down from the ceiling?'

She permitted herself a little smirk. 'Unless it's changed since I was last up there.'

'How do you switch it on and off?'

'There's a switch by the door, and there's a cord hanging from the ceiling over the bed.'

He raised his eyebrows and looked slightly puzzled.

'Some people like to read in bed, you see,' she went on, the smirk broadening, 'or sometimes they like to do other things with the light on.'

'I see.' He made a note, completely unnecessarily because Joan was recording the whole exchange. 'Now what's really confusing me is the switching. If you turn it off at the door, you can't turn it on at the bed — but not vice versa. Is that right?'

She shook her head. 'You can only turn it on from where you last switched it off.'

'Could you switch it on at the door on Tuesday night?'

'No —' She broke off, realising what she had said. For an instant she drew back her lips like an animal at bay, revealing yellow teeth and pink, swollen gums. 'You tricked me into that. But you're wrong. I thought you meant the last time I was up there, which was Tuesday afternoon.'

'It was broad daylight then. You didn't need the light. Anyway, Jane took him up there.'

'I wanted to check everything was OK, didn't I? And I tried the light to check it was working. I thought—'

'I know what you thought, Gloria,' Thornhill said, abandoning the 'Mrs Alvington' he had used since the beginning of the interview. 'And I know you went up to see Cameron Rowse some time in the early hours of Wednesday morning, just as your husband and your stepdaughter say you did.' He watched her eyes narrowing and darting to and fro, as though looking for an escape route. 'Maybe you called his name, and there was no answer. But you'd probably have been able to see him lying on the floor if the light at the bottom of the stairs was on. Maybe you tried the light switch, just to make sure. Well, you must have done if you knew it wasn't working. The real question is, was he dead on the floor when you arrived as well as when you left?'

'For God's sake,' she said and stopped. She licked her lips. 'All right, all right. I did go up there. Look, Mr Thornhill, there's no reason why this need come out, is there? I thought he looked peaky, when he went upstairs, you see. He'd had a drop to drink, maybe a bit too much, and I couldn't get to sleep for wondering if he was OK. I used to know this bloke who was sick one night and choked on his own vomit. So I thought I'd better check. I swear to God, though, I—'

'Tell me what happened,' Thornhill snapped. 'Was the light on at the bottom of the stairs?'

She nodded.

'Yes or no?' he barked.

'Yes.'

'Were the bolts drawn across on the back door?'

'I can't remember. Should have been.'

'You went upstairs. And then what?'

'I could see him on the floor. And I thought—'

'Never mind what you thought, Gloria. What did you do?'

She looked across the desk at him, her eyes wide, reminding Thornhill of a cowed dog. 'I tried the light switch. Nothing happened. So I pushed the door open as wide as it could and then went in. He was – he was lying there. I thought he was asleep. I could see his mouth, and he hadn't been sick, so that was all right. I loosened his tie, just to make him a little more comfortable. And then I went back to my room.' Suddenly she laughed, a harsh sound like the scrape of fingernails. 'There was no point in me staying, was there? But I didn't realise quite how pointless it was.' She turned her head away, one hand reaching for her cigarettes. 'Oh Christ,' she said in a muffled voice, 'what a bloody mess.'

'Well, what do you want to do?' Charlotte Wemyss-Brown asked.

She stared down at Jane Alvington. They were in the kitchen at Troy House. Susan was sitting in the rocking chair beside the Aga, swaying to and fro and listening to the conversation with shameless enjoyment.

'I want to go home.'

'Yes, dear, I'm sure you do. But I think you should consider my little proposal very carefully before you decide.'

The kettle was coming to the boil. Charlotte turned away to make the tea. She was glad of the breathing space – her exasperation had been coming to the boil as well. After her victory at the Bathurst Arms, and the summoning of the police, Charlotte had gone to the Bull Hotel, where she was just in time to have coffee and a celebratory brandy with Philip and Councillor Broadbent. (Charlotte was now on Christian-name terms with Mr Broadbent who, despite a few rough edges, was clearly one of nature's gentlemen.)

On the walk back from the Bull, she and Philip – or, to be more accurate, Charlotte alone – had been making plans. Not for themselves, but the unfortunate family at the Bathurst Arms. Harold Alvington was obviously too ill to be at home, particularly now that Gloria was revealed as the slut she really was. Nor could Jane be expected to nurse her father all by herself. On consideration, Charlotte thought it best that Harold Alvington should be moved to the RAF Hospital. The pub would close unless the brewery wished to put in a temporary manager, and Jane could come and stay at Troy House for the time being.

'She's really quite an intelligent girl,' Charlotte had told Philip as they reached Troy House. 'One could make something of her. I wonder if she's considered domestic service?'

Jane, however, was resisting Charlotte's proposals. 'It's very kind of you, Mrs Wemyss-Brown,' she said, staring at the floor. 'But really I've got to get back.'

'But things would be much better if—'

'I'm sorry. But Dad needs me.'

'They could look after him much better at the hospital, dear.'

'I know, but he hates hospitals.'

Charlotte sighed. 'And what about your stepmother?'

'I've got to face her sooner or later.'

'Well, I can't stop you,' said Charlotte regretfully, 'but—'

The kitchen door opened and Philip came in. 'There's a police car outside,' he said, glancing warily at Jane. 'I think it's Thornhill.'

'We'd better see what he wants.'

Charlotte reached the front door before Thornhill had time to ring the bell. He was accompanied by a young woman police officer. Charlotte knew she was old-fashioned, but she could not help thinking that there was something rather unnatural about police women. There were some jobs – soldiers, for example, prime ministers, priests – which she instinctively felt were better done by men, though of course the best of men generally had a woman lurking as an eminence grise in the background.

'Is Miss Alvington still here?' Thornhill asked.

'She's in the kitchen, Inspector.'

'I wonder if I might have a word with her.'

Charlotte fetched Jane.

'If you don't mind, Mrs Wemyss-Brown, I'd like to talk to Miss Alvington alone.'

'Oh. Yes, of course.'

Charlotte left the room and lurked in Philip's study. A few minutes later, she heard the front door closing. She went into the hall and found Jane looking puzzled.

'What did Mr Thornhill want, dear? You don't mind me asking?'

'No, of course not. He just wanted to know what Mr Rowse used to light his cigarettes.'

'Oh.' Charlotte raised her eyebrows, aware that her knees felt suddenly shaky. 'And what did you say? Can you tell me?'

'I don't see why not. He had a silver lighter.'

'Oh really.' Charlotte sat down heavily on the chest by the front door. 'And when did you see him use it?'

'That's what Mr Thornhill asked.' Her face thoughtful, Jane stared at Charlotte. 'It was quite late on. Him and Gloria were in the lounge bar while I was tidying up in there. It was then.'

'After he got back from the Bull?'

'Yes. But why do you want to know?'

'Hallelujah,' said Charlotte, surprising herself as much as Jane, and told her.

Chapter Fifty

Mrs Veale was a creature of habit. For more than twelve years, she had taken Freddy for a walk, morning and evening, rain or shine. The routine had begun when Freddy was a puppy. By the time Freddy was a few months old, he had been quite capable of exercising himself off the lead. Nevertheless, Mrs Veale maintained the routine of morning and evening walks.

The routine outlived Freddy. Morning and evening, rain or shine, Mrs Veale walked round the green and often much further afield. The Mixed Infants were creatures of habit as well. They did not let Freddy's death prevent them from chanting 'Mrs Nipper! Mrs Yipper! Mrs Yapper! Mrs Crapper!'

Late on Saturday evening, the weather changed: the wind blew in gusts from the south-west, and the sky clouded over. Despite this, Mrs Veale had a rather longer walk than usual in the hope of satisfying her curiosity. There was still no sign of Mrs Portleigh or her companion. Rochester House was in darkness. The police cars were gone from the drive. But Mrs Veale suspected that there was someone inside. On an earlier excursion, while it was still light, she was sure a curtain had moved at one of the bedroom windows. She had not seen Peter Porter since the afternoon, which was a pity – she was reasonably certain that she could worm whatever she wanted out of Peter Porter, given ten minutes alone with him and no distractions. The impudent whippersnapper who had manhandled her down the drive was another matter. Not a local man, by the sound of him. Mrs Veale was seriously contemplating an official complaint.

She drifted twice round the green, visited her husband's grave in the little churchyard, walked down to the main road and followed it part of the way into Lydmouth. In truth, she was glad of the walk. It gave her something to do. Being outside was preferable to being at home. At the cottage, the rooms were too silent. Everywhere she looked, there were empty places.

It began to rain as she was walking back towards Edge Hill. The rain grew steadily harder, whipped by the gusts of wind. Mrs Veale raised her umbrella. Though it was Saturday night, there were few people around. She brushed a drop of water from the end of her nose. It would be a different matter when the pubs closed, she thought – then you'd see all the riffraff. You'd hear them, too.

The rain grew heavier and heavier. Even Mrs Veale, who quite liked bad weather on the grounds that it confirmed her belief that life was awful, felt that the rain was going too far. She was wearing her lightweight raincoat, which was really capable of withstanding only a shower. Muttering under her breath, she accelerated, skimming along the glistening pavement past the pebble-dashed houses which attached Edge Hill to Lydmouth, as the lead had once attached Freddy to Mrs Veale.

Just as she reached the green, tragedy struck. The wind caught the underside of the umbrella and, with a wrench that nearly tore the handle from her hand, blew it inside out. The rain smacked into her face. Panting, Mrs Veale ducked into the bus shelter to get her breath back.

The area was well lit because of a street lamp, though the shelter itself was dark. Mrs Veale huddled at one end of the bench. Her thick woollen stockings were soaking, thanks to the spray from a passing lorry. She stared across the road at the dark expanse of the green, wondering whether she should make a dash for her cottage at the far end. As if sensing her thoughts, the rain increased still further in intensity, thrumming and tapping upon the asbestos roof of the shelter.

Suddenly Mrs Veale was not alone.

A woman appeared in the doorway and peered inside. She looked even wetter than Mrs Veale. She was wearing a heavy overcoat and an old-fashioned hat with a veil attached. She gave a harsh sob which ended in a sudden intake of air when she realised she was not alone.

Mrs Veale stood up and advanced towards the doorway. 'It's not –? Mrs Portleigh? Is that you?'

She would have recognised that hat anywhere. Mrs Portleigh had had it for at least twenty years. It had a half veil and a distinctive brim, which curved lugubriously downwards at either side.

'Fuck off.'

Mrs Veale stopped as though she had collided with a wall of glass. It wasn't just the obscenity: it was the voice, which was low and unmistakably masculine.

'I beg your pardon,' Mrs Veale snapped, rapidly regaining her wits. She thought she recognised the coat now, as well. Nameless perversions streaked through her mind. 'And what might you be doing in Mrs Portleigh's clothes?'

The man leapt at her, his hands outstretched towards her throat. Mrs Veale raised the ruined umbrella and jabbed it like a rapier at his face. He recoiled with a howl of pain.

Rage welled up inside her. How dare he attack a poor defenceless old lady? The pervert was now covering his face with his hands and backing outside the shelter. Mrs Veale stabbed once more in the direction of his face and was rewarded with another howl. The man ran outside. Mrs Veale followed, borne along by her rage, as helpless as a piece of driftwood on a spring tide. The pervert fled into the shadows of the building site, slithering in the mud. He tripped and fell full-length. Mrs Veale reached him as he was trying to stand up and belaboured his bowed back with the remains of the umbrella.

He lunged suddenly at her arm, taking her by surprise. He dragged her down on top of him. Mrs Veale poked her elbow at his face. There was a foul smell in her nostrils.

'Help!' she cried. 'Help!'

In the split second that followed, she knew that she was doomed. The pervert would kill her, and she would never know why, let alone who he was. In that split second, she also knew that she did not really care. But she wasn't going to make it easy for him. She felt his hand close over her mouth and bit down on his finger as hard as her dentures would allow. She heard him squeal and felt a fierce satisfaction. He whipped his hand away which gave her an opportunity to cry out once again. The rain poured down from the invisible sky. She tried to pull herself away, but slipped in the mud. The pervert hooked her head in the crook of his elbow and began to squeeze.

'What's all this then? Here, stop that. What's going on?'

Despite the pain and confusion, Mrs Veale recognised the shouting voice. Her assailant's hold slackened. She seized the opportunity to drive her fist in the general direction of his belly. She heard footsteps splashing through the mud. The beam of a torch swooped over her, momentarily dazzling her.

'Here, you, what's all this? You can't do that here!'

Suddenly it was over. Mrs Veale lay back in the mud. The man in Mrs Portleigh's clothes writhed in the massive arms of PC Peter Porter. She wondered whether Peter had really believed them to be a courting couple enjoying a strenuous session in the rain.

'Well, Peter,' said Mrs Veale in a trembling croak she barely recognised as her own voice. 'So you can do something right after all.'

Chapter Fifty-One

'Looked like an old lady,' said the young soldier, 'but smelt like a fox.'

Thornhill glanced at the boy, who was fair and had features too large for his face. 'You're sure you can find the place again?'

'Yes, sir. It's not far. Just a hundred yards or so.'

For a moment, the line of men walked in silence. There were seven of them altogether. Williamson was there, looking washed out, and a couple of uniformed constables. At the rear came a redcap, a Sergeant with a startling resemblance to Hermann Goering, and a young subaltern. After last night's rain, the sky was a crisp, hard blue and the air smelled as though it had been washed. In the valley below, on the other side of the river, the bells of St John's were summoning people to morning service. Edith, David and Elizabeth would probably be among the congregation.

Thornhill had contacted the commanding officer of Farnock Camp the previous afternoon. It was a long shot, but the officer had agreed to circulate a description of Simcox and ask his men to report any suspicious strangers near the camp. The news of the old lady who smelled like a fox had reached Police Headquarters only an hour earlier.

An old lady who had emerged as if by magic from a

crack in the rocks. An old lady wearing a hat with a veil. An old lady who, seeing three young soldiers, gathered up the skirts of her tweed overcoat, revealing Wellington boots and corduroy trousers, and vanished. An old lady who was now in police custody. An old lady who wasn't old and certainly wasn't a lady.

'Like an Olympic sprinter, sir,' the soldier went on, reliving and probably magnifying the glory of it. 'Went like the bleeding wind.'

Thornhill nodded. They were walking up a field that sloped to the Forest. Farnock Camp was immediately behind them. He had not slept, but he did not feel tired. This was often the way when the last pieces of an investigation were at last falling together. Perhaps hunters felt like this, Thornhill thought, when they knew that at last the fox could not escape them. Tiredness would come later, when the fox was captured and disposed of.

The astonishing news that PC Porter had single-handedly arrested Howard Simcox, conman and probably murderer, and saved the life of an old lady into the bargain, turned more than the investigation upside-down.

Thornhill felt a tap on his shoulder and turned to see Superintendent Williamson just behind him. He dropped back and for a moment the two men walked side by side in silence. Williamson was already out of breath.

'The lab phoned just as we were leaving,' he murmured to Thornhill. 'Drawn a blank with Mrs Portleigh, I'm afraid.'

'A natural death?'

'Heart attack. She had a history of it. No sign of anything else, though she definitely didn't die where we found her.'

'Mrs Richards says that Simcox frightened Mrs Portleigh to death in the kitchen.'

Williamson looked sharply at him. 'Not the sort of thing that shows up in an autopsy, I'm afraid. But there's some bruising which occurred around the time of death. That fits in with the idea of a fall on to the kitchen floor.' His face brightened. 'Still, we don't need that now, do we? Not with that camera.'

They now knew beyond all possible doubt that the Contax in Simcox's bag had belonged to Cameron Rowse. It had Rowse's fingerprints on the inside as well as the outside, and it had contained Rowse's film. DC Flack had processed the film overnight, and one of the shots near the end of the reel had produced a sharp and perfectly recognisable print of Howard Simcox's face.

'What about Coalway, sir? That knife is a difficult thing to argue away.'

Williamson shrugged. 'He must have been telling the truth. Maybe he did find it by the river.'

They were at the edge of the Forest now. Thornhill hung back with Williamson. One by one the others clambered over the stone stile.

Williamson said quietly, 'But we'll hold on to Coalway for a while. He stole those tools – he's not going to wriggle out from that.'

'And Vance?'

'Not up to me what happens to him.' Williamson heaved himself over the stile. 'You know something? What really makes me happy is that Post Office Book. The ration book. The watch. All there in Simcox's coat pocket. Like a bloody miracle, eh? Talk about stupid.' He glanced at Thornhill and added unexpectedly, 'And you did well, tying in the timing of the two cases. Oh yes, it's all very satisfactory.'

Birds fell silent as the little party climbed slowly among the trees. Their feet crunched on last year's leaves. They were following a path of sorts – not a man-made one, Thornhill thought, but one worn by small paws.

'I think this is it,' the young soldier said, glancing back at Thornhill. 'Yes, I'm sure.'

They were in a clearing, a flattened area the shape of a horseshoe in the side of the hill. At the rear was a curving wall of rock. A huge beech tree towered above the clearing and several of its roots had snaked down the rock and burrowed into the ground.

'See that?' The soldier pointed to the ground, at an empty cigarette packet, its colours still fresh. 'That's mine.'

'Where did you see him, son?' Williamson demanded. 'And where were you?'

'We were lying over there, sir.' The boy waved at the opposite side of the clearing from the beech tree. 'Ned and Steve were dozing but I was awake having a smoke. And I heard a rustling – thought it was a sheep, or something. And I looked up, and there he was.' He nodded towards the beech tree. 'I looked at him, and he looked at me. Then he ran like buggery.'

Williamson and Thornhill walked over to the beech tree with the soldier trailing behind. Here, by the roots of the beech, was a triangular recess in the wall of rock.

The soldier pointed at a crack near the base. 'I reckon he must have been in there.'

'There's not enough room,' Thornhill said.

Williamson shook his head. 'Don't you believe it. Looks like an old iron working. My old dad used to say they tunnelled for miles under the rock, following the ore.'

Thornhill crouched and pulled aside the heap of dead leaves which obscured the bottom of the hole. The opening became slightly larger. He sniffed, and wrinkled his nose.

'See what I mean?' the boy said. 'That's fox, I reckon.'

Thornhill turned. The soldiers lying on the other side of the clearing would not have been able to see the opening because it was in the recess. But as soon as Simcox had taken a couple of paces away from it, he would have been instantly visible.

'We've peed in them leaves,' the soldier said. 'Seems funny now, don't it?'

Thornhill stood up, brushing his hands on his coat, and looked at one of the constables. 'Give me a torch, will you?'

He knelt and poked his head and shoulders into the hole. The smell was stronger here, the stench of decay, and for a moment he thought he might be sick. The torch beam swept ahead of him, revealing dry, dusty walls of pinkish rock. The tunnel was little more than a foot high, though nearly a yard wide. It slithered into the earth. Thornhill thought it became wider and taller as it went on. He swallowed. He did not like enclosed places.

'Well?' Williamson said, his voice muffled and oddly distant. 'What can you see?'

Thornhill returned to the sunlight. 'Just rock, sir.' He glanced at the others. He was the smallest and slimmest of them all. 'I think I'd better crawl a little way in.'

Williamson gave him a smile. 'Good idea.'

Thornhill wriggled into the tunnel. He tried to imagine what it must have been like to work in conditions like this. Even though he knew that he was only a yard away from six men, he felt very lonely. The smell had a sour quality and he wondered if part of it was Simcox's fear. He pulled himself completely into the slit between the rocks. At this point it curved round to the right. His outstretched hands palpated the floor of the tunnel: rubble and loose earth. The torchlight wavered, revealing a dusty, almost monochrome world. He forced himself a little further in. His fingertips danced ahead along the floor of the tunnel. His hand closed on something that did not feel like rock or earth. His stomach lurched as he pulled it free and examined it in the light of the torch.

It was a sandal, one of those solid ones which enclose the foot. He shook it gently and there was the rustle of something moving inside. He pushed in his thumb and forefinger and they closed, pincer-like, on the rounded edge of a bone.

'So now we know,' he said, and he wasn't sure whether he spoke the words aloud or only in his head.

He closed his eyes for a moment. Then he began to struggle backwards, taking the sandal and its contents with him. Heather Parry was coming home.

Chapter Fifty-Two

'I've no idea what he wants,' Charlotte Wemyss-Brown said, overtaking a pair of cyclists, 'Jane didn't say.'

'It must be a very difficult time for him,' Jill said. 'Do we have to go quite so fast?'

Charlotte dropped a gear and accelerated past a dawdling lorry. 'I want to find out what this car is capable of. So far, I'd say not very much. It's about as nippy as a − as a suet dumpling.'

Nevertheless Charlotte slowed down as they drove along the High Street, nearly deserted on a Sunday afternoon. She and Philip had agreed to waive charges against Joe Vance. In return, he was going to replace the slashed tyres of the Rover for free and had also lent the Wemyss-Browns an elderly Riley until the work was done. All in all, Charlotte was quite pleased with the way things were turning out. Her frontal assault on the Bathurst Arms yesterday afternoon had been an unorthodox tactic, but it had proved surprisingly successful. In church this morning, Charlotte suspected that people were treating one with added deference because of the victory. One wasn't vain, of course, but it was nice to know that one was respected.

'I hope you don't mind my asking you to come,' she said. 'But I thought it could be rather awkward otherwise − because of yesterday. And having you there will make the situation easier to cope with. Of course if I'd known about the kittens ...'

'I think Alice would rather be left on her own. After all, she's the expert.'

'What will you do with them?' Charlotte asked, momentarily diverted.

'Edith Thornhill's interested in at least one of them.' There, Jill thought, she had said the name Thornhill in a perfectly normal fashion. 'Do you know what Mr Alvington wants?'

Charlotte shook her head vigorously. 'No idea. Poor man! How he's changed. Until yesterday, I hadn't seen him for months. You wouldn't think it now, but he was rather good-looking as a young man. The family were quite respectable, in their way. But then the first Mrs Alvington died, and I'm afraid things went downhill.'

The Riley turned right into Lyd Street and rolled down towards the river.

'There's always the possibility that things might turn nasty.' Charlotte glanced at Jill and added in a lower voice, 'Especially if that woman's around. One might need a witness.'

Charlotte was aware she was saying only part of the truth. Though Jane's gratitude was flattering, Charlotte had no wish to spend her afternoon beside the sickbed of a dying man whom she hardly knew. Jill would know what to do or say; she was that sort of person. There was also the point that if one was going to play Lady Bountiful in some as yet unknown capacity, it would be pleasant to have an audience.

Charlotte pulled up outside the Bathurst Arms. Suddenly she wished she had found an excuse not to come. The building looked drab and lonely, as pubs usually do outside opening hours. Beyond it the river lapped brown and sluggish beside its banks; the level was higher than usual because of the heavy rain during the night.

The two women climbed out of the Riley.

'Aren't the flowers lovely?' Charlotte said, postponing what would probably be a harrowing scene. 'See? Down by the river.'

'Yes, aren't they?' Jill was already walking round the side of the pub. 'I wonder which door we should try?'

'The honesty's early. We've got some at the bottom of the garden – so pretty. Did you know it's also called moonwort? And satinpod, too, I think.'

Charlotte broke off as a door at the side of the building opened and Jane came out, wiping her hands on an apron. Her face anxious, she hurried towards them.

'Thanks ever so for coming.'

'Not at all, dear.' Charlotte rose to the occasion and patted Jane's arm. 'I hope you don't mind – I've brought Miss Francis with me.'

Jane smiled at Jill. 'Of course not.'

She led them into the building.

'How is your father?' Charlotte murmured.

'No better. All this has taken it out of him, I think.'

'At least it's over now.'

Jane stopped, her face startled. 'What do you mean?'

'I thought you would have heard.'

'I've been with Dad most of the day. We didn't open up at lunchtime – no one's been in since last night.'

'A man called Howard Simcox has been arrested.' Charlotte had heard from Philip, who had heard from Sergeant Fowles. 'They think he may be charged with several murders, including Cameron Rowse's.'

Jane's right hand twitched, as though she were brushing away a fly. 'Hardly seems real. I'm sorry.'

'Nothing to be sorry for, dear. Now – what can we do for your father?'

Jane blushed. 'He's got a favour to ask, I think.' She opened the door of the living room which was now the sickroom, cutting off the need to say more. 'They're here, Dad,' she said in a bright, firm voice, quite unlike the mumble she had used in the hallway. 'Can we come in?'

The three women filed into the room. It was uncomfortably hot and smelled unpleasantly of stale air and what Charlotte thought of as bodily functions. Harold Alvington was propped up in bed. Despite herself, she was shocked by the change in him. In twenty-four hours, he seemed to have moved several years closer to death. His face was grey, the bones poking at the skin as though trying to escape. But his hair had recently been brushed, Charlotte was pleased to see, and he had shaved.

'Mr Alvington! How are you?'

He waved the question away with a twitch of his hand, an irrelevancy.

'You remember Miss Francis, I expect?' Charlotte knew that she was speaking too loudly, that her voice was too cheerful. 'I hope you don't mind my bringing her with me.'

'Jane.' Harold's voice was like the scrape of sandpaper on wood. 'Chairs.'

Jane brought over two dining chairs and set them beside the bed. 'Dad – they got the man who killed Mr Rowse.'

He looked puzzled. 'Who?'

'A man called Simcox,' Charlotte said. 'They think he also killed that poor girl Heather Parry. Do you remember? She went missing about three years ago. And it's possible he also killed an old lady in Edge Hill. A thoroughly nasty piece of work.'

Charlotte and Jill sat down. Her hands clasping the strap of her handbag, Charlotte smiled with ferocious benevolence at Harold Alvington. Jane hovered at the foot of the bed, her eyes moving from face to face.

'Now – what can we do for you, Mr Alvington?'

But Harold was looking at Jane. 'Gloria?'

'Upstairs.'

Harold nodded. He fixed his eyes on Charlotte, who felt increasingly uncomfortable, as though buttonholed by an Ancient Mariner. 'It's not for me, Mrs Wemyss-Brown, it's for Jane.'

'Oh Dad—'

He did not look in her direction, but raised a hand to silence her. 'When I die, there's nothing for her here. Gloria don't get on with her. You know that.' He licked his lips. 'Anyway, the brewery probably won't want Gloria as their tenant.' He threw the ghost of a smile at his daughter. 'You never liked bar work, did you? Can't blame you.'

Charlotte frowned, suspecting that Harold's mind was wandering. 'So how can we help Jane?'

'Help? It's not charity I want,' he said, his voice suddenly fierce. 'Our Jane has got a head on her shoulders. She was at the High School, she did well, they wanted her to stay on, maybe go to college. But then her mum died, and things changed. It was her mum who wanted her that.' He coughed, and Charlotte wondered if he had lost the thread of what he was saying. 'When I go,' he went on, 'there'll be a bit of money, not much. But most of it will come to Jane. So she won't be penniless. She could pay her way at first, like.'

'Mr Alvington,' Charlotte said, bewildered. 'I'm afraid I don't understand what you mean.'

He stared at her with eyes which seemed very blue because the pupils were no more than tiny black dots. 'I want her to be a journalist. She was always good at English. I know that's what she wants, because she told me. Years ago.'

Jane had gone red. She shifted from one foot to the other and glanced out of the window, as though looking for a means of escape.

'If she could get a bit of training, for which she could pay, I reckon she could do well.' Harold stared at Charlotte with those blue eyes. 'It's a business proposition. What do you say?'

'Well, it's — it's certainly an idea. What do you think, Jane?'

'I'm not sure I'd be much good. But perhaps I could do filing and things. I don't mind work.'

'That's half the battle,' Jill said, glancing at Charlotte. 'And of course you know the area, which is always a help on a local paper.'

'Perhaps we could arrange a trial period,' Charlotte said slowly. 'I shall have a word with my husband.'

'Not charity,' he reiterated. 'I don't want that.'

'No. But if Jane settles in at the *Gazette*, then everyone will benefit. And if not, there's no harm done.'

Harold nodded slowly. He let his head fall back on the pillows. His eyelids drooped. Charlotte looked at Jill, wondering if they should slip away.

'Jane,' Charlotte murmured, though keeping her voice down did not come naturally to her. 'Should we——?'

'Stay a bit,' said the man on the bed, his eyes opening once more. 'Jane, will you leave us for a moment?'

'But Dad——'

She broke off and looked at her father. At that moment, seeing the two faces in profile, Charlotte realised how similar father and daughter were. The father's face was now stripped to its essentials of skin and bone, while Jane's was swathed in puppy fat and surrounded by fluffy brown hair. Still, the likeness was extraordinary, and the differences only accentuated it.

Jane picked up a folded blanket from the bed. 'Just for a moment, mind. You know what doctor said.'

Harold nodded. His eyes followed her as she left the room. The door clicked behind her.

'I'm worried about her,' he said to Charlotte. 'When I'm gone, anything could happen. Gloria might try and fight the will.' His fingers picked at the sheet. 'Will you——?'

'Yes,' said Charlotte. 'I can promise you that Jane won't be without friends.'

'It's my fault. I shouldn't have married Gloria. She can't help it, look. I think she needs a man to make herself feel real.

And the more important she thinks a man is, the more real she feels.' He blinked; his eyes were full of moisture. 'Sorry – mind's wandering all over the place. Thirsty.'

Charlotte sat forward in her chair, picked up the glass on the table by the bed, and held it to Harold's lips. He sipped once, and then again. To her surprise, Charlotte felt tears pricking against her own eyelids. She put the glass carefully back on the table. It was absurd to feel grief that a man one hardly knew was dying. But then, she thought, with a shiver of self-knowledge, much of what one felt was absurd.

Harold's eyes were closed, but his lips moved. 'They got the man that did it, then. So it wasn't Sid Coalway, after all?'

'No – they think that for once Coalway was telling the truth: that he picked up the knife on the river bank. Probably Simcox threw it at the river as he ran away. But it was dark, and he didn't see where it landed.'

'Under the honesty.' Harold wheezed, a sound that might have been the next best thing to a laugh. 'Just his luck.'

As he was speaking, the door opened with such force that it slammed against a table. Gloria burst into the room. She was immaculately made up, encased in a tight electric blue dress and equipped with a cigarette in one hand and a glass in the other. 'What's going on here?' she demanded. 'You're all planning something, aren't you? Behind my back.'

Charlotte stood up. 'Mrs Alvington, I can assure you—'

'You cow,' Gloria said.

Jill stood up. 'I think we should leave now.'

Harold turned his head so that he faced the wall.

Jane appeared behind Gloria. 'Get out of here.'

Gloria glared at her stepdaughter and then at Charlotte and Jill. Her eyes swivelled to and fro behind the cosmetic mask. The glass quivered and drops of liquid spotted the carpet. 'I've said all I want.'

She pushed past her stepdaughter and walked away, her heels clacking on the linoleum of the hall. Charlotte and Jill said goodbye to Harold Alvington, who nodded slightly, but otherwise gave no sign he could hear them. Jane waited by the door.

'Is there anything we can do?' Charlotte whispered to her as she passed. 'I still wonder if he might be more comfortable in hospital.'

'Away from Gloria, you mean?'

Charlotte nodded.

'He wants to die here. He was born here – did you know that? His dad had the lease before him.' Jane's face twitched. 'I think he wanted me to be a boy. Or marry someone who'd want to carry on.'

'Yes, dear.' Charlotte was uncertain how to deal with this. 'I'm rather worried about your stepmother. Will you ring me if I can help?'

'With Gloria?' Jane looked up at Charlotte. 'Don't worry. I can deal with her.'

Chapter Fifty-Three

The press conference on Monday morning was a triumphant affair. Though the Chief Constable was present, Superintendent Williamson did most of the talking and appropriated most of the glory. Ivor Fuggle of the *Evening Post* came in after Jill and Philip and sat as far away as possible. Few people talked to him. Journalism had its own code, and Fuggle had sinned against it.

The investigation, Williamson said as flashbulbs popped, had been a textbook example of how a relatively small provincial CID could achieve first-class results without calling on outside help. All it took was well-trained officers, co-ordination and persistence.

'And leadership?' Ivor Fuggle put in at this point.

Williamson nodded, graciously accepting the addition. Though Heather Parry had vanished more than three years ago, the case was still open, still actively pursued. That was how they did things in Lydmouth. Cameron Rowse, on the other hand, had been murdered less than a week ago. The police had already succeeded in making an arrest.

As everyone in the room knew, Howard John Simcox was now helping the police with their inquiries. He had been charged with theft and assault at Lydmouth Magistrates Court earlier this morning and remanded in custody. The arrest had been made by a young officer, PC Porter, who had saved the life of an old lady in the process. Documents belonging to Heather Parry had been found in the pocket of the coat he was wearing. During the previous day, a soldier from Farnock Camp had seen him lurking in the Forest. Yesterday morning, Williamson had himself led a team of officers who investigated this sighting, which led to the discovery of Heather Parry's body. Items belonging to Cameron Rowse had been discovered among Simcox's possessions.

As Williamson talked, Jill made notes. Occasionally she stole a glance at Thornhill, who was sitting on Williamson's left. Once he looked up and met her eyes. Jill hastily looked away. In that instant, something had passed between them, but she wasn't sure what it was. All she knew was that if you could convert it to electricity you could light a town the size of Lydmouth as well as Piccadilly Circus.

Afterwards there was a sense of celebration. Williamson announced his intention of dropping into the Bull for a drink at lunchtime, and it soon became clear that most of the journalists who had been at the press conference would be able to join him. The crowd of people, journalists and police officers, eddied out of the Conference Room into the reception area, and out into the High Street. Waiting for Philip, who was talking to Williamson, Jill found Richard Thornhill at her elbow. He was hollow-cheeked with tiredness.

'Richard – are you all right?'

He nodded. 'I wondered if . . .'

'What?'

'I – I would like to see you,' he said.

'Yes. When are you free?'

'Would lunchtime be possible?'

'Yes.' The strangest thing about this conversation, she thought, was that it did not seem strange. 'Where?'

'I don't know. What do you think?'

'The kittens have been born. Perhaps you'd like to see them?'

'What?'

'David and Elizabeth might have a kitten. Possibly one each.'

'Eh? Oh yes – Edith said something.' His eyes were very bright. 'Yes, I'd like that.'

'The cottage, then?' she murmured. 'At about one?'

His face changed, as though a shutter had descended. 'I'm afraid an interview would be out of the question. You'd have to approach the Chief Constable.'

'Ah,' said Williamson clapping Thornhill on the shoulder. 'Enjoying the company of our lovely Miss Francis, eh?'

Thornhill smiled, as one does when superior officers make a joke.

'I'm glad I've caught you both, actually,' Williamson went on. 'I've got a piece of news. There'll be a public announcement later this week, probably, but I'd like you to know before that.'

Smiling wolfishly, Williamson lowered his voice and told them.

Richard Thornhill was appalled by his own behaviour. He walked quickly down the High Street, passing the Bull Hotel where Williamson was already holding court. He had no doubt that his own absence would be noted, and possibly Jill's.

The day was unexpectedly warm, a foretaste of summer all the more welcome after the hard winter. He turned into Church Street, glancing over his shoulder as he did so. He knew what he was doing was not only morally indefensible: it was dangerous as well. He had noticed Kirby watching as he and Jill were talking outside Police Headquarters. What if Brian guessed?

He knocked on the door of Church Cottage. It opened almost at once. Jill stood back against the wall of the little hall to let him pass. She was wearing a light, summery dress and as he passed her he smelt her perfume, or rather he smelt that mixture of perfume and Jill herself which he could have recognised with his eyes shut. She closed the door and followed him into the sitting room. They looked at each other for a moment and Thornhill felt panic rising like sap.

'So it's all over bar the shouting?' Jill said. 'I've never seen Williamson looking so happy.'

'He's leaving on the crest of the wave.'

Thornhill was looking at her, and she was looking at him, and their eyes were speaking a different language from their mouths.

'It's so very neat. Such a tidy ending. Can you talk about it?'

He shrugged, knowing that if he couldn't there was little point in his being here. 'There's no doubt that Simcox killed Heather Parry, and that he was there when Mrs Portleigh died. He denies it, of course, but that sort always does. But I wish the evidence linking him with Rowse's death was a little stronger.'

'What about Sid Coalway?'

'He's finally admitted stealing the tools and the eggs. He'll be charged with that.'

'But not with Rowse's murder?'

'No. It's not our decision, of course, but I'm sure the DPP will agree with Williamson: that Simcox killed Rowse – Rowse probably surprised him when he was looking for the camera. And Simcox tried to throw the knife in the river, but missed.'

'Where exactly did Coalway say he found the knife? Can you tell me that?'

He smiled at her. 'I tell you far too much.'

She smiled back. After a moment she went on, 'I have a reason.'

'If you follow the towpath upstream from the Bathurst Arms, there's a bench near the water's edge. Not far, maybe twenty yards.'

'I know.'

'It was in a clump of weeds, at one end of the bench.' Thornhill frowned, remembering. 'According to Sid, they were tall ones with little purple flowers.'

'People grow them in their gardens. They're called honesty.'

'Why are you asking?'

Jill sat down and looked up at him. 'Richard, Coalway said he found it there: but that's not general knowledge, is it?'

'No. Why?'

'Because that's where Harold Alvington said the knife was found. I went to see him yesterday afternoon with Charlotte Wemyss-Brown.'

'But — Alvington's more or less bedridden.'

'He is now. But on Wednesday morning I met him on the riverbank.'

'Where?'

'He was sitting on that bench. He looked dreadful. Dr Bayswater and I helped him back to the pub.'

'So perhaps he was trying to throw the knife in the water? But he ran out of strength before he got there? He's a proud man, and I think a jealous one.'

Thornhill walked to the window, then turned back. 'If he could reach the riverbank, he could have climbed up to Rowse's room.'

'But he's *dying*.'

Jill shook her head. 'People don't change their nature just because they're dying. Suppose he heard Gloria agreeing to go to bed with Rowse under his own roof. Suppose Alvington was angry enough to do something about it ... Why should he care? As you say, he's dying. The only problem is, surely he wouldn't have been strong enough to stab Rowse?'

'He wouldn't have needed much force, not if he took him by surprise. Rowse was drunk. It's only the first thrust that's hard. The one that penetrates the skin.' Thornhill sat down on the little sofa, suddenly weary. 'I didn't expect all this.'

'No. But it has to be said.'

He looked at her and thought, *That's why I love you.*

'What will you do?' she asked

'Tell Williamson, I suppose, though he's not going to be pleased. He likes a tidy ending. Anyway, I doubt if it will make any odds.'

'Why not?'

'No jury on earth would convict Alvington on that evidence. It's not the sort of thing you can hold up in court and say "This is Exhibit A". It's not like the knife they found on Coalway's wardrobe or Rowse's camera in Simcox's bag.'

She slipped out of the chair and joined him on the sofa. Her nearness distracted him.

'Will Simcox hang?'

He wanted to nuzzle her neck like a horse looking for sugar. 'Probably.'

'And he killed Heather?'

'Yes.' He twisted on the sofa, so he could face her. A man could drown in those eyes. 'You're saying that Simcox is going to hang anyway, so why upset the applecart?'

'Yes. What good would it do?'

He shook his head. 'I'm sorry.'

'Why not leave it? You just said you wouldn't be able to get a conviction. All you'd achieve is upsetting a dying man and his daughter.'

He snorted. 'Not to mention Mr Williamson.'

'Damn Williamson.'

'Jill, I'm going to talk to Alvington about this. And depending on what he says, I may have to take it further.'

'If it was Harold, and I think it was, then it was a perfect murder. Or as perfect as things get in this world.'

'Why?'

'Jane Alvington phoned Charlotte this morning. He's in a coma.'

For a moment Thornhill said nothing. Then he held out his

hand as though they had concluded an agreement and needed to seal it by shaking hands. She took his hand and stood up. He looked up at her.

'I'll show you the kittens,' she said.

Hand in hand, they went into the hall. In the doorway, her thigh brushed against his. Jill stopped by the door to the cupboard under the stairs, which was slightly open. She opened the door a little further and the cupboard filled with light. There was a box on the brick floor and in it lay Alice, looking up at them. Four tiny bundles were locked to her belly.

'They're so small,' he said. 'Not like cats at all.'

'They're blind at this age.'

Jill crouched and, still holding on to Thornhill's hand, stroked Alice's head. Then she straightened up. He put his arms around her and felt her arms circling him. They kissed. She tasted sweet and smoky.

EPILOGUE

<hr/>

LYDMOUTH POLICE CHIEF TO RETIRE

Detective Superintendent Raymond Williamson, Head of the Lydmouth CID for the last eleven years, has announced his intention of retiring at the end of June. It will bring to a close a career which has seen many successes. Mr Williamson, who was born and bred in the county, says that he and his wife will stay in Lydmouth after his retirement.

Announcing his decision, Mr Williamson commented today, 'All our friends are here, both inside and outside the Force. I shall keep busy – I plan to write my memoirs, and I shall need to do that in Lydmouth so I can check my facts.'

DEATH OF WELL-KNOWN PUBLICAN

Harold Alvington, landlord of the Bathurst Arms, Lydmouth, died at home yesterday afternoon after a long illness. He was 63. Mr Alvington was a familiar figure in Lydmouth, where his father had kept the Bathurst Arms before him.

He leaves a widow and a daughter. The funeral will be at St John's, 2.30 p.m., on Monday. Flowers should be sent to Jones and Whittakers, Castle Street, Lydmouth.

The *Lydmouth Gazette*, 27 April